Those Who Know

Alis Hawkins' first novel, *Testament*, was published by Macmillan after winning a national competition. She works for the National Autistic Society and is a member of the Society of Authors and the Crime Writers Association. She lives in Coleford, Glos., in the Forest of Dean.

Also by Alis Hawkins

The Teifi Valley Coroner Series

None So Blind
In Two Minds
Those Who Know

Alis Hawkins
THOSE
Who KNOW

CANELO

First published in the the United Kingdom in 2020 by The Dome Press

This edition published in the United Kingdom in 2021 by

Canelo
31 Helen Road
Oxford OX2 0DF
United Kingdom

Print ISBN 978 1 80032 271 4
Ebook ISBN 978 1 80032 239 4

Look for more great books at www.canelo.co

Printed and bound in Great Britain by Clays Ltd, Elcograf S.p.A.

For Rob and Flo

Wishing you both all the happiness in the world

Those who know do not speak, those who speak do not know.

Lao Tzu, *Tao Teh Ching*

Glossary of Welsh terms

bara brith: speckled bread, a fruit cake

betgwn: the outer garment of most Cardiganshire working women in the nineteenth century. It featured a tight, low-cut bodice, worn over a blouse, with a long back, sometimes gathered up into a 'tail', and was worn over petticoats and an apron

ceffyl pren: wooden horse. A traditional form of folk justice in the area

cymanfa ganu: a singing meeting, usually to sing hymns at chapel

gwylnos: watchnight, a night sitting in vigil with the dead

plwyfwas: parish servant, a parish constable

Shoni Goch: Red John

swci lamb: a lamb whose mother has died and which has been hand-reared

Part One

John

If Llanddewi Brefi's parish constable hadn't been so keen to keep his job, we'd never have got involved in Nicholas Rowland's death. It just would've gone down as a tragic accident and we'd have been spared a lot of trouble.

My boss, Harry Probert-Lloyd, didn't have time to be looking at bodies just then. He'd been acting coroner for three months and he'd just got started on his campaign to be elected coroner for the Teifi Valley in his own right. An inquest was the last thing he needed.

When news of the death came, we were standing in Tregaron's town square where carpenters were putting up a stage for the election meeting at the end of the week. Harry's election agent, Jonas Minnever, had dragged us up there to do some canvassing.

Minnever. Even after knowing him for a month and more, I still didn't know what to make of him. He'd just turned up at Glanteifi one day and, before we knew where we were, he was a fixture. Forever asking questions, making arrangements, insisting on things.

I know you're not supposed to look a gift horse in the mouth but there is such a thing as buying a pig in a poke, isn't there? Fair enough, Minnever might be more horse than pig but, in my experience, if a man you don't know offers you something you haven't asked for, he's probably got a plan for you that you're not going to like.

Mind, he was good company, as far as that went. Cheerful, witty, always asking your opinion and making you feel clever. But that was suspicious in itself, wasn't it? Why would a man like him – somebody who knew everybody who was anybody in the county – go out of his way to make me feel important?

I never put the question to Harry because I knew what he'd say. That I'd come up in the world. That I wasn't just the temporary coroner's borrowed assistant any more. Nor Mr Solicitor Schofield's clerk, either. That I might only be twenty years old but I was under-steward to the Glanteifi estate and about-to-be-qualified solicitor.

Which was all true. But Minnever's back-slapping still put me on edge. And, whatever he said, Harry wasn't really any happier to have him about the place than I was. Called him a *necessary evil*. Still, like him or not, Jonas Minnever had long pockets filled by powerful men.

So, there we were, standing about watching men work and listening to Minnever wanting to know when the stage'd be finished, could we put up an awning in case it rained, where were the chairs and lectern coming from, when one of the nameless Liberal Party hangers-on piped up.

'Done much public speaking before, Mr Probert-Lloyd?'

Harry turned to him. 'Before I went blind, I was a barrister, so my job consisted of very little *but* public speaking.'

But Mr Ears-on-a-stalk Minnever wasn't having that. Left off what he was saying to put Harry right. 'Speaking in public isn't the same as public speaking, Harry. Electioneering is all about carrying a crowd with you. More like rabble-rousing than reasoned argument.'

I turned away to watch a carpenter mitring the end of a plank. We'd been in Tregaron two days already and I was sick of it all. Sick of the election. Sick of Minnever and the endless people who seemed to be working for him. Sick of being introduced to men who Minnever always called 'one of us'. *This is Mr So and So – he's one of us.* Liberal Party supporters, he meant. Was *I* one of us? I didn't know, to be honest.

Most of all, I was sick of having nothing proper to do. For the last couple of months I'd got used to working flat out, whether it was learning the stewarding trade or studying for my solicitor's exams or going all over the Teifi Valley with Harry as coroner's officer. But here, on what Minnever called 'the canvass', I was nothing more than a note-taker and noticer of things Harry couldn't see. And unwilling ally to Jonas Minnever.

'What do you think, Mr Davies?' he'd ask every time Harry looked unhappy about something he'd been asked to do. I knew he just wanted me to talk some sense but, every time he asked for my opinion, it felt as if he was trying to get me on his side against Harry.

I watched the carpenter putting his two mitred planks together in a right angle and longed for some honest work that didn't involve telling people what they wanted to hear. I didn't know it but I was about ten seconds away from salvation. And the person who was going to save me was clumping across the square on heavy legs.

'Excuse me.' The boy might be panting like a sow in the sun but somebody'd taught him his manners. 'I'm looking for the coroner.'

I stepped forward. 'This is Mr Probert-Lloyd, the acting coroner,' I said. The boy'd asked the question in Welsh so he probably didn't speak English. 'Who's died?'

'Mr Rowland. Our teacher down in Llanddewi Brefi. Fell out of the loft, he did. Mr Jones, the *plwyfwas*, sent me.'

'The *plwyfwas* has done the right thing,' Harry told him. 'Has the body been moved?'

Llanddewi Brefi might be a bit out of the way but I was pretty sure that the parish constable, this Mr Jones, would've heard that the acting coroner was fussy about his corpses. There'd been a case a few weeks before where Harry hadn't been called in until the body'd been taken home, washed and laid out. Nobody in the Teifi Valley would be making that mistake again.

You could see that the boy was thrown by Harry speaking to him in Welsh. 'No, sir,' he stammered. 'Mr Jones said we should leave it for you to see.'

Harry turned to Minnever and the others. As usual, politeness put him at a disadvantage because the more directly he looked at them the less he'd be able to see. 'Gentlemen, I'm afraid there's been a death that requires my attention so I shall have to take my leave. Will you excuse me?'

Minnever wasn't having any of that. Rubbed his hands together as if he hadn't heard better news in a week. 'Excellent,' he said, 'an *in vivo* demonstration of your methods! Who could have wished for better?'

Harry

I would not have admitted it to anybody, even to John, but I welcomed Schoolmaster Rowland's death like a gift from the gods. For weeks now, Minnever had been taking me about, praising me to party supporters, discussing strategy and introducing me to the men who would organise public meetings in the fortnight running up to nomination and polling day; and though my determination to secure the coronership had not wavered, I found myself ill at ease with the election process.

From the outset, I had had misgivings about becoming embroiled in politics, an attitude Minnever clearly found naïve.

'Despite a general sympathy for your recent bereavement,' he'd said on his first, unannounced, visit to Glanteifi as he moved restlessly around the drawing room. 'I fear you lack *allies* in Cardiganshire, Mr Probert-Lloyd. And you're going to need support. Substantial support.'

I had not known how to respond to his oblique reference to my father's recent death, or how to ask what kind of support he had in mind; I feared sounding embarrassingly ignorant but Minnever continued as if my very lack of response had been an answer.

'If you're going to successfully oppose the Tories, you'll need—'

'The *Tories*?'

'Yes.' Minnever's tone suggested that he was not sure what exactly my surprise signified. 'Their candidate, Montague Caldicot, has moved down from London and is waiting in the wings.'

I had seen no public announcement from this Caldicot and his existence as a rival candidate was an unpleasant surprise. 'But why the party affiliation? This isn't a political election.'

Minnever sighed audibly and ran a hand over a pate that seemed, to my limited vision, to be completely bald. 'Mr Probert-Lloyd, believe me when I tell you that there is *no such thing* as a non-political election! The Tories will be out in force behind their man. And they're not accustomed to being beaten. Not here.'

I was finding it difficult to assimilate what Minnever was telling me. Having been asked by the county magistrates to act as coroner during the previous incumbent's final illness, I had expected to stand unopposed in the subsequent election to the post. The notion that I had been a mere placeholder while the Tories manoeuvred their favoured candidate into place was humiliating.

'Suppose,' I said, 'that I accept that political support might be useful. What would the party want in return?' Though there was absolutely no prospect of my being able to fund an election campaign on my own behalf – not with the estate teetering towards bankruptcy – I was unwilling to enter into some species of Faustian pact.

Minnever hesitated before answering. 'There's going to be a general election next year,' he said, rocking on the balls of his feet in front of the fire, as if he would like to break into a run. 'And, for the first time in a generation, both the borough and the county seat will be contested. We want to see how much work we'd need to do in order to carry the day in both constituencies.'

He paused, presumably expecting derision at the idea of anybody but a Tory winning an election in the county seat, but I had no intention of fulfilling his expectations.

'This election is important for you,' he said, when I failed to react. 'And next year's is important for us. We can help each other. What do you say?'

I had seen no alternative but to acquiesce and, as a result, I had not been the master of my own fate since.

Now, however, there was a body, and I could go about the job for which I had discovered such an aptitude. Minnever's motives for backing my campaign might be entirely political, but having the opportunity to witness my competence could only make his support more wholehearted. Or so I hoped.

John

It wasn't only Minnever who rode down to Llanddewi Brefi to see the body with us. So did Benton Reckitt – workhouse doctor, anatomist and Harry's preferred medical witness. Dr Reckitt looked at corpses and gave us his opinion on how they'd died. At length, if we weren't careful.

He wasn't in Tregaron by accident. Far from it. Reckitt had taken it into his head to try and get himself elected coroner. The fact that he was Harry's friend didn't seem to have struck him as a reason not to.

He was an oddity, Reckitt.

The boy who'd come for us rode pillion behind me. I was glad we had a headwind – the whiff I'd got off him as I hauled him up on to the mare's back had been ripe. The stale smell of smoke from a fire that's mostly turf. Damp homespun. Linen not washed enough and only in water. And a body barely washed at all. The fact that I knew I would've smelled exactly the same at his age didn't make him any sweeter. My life'd changed since then, thank God. Changed out of all recognition.

While Minnever listened to Harry explaining what would happen when we got there, and Reckitt concentrated on staying in the saddle, I had a little chat with my passenger. If previous sudden deaths were anything to go by, there'd be plenty of people who'd want to put their tuppence in, but children see the adults around them in a different way. Sometimes more clearly.

Enoch, the boy's name was. I commiserated with him about having to run all the way to Tregaron with the news of this teacher's death and, in return, he told me everything I wanted to know. Turned out that the dead man, Mr Rowland, had come to teach in Llanddewi a bit more than three years ago. His school was popular – between twenty and forty children at any given time, Enoch said – because he'd never turned anybody away, even if they couldn't afford their teacher's pence.

'Dic Penwarren came to school for a whole winter without ever paying a penny,' he told me. 'He'd bring an egg in his pocket for Mr Rowland every day and Mr Rowland said that was enough. And Mr Rowland got Anna Dangraig specs!'

'Did he indeed? Doctor as well, is he?'

'No! He saw her screwing her eyes up to try and make the letters clear and he took her to Miss Gwatkyn. It was Miss Gwatkyn that got her the specs really,' Enoch admitted. 'But she wouldn't have known about Anna if Mr Rowland hadn't told her, would she?'

'And who's this Miss Gwatkyn, then?'

'Miss Gwatkyn, Alltybela,' he said as if that explained everything. 'The big house.'

The big house. The mansion. Miss Gwatkyn was obviously somebody to be reckoned with locally.

According to Enoch, Mr Rowland never used the birch – not like some, he said – and he didn't just make them read by rote. 'He told us what we were reading about – explained things.' And he hadn't only taught them to read and write. 'Nobody'll be able to swindle me any more,' Enoch boasted. 'Mr Rowland taught us our pence tables as well. And how to reckon money.' And, apparently, the teacher had always talked about how it was a big world. 'We've got a map of the world on *Mercator's projection*,' Enoch told me, producing each syllable carefully.

'Do you know any English?' I asked.

'Only a bit to read. Not to speak,' he told me. 'Mr Rowland says we should learn in our own language first, then, if we want

8

to carry on, we can learn English. He says how can we know what we're reading if it's in a language we don't understand?'

That took me back to my first proper day school, sitting in a ragged row with a strange English book that none of us understood a word of to begin with – *The Ready Letter-Writer*. To this day, I remember copying out 'A letter from a young gentleman to a lady, begging her acceptance of a present'. I don't know where that winter's teacher'd got hold of it but that'd been our only English primer.

'Do any of the pupils stay on to learn more – geography or history?' I asked, following Enoch's lead and referring to the school in the present tense. Best not to upset him with thoughts that Mr Rowland and his school were both in the past, now.

'Some, yes. The ones with parents who can afford it.'

The children of Llanddewi Brefi were unusually fortunate. In most schools that came and went with the seasons you were lucky if you learned anything but how to read the Bible and write your name. Your parents'd pay for you to go for two or three terms and then the money'd go back to paying for things the family'd gone without for you to learn your letters. Soap. Tea. Shoes.

From Enoch's prattling, it sounded as if his family was better off than most. He'd attended the school ever since Mr Rowland had arrived in Llanddewi Brefi, three years ago. Apart from the times when he'd been needed to work in the fields, obviously.

'Did any of the older pupils help with the teaching?' I asked him. They might well have done if Mr Rowland had been taking the brighter ones beyond the basics.

'No. He had Miss Walters and Miss Eynon for that.'

I stored that information away. Mr Rowland must've had ambitions beyond his score or two of pupils if he'd been taking on assistants.

'So, did everybody like him?'

Enoch hesitated. 'Nearly everybody. Not Mr Hildon, though. The vicar.'

'Why's that, then?'

'Mr Hildon wants a different kind of school. A church one.'

'Chapel was he, Mr Rowland?'

'Yes. Unitarian.'

I nodded. The Unitarians were big believers in education. I decided to poke a bit more at that *nearly everybody*. 'So,' I said, 'no enemies, eh?'

Enoch would never've told Harry, but I was different. I'd asked the boy questions that told him I'd been like him once upon a time.

'Only Old Mattie,' he said.

I soon had the whole story. Old Mattie'd been the local teacher before Mr Rowland came. Hadn't been much good at his job, from what Enoch said, and none of the children'd liked him.

'What does he do now?' I asked.

I felt the boy shrug against me. 'Past couple of months, I think he's mostly been threshing.'

Threshing was what kept the poorest out of the workhouse in winter. Old Mattie must've had a thin time of it after Rowland and his progressive ideas arrived. 'Enemy' probably wasn't far off the mark.

–

Llanddewi Brefi turned out to be a small village. The whole place looked as if it had washed down out of the hills, every shop and dwelling separate from its neighbours, with the church stranded on a rise above the houses. Rooks were flying around the square tower like a ragged black cloud, cawing as if they hadn't seen each other for a year.

Unusually for the time of day, everything was quiet, almost tucked up. Perhaps people were keeping silent out of respect. Whatever the reason, we were almost through the village and out the other side before we saw a soul. An old man with a peg-leg was sitting on a milking stool in the only open doorway, whittling a piece of wood.

He looked up as we went by. 'Here for Master Rowland, is it?' he asked, in English.

I nodded but didn't stop.

Of course, he'd know what'd happened. He'd have seen the boy running past his door and asked him where he was going in such a hurry. We'd be lucky if there wasn't a crowd of people waiting for us when we got to the schoolroom.

'That was him,' Enoch said, once we'd left the man behind.

'Who?'

'Old Mattie.'

Was it indeed? I had a pretty shrewd idea Harry'd want to talk to the nearest thing Mr Rowland'd had to an enemy, and now I knew where to find him.

I turned my head back to Enoch. 'Where's the school?'

'Little way yet,' he said. 'Just keep on going and I'll tell you where to turn.'

—

Mr Rowland might have been a popular teacher but his schoolroom wouldn't have won any prizes. Before being turned into a school the building had been a cowshed with a half-loft. About eleven or twelve yards long and half as wide, it had a teacher's desk and some cupboards at one end, two biggish tables under the windows, Enoch's map of the world on one wall and the rest was just scattered benches. The only real improvements anybody'd made to it had been to give it a proper flagstone floor, glass in the windows to keep the weather out, and an iron stove to stop Rowland and his pupils freezing to death. It stood in the middle of the room with its flue running up into the loft.

The teacher's body was lying on the floor, arms flung out, a ladder lying on top of it. I moved closer. The dead eyes were open, cloudy and empty. Whatever it is that makes us alive had gone.

Why hadn't somebody closed his eyes? Fear probably. *Don't touch the corpse or Mr Probert-Lloyd'll have your hair off!*

I took my notebook out and started jotting things down.

Body some way from loft edge. Left ladder rail under corpse's chin.

The *plwyfwas*, who'd introduced himself as Simi Jones, noticed me writing and shuffled towards me as if he was going to ask what I thought I was doing. He wouldn't have moved so much as a muscle if it'd been one of the gentlemen taking notes.

I snapped my book shut and looked him in the eye. 'So. Some poor child came in this morning and found him like this, did they?'

Before he could say anything, Harry jumped in. 'I'm sure Mr Davies didn't mean to sound critical, Mr Jones. It's just upsetting, isn't it? The thought of children coming for their lessons and finding him like this.'

Simi Jones didn't reply. Just gave me a look fit to bruise flesh. I gave him it back, too. Right in his face. And a thin, ratty little face it was. The face of a man who couldn't be bothered to keep his razor sharp. Probably wasn't married. Mind you, man of his age didn't need to keep a smooth chin, married or not. Past all that.

His narrow eyes flicked away from me and fastened on Harry. 'Came straight to me, the children did, Mr Probert-Lloyd. They knew what to do.' You could see he wasn't comfortable speaking Welsh to a gentleman but Harry'd greeted him in Welsh so that was that.

'And you did the right thing, too,' Harry said. 'You called the coroner.'

Jones's sloping chin went up. 'I know what's to be done, sir, don't you worry.'

He could say what he liked. Truth was, with us up the road in Tregaron, Rat-face wanted to show that he did things by the book. Now that we had the county police, parish constables only held on to their job if they really earned it.

He wasn't that keen on still being there, though. Shifting from foot to foot, waiting for us to tell him he could go. Whatever he did for a living, he was losing money every moment he stood there.

Harry noticed the foot-shifting. 'We needn't keep you any longer,' he said. 'Where can we find you if we need to call a jury?'

Jury? Jones's ratty little eyes almost crossed. Could see a world of trouble on the way, now, couldn't he? All he'd wanted was for Harry to come and say, 'Tragic accident, well done for observing proper procedure, just ask a doctor to come in and certify it for the register.' But, if Harry ordered an inquest, Rat-face Jones'd be the one the magistrates called on to give an account of himself.

The magistrates didn't like the sudden increase in costs since Harry'd taken over as acting coroner. Muttered about wasting ratepayers' money. But, if you want my opinion, what *really* got up their noses was Harry making them look like a bunch of negligent fools who'd spent years not giving a damn about how ordinary people'd died.

I looked down at the body again. Looked like an accident to me. The ladder wasn't secured. Somehow or other, Rowland had pulled it away from the loft as he was climbing up. And back he'd gone onto the flags.

Trouble was, if there was one thing working with Harry had taught me, it was that people see what they expect to see.

Or what they want to see.

'Who's the local registrar, here?' I asked Rat-face as he turned to scuttle off. 'We'll need to talk to him.'

Jones gave me a nasty, yellow little smile and jerked his thumb over his shoulder. 'Him,' he said. 'Mr Rowland. He'd been the registrar in Llanddewi for just over a year. Bench'll have to find a new one now.'

Just what the magistrates loved, making sure there was someone to fill all the local jobs.

Once Rat-face'd gone, Harry half-turned to me. 'Any particular reason you don't like him?'

I didn't answer. I knew he was telling me off. *Don't let your personal feelings get in the way.* It was a song he'd sung before. All very well for him, he couldn't see how people were looking at him, judging him. But, point made, he left it.

'Gentlemen,' he said, switching back to English, 'if you'd be so good as to step to one side while John and I do what's necessary?'

I half-expected Dr Reckitt to object but he didn't. Perhaps he was learning sense – Harry'd find it a lot easier to ask for his opinion now he hadn't tried to force it on us.

'Right,' Harry said. 'Let's have a look at him, then.'

Harry

We stepped forward and, positioning himself at the corpse's head, John began to describe the dead man for me.

'Deceased is in early middle age. He has a full head of hair without any grey but his beard has started to turn. His face is beginning to show lines – he's not young any more.' He took two deliberate paces along the side of the body. 'A little under six feet tall. Slim build.' He squatted down. 'He's wearing a well-cut suit of clothes but they're not new.'

'Do we know where his jacket is?' I asked. In my peripheral vision, I could see that the dead man was dressed only in his shirt and waistcoat.

'No. Do you want me to look in the loft?'

'Later. Carry on.'

'He's still wearing his necktie,' John continued, 'and his boots. Riding boots,' he added, 'not ordinary ones.'

I left the subject of boots on one side for now. 'Any indication that he was drunk?'

John knelt and leaned over the dead man's face. 'No smell of alcohol.' He stood again. 'His arms are flung out to the sides, as if he was falling backwards.' He sketched a vague windmilling of his arms in demonstration.

'But the ladder's lying right on top of him,' I pointed out. 'If it tipped backwards and he let go to try and save himself, you'd expect it to have bounced away from him, wouldn't you? It wouldn't land on top of him unless he'd been clinging to it.'

I heard John take a long breath through his nose. Thinking. 'Unless he only let go at the last moment?'

'Perhaps. Obvious injuries?'

John bent over the dead man again. 'A swollen lump on his forehead. Right hand side, just below the hairline. D'you want me to turn him over?'

I weighed my options. The position of the body relative to the ladder disturbed me. It was too early, as yet, to cry foul play but an inquest already seemed inevitable; there were clearly questions to be answered as to how this man had died. It would be prudent to assemble a jury today so that it could examine Rowland's body *in situ*. That would be much more compelling – and evidential – than viewing the body elsewhere and simply hearing the scene described.

I nodded to John to turn him over. 'But make a note of exactly how he's lying and where the ladder is so we can recreate the scene for the jury.'

Having lifted the ladder away and leaned it against the wall, John stooped over the dead man and attempted to move his right arm into his side so as to roll him over. It was quickly clear that the body was stiff with the rigor of death.

Reckitt strode forward. 'Let me help you.'

In the event, such was the corpse's unwieldiness that Minnever's help was also needed to turn it. Once this was accomplished, an 'Ah' from John and a muffled grunt from Reckitt told me that a possible cause of death had been revealed.

'The back of his head is matted with blood. And there's an obvious wound.' John's voice was carefully firm; he had yet to overcome a certain natural squeamishness.

'May I?' The request came from Reckitt.

'Please, do.' I knew he could be relied upon to see things that might otherwise go unremarked.

With an audible effort, Reckitt lowered himself to his knees and bent to examine Rowland's head wound. After a minute or so, he struggled to his feet again and asked if John and Minnever would be so good as to help him return the body to its original position.

The dead man on his back once more, Minnever retreated while John and I watched Reckitt bend over the corpse, first on one side, then the other.

'This man's hands are badly damaged.'

'By the fall?' I asked.

Reckitt's head stayed bent over the hand he was examining. 'No. These are old injuries. If I had to guess, I'd say his hands had been crushed beneath a heavy weight.'

'But those grazes look recent,' John pointed out.

'The superficial injuries were probably caused by the fall,' Reckitt agreed, 'but the earlier damage was much greater. You'll need to ask people who knew him how much use he had of his hands. It's hard to be sure while I'm unable to move them, but I'm certain his fingers wouldn't have functioned normally.'

'That would explain the beard,' John said. 'He couldn't shave.'

'And his stock has no bow,' Reckitt agreed. 'He's just knotted it and tucked the ends in clumsily.' With a grunt, he straightened up. 'John, be a good fellow and see if his waistcoat is loose enough to put on over his head.'

John did as he was bid. 'Very loose. You could get two of him in there.'

'Explains why he was a schoolteacher at any rate,' Minnever volunteered from behind us.

'Possibly.' If Rowland had been a pauper, I would have agreed without hesitation. There were precious few occupations for a working man with crippled hands. But John had said that Rowland's clothes were well cut, if old. He had been better off, at one time, than he was now.

'Can we go back to the grazes on his hands?' I asked Reckitt. 'How did he graze them if he fell backwards?'

'I'm quite sure he didn't fall backwards. The pattern of the grazes indicate that he put his hands out to save himself. Like so.' Reckitt thrust his arms out. 'His hands would have been the first part of him to hit the floor and, if that's the case...' Once more, he lowered himself to his knees and put his hands to the dead man's chest. 'Yes. Broken collarbone. Classic injury when taking a precipitate fall from height. The hands go out, instinctively, to save the head from hitting the ground. You see it in steeplechase riders when they've come to grief over a particularly nasty hedge.'

Reckitt was a fount of arcane information. What was his connection with steeplechasing? He was hardly an avid rider himself, preferring carriage to saddle where at all possible.

'So he didn't fall backwards? You're quite sure?'

Reckitt rose laboriously. He was a big man and, though he was light enough on his feet when upright, rising from a kneeling position clearly troubled him. 'All I can say for certain is that he first fell forwards, probably out of the loft given the clavicular fracture and the extent of the superficial damage to his hands. Whether he would have been able to climb the ladder after that I can't yet say – I'll need to examine him more closely.'

'But if he fell and hurt himself,' John objected, 'why would he try and get back up the ladder? He'd go for help, wouldn't he?'

'He might not have realised how badly injured he was. Might have thought he could sleep it off.' Reckitt's tone was that of a man speaking to his equal; it was his habit to distinguish people purely on the basis of whether or not they were prepared to deploy their intelligence in a rational manner.

'So, in his injured state, he might have tried to climb back up to the loft, misjudged it somehow and fallen, pulling the ladder back on himself?' I suggested.

Reckitt's attention was still on the body. 'Possibly.'

While he deliberated, I turned an apologetic face to Minnever. 'I'm sorry about this.'

'Don't be, Probert-Lloyd. It's quite fascinating.'

Reckitt knelt once more at the dead man's side, this time at his head. 'Bruised lump just below the hairline as John observed,' he said. 'So, despite putting his hands out, he still struck his head.'

In my peripheral vision, I watched Reckitt push his fingers into Rowland's hair and pull them out slowly, as if he were searching for nits. He did this several times before apparently parting the corpse's lips and peering at them.

Frustrated by my inability to see what was happening, properly, I bit my tongue and waited for him to finish.

John, however, had no reservations about squatting next to the doctor and asking for an explanation of his methods. In a previous life, Reckitt had been an anatomy demonstrator at Guy's Hospital and only the slightest excuse was required to set him off on an *ad hoc* lecture.

'D'you see here,' he said, 'on the inner aspect of the lips? The man was a habitual lip-chewer. Makes it almost impossible to distinguish any new bruising or laceration.'

'And if you could see bruising, what would that mean? That he hit his mouth as he fell?'

'No. It would mean that somebody held their hand over his nose and mouth while he was insensible in order to smother him.'

The silence which greeted these words told me that I was not the only person to have been shocked. 'But you can't tell?' John asked.

'No.' Reckitt's head moved again, as if he was trying to bring something into the light. 'I can't see any bruising to the nose, either, but that's not conclusive. You have to pinch nostrils extremely hard to bruise them and, if he was in no position to offer resistance, that degree of force would have been unnecessary.'

'But you think somebody might've smothered him after he fell?' John persisted.

'It's possible. The evidence suggests that, after he fell, somebody held him by the hair and banged his head on the ground. Repeatedly, in all likelihood. Why do that and then leave his death to chance?'

'Held him by the hair? How can you possibly claim to know that?'

I suppressed a smile. Minnever's incredulity was typical of the reaction Reckitt tended to produce in people.

Reckitt beckoned him over. 'When we arrived, did his hair look like this?'

'More or less, I suppose.'

'No,' Reckitt said, 'it did not. We disarranged his hair in moving him. When we arrived, it was combed back in a neat manner. But this man had recently fallen from a considerable height and hit his head hard enough to cause the frontal damage. His hair would have been considerably disordered.'

Minnever was not convinced. 'But mightn't he have come to his senses after a while and run his fingers through his hair? To get it out of his eyes so he could see to go back up the ladder?'

'You will have observed my running my fingers through his hair, just now?' There was a pause during which I assumed that Minnever had given some kind of assent. 'In doing so,' Reckitt went on, 'I satisfied myself that manual rearrangement would not have been sufficient to achieve the level of neatness we first observed. And besides,' the doctor moved to one side, 'observe this hand, if you will. I shall need to examine him again once rigor mortis has subsided but I believe it's unlikely that he had much movement in his fingers. I doubt whether he could straighten them properly, for instance.'

'How do you come to suspect that?' Minnever asked. 'When your hand is relaxed, doesn't it fall into that shape naturally?' He held his hands out, palms up, fingers presumably curled, to illustrate his point.

Reckitt demonstrated neither discomfort nor irritation at being cross-examined. 'Look at the recent damage to his hands. When he sustained his fall – forwards – he didn't put his hands out, palms flat, fingers straight, as you or I would have done by reflex action. He couldn't. So the grazes are to the heels of his hands and the dorsal aspect of his fingers.'

Minnever crouched down to look at Rowland's hands. He might as well not have bothered; Reckitt was constitutionally incapable of misrepresenting anatomical findings. But the need to see with our own eyes is surprisingly strong, as I had discovered to my own immense frustration since my ability to examine things visually had failed me.

'All of which suggests,' Reckitt continued, 'that, after his fall from the loft – presumably as a result of being pushed – his killer took advantage of his injured and groggy state to take hold of his hair and bang his head on the floor until he was insensible.'

'Then made sure he was dead and smoothed his hair back into place to hide the evidence,' John finished.

'Not simply smoothed. As I indicated, a brush or comb was used.'

'Bravo, Doctor! But surely that's a great deal to infer from the way his hair was arranged?' I could hear the smile in Minnever's voice.

'The boy's description of events when he came to summon us has coloured your judgement, sir. He informed us that his teacher had fallen from the loft. That has worked upon your mind and you are looking for evidence to confirm an accidental fall and rejecting other evidence as fanciful.'

Ignoring Minnever's harrumph of protest, I made a decision. As 'fanciful' was the last adjective one might ever apply to Reckitt, a jury would have to be called and an inquest convened.

After Benton Reckitt'd said his piece, we left the corpse in the cold schoolroom and went back out into the sunshine. While Harry relieved Enoch of his horse-minding duties and sent him off to fetch Rat-face Jones again, I leaned back against the wall of the schoolroom, closed my eyes and turned my face up to the spring sun. The year was coming to life. I could hear birds singing their feathery little hearts out and, on the way over here, we'd seen blackthorn out everywhere, like spring snow in the hedges. Even the grass was beginning to brighten again after a mud-coloured winter.

'How long's this viewing going to take?' I heard Minnever ask. Keen to get Harry back to the voters in Tregaron, wasn't he? But he was in for a shock if he thought Harry was going to hurry things up for the sake of electioneering.

The warmth on my face suddenly cooled and I opened my eyes. A fat cloud had covered the sun. April's a treacherous month. Snow up here in the next few weeks'd be nothing unusual.

It'd been a treacherous time for schoolteacher Rowland as well, if Reckitt was right. And I had no reason to think he wasn't. Like a university education, it was, watching Benton Reckitt work. Between him and Harry they were giving me such a course in the business of suspicious death that I'd be an expert by the time I came of age.

I heard a sound and looked round. 'Simi Jones is back,' I told Harry. 'And he's not looking very pleased.'

–

Harry hadn't just called Jones back to tell him to get a jury together – he could've given Enoch that message. No, he wanted to make sure nobody'd tidied the corpse up.

'Mr Jones, as far as you know, did anybody comb Mr Rowland's hair while he was lying there?'

Rat-face looked at him as if he was off his head. 'No. That'd be for the laying out, wouldn't it?'

'You're quite sure none of the children could have done it?'

Rat-face gave a pinched look at Enoch. 'Well? You were here, weren't you?'

The boy shrugged. 'Nobody touched him. Came straight for you, Mr Jones.'

Simi Jones looked back at Harry with an expression somewhere between *told you so* and *always finding fault, the gentry are.* Wasted on Harry, of course. But then, if Rat-face hadn't known that, he wouldn't have dared give him the look in the first place. It wasn't only Harry's reputation as a stickler with corpses that had gone up and down the Teifi Valley. People'd heard all about how he couldn't see properly as well. *Can't see your face, Mr Probert-Lloyd can't. If he looks straight at you, he can't see you at all. Has to look at you side-on.*

'Thank you, Enoch,' I said. Then I turned to Rat-face. 'And you, Mr Jones.'

Narrowed his eyes at me then, Simi Jones did. Didn't like me speaking for Harry. Thought I was giving myself airs. And I knew there were plenty of others who thought the same thing since Harry'd asked me to be under-steward. Well, they could think what they liked. When I took over the running of Glanteifi with Harry, they'd have to call me *Mr* Davies and smile to my face, whatever they said behind my back.

'Very well,' Harry said. 'I need you to call a jury, Mr Jones. We'll do the view this afternoon — as soon as you can find enough men. The bare twelve will do. We don't want to have to wait any longer than necessary.'

Rat-face opened his mouth, thought better of it, and turned back towards the village with Enoch in tow. I saw Minnever draw breath to speak but, before he could, Harry turned to me. 'Right, before we have to put the ladder back for the jury, let's have a look in the loft.'

I didn't look at Minnever. Didn't want him to try and get me to change Harry's mind. Just went back into the schoolroom and up the ladder. It was the first time I'd been in a cowshed's loft for years and it brought back a lot of memories I'd rather not have had, to be honest. Still couldn't think of my family without feeling the pain of loss under my ribs. Stupid really, I'd been an orphan almost half my life.

The loft barely covered half the ground floor but, even though it wasn't partitioned, you couldn't see into it from the ground. It was set quite high up and didn't have much head-room. No headroom needed for hay, is there?

Down below, Minnever started on at Harry about going back to Tregaron with him and leaving the viewing of the body to me. I hesitated at the top of the ladder to hear what Harry would say.

'Go back by all means, Minnever. There's really no need for you to stay. But this is coroner's business and I'm not going to shirk it.'

I looked about. Rowland's living quarters were barely any better furnished than the schoolroom beneath. Rough boards, threadbare rug, narrow iron-framed bed with a battered wicker trunk pushed up against the wall on one side of it, a scratched but clean table on the other. Rowland had used the end of the table directly under the loft's one small window as a washstand. A bowl and jug stood there, with a small mirror hanging from a nail on the wall. A ladderback chair was pulled out from the table with Rowland's jacket draped over it.

At the back of the table there was a collection of books on bare plank shelves. I peered at them in the dim light. Didn't recognise the titles but the spines were scuffed and battered, as if they'd knocked about the place for a good while. Rowland's bowl and jug were decent and matching, though. And the soap was dry, not sitting in a pool of its own melted fat. The word *fastidious* came to mind, along with the face of my previous employer, Mr Schofield. That was the sort of word he liked to use.

I half-turned. Rowland's bed was more or less made and, if the blankets weren't very neatly tucked in, the man's hands explained that, didn't they? I pressed down on the mattress. Feather. No horsehair or straw stuffing for Schoolteacher Rowland.

'Harry?' I called, looking over the bed to the trunk on the other side.

'Yes?'

'There's a trunk up here – do you want me to open it?' Always wise to have the boss's say-so before you go poking about in a man's personal possessions.

'Is it locked?'

I moved round the bed. 'No.' It was fastened with two straps. No lock.

'See what's in it, then.'

I undid the buckles and flipped the lid up. Clothes. I pulled an overcoat out and laid it on the bed. Then a spare suit – just as well made, and just as worn, as the one he'd died in. Some neckties, much more fancy than the white stock he'd been wearing. A pair of shoes that wouldn't have survived five minutes on the roads around Llanddewi Brefi, and a second pair of riding boots, stiff from lack of use.

'Just clothes,' I shouted down. But when I dropped the boots back in to the empty trunk the sound they made was wrong. I took them out again and leaned into the trunk. I got my fingers under the edge of the base in one corner and pulled it up. Underneath was a linen bag. When I lifted it out, there was the unmistakeable clink of coins. I untied the neck and looked in.

Money. A *lot* of money.

Harry

If the cash hidden in Rowland's trunk was surprising, I found John's request that one of us come up and witness his removal of it even more so.

'That's not necessary, John,' I called up to the loft in response.

24

Jonas Minnever cleared his throat in that way people do when they are about to say something that others might find less than entirely acceptable.

'Perhaps the boy's wise to be cautious. Money tends to make people mistrustful.'

The boy: John would not like that. No more than I liked his probity being called into question, however obliquely. I took a breath and composed my face into a bland agreeableness. 'Very well.'

'I'll go up,' Reckitt offered.

I kept him in the corner of my eye as he moved his bulk up the ladder and, with some grunting and muttered oaths at the ladder's instability, on to the floor of the loft.

Though lofts pressed into service as living quarters generally merited a fixed ladder, I could see that, here, such a thing would have presented an obstacle to the free movement of children below. Easier by far simply to lean the ladder out of the way during school hours and replace it at need.

Reckitt had scarcely clumped across the floor overhead before our attention was diverted.

'Good day to you, gentlemen.'

The newcomer hovered between us and the daylight, rendering him nothing more than a silhouette to me. Fortunately, Minnever was not so disadvantaged.

'Good day, Reverend…?'

The gentleman stepped further in, allowing me to make out the sober black and white clothes that had prompted Minnever's guess.

'Hildon. Tobias Hildon. Vicar of St David's. I gather,' he said, not waiting for us to introduce ourselves, 'that there is some suggestion that Rowland's death was not an accident.'

Simi Jones, the *plwyfwas*, must have gone straight to the vicarage before beginning jury-recruitment, damn him. I stepped forward before Minnever could speak. 'Good day, Mr Hildon, I'm Henry Probert-Lloyd, acting coroner for the Teifi

25

Valley. And I'm afraid you're right. There's evidence of foul play.'

'You mean he was murdered?' Hildon's tone indicated no shock at the news, only irritation with the way I had expressed it.

'That's for an inquest to decide.' I would not be responsible for 'murder' being bandied about the village and the jury's judgement prejudiced. 'Meanwhile, we're trying to understand as much as we can. By good fortune, we have a doctor on hand who is experienced in post-mortem examinations.'

'No, no, not I,' Minnever said, in response, presumably, to an enquiring look from Hildon. 'Doctor Reckitt's up there, with Mr Probert-Lloyd's assistant.'

As if his words had brought it into being, a faint chinking came from the loft. The sound of coins being counted and stacked on a hard surface.

Hildon obviously heard it, too, because he whipped around and addressed me. 'What exactly is taking place here?'

I responded to his abruptness with a considered calm. 'My officer discovered a certain amount of money amongst Mr Rowland's possessions. It's being counted before we remove it from the premises as evidence.'

'May I ask why?'

Unsure as to whether he was asking for an explanation for the money's being counted or its removal, my answer did duty for both. 'The fact that a large amount of money was found in his living quarters argues against a pecuniary motive for Mr Rowland's death.'

'I thought I understood you to say that you were undecided as to the manner of his death?'

I disliked his combative tone but was saved from making an unwise rejoinder by the shifting of the loft ladder.

'It's all right, I'll hold it.' John's words produced a grunt of relieved thanks from Reckitt; coming down an unsecured ladder is worse than climbing up.

Once at the bottom, Reckitt planted a foot on one of the ladder's rails to hold it firm while John came down. This he did with considerably more agility than the doctor, despite being encumbered with a decent-sized linen bag.

'How much?' I asked, as he turned around.

'Almost three hundred.'

'*Pounds?*'

Had I been able to see properly, John would probably have glanced at me to ask whether I wished to field Hildon's incredulous question; as it was, he simply took it upon himself to decide.

'Yes, Mr Hildon. Two hundred and ninety-eight pounds, thirteen shillings and sixpence to be exact.'

'I heard coins,' I said. 'Is it all small takings?'

'No. Most of it's in banknotes but there are some sovereigns and smaller stuff – crowns and half crowns. Nothing less than that, though.'

In other words, Mr Rowland's bag of money did not contain his daily teacher's pence.

'Can you write a receipt and have it witnessed by Dr Reckitt, please?' I asked.

John took out his pocket book and began writing.

'You'd better leave the money with me.'

I turned, slowly, towards the vicar and his peremptory tone. 'Do you believe you have a claim on this money, Mr Hildon?'

'Not at all. But it should be taken in trust for his family, when they can be found.'

'Mr Rowland had no relatives in the village?' It was the obvious inference but it was as well to be sure.

'No.'

'Do you happen to know where he is from?'

'I do not.'

'Might there be somebody who could give us details of his family?'

'Miss Phoebe Gwatkyn is your most likely informant. They were as thick as thieves.'

In my peripheral vision, John held his pencil over his pocket book, the very picture of a diligent amanuensis.

'And where would we find Miss Gwatkyn, Mr Hildon?'

The vicar turned and pointed through the door. 'Over there. Alltybela mansion. If you look hard, you can see it on the edge of the hill above Pentre Rhew. Any of the villagers'll show you the way.'

A favour which he neglected to offer. Mr Hildon, apparently, was not cut from the servant-of-all clerical cloth.

'Thank you,' I said. 'Doubtless we'll find somebody who can introduce us to the lady in due course.'

'When will you hold the inquest?'

Damn the man – did he always bark instead of speaking? 'Simi Jones, the *plwyfwas*, is already out gathering a jury. Beyond that, no decisions have been made.'

'With any luck,' Minnever said, 'Mr Probert-Lloyd will be able to conclude this sad business as swiftly as possible. You'll be aware that we're in the middle of an election, and he is to speak at a public meeting next Saturday.'

I sighed. Given Reckitt's opinion on how the teacher had come by his various injuries, it seemed unlikely that an inquest into Rowland's death would be concluded anything like as swiftly as Minnever would like. Worse, now that electioneering had begun, the press would be more avid than usual.

John and I would have our work cut out to stop the whole thing becoming a fairground attraction.

John

Dr Reckitt might be convinced that the teacher'd been murdered but I was pretty certain the jury'd see it differently. I might not have been coroner's officer for long but I already knew that juries were apt to explain away signs of foul play.

28

Especially if they thought the dead person was so loved and respected that nobody in their right mind would want to hurt them.

Must've been an accident, they'd say. *Poor dab, terrible thing to happen, couldn't be helped though.*

But, if anybody could make them look beyond what they wanted to see, it was Harry. I knew that because I'd watched him do it, again and again. In the ten weeks or so since he'd been asked to stand in as coroner, Harry'd held more inquests than there'd been in the Teifi Valley during the previous year and a half.

As our jury gathered in the schoolhouse that afternoon, I wondered how he was going to conduct the view. 'Are you going to get Dr Reckitt to tell them what he thinks?' I asked.

He shook his head. 'I'm just going to let them look at the body. Reckitt can speculate at the hearing.'

An inquest jury was required to look at the body and bear witness to any and all injuries to its surface. Post-mortem examinations might come later – and Doctor Reckitt certainly thought they should – but the jury's job was just to look at the body's condition as soon after it'd been found as possible. Preferably before it'd been moved or tidied up in any way. Trouble was, juries didn't always notice things like broken collarbones. Or know what to make of them, if they did.

I watched as the jurymen dribbed and drabbed in. From the look of them, there were more farmers than usual. We were in the back of beyond, out here, and there weren't many shopkeepers and tradesmen to call on. Mind, that wasn't the only way this lot were different. Most juries didn't get anything like as upset.

It started as they came in. They looked around at the school-room and saw what we'd seen when we first came in. A cowshed that hadn't had much done to it to make it fit for teaching in.

I saw one man looking at the walls. The thin coating of lime-wash they'd been given hadn't been anything like enough and the shit that'd been left after a quick clean had come through. Ugly brown stains travelled two feet up the wall in most places, as if there'd been a flood.

God, what must these gentlemen think of us, you could see the jury thinking, *if this was the best we could find him in the way of a school? Only one room for everybody, no proper desks or chairs. And where are the books the children were supposed to be reading?*

I knew the answer to the last question because I'd looked around earlier. They were in a low, battered cupboard in the far corner of the room. And, fair play, they were proper reading books, not just old copies of the Testament or whatever somebody'd had lying about. Far better than anything I'd had, I knew that.

I watched the jury glancing up at the loft where Rowland had lived. It was as if they thought their eyes were tricking them and, instead of lying there sprawled and stiff on the ground, he was still up there, watching them.

Or maybe it was just the thought of the fall. If they all knew about his hands, how useless they were, perhaps they thought this was an accident that'd been waiting to happen.

'A shaky ladder?' The first man to speak looked from Rowland, with his ladder on top of him, to Harry and me. 'Is that what's killed him?'

Then they were all at it.

'Best teacher we've ever had in Llanddewi. The things my Twm used to come and tell us!'

'No thought for himself, ever. Only for the children and his new school.'

'*Duw!* The new school – what's going to happen to that, now?'

What new school? If it'd been up to me, I'd have asked, but I knew Harry'd want to get the view over with before we started on other questions. He was a great one for not accidentally putting ideas into the jury's heads. And, anyway, we'd waited long enough already. He'd refused to go back to Tregaron while

Simi Jones drummed up his jury so we'd found a decent public house in the village and persuaded the landlady to find some bread and cheese for us while we waited.

Once we'd sworn the jurors in and Harry'd explained what was required, they all shuffled round, looking at how Rowland was lying.

'Notice the position of the ladder,' Harry said. He was speaking Welsh, as usual. I'd told him a hundred times to let me do the talking, that it made people nervous to hear a squire speaking their own language, but he wouldn't listen. Didn't want to be thought of as a gentleman, did he? Just as the coroner. As if that wasn't the same thing.

'I want you to think about that ladder,' he said. 'If it fell backwards with Mr Rowland on it, is that how you'd expect it to be lying?'

So much for just letting them look at the body.

I watched the men glancing at each other. They'd all taken their caps off, in deference to Harry as much as to the corpse, so I could see the looks they gave each other. *What does he mean – how does he expect a ladder to lie?*

Even if their imaginations didn't get much work from one week's end to the next – unless it was to imagine how close the workhouse doors were getting – they did their best. They fixed their eyes in one spot and tried to put themselves on that ladder. To feel it toppling backwards, their weight pulling them to the ground, their arms going out to save them, the ladder coming down, bouncing, skidding away. Then they looked at the body again, saw the ladder lying there, pointing up under his chin. It meant something, but what?

The sky had clouded over since Rowland's examination earlier and there wasn't as much daylight coming in through the door, so Harry decided to move the body outside where the jury could see it more easily. Four men carried one of the heavy schoolroom tables out on to the muddy lane and two others brought the corpse.

It wasn't the first time Harry'd done this with a jury. If the place where somebody'd died was poorly lit, it was better to bring the body into the light than to take a lantern to it.

The jury'd all have seen dead friends and relatives laid out, of course, but not a body stiff and awkward like this. There was something not quite human about the way Rowland's limbs were frozen.

'Stiff as a plank,' one man said. 'He didn't fall out of that loft this morning.'

Harry turned to Benton Reckitt. 'Doctor?'

Reckitt stumbled a bit over his Welsh but it wasn't a bad attempt, fair play. As attending physician at Cardigan work-house, I suppose he'd had to learn enough to speak to his patients. 'I'd say he's been dead at least since last night – some-time before midnight – maybe longer. It'll be easier to tell as we see when the stiffness goes off.' Speaking poor people's Welsh, Reckitt sounded a lot less stuffy than he did in English.

'Did anybody see Mr Rowland yesterday?' Harry asked.

I caught one man's chin-cocked response. 'You did, did you?' I asked.

He nodded. 'At chapel.'

'The Unitarian chapel, is that?' Harry asked.

Another nod. Our Unitarian friend was a man of few words. No bad thing, generally. The less you say, the less people can find fault with you.

'And after that?' Harry tried to give the impression of looking round at the jury. They probably all knew about his odd sort of blindness but he always tried to make it look as if he could see. Kept people guessing about how much sight he still had.

Looks darted round the group. Heads shook.

'Nobody?' I wanted to make it clear for Harry. 'None of you saw him after chapel yesterday?'

More head shaking. Mumbles to the same effect.

'Do any of you know what Mr Rowland would normally do on a Sunday afternoon?' Harry asked. 'Did he have a Sunday school for the adults at his chapel?'

'There *is* a Sunday school,' the Unitarian said, 'but Mr Rowland isn't – wasn't – the teacher any more.'

'Does anybody know where he might have been yesterday afternoon?' Harry asked. 'Who he might have seen?'

I watched them shuffling, scratching their heads, jamming their hands in their pockets. All waiting for somebody else to speak first.

'Might've gone to see Miss Gwatkyn,' one of them said. Mutters of agreement came straight away. Miss Gwatkyn of Alltybela. Gentry. Above suspicion. It was all right to mention her.

'Was he a frequent visitor there?' Harry asked.

Thick as thieves, Tobias Hildon had said.

One man spoke up. 'She owns this place. Paid Mr Rowland to run the school.'

That was worth knowing. Had some of the money in the trunk come from Miss Gwatkyn? I made a note in my book. Didn't really need to, but it's just as well to let people see you doing your job.

'Very well,' Harry said, 'let's proceed. Will somebody be good enough to remove Mr Rowland's clothes so that his body can be examined?'

Nobody stepped forward so, in the end, I just picked the two men standing nearest to the table and told them to do it.

'Has to be done,' I said. 'The jury has to look for marks on the body. And none of us wants to be here all day, do we?'

His trousers and drawers came off easily enough once they'd unbuttoned his braces but, with his arms as they were, getting his shirt off was virtually impossible, never mind his underlinen. Harry decided that we'd have to cut it off.

'But those are good clothes!' somebody protested.

'They're the clothes he'll be buried in, unless somebody comes forward to tell us otherwise,' Harry said, 'so it's not going to make any difference.'

Somebody pulled out his knife and cut the clothes so that they lay around Rowland's body. The paleness of his skin was striking against the dark body hair that curled down in a narrowing trail from collarbones to privates. Rowland had been a wiry type of man, not showing a lot of either fat or muscle. His arms, particularly, looked weak. But then, with his hands as they were, I didn't suppose he'd been able to do much.

Harry asked the jury to choose a foreman to describe the wounds so I could write them down.

'Go on, Llew, you do it,' one man said. All the others quickly agreed and a small, well-fed man stepped forward.

'Llewelyn Price,' he said when I asked for his full name for the record. 'I keep the grocer's shop in Llanddewi.'

Llew Price turned out to be a good choice of spokesman. Years of examining the goods that came into his shop'd given him a sharp eye and quick judgment. In no time he'd described grazed hands and a purplish lump where Rowland's collarbone'd broken. There were also bruises on the dead man's right hip and knee from the fall.

'Before we go on,' Harry said, 'can you describe how his hair looks, please, Mr Price?'

I saw Llew Price flick a glance at Harry then, quickly, he moved it to me. I just nodded at the corpse for him to get on with it.

The grocer peered at the dead man. 'Well. He's always had a good head of hair, Mr Rowland. It's a bit longer than he usually had it – probably hadn't been up to London for a while.' He turned to me. 'Always used to get his hair cut whenever he went to London.'

That was an interesting piece of information. Not the hair cutting – everybody has to get their hair cut – the bit about going to London regularly. I made a note of it, which seemed to satisfy Llew Price because he went back to doing what he'd been asked to do.

'It's brushed back off his forehead. Used a bit of oil to keep it tidy by the looks of it. Not much but there's something there.'

'And you'd say it was tidy, now?' Harry asked. Before the jury arrived, Harry'd asked me to fetch a comb or brush from Rowland's loft and make his hair look like it had before Reckitt'd started fiddling with it.

Llew Price looked back at the corpse. 'Yes. Neat. Like he always kept it.'

Harry nodded. 'Thank you. Examine his head, now, if you would, Mr Price, before we turn him over.'

Price peered down at Rowland's face. I wondered if he felt the same need I had to reach out and close the teacher's eyes.

'Reddish lump where the hair meets his forehead on the right-hand side,' he said, peering at Rowland's forehead without touching it, just like I had. He walked around the table so he could see the other side of the corpse's head properly. 'Can't see anything else.'

Harry asked for the body to be turned over and, after he'd explained to the jury that what looked like bruising all over the dead man's back and legs was just the blood in him settling to the lowest parts, they calmed down and got on with looking at the bloody wound on his head.

'It's wide and deep,' Llew Price said when Harry asked him to describe it. 'There's a dent where you can see the skull's broken,' he swallowed. 'And there's blood in his hair.'

'How big would you say the wound is?' I was duty bound to ask. Any wound's dimensions had to go down on record.

Price held a finger edge-on to the wound. 'An inch and a half, or so, from one broken edge to the other.'

'Are there any wounds or bruises to the back, otherwise?' Harry asked.

I watched Price look. He was careful and thorough. He might only be small, but Llew Price was one of those men people give way to. He had something about him. Presence, I suppose you'd call it.

'No, nothing else,' he said when he was sure.

Once the body was on its back again, Harry carried on. 'I want you to look at his hair, now we've turned him over again,' he said. 'See how untidy it is, just from the body being moved? How do you think it would have been if he'd just fallen from the loft?'

I watched the jury looking at each other. Those who were capable of it did some imagining. The rest shuffled their feet.

'The wound on his head, his grazed hands and his broken collarbone all mean that he must have fallen forwards out of the loft,' Harry said. 'But Dr Reckitt tells us that it was the injury to the back of his head that killed him.'

All right, he wasn't letting Reckitt speculate but this was a long way off just letting the jury look at Rowland's wounds, wasn't it?

Llew Price ventured a question. 'Begging your pardon, Mr Probert-Lloyd, if he fell forwards, how was the back of his head injured?'

'Clearly, after he'd fallen out of the loft, somehow the back of his head hit the ground, very hard.' Harry waited while they looked at each other then asked, 'Which of you knew Mr Rowland best?'

After some muttering, the Unitarian was pushed to the front. 'Gambo saw him at chapel. And Mr Rowland taught him to read in Sunday school.'

Harry turned his eyes in the direction of the man called Gambo. 'Is that right?' I could see where the nickname'd come from – he was unusually tall and bony, like the long, bare-ribbed haycarts we called *gambos*.

A nod.

'Could Mr Rowland straighten his fingers, like this?' Harry held his hands out, palms down, fingers stretched long.

Gambo shook his head. 'No. His hands were twisted, sort of. Closed up. Like this.' He held his hands out, fingers curled.

'So, he couldn't have done this?' Harry combed straight fingers through his hair.

I was watching the other jurymen. You could see the light dawning on a few faces, like turning the wick up on a lamp. *He couldn't have tidied his own hair after he'd fallen. Somebody else must've done it.*

'No, sir,' Gambo said. 'His fingers wouldn't do that.'

Harry just let them think about that. The ones with imagination would have to tell the ones without what he was getting at, later.

'Deciding how Mr Rowland died is the job of the inquest,' he said. 'I don't want you talking about it with anybody else before then. I'm going to adjourn proceedings, now, until the end of the week. We'll hold the inquest here, in the school-house, on Friday.'

'Pardon me, Mr Probert-Lloyd,' one of the jurors said, 'but couldn't we have the hearing sooner? It seems as if we might have all the information we need to decide on a verdict, now.'

Harry turned to him. 'I understand, but I want to allow time for two things. Firstly, for any witnesses to what happened here to come forward. And secondly, to allow time for me to discover what family Mr Rowland had and inform them. It's a terrible thing to learn of the death of a loved one from the newspapers.'

He could tell them that if he liked. I knew the truth.

Harry wanted to find out who'd killed the teacher.

Harry

The jury having been dismissed, I turned to Minnever. 'If you wish to make your way back to Tregaron, I shall quite understand. But I will be detained a little longer.' I had hoped that he would leave John and me to quiz Reckitt in private but Minnever was not to be dismissed so easily.

'No, Harry. There's very little to be gained in Tregaron, now, without you. I'll wait and we can ride back together.'

I acquiesced with the best grace I could muster and turned my attention to Simi Jones. 'There's the question of where the body should lie until the inquest is complete.'

Though Rowland's body was unclaimed by any immediate family, it seemed entirely inappropriate that he should lie, abandoned, in a converted byre. 'Is there anybody in the village that we could ask?'

Jones shifted his feet uncomfortably. 'Plenty of people'd be honoured, Mr Probert-Lloyd, but that's the trouble, isn't it? Whoever you asked, everybody'd want to know why *they'd*been chosen. There'd be bad feeling.'

It was a more forthright answer than I had expected from him and I was reasonably certain that he would not have volunteered such information in English.

'What about the Unitarian chapel?'

'That's miles away, sir.'

'But we'll need a cart, so would that matter?'

Simi Jones was spared the necessity of responding by the arrival of a horse and trap. Its driver jumped down to help the lady passenger and, just for a moment, a thought flashed through my mind that it might be Lydia Howell, newly arrived from Ipswich via Glanteifi and in search of us. But I dismissed the notion as soon as it came. When Lydia and I had agreed, in January, that she would come to Glanteifi to work as my private secretary, she had been uncertain as to the period of notice she would be obliged to work. 'And, besides,' she had said, 'I wouldn't want to leave the children until I knew they were in good hands. I'll write as soon as I can name a date.'

This lady could not be Lydia.

I watched the new arrival descend from her trap out of the corner of my eye. Small and slight, the figure was quick and light on her feet as she came towards us.

Suddenly remembering the naked state of Rowland's body on the table, I gave Jones swift instructions to cover him before addressing the lady. 'Good day. Whom do I have the honour of addressing?'

'Good day to you. Phoebe Gwatkyn, of Alltybela.' She did not introduce the man who had given her his hand to help her down from the trap, though, as he moved back to the horse's head, she thanked him with a '*Diolch*, Gwilym.' A servant, then.

'Mr Probert-Lloyd, is it?' she asked. 'The acting coroner?'

For some reason, hearing her described as Rowland's patron had led me to believe that Miss Gwatkyn must be an elderly lady but her clear voice and the fluidity of her movements said otherwise.

The necessary introductions concluded, Miss Gwatkyn came straight to the point. 'Mr Probert-Lloyd, where do you intend that Mr Rowland should be laid out, now that the viewing of the body has been carried out?'

'Given that he had no family in the village,' I said, 'that represents something of a dilemma.'

'No family, but a sincere friend in me. I would consider it a great favour if you would allow me to take his body back to Alltybela.'

Her request, though a trifle unorthodox, offered a more satisfactory solution than having Rowland's body lie at a distance in the Unitarian chapel and was unlikely to stir up resentment in the village, particularly as the friendship to which Miss Gwatkyn laid claim seemed to have been generally acknowledged.

Neither of us asked Simi Jones for his opinion. Far better for him if he was able to go back to the village and report that the matter had been taken out of his hands by the gentry.

Once her custody of the body had been agreed, Miss Gwatkyn turned to her driver and spoke in Welsh. 'Gwilym, could you and Simi manage to put Mr Rowland in the trap?'

But Simi Jones spoke up. 'I'm sorry, Miss Gwatkyn, the body's in no state to go into a trap. Better if you send a long cart round.'

Somewhat to my surprise, Miss Gwatkyn took no apparent offence at being contradicted in this way. 'Very well,' she said,

'I shall see to it. Meanwhile, could you ask Gwenllian Walters and Mari Eynon to come over to Alltybela later, and lay him out? I think their daughters might like to help, too.'

And with that, she bade us good day.

–

Twilight was creeping quietly toward the hills as we left to return to Tregaron, and the setting sun moved long shadows with us through the lanes, so that, in my peripheral vision, we seemed to be escorted by a silent troupe of ghostly, stretch-limbed riders.

The countryside around was unfamiliar to me as, despite being a Teifi Valley native, I had never been to Tregaron before that week. It makes me sound as parochial as the least well-travelled of my fellow-countrymen, but I have to confess that anywhere further upstream than Lampeter felt like a foreign land.

As the cowshed school fell away behind us and I tried to gather my thoughts about Rowland's death, I heard one of the other horses breaking into a trot to catch me up. I looked around expecting to see John's dark hair and glasses in my peripheral vision; it had become our custom, on the way home from viewing a body, to formulate a list of potential witnesses for the inquest. However, the horse that trotted up alongside mine was not John's little mare but Minnever's rangy grey.

He came straight to the point. 'After spending so much time on that, we'll have a lot of ground to make up tomorrow. I'd arranged meetings with some important people today – there will be ruffled feathers to smooth.'

Minnever's crassness made me want to punch him. He had just dismissed a man's death in a single word: 'that'. Almost as bad was his relegation of the inquest's importance to a status beneath that of courting voters.

Oblivious to my silence or choosing to ignore it, he went on. 'It's a good thing the parish constable's already involved.

He and John can be down here attending to witnesses and so forth while we're in Tregaron—'

'No.' I could not bear to let him finish his sentence. If he had said 'making up for lost time' or, worse, 'on more important business,' I believe I would have dismissed him there and then. 'You just heard me making arrangements to visit Miss Gwatkyn first thing tomorrow—'

'John can do that. He almost passes as gentry and, in the circumstances—'

'The *circumstances* are the death of a man who was her friend. *I* will go and see her.'

Minnever huffed an impatient sigh. 'Very well then, if you must. At what time can I assume you'll be back so that I can arrange meetings?'

A sudden silence fell between John and Reckitt behind us. Our argument had obviously brought their conversation to a halt. Much though I wanted to shout at Minnever, I lowered my voice; this was election business and, however improbable it seemed, Reckitt was a rival candidate.

'You don't seem to understand, Minnever. I am the coroner. I investigate deaths. John is my officer. He accompanies me.'

'But he's often gone off to investigate when you've had more pressing business—'

'I have been forced to allow him to deputise for me, *occasionally*,' I hissed. 'But only when it's been unavoidable. However,' I raised my voice slightly as he tried to interrupt, 'I do *not* consider meetings with political supporters to be unavoidable.'

'Then you're a fool. These are men who can make or break your campaign.'

'You speak to them, then! Tell them I'm doing my job – if they're worth their salt they'll understand, surely?' I turned my gaze in his direction and he disappeared into the odd patch of blindness at the centre of my vision that I privately called 'the whirlpool'. Somehow, it still felt right to give people the impression that I was looking at them.

'No, Harry, that's where you're wrong—'

'How can I possibly demonstrate greater commitment to the post than by going about coroner's business to the best of my ability?'

The silence that followed was uncomfortable. I was used to garrulousness from Minnever. 'I'm afraid,' he said, eventually, 'that that question indicates how far you are from understanding your situation.'

A chill spread from the nape of my neck to the rest of my body. 'My situation?'

'Why do you imagine that the Tories have raised their own candidate?'

'For the same reason that you and the Liberals are backing me – because they want to test the waters for the general election next year.'

Minnever sighed. 'I don't suppose for a second that it's crossed the Tories' minds that we'll try and take the county seat from them. No, they're putting Caldicot up to oppose you because they're unhappy. You refuse to work with them on the bench, you appoint your own coroner's officer instead of using police officers, you hold three times as many inquests as your predecessor—' He pulled himself up. 'If you'd expressly set out to annoy the magistrates, you could scarcely have come up with a better strategy.'

'And if I'd set out expressly to *please* the magistrates,' I said, stung, 'I wouldn't be doing my job! A coroner's job is to represent the dead and bereaved—'

'That may be so. But, unfortunately, neither the dead nor, as a general rule, the bereaved are liable to pay county rates. Those who pay don't benefit and those who benefit don't pay. Do you see the conundrum, Harry?'

'I see very well. The magistrates would like to stop people grumbling about the rates. But I can't help that. Accidents can and should be prevented. Murders can and should be investigated—'

'Harry, please listen to me. In the Teifi Valley, the post of coroner has always been in the gift of the magistrates. There hasn't been a contested election here in living memory. And even when there was, the franchise was so limited that it was a foregone conclusion. You are the first man to challenge the Tories on this.'

Though I wanted to argue that the county magistracy was not the same as the Tory party, I knew he was right. There would be scarcely a man in ten on the local bench who would describe himself as a Liberal.

'Think very carefully before you snub the men who can help you, Harry. Think very carefully indeed.'

Harry

I had assumed that my argument with Minnever was the last one I would have that day but I was wrong. Though my agent had arranged to dine elsewhere – no doubt in an attempt to unruffle some influential feathers – John and I were not to be left to eat our dinner in peace.

We had scarcely changed and come down to the room that had been made available for our private use in the Talbot Inn, when Benton Reckitt appeared, still, as far as I could tell, in his riding clothes. His spurs were not properly fastened and they moved audibly with each footstep.

'Ah, excellent. You're here!' He made straight for the fire and bent towards it. 'I'd like to be allowed to examine the body again.'

I had become accustomed to Reckitt's direct manner of approaching things and found it oddly restful. It obviated the need for analysis; one simply opened one's mouth and replied.

'Why?'

Reckitt straightened up and pulled a chair from under the table. But instead of sitting on it, he seemed to rest his weight on its back, as if he required an anchor of some kind. 'Do

43

you remember asking, when I examined the body on Tresaith beach, if I could tell whether he'd been smothered?'

It was typical of Reckitt to remember the details of the first post-mortem examination he had carried out for me but not the name of the victim. 'I do,' I said, 'very well.'

'I believe I told you then that, in the absence of evidence on the body's surface, I knew of no physiological signs that would indicate such a thing?'

'You did.'

'*This* death – this *murder* – offers me the opportunity to begin documenting such physiological signs. It gives us an unparalleled opportunity to document the resulting damage to bodily tissues.'

I sighed inwardly. Reckitt was asking me to bend the law; the dissection he was proposing was not necessary to determine the cause of death. 'Reckitt, this man is respected – revered – by people here. What would they think if they knew I'd allowed you to butcher his body for your own satisfaction?' I disliked putting it so crudely but I wanted him to understand how such a thing would be seen.

'It's not for my own satisfaction! It's for the advancement of medical science.' Reckitt relinquished his hold on the chair and stood up straight. 'You know perfectly well,' he said, 'that if we hadn't been summoned to see the body today, it would have been put down as accidental death. Some quack would've signed the death certificate – sight unseen as likely as not – and that would've been an end to it.'

He began to pace and the little room in which we sat suddenly seemed smaller, filled with his seething frustration. 'We need *properly appointed* medical witnesses to certify death. And they need to be properly trained. Which they would be if we had more knowledge. Knowledge which can only be gained from routine post-mortem dissections.'

I sighed. This was a familiar theme from Reckitt who believed that all deaths should be fully investigated by a doctor, that no death certificate should ever be completed on the basis of supposition or likelihood. And, as I should have known, he had not finished.

'It's absolutely ludicrous that only in exceptional circumstances are we permitted to determine exactly how a person has died! The government brought in death certification to give them data to improve public health but we're simply not collecting those data!'

'Perhaps people'd rather bury their relatives in one piece and stay in ignorance,' John said.

Reckitt's silence told me that he had been taken aback by the interruption. Was he wondering, as I was, whether John was defending my own recent actions? For, after my father's death from repeated apoplectic strokes, I had balked at allowing Reckitt to dissect his brain.

I swallowed and opened my mouth to say something but Reckitt was there ahead of me. 'It's precisely because people make irrational decisions that the government must legislate,' he said. 'If a murderer must be prevented from killing again, why must a disease be allowed free rein when knowledge might stop it in its tracks?'

'But cutting up a body isn't going to *let* you stop disease, is it?' John sounded agitated. 'Finding out what's killed a person doesn't mean you can prevent anybody else from dying from the same thing! If somebody gets typhoid fever, they either die or they don't! Knowing what it is makes no difference.'

Typhoid fever. It was no mere illustration on John's part. An outbreak had killed his parents and little sister.

'If we were allowed to perform autopsy examinations in order to understand diseases, we might – in time – be able to cure them!'

'But where will it all end, this mania for cutting people up?' John's agitation had become anguish. 'I read that book – *Frankenstein* – about sewing bits of dead bodies together and bringing the whole thing to life. Is that where we're going – to a world where we make new people out of dead ones?'

I do not know which surprised me more, his previously unvoiced apprehension or his having read Mary Shelley's book; *Frankenstein* had been old hat even when I had read it at school.

'That's a work of fiction,' Reckitt said. 'As far as I'm aware, nobody is seriously thinking of attempting to create life.'

'All right, maybe not *create*, but what about using this electricity to bring dead things back to life?'

'If you're talking about Galvani, he didn't bring his dead frogs back to life, just made them twitch! And those party tricks have come to nothing. Do you honestly think that, in fifty years, we wouldn't have found a way of reanimating corpses if it could be done? Galvani's experiments are a byway of medical history. They have nothing to do with the proper, scientific study of anatomy and physiology.'

John folded his arms. 'You can think it's a byway if you like, but I think it's the thin end of the wedge. Experimenting, cutting everybody up after they've died – where's it all going to end?'

I intervened lest Reckitt should attempt, in all seriousness, to answer John's rhetorical question; our medical friend in full didactic flight was the rhetorical equivalent of being hit over the head repeatedly with a blunt instrument. 'I fear John's reaction is likely to be representative of public opinion, Reckitt. People still associate dissection with criminality.'

'But that's nonsensical!'

'Is it? It's not much more than a decade since the Anatomy Act—'

'Nearly two decades, actually.'

'—and you know better than anyone that, before that, dissecting rooms were full of hanged felons and corpses stolen from their graves!'

'Full? The "dissection rooms" as you call them were never full! If doctors are poor diagnosticians and worse anatomists, it's because they were lucky ever to see the inside of a cadaver!'

Next to me, John's tension was palpable, but before he could speak again, the door opened and we were saved by the arrival of dinner.

John

Alltybela was the oddest mansion I'd ever seen. It wasn't so much its situation, though, to be honest, I wouldn't have built a house right at the top of a ridge, view or no view. No, it was the way it was constructed. It had two fronts. As you came up the drive, you saw an old-fashioned hall, like something from the time of Queen Elizabeth. Two storeys of tiny-paned windows, glinting in the sunshine. But, instead of taking you up to the old front door, the drive swept you past the hall. And there, around the corner, on a right-angle, was another, much more modern wing.

And the oddness of the place didn't stop at the front door. Once we were inside, I looked about the grand entrance hall while a footman took our coats and hats – fair play to him he didn't so much as turn a hair at Harry's awful Mackintosh coat – and I realised there were no portraits of ancestors on the walls. Just maps, something that looked like a cape made of animal skin with bright binding on its edges and a pair of oval-shaped wooden frames with a kind of twine lattice. I couldn't imagine what they were for.

'Miss Gwatkyn is in the morning room, gentlemen. If you'd care to come this way.'

The Alltybela butler was a lot friendlier than Moyle, the butler at Glanteifi. Ever since I'd moved into the mansion when Harry made me under-steward, Moyle'd been treating me as if I was a guest he couldn't wait to see the back of.

The morning room wasn't big but it was full of light. The long windows drew your eye as soon as you walked through the door and, instead of looking around the room, you found yourself looking out over a few acres of parkland in front of the new wing. Which was just as well, to be honest. The furniture was old and I was sure that the fashionable ladies of the parish, if they ever came here, would tut over chairs that needed re-upholstering and raise their eyebrows at the age of the rugs. Exotic they might be, with their designs and colours, but they'd been trodden to bare threads in parts. And what Llanddewi Brefi's ladies made of the fact that there was a harp in the corner of the room where you'd expect to see a piano was anybody's guess.

While we were waiting for tea to be brought, Miss Gwatkyn and Harry had the kind of chat that the gentry have. Miss Gwatkyn offered Harry her condolences on his father's death and he thanked her and changed the subject by asking how long the family'd been on the estate. Turned out the Gwatkyns had been here since Henry Tudor's time.

'I'm sure my ancestors were here before that,' Miss Gwatkyn said, 'but that was when the estate, as it is now, was granted to Sir Iorwerth Gwatkyn.'

Harry grinned. 'Grateful thanks for supporting the new king's claim to the throne, I suppose?'

'Undoubtedly.' Miss Gwatkyn's whole face changed when she smiled, took ten years off her. I was no great shakes at guessing ladies' ages but I thought she must be in her middle thirties, at least. Generally, her face had quite a serious cast, as if she was considering everything you said very carefully, but her smile lit her up. She must've been very pretty when she was younger and didn't have the millstone of managing an estate around her neck.

The tea arrived on a big tray. I got the impression that the maid who brought it – a tall, handsome kind of girl – wasn't the one who'd usually bring tea up because Miss Gwatkyn said, 'Oh, Susan! Thank you,' as if the maid had done her a favour. Perhaps the butler thought we needed impressing.

Susan gave her mistress a warm smile. Wouldn't let me catch her eye, mind. One of the disadvantages of being seen as a gentleman. Maids behaved as if you were floating six feet above their heads, not treading the same floor as them.

'May I ask where Mr Rowland's body is lying?' Harry asked after Susan had left. It was as good a way as any of reminding Miss Gwatkyn that this wasn't exactly a social call.

'In the old hall.' She dipped the sugar tongs into my tea to let the sugar go without a splash. 'The carpenter's already taken measurements for the coffin.'

I wondered if Harry was thinking of his father, who'd been laid out in his dressing room. If he was, he gave no sign of it. Apart from thanking Miss Gwatkyn for her condolences two minutes before, he hadn't mentioned his father once since the funeral. Not once.

'Miss Gwatkyn,' he said, 'without wishing to pre-judge the outcome of the inquest, between ourselves, it seems that Mr Rowland's death may not have been an accident.'

Miss Gwatkyn's eyes didn't leave the spoon she was stirring her tea with. It wasn't a surprise to her, I could see. Somebody'd brought her that news already. 'May I ask how you reached that conclusion?'

Harry didn't reply straight away but she wasn't going to be put off. 'Please don't try to spare me, Mr Probert-Lloyd. It's entirely unnecessary, I assure you.'

I watched Harry's face. Poor dab, his upbringing was getting in the way again. Living in London, Harry'd moved in circles that believed that women were the equal of men. Not in working strength, I don't mean that. But as far as intelligence and ability to reason were concerned.

It wasn't something he talked about a lot but I'd asked him to explain it to me, once, and the floodgates'd opened, as if he'd just been waiting for a chance to convert me to his way of thinking. Chapter and verse, I'd got, about how society kept women back, treated them like children. He'd quoted writers I'd never heard of. Mary Wollstonecraft. Jeremy Bentham. William Godwin. And he wanted to believe it, I could tell. No, to be fair, I think he *did* believe it. Trouble was, his upbringing had given him different ideas entirely. Been brought up to see ladies as delicate, tender flowers who're easily bruised, hadn't he? I'd watch him having to slap those attitudes down, like a man with a dog he's been too soft with.

But he'd been getting a lot more practice recently. I'd had to read Lydia Howell's letters to him. The two of them had been writing back and forth every week or so for months. Ever since we'd met her when we went to Ipswich in search of her brother, Nathaniel. Of course, after Miss Howell had turned up at Glanteifi unannounced and they'd decided that she was going to come and work for him, the letters'd got even more frequent. Not to mention more personal. Nothing improper, I don't mean that. Nothing I'd even blushed to read to him. There were just a lot of opinions expressed and, presumably, Harry'd done the same in his. Mind, Miss Howell must've had the devil's own job to read Harry's scrawl. I'd seen what he could produce with the sight he had left and it wasn't what any teacher would've approved of, even when he was taking his time. Goodness knows what it was like when he was hurrying to keep up with his thoughts.

I half-listened while Harry took Miss Gwatkyn at her word and gave her a decent summary of what Reckitt had concluded but the other half of my brain couldn't leave the subject of Lydia Howell alone. What did she think she was going to *do* as Harry's private secretary? I could see that, with me out and about with Mr Ormiston, he needed somebody to help him with paperwork and so on, but why couldn't he call on Mrs Griffiths, the housekeeper? She'd known Harry since he was a baby and there was nothing she wouldn't do for him. But no. After Lydia Howell's flying visit at the end of January, it'd all been decided. She was going to come and live at Glanteifi and work for Harry. Just like that.

Well, whatever it was she thought she was going to do, we'd all see soon enough. Harry was just waiting for a letter to say she was on her way.

While Harry finished explaining Benton Reckitt's theory about Mr Rowland being smothered, I kept my eyes on Miss Gwatkyn. She was giving nothing away. No 'oh my goodness' or fingers to the lips for her. Just sat waiting for the next thing.

Harry put his teacup down. 'Is there anybody you can think of,' he asked, 'who might have wanted to harm Mr Rowland?'

Miss Gwatkyn gave the question some thought. She was another one in the Lydia Howell mould. Used to being in charge. But Phoebe Gwatkyn was eccentric with it. You could tell that by what she was wearing. She might have a perfectly respectable gown on but, over the top of it, she was wearing a long, dark blue, woollen tunic with a full skirt. It had deep red and yellow edging around the open part at the top, and hoops of red and yellow at the bottom of the skirt which came down to just below her knees. It looked outlandish. And the boots she was wearing were just as odd. They were made out of animal hide with the hair still on. Made her look as if, from the waist down, she might be some kind of mythical creature under her clothes.

'Nicholas – that is to say, Mr Rowland – was well liked in the village,' she told Harry. 'You'll have gathered that much already. The only person in Llanddewi Brefi who's likely to speak ill of him is the other teacher, Mattie Hughes.'

Mattie Hughes. Enoch's Old Mattie.

'Do you think he'll take over the school, with Mr Rowland gone?' I asked.

She hesitated. 'I don't think so. There are others, now, who might do that.'

'The assistant teachers Rowland had been training?' Harry suggested.

'Yes. The plan was for them to take over later this year anyway, after the summer, so that Nicholas could devote more time to the establishment of the new school.'

That was the second time a new school'd been mentioned and, this time, Harry didn't let it go.

'Can you tell us about this plan for another school, Miss Gwatkyn?'

She smiled and stood up in her little, furry boots. 'I think, if we're going to start down that long and torturous road, we shall need more tea.'

—

We drank another two cups of tea, each, and heard the tale of Nicholas Rowland which, as it happened, wasn't so different from Harry's story. Like Harry, Rowland had left Cardiganshire for London to make his fortune. Only, where Harry had become a barrister by way of the university at Oxford, Rowland had ended up teaching at London's new University College.

'Then,' said Miss Gwatkyn, 'came 1847 and the Report.'

The Report. Or, to give it its official title, the Report of the Commission of Inquiry into the State of Education in Wales. Just hearing Miss Gwatkyn mention it made my jaw clench and my stomach knot up.

Was that why Nicholas Rowland had come here, I wondered, to prove that the commissioners were wrong? Or had he come because he'd been afraid they were right?

But I'm getting ahead of myself. Unless you lived in Wales at that time, a government enquiry probably wouldn't have been of much interest to you, so to understand the treachery of that 1847 report, you need to know how it came to be written in the first place.

Because of all the unrest on the continent – there was always a revolution brewing somewhere or another from Italy to Prussia – the authorities were constantly terrified of the same thing happening in Britain. Especially with the Chartists and their petitions for radical change. The government was afraid of sedition – saw it everywhere, whether it was really there or not, and nowhere more worryingly than here, in Wales.

To be fair, they had a point. Twenty years ago we'd had the Merthyr rising, with the miners defying Crawshay and running riot through the town. Then we'd had the Chartists in an armed stand-off with the military in Newport. And, most recently, there'd been the scandal of Welsh farmers defying the authorities night after night for the better part of a year and a half as they went out to destroy tollgates and intimidate people they didn't approve of – in other words, the rebellion known as the Rebecca Riots. Why, the government wanted to know, had our previously docile farmers rebelled like that? And how had they been able to organise themselves so effectively?

And the harder the government looked, the more clearly they saw two things. Our language – which, as far as the English are concerned, we only speak to annoy them – and our chapels. Chapels that encourage dangerous thinking like all men being equal in the sight of God. Chapels which run Sunday schools to teach people to read and which have ministers who might take it into their heads to encourage folk to read things other than the Bible. Newspapers, for instance. Some of which are in our own annoying language and speak to people about their own lives, their own country, which, until then, they'd barely separated in their minds from England.

The government wasn't in favour of that kind of education. Not at all. So they sent in commissioners of enquiry to take a long, hard look at every school in Wales. Three church-going, landowning English gentlemen who didn't have a word of Welsh between them, were authorised to sit in judgement on how poor, chapel-going Welsh people with little or no English scratched a bit of an education for their children.

I don't know what they expected to find. Lines of children chanting, 'Down with the Queen and her English ministers', perhaps, or, 'The church of England is the antichrist'.

But, of course, that wasn't what they found. What they discovered was a system – if you can call it a system – of schools that popped up with the seasons in all kinds of unsuitable build-ings. With teachers who sometimes had little more in the way of learning than the children they were supposed to be teaching. A system run by chapels and churches, charitable ladies, dedicated men and desperate paupers. Fair play, some of the schools were praised but, according to the commissioners, the vast majority were a disgrace.

The trouble was, those three Anglican gentlemen didn't come in with an open mind about education. No. They were looking for something quite specific: scriptural knowledge and children who could rhyme off the church's catechism – that, according to them, being the main point of the poor going to school. What they found were schools in which, nine times out of ten, the pupils' grasp on any of that was weak. And that was putting it kindly.

The reports from each county were more or less alike in the way they condemned pupils' lack of understanding of basic Christian doctrine. But it wasn't the children's fault, was it? If those commissioners'd bothered to spend five minutes with two chapel ministers from different denominations, they'd have heard two pretty different versions of what Christianity was, so how children were supposed to get to grips with it all was beyond me. I suppose children in England just learn the vicar's catechism by rote and parrot it back as required. Well, if that's understanding, I'd rather have our ignorance.

But it wasn't only religious knowledge that the commissioners found fault with. They complained that children couldn't do simple sums, couldn't say how many pence they'd have to pay if this was priced at x pence and that at y. Well, the poor children must've been baffled to be asked! They didn't think they were going to school to learn to count and neither did their parents. School was for reading and, if you were lucky, a bit of writing.

Worst of all was the commissioners' attitude to our language. They decided that speaking Welsh was holding the whole nation back. Worse, it was encouraging backward thinking and immorality. Because, even though they were only supposed to be reporting on education, the commissioners had decided that it was their right to comment on our morals and conduct, too.

According to their report, our mothers were women of low morals who passed on their sinful ways of thinking to their children through our mother tongue and, until our language was replaced by English and our ways amended by education in a proper, decent language, we'd never prosper and Wales would be a festering sore on the western edge of Her Majesty's dominions.

Well, all right, they didn't *exactly* say that, but it's what they meant.

We welcomed those commissioners into our schools and told them everything they wanted to know. Then they twisted our words and lied about us.

Treacherous bastards.

I unclenched my fists and tried to concentrate on what Miss Gwatkyn was saying.

'When Nicholas read the commissioners' report, he felt compelled to act and he decided to set up his own school to show what could be achieved.'

'But what was it that brought him *here*, to Llanddewi Brefi?' Harry asked. 'This wasn't his family home, I understand?'

Miss Gwatkyn got up to feed the fire. 'No. He came here because of Lampeter and St David's College.'

I watched her picking balls of culm out of the copper scuttle with a big set of tongs. That wouldn't have happened at Glanteifi. If Harry or I lifted a finger to feed the fire or light a lamp, the servants took it as a criticism of them. Alltybela's servants were on a different footing, seemingly.

'Did you know that the college was originally supposed to be here, in Llanddewi Brefi?'

Harry shook his head. 'No.'

Miss Gwatkyn sat down again. She looked like a pixie in her woollen tunic and heathen boots.

'There's a very long tradition of scholarship in Llanddewi,' she said, 'stretching all the way back to St David and beyond. There was a centre of learning here for almost a thousand years until the vandals of the Reformation destroyed it. So, when Bishop Burgess decided to set up a university college in Wales, Llanddewi was the obvious place.'

'What changed his mind?' Harry asked.

'Money. Or land, which comes to the same thing. The bishop was offered a prime plot in Lampeter.'

'So they got the college and prospered, and Llanddewi Brefi stayed a backwater?' I said. We'd ridden through Lampeter on the way to Tregaron and if ever I saw a town on the up-and-up, that was it. Lots of big, new houses, thriving shops, streets full of well-dressed people, building going on pretty much wherever you looked.

'That's the difference a college like St David's makes to a place,' Miss Gwatkyn said. 'Lampeter's usurped Llanddewi as Wales's seat of learning.'

'And Mr Rowland wanted to reinstate it?' Harry said.

Miss Gwatkyn hesitated and blinked rapidly several times. But, if she was fighting back tears, it didn't show in her voice. 'To some extent, yes. But not with any kind of university. Nicholas's vision was for a collegiate school combining elementary and grammar education. He wanted students with the necessary aptitude to be able to progress from one to the other entirely on merit rather than on the basis of whether their parents were able to pay.'

'A school funded by endowment, then?'

'Precisely.'

'And who was going to endow it?'

Miss Gwatkyn sighed. 'Initially, things seemed promising. Nicholas had letters of introduction to some of the county's more influential families and his vision did capture a few imaginations.' Her eyes moved from Harry to me, as if she was looking for understanding. 'A different man might have waited until he had sufficient backing to build his school, but not Nicholas Rowland. He was determined to begin teaching immediately. He felt that if he could make his mark as a teacher, even in the least promising circumstances, he might more easily find patrons.'

'The least promising circumstances being the cowshed schoolroom, I assume,' Harry said. 'You gave him the byre, I gather?'

'Yes. It was all he asked for. I hadn't intended him to live there, too, but he said it suited him.' She turned away from us to look into the fire. 'I don't imagine he thought he would still be there more than three years later.'

Three winters living in that draughty loft, with only the stove downstairs between him and freezing to death. The place'd been chilly enough yesterday, in the spring sunshine. I didn't want to think what it must've been like in January.

'The initial enthusiasm for his project came to nothing, then?' Harry suggested.

Miss Gwatkyn didn't reply for so long that I thought she wasn't going to give him an answer. But I was wrong.

'When it became clear that there was support for his collegiate school proposals,' she said, as carefully as if she was picking her way, barefoot, through thistles, 'an alternative scheme suddenly emerged. A National School, here in Llanddewi.'

'A National School,' Harry repeated. 'It was a church scheme, then?'

'Yes.' It sounded like a truth Miss Gwatkyn regretted having to tell. 'Instigated by Mr Tobias Hildon.' She waited for Harry to say something but he kept quiet and I followed his lead so she had to go on without help. 'Enthusiasm for Nicholas's college immediately fell away,' she said. 'Many gentlemen who had previously offered their support felt that it was their duty to support a church school once it had been mooted.'

'Couldn't Mr Rowland have joined in the effort for a National School?' I asked. 'Or wasn't he allowed to, as a Unitarian?'

Miss Gwatkyn shook her head. 'It wasn't that. Nicholas objected to the ethos of the National Schools. He wanted

57

a more liberal kind of education. One which didn't just fit people to be useful citizens but which encouraged freedom of thought.'

Ah. Sounded as if Harry and Schoolteacher Rowland would've got on like a house on fire. Free thinkers, the pair of them.

'Had Mr Rowland garnered more than just enthusiasm for his collegiate school?' Harry asked. 'We found a significant sum of money in his living quarters.'

Miss Gwatkyn got up to fiddle with the fire again. It obviously wasn't burning to her satisfaction at all. 'As I said, Nicholas managed to secure some interest when he first mooted his idea. I understood that there was a not inconsiderable sum of money in the bank. But…' she hesitated. 'He'd given me the impression, recently, that he was pursuing other means of raising funds.'

'Do you know what those means were?'

She turned to me. 'No, Mr Davies, I'm afraid I don't. But I do know that Nicholas Rowland wasn't one to give up easily. He was convinced that he could persuade influential people to his side, once they saw the success of what he liked to call his cowshed academy.'

Harry nodded, as if he was thinking it all through. I watched him, waiting to see what he'd say next. Compared to Miss Gwatkyn's eccentric dress, he looked relatively normal without his rubberised coat, even if his beard still made him look like a foreigner. But then, he only had it because he couldn't see to shave himself and wouldn't employ a valet. Schoolteacher Rowland had had his beard for similar reasons and I wondered if he would've refused help, too, if it'd been on offer. Probably. He sounded as pig-headed.

Before Harry had a chance to put whatever thoughts he was having into words, Miss Gwatkyn spoke again, her head cocked as if she'd just heard a suggestion she didn't like. 'You don't imagine that somebody murdered him over the matter of his school?'

'As yet, I have no idea as to motive. But, when I practised at the bar in London, I certainly saw men killed for less.'

'Yes, but London's different.'

'People are people, Miss Gwatkyn. Wherever they live. And what might not represent a motive for murder to you or me might very well drive another to desperate acts.'

Harry

As we rode back from Alltybela towards Llanddewi Brefi, I was struggling with a small crisis of confidence. Despite the evidence I had presented to Miss Gwatkyn, she had remained unconvinced that Rowland's death could be anything other than a tragic accident.

'I'm not discounting what you've told me of Doctor Reckitt's examination, Mr Probert-Lloyd,' she had said, 'it's simply that, when weighed against the evidence of the esteem in which Nicholas was held locally, I find it insufficient.'

Perhaps, I reflected, I had become too ready to accept Benton Reckitt's opinion without question. Yesterday, his absolute conviction as to the nature of Rowland's injuries had seemed to leave no room for doubt but, as I recounted his reasoning to Miss Gwatkyn, I had found that it seemed less convincing. Was I really going to look for a murderer because the schoolmaster's hair had been re-arranged?

Still, she made no objection to furnishing us with the names and addresses of Rowland's assistant teachers.

'Morgan Walters, Nan's father, keeps the Three Horseshoes in the village and Ruth Eynon's family lives over at Pantglas Farm, a mile or so up the valley.'

Though John sighed when I told him that we were going to the Three Horseshoes, he did not attempt to persuade me to fall in with Minnever's wishes and return to Tregaron, for which I was grateful. Minnever's demands would ensure that my life was quite full enough of contention.

My experience of the Teifi Valley's public houses had grown tenfold since becoming acting coroner so I was able to rate the Three Horseshoes as unusually well furnished and welcoming. Though it had only a room or two available for travellers, it still had the air of somewhere that saw people from hither and yon and was, therefore, far superior to a run-of-the-mill alehouse.

The effusive welcome we received from the landlord's wife, Mrs Walters, marked her husband as one of Minnever's endless 'local men'.

'Gentlemen! Are you here about the meeting in Tregaron? I know my husband's got plans to bring the whole village up there for you—'

'No, actually,' I interrupted. 'We're here on more sombre business.'

Her tone changed immediately. 'Oh, of course! Poor Mr Rowland. I'm sorry. Listen to me going on about elections when the poor man's lying dead at Alltybela.'

Her reference to the mansion recalled to mind Miss Gwatkyn's request that two women come and help lay out Nicholas Rowland's body.

'I believe you and your daughter went over there yesterday to help with the laying out?' I said.

'That's right. Such a terrible thing, the accident. Terrible.'

The accident. Given her husband's trade, it was inconceivable that Mrs Walters would not have heard the mutterings of 'murder' that would have run the length and breadth of the parish by now. Evidently, like Phoebe Gwatkyn, she chose not to believe them.

'Is your daughter here at the moment?' I asked.

'Sit down a minute, Mr Probert-Lloyd, Mr Davies. Let me draw you a mug of beer. Keep you going while you're about your work.'

I pulled out a chair. There are few better ways to ensure people's co-operation than to enrich them, even by as little as the price of a pint of beer.

But John was not to be put off. 'Is your Nan here?'

Mrs Walters put the mugs in front of us. 'Not at the moment, I'm sorry. Her father's gone to Tregaron for the post and she and Ruth have gone in the trap with him.'

'Do you know when they'll be back?' I asked.

'Morgan will be back within the hour but Nan and Ruth have only gone with him as far as Efail Fach. They're going round the parish to tell the pupils to come back to school next week. After we've buried poor Mr Rowland.'

I nodded. 'We understand that your daughter and Miss Eynon were Mr Rowland's assistants?'

'Yes. He was training them. Thought the world of Nan and Ruth, he did. Of course, our Nan'd already had an education before Mr Rowland came here. We've always sent both our children to school – Nan and Billy, her brother.'

I nodded as I sipped at the beer. 'You said your husband was going to Tregaron for the mail – does he deliver it, too, or do people come here to collect it?'

'If they drink here regularly, people generally come and collect their letters. Otherwise, he either delivers if he thinks they'll have the money or sends Billy out to tell them there's a letter waiting for them. People haven't always got a penny to hand, have they?'

A penny a letter. In London, correspondents only paid once, for the stamp. Here, the cost was doubled by the charge made for delivery. But, of course, the sheer volume of correspondence in London made it feasible for the Post Office to employ letter-carriers. In rural areas like this, the cost would bankrupt the entire system, leaving entrepreneurs like Walters to fill the gap.

'Did Mr Rowland get much mail?' John asked.

Mrs Walters applied a cloth to the barrel's tap, then tucked it over the waistband of her apron. 'Some,' she said. 'I wouldn't say a lot.'

'Difficult to keep up a correspondence, I daresay,' John suggested, 'without the proper use of his hands.'

'Yes, poor dab. Couldn't write with a pen. Managed with chalk on the board, just about. But Nan and Ruth had to write his letters for him.'

'Family correspondence?' I asked. Rowland had, seemingly, been universally loved in Llanddewi Brefi but I was eager to canvass his wider connections if I could.

Mrs Walters sat down on a stool facing us. 'No. For the new school, mostly. To gentlemen, asking for their support. Mind, Nan never told us who he wrote to. She wouldn't, those letters were private. Mr Rowland knew he could trust her. And Ruth. Never had a favourite between them. Always treated them exactly the same.' She paused briefly. Was she looking at us, waiting for some encouragement to go on? But it seemed that she had simply needed to retrieve her thread for she set off again without intervention.

'But – and this isn't gossip, this is fact – he didn't write to his family. Must've been a falling out, mustn't there, for him not to write to them?'

Indeed. Finally, evidence that not everything in Rowland's garden had been entirely prelapsarian.

'Do you know where his family is, Mrs Walters?'

I trained the grey opacity of my blindness on the rim of my beer mug. Above it, I could see the landlady well enough to catch her shake of the head. 'I don't, Mr Probert-Lloyd, I'm sorry.'

I had meant to ask Miss Gwatkyn about Rowland's family but had been distracted by our discussion of his proposed school. Still, there was a remedy at hand. 'Is your son at home?' I asked. 'I have a job for him.'

While she went to find the boy, John took out his pocket book and I dictated a brief note to Phoebe Gwatkyn. He had not yet finished writing when the back door opened and in strode a half-grown lad with bright red hair.

John held out the note. 'Have you been to Miss Gwatkyn's house before?'

'Yes, sir.'

Sir. John would like that.

'So you know where the servants' quarters are? Right, ask whoever answers the door to give this to Miss Gwatkyn straight away and say you've got to wait for a reply and bring it back to Mr Probert-Lloyd. If you're lucky, they'll give you something to eat while you're waiting. Look hungry is my advice.'

Billy Walters dashed off before his mother could add to his burdens by remembering something he could do for her on the way, and John and I rose to take our leave. We had other people to see in Llanddewi Brefi while we waited for Miss Gwatkyn's response.

'Who'll take on the job of local registrar, now,' I asked Mrs Walters, 'with Mr Rowland gone?'

'My Morgan'll have the job, if he can,' she said. 'Going to see about it this afternoon, he is.'

I nodded. Morgan Walters would be well placed to make sure that all births, marriages and deaths were duly recorded. Evidently, very little happened in the parish without his knowledge.

'If that's the case,' I said, 'it would be as well if he came to the inquest at the school on Friday.'

Mrs Walters folded her arms. 'Yes, the inquest. I know he wanted to speak to you about that. Shouldn't it be here, Mr Probert-Lloyd? We're the biggest public house in the village. And the cleanest.'

I had anticipated some objection to the break with custom. 'Even your establishment is still not as big as the school, Mrs Walters.'

Actually, my principal aim in holding the inquest in the school was to remind the jury of the circumstances in which Nicholas Rowland had died but that was a fact I did not wish to share with Mrs Walters.

Keen to remove myself from the Three Horseshoes before her husband could return and berate me on his own account, I moved toward the door but, before I could reach for the latch, the door swung inwards and Minnever's unmistakeable form appeared with an exclamation of satisfaction.

John

Jonas Minnever wasn't in the best of moods.

'It seems that Mahomet won't come to the mountain, so the mountain has postponed meetings, yet again, in order to come to Mahomet,' he said.

'As I told you yesterday, Minnever, I have a job to do.'

'What you don't seem to grasp is that you won't have it for much longer if you pay no attention to the election. You can't keep avoiding people.'

'I'm not avoiding people.' Harry was irritated that Minnever'd followed us. And maybe a little bit embarrassed. But he was going to have to listen to him whether he liked it or not. You can't have an agent and then ignore him, can you? Not if he's doing most of the work for you. Minnever had men out everywhere drumming up support for the election meeting at the end of the week. Today was market day in Tregaron and his minions would be buying plenty of drinks in the hope that people'd come back on Saturday in search of more. Minnever wanted his candidate in town where he could be seen.

'Harry,' I said, 'why don't you wait here for Billy, and have a chat with Mr Minnever, and I'll go and see Mattie Hughes? That'll save time.'

Minnever took Harry by the arm. 'Excellent notion. Mr Davies has a habit of talking sense. You should listen to him.'

Mattie Hughes was sitting in the doorway of his cottage making the most of the light, just like he had been the day before. This time, I could see what he was whittling. A spoon.

'Back, then?' he said, when he saw me walking his way.

'Bad pennies. That's us.' The smile I gave him was wasted. He didn't look up, just carried on pulling the curved blade of the knife back towards his thumb, shaving off curls of pale wood.

I leaned against the wall of his cottage and watched him for a bit. Always nice to watch somebody doing something they're good at.

'Wanted something, did you?' he asked, in the end. 'Thought you were just passing.'

'No. Came to see you.'

'Want to know if I pushed him out of the loft, is it?'

Since you ask… 'Did you?'

'No. But you won't believe me just for saying it, will you?'

Of course I wouldn't just take his word, but there was something he could show me that might back it up. 'Can I come in and have a cup of tea?'

For the first time, he looked up. 'Cheeky pup! Not backward in coming forward, are you?'

I shrugged. 'I can do without the tea if there's none on offer, but I'd rather not talk about your business in the street. Never know who's listening.'

He sighed, pocketed spoon and knife and hopped up on to his one good leg. Then he did an awkward kind of lifting movement with his hip to get the wooden one in place. 'You'll have to take me as you find me.'

He picked up his stool and swung himself around and through the door.

The cottage wasn't big – only one fair-sized room deep – but, despite what he'd said, the place was as neat and clean as a spinster's parlour. He didn't have much in the way of possessions but what there was looked workmanlike. A place for everything and everything in its place.

Next to the big, old-fashioned fireplace there was a stack of turfs as tall as me. Good and burnable, they looked, as if they'd been drying somewhere all winter. On the other side of the hearth, pots were hanging from the beam. One looked big enough for washing. Mattie Hughes didn't boil his own linens, did he? Then again, looked like there was nobody else here to do it. And, if Enoch was right about him not having much work, he wouldn't be able to pay.

'Not married?' I asked.

Mattie shook his head as he swung the kettle over the fire. 'Left it too long.'

For what? To come back from soldiering? To ask the right woman? To be bothered any more? He didn't explain and it wasn't my place to ask. If there wasn't a Mrs Hughes then she hadn't pushed Schoolteacher Rowland out of his loft to get her husband back into steady work. That's all I needed to know.

And it didn't look as if Hughes would've been able to push Rowland out of the loft himself. The reason I'd wanted to see inside his house was standing in the corner. Mattie's bed. He was the sort of man who'd have it out of the way in the loft if he could, I was sure of it.

He saw me looking but didn't say anything.

'Stairs are difficult, I expect?'

Mattie sucked his teeth. He knew what I was asking. And why. 'I can manage proper stairs but not a ladder. Morgan Walters pays me for use of the loft. For storage.'

'What's he storing?'

'All sorts. Got his finger in any number of pies, Morgan Walters.'

'You ever do any work for him?'

'Now'n again.'

He step-tapped to an old, dark-wood sideboard. There were a few tin pots standing on top, some with lids and some without. He opened one and shook some tea into a stained and battered pan. It looked like what you'd get if you asked somebody who'd only ever seen cooking pots to make you a skillet. Straight-sided, shallow, a kind of handle-frame on a hinge. Mattie took it over to the fire and bent down to put it on the hearth. Because of his leg, I suppose, he bent from the waist in a way you wouldn't expect a man of his age to be able to manage. He was fit, supple.

Maybe he was lying about his difficulty with ladders. I tried to imagine it in my mind's eye. He'd have to hop up each rung, wouldn't he? Impossible. Or would he be able to go up backwards, using his arms and arse? But, again, if he could, I was pretty sure he would've done that and kept his bed upstairs.

'Odd-looking teapot.'

'It's a mess tin.'

The kettle must've been warm before he put it back over the fire because it was boiling now. He poured the spitting water on to the tea leaves and fitted what I'd taken for a plate snugly over the top of the mess tin, like a lid.

'Clever,' I said.

'Don't want to carry an ounce more'n you need to when you're marching.'

I could see the sense in that.

'Sit down.' Mattie chin-pointed at the stool which he'd left under the street-side window. I dragged it up to the fire opposite a chair which, going by the arse-shaped dent in the folded blanket on its seat, was where he always sat.

'Think you'll go back to teaching, now Rowland's gone?'

He snorted. 'Not while there's anything better on offer.'

'You didn't like it much, then?'

He swirled the tea in the pan. 'Beggars can't be choosers.'

A sudden thought came to me. 'Where did you used to have your school?' If Miss Gwatkyn had given the cowshed to Rowland, presumably Mattie'd had his somewhere else.

'Here,' he said, not looking up.

I could see the sense in that. His house was warm and dry and if it didn't have desks or a teacher's table then it was no worse than half the schools in the country. Rowland must've been a far better teacher for Llanddewi Brefi's children to've chosen his cold, dark shed over this snug little house.

'Did you teach Nan Walters?'

He glanced at me and I thought he might be about to laugh. 'No, I never taught Nan. Her father sent her to some ladies' school down in Lampeter. Wanted her out of the way of the men who drink at his place till she was old enough to've learned sense.'

I nodded. Sounded as if Nan Walters might be a bit of a flighty piece. That would explain why she'd been sent away to school while her brother stayed home. Then again, he'd need to be learning the family trade. 'Did Morgan Walters support this new school idea of Mr Rowland's?' I asked. If he had his fingers in various pies, it'd be in Walters's interests to see Llanddewi Brefi flourish, wouldn't it?

Mattie nodded. 'Mustard-keen. Hedging his bets, mind, like always.'

I raised my eyebrows. *Tell me more.*

'Giving support to Mr Hildon's idea of a National School, as well, wasn't he? Just in case Nicholas Rowland's ambitions came to nothing.'

'Is that what you thought would happen?'

He grunted. 'Mr Hildon'll have the gentry on his side, won't he?'

Which was exactly what we'd heard from Miss Gwatkyn. 'How did you get on with Nicholas Rowland?' I asked. Llanddewi Brefi was a very small place. They'd have got on one way or another, well or badly.

Mattie Hughes stared at me, watching without giving anything away. 'Still think I might've killed him?'

I shrugged. 'Not really. Don't see how. But everybody seems to've liked him from what we've heard so far. Makes me a bit suspicious, if I'm honest. As if he was too good to be true.'

All right, maybe I egged it a bit to get him to talk but there *was* a part of me that was a little bit sceptical.

Instead of answering, Mattie went back over to the sideboard for two cups. Seemed pretty nimble on his peg-leg.

'You don't use a crutch, then?'

'Suspect me less if I did, wouldn't you?' I gave him his grin back, caught out. 'Use one for walking any distance. Mostly learned to manage without. Been without that leg longer'n I had it, now.'

I wondered what age he'd been when he'd had it amputated but it didn't feel like my business to ask. How old was he, anyway? I wasn't good at guessing people's age – his hair was grey but thick. He could've been anything from fifty to seventy.

He poured the tea carefully. No saucers, I noticed, but the cups were clean. No milk, either. Was that the way soldiers drank it? Maybe he'd just learned to do without to save money.

'So?' I pushed. 'What was he like – Nicholas Rowland?' I blew on my tea and took a sip. Strong enough to set your teeth on edge so he wasn't scrimping on leaves.

'I was a private soldier,' Hughes said. 'Rowland was the sort who would've been an officer.'

I sipped the teeth-coating tea and waited.

'Offered me a job. Thought he could make me into the sort of teacher he was.'

He didn't have to go on. Charitable gesture or not – and Rowland might just've been trying to put Mattie Hughes in his place – he wouldn't have been able to stomach working for Rowland after running his own school.

'Any idea who might want to push him out of his loft?' I asked.

Mattie looked me in the eye. 'That's for definite, is it? Somebody pushed him?'

'Jury's yet to say, but...'

He nodded, eyes still on me. 'I thought your boss must've reckoned something wasn't right for him to've done the view there, in the school.'

The light from the front window dimmed for a second or two as a cart went past. It was a reminder that I shouldn't be there too long. Billy'd be over to Alltybela and back within half an hour if he gave it a clean pair of heels.

'Might've been an argument,' I said. 'Maybe a bit of pushing and shoving. Not an accident exactly but not stone-cold murder, either.'

Mattie said nothing but I thought there might be something he wanted to say.

'Is there anybody he'd be likely to argue with?' I asked.

He shook his head. 'Not for me to start pointing fingers. You'll know the lie of the land soon enough if you speak to those who had business with him.' He hesitated. 'You'll be speaking to those girls and their families, I'm sure.'

In the normal run of things, of course, we'd do exactly that. But, with Minnever wanting Harry in Tregaron, I wasn't so sure. 'If there's something you know, you need to tell me.'

He looked me in the eye like an old dog faced with a bumptious child. 'I don't know any more than anybody else in the parish. If your boss does his job right, he'll find out everything he needs to know.'

—

I was ten yards away from the Three Horseshoes when the door opened and Mr Minnever came out. He was banging the brim of his hat against his leg as if there was something in there that he was trying to dislodge. Something unpleasant. Then he clapped eyes on me.

'Mr Davies. Could you please attempt to talk some sense into your employer? At the moment he's going the right way about losing this election.'

His shiny bald head made him look defenceless, somehow, like a chick coming out of its shell. I was glad when he put his hat on and knocked it down into place.

'What is it you want him to do?'

'I want him to come back to Tregaron! It's market day. The place is heaving. He should be there, talking to people, buying drinks, winning them over.'

'I know.' I did. But I knew Harry, too. 'Trouble is, we've got an inquest to prepare for.'

Minnever shook his head. 'Only in his mind! Other coroners don't *prepare*. They rely on their officers to bring the appropriate people to the hearing and then they simply preside over it. He should be relying on you, not doing everything himself.'

He waited for me to say something. But I wasn't going to get into an argument with him.

'Harry needs to mend his ways,' he said. 'And not just to win the election. He's going to have a fight on his hands even if he *is* elected. The magistrates aren't happy about the way he constantly sees doubt where everybody else just sees death.'

I knew what he meant. The magistrates wanted a coroner who agreed with Minnever's description of the job. But I knew Harry'd never stand for that. *In every case there are too many people with too much to lose,* he'd say. *That's why the coroner needs to dig. Find out what people know but won't volunteer. Then put them on oath so they can't avoid telling the truth.*

Trouble was, he wasn't going to be doing any more digging if he didn't get elected.

I nodded. 'I'll see what I can do.'

Harry

Minnever had barely shut the door on our conversation before he was making an all too audible attempt to recruit John to his cause. How dared he? This was exactly the kind of thing I had feared when he first came to see me: that I would find myself no longer the master of my own fate.

Well, I would not have it.

I moved restlessly around the taproom, unable to sit and simply wait for John. In one corner, Mrs Walters was shovelling soiled sawdust into a bucket and, even from a distance of two or three yards, I could smell a pungent mix of odours. Sawdust, stale beer, pig and horse shit, pipe dottles.

How much longer was John going to be? Damn him, he worked for me, he had no business allowing Minnever to bend his ear.

My state of mind was in no way improved by the fact that Mrs Walters had overheard my argument with Minnever and would, without doubt, relay it to anyone who would listen from now until the election.

Finally, John came in. 'Billy not back yet?'

'No.'

Ignoring my terseness, he drew me to one side and spoke in an undertone. 'I don't think we need to look at Mattie Hughes any more. He can't climb a ladder. His bed's downstairs when he's got a perfectly good loft. He wouldn't sleep in his kitchen like an old man unless he had no choice.'

Apparently, John was going to ignore Minnever's appeal for help, at least for now. 'Did you get anything else interesting out of him?' I asked.

'Not much. Bit tight-lipped to be honest. But he did say that not everybody thought Rowland was the white hen's chick. Didn't name names, but he was pretty definite that, if we asked the right questions, we'd find someone with a motive.'

So Hughes, at least, thought I should be speaking to witnesses and not courting voters' favour. 'D'you think he suspects somebody?'

'Might do. But he said anything he knew was common knowledge.'

'And if we call him as a witness, ask him what he knows?'

John tried to perch on the edge of a table which tilted alarmingly, causing him to straighten up with a muttered oath. 'We'd need to know what to ask him, wouldn't we? You wouldn't get far with, "we think you know something, tell us what it is".'

'All right. We'll talk to him again once we know more. What we need to do now is wait and see whether Miss Gwatkyn can tell us where to find Rowland's family.'

'Don't you think we should be speaking to Miss Walters first?' John asked.

'You could have a long wait, Mr Davies,' Mrs Walters's voice came from behind me. 'Nan and Ruth could be out most of the day. There's a lot of farms for them to get round.'

I turned towards her but, before I could say anything, John put a hand on my shoulder. 'Shall we step outside for a minute, while we wait for Billy? The sun might not make another appearance for weeks.'

I followed him out. And, tactful diversion though his suggestion undoubtedly was, the day did make me glad to be outside. The sunshine was bright and warm, setting the whitewash of Llanddewi's cottages aglow against the mud of the main street, like snowdrops pushing through dead grass in January.

I looked around, taking in the dwellings on one side of us, the church away to the right. Despite the brightness of the wild daffodils that spring had tossed amongst its grey headstones, the cold stone bulk of St David's church loomed over the little houses of the village like a dyspeptic uncle. Grey, squat, brooding. No soaring spire to raise the eye to heaven, just a low, square tower which, at least in my edge vision, had something of the fortress about it.

I closed my eyes and let the April sun warm my face. Somewhere nearby, I could hear the rhythmic sound of a blacksmith's hammer, blows alternating between his anvil and the metal he was working. The sound set off a Welsh proverb in my mind. *Dyfal donc a dyr y garreg.* Dint after dint will break the rock.

An appropriate proverb for the post of coroner, perhaps. The stone of unexplained death, the dint of question after question, witness after witness. The unyielding stone finally gives way and the truth is uncovered.

But when the goal was not a jury's verdict but election to the post of coroner, the necessary dints became a matter of contention. I wished simply to do my job and let my record speak for itself. Minnever argued for pressing the flesh, standing in public houses buying beer for all and sundry and spouting party puffery.

But what Minnever could not know was the soul-eroding effect of hours spent in the company of strangers whose reactions could only be guessed at and whose puzzled, appraising or embarrassed looks were a constant, invisible assault. *Dyfal donc.* Relentless, tiny dints in one's personal armour.

Beside me, John drew in a deep breath. I tensed, waiting for him to speak but he just let the breath out again, as if he had thought better of it. I could not bear it any more. 'Aren't you going to try and persuade me round to Minnever's way of thinking?'

'What's the point? Trying to persuade you to do something you don't want to is like trying to make water run uphill.'

'So you think Minnever's right? You think I should be buying beer for farmers and asking them what they want in a coroner?'

John leaned his head back against the wall. Did he close his eyes, feel the warmth on his eyelids? 'You don't *want* to know what farmers think a coroner should be, Harry. Or what anybody else thinks, for that matter.'

The blacksmith's hammer, having fallen quiet while the metal was back in the coals, now rang out again, its regular strokes insistent on the still, warm air.

John sighed as if in capitulation. 'Obviously you *should* speak to the people who can vote you in,' he said. 'But maybe it'd be better after the meeting on Saturday. When people've heard your speech. When they've got questions.'

Before I could reply, I heard the sound of running feet and looked up to see Billy Walters's red hair. Had he started running when he saw John and me or had he run all the way?

'Mr Probert-Lloyd!' He skidded theatrically to a stop in front of us and doubled over, hands on his knees, panting in a way that seemed too laboured to be real. 'Got your answer from Miss Gwatkyn!'

John took it and Billy stuck his hand out. I reached into my pocket for a penny and, once the boy had moved out of earshot, John unfolded the note.

'*Dear Mr Probert-Lloyd,*' he read.

'*As regards Mr Rowland's family connections, I know only of his father, who was, and may still be, a ship's chandler in Aberaeron. I know, also, that they had not spoken for many years. If you wish to travel to Aberaeron to see him, as I presume you may, I would be more than happy to accompany you. I am a frequent visitor to the town and am accustomed to navigating via a swift route which you might, without guidance, struggle to follow.*

In answer to your other question, yes, Nicholas Rowland had indeed made a will. You will find it lodged with Mr Silas Emmanuel, attorney, in Lampeter.'

'She's just signed it *Gwatkyn, Alltybela,*' John said.

I nodded, thinking rapidly. 'Right. This is what we'll do. We'll write to Miss Gwatkyn, now, and accept her kind offer. Apart from anything else, I wouldn't mind talking to her again. And then, we'll go down to Lampeter and talk to the attorney about Rowland's will.'

'And Mr Minnever?'

'Minnever will just have to get on with his job while I do mine.'

John

The sun was shining as we set off for Lampeter. I'd tapped the Talbot's barometer first thing that morning and the arrow'd shivered but stayed where it was – on *Set Fair*, somewhere between the numbers thirty and thirty-one.

'What are these numbers counting?' I'd asked Harry.

'Inches of mercury.'

'I'm none the wiser.'

'Air pressure. Makes the mercury rise up the tube. The higher the pressure, the nicer the weather. Don't ask me why. That's all I know.'

I might've reached the limit of Harry's knowledge but I was pretty sure Dr Reckitt'd know why air pressure affected the weather. What he called *physical phenomena* were better than meat and drink to him. I'd ask him when he came back for the inquest and the election meeting.

The thought of Dr Reckitt made me grin to myself. I was looking forward to watching him tell people why he thought he should be coroner. When he started talking about cutting everybody up to find out exactly what they'd died of, he'd be lucky if he didn't get things thrown at him.

It's an hour's ride from Llanddewi Brefi to Lampeter if you don't dawdle. And, if you're not dawdling it's hard to talk, so Harry and I didn't say much on the way to see Silas Emmanuel.

We cantered along, the hillside sloping up on our left and flattening out towards the river on our right. Cattle were back in the fields after a winter in the byres and I could see them, winter coats still caked with shit around their bellies and legs, standing in the river meadows, pulling at the new spring grass and putting their heads up to the warmth. All they'd have had during the winter would've been hay and, if they were lucky, some gorse and oats. The spring grass would give them the proper squits.

But I shouldn't be thinking about shit, should I? I had to start thinking more like a steward. When I looked at cattle, I should be pricing them up, wondering how many acres it'd take to rear them till they were ready to go for fattening, or how many milking cows the acreage would support. That was the way stewards had to think – in figures. When I started working with Mr Ormiston – Harry's steward and my boss – he'd been straight with me. We had to make every acre pay, every quarter. If we didn't, the mortgage Harry's father'd taken out to improve the estate was going to ruin us.

By rights, Harry shouldn't have taken me on as under-steward. The estate couldn't afford another employee. But we'd got around it. I lived in at the mansion so I only cost the food I ate, and I'd agreed to work for my keep for a year while I learned the stewarding trade and took my solicitor's exams, at Harry's expense, as insurance. So everything was found for me, right down to the clothes I was wearing. I'd never in my life had more than one decent suit of clothes at a time before but, here I was, in a suit made just for riding about in. I had other clothes for wearing when I wasn't on a horse, and I understood, now, why gentlemen changed for dinner. The ladies they sat down with didn't want to smell saddle oil and horse sweat while they ate their dinner, did they?

Not that there had been any ladies at Glanteifi for a long time. But we'd soon be lighting a fire in one of the damp, neglected bedrooms and it'd be aired for Lydia Howell.

Going to be a nine days' wonder, Lydia's arrival was. The people of Newcastle Emlyn wouldn't know what to think.

Harry Glanteifi's employed a woman *as his private secretary!*

And not just any woman. The sister of Nathaniel Howell, minister and rabble-rouser, who'd run away when the rabble he'd roused during the Rebecca Riots had turned nasty.

We pulled up at the top of a hill to let the mares catch their breath. It was midday. The sun was warm and the primroses on the bank beside us turned their pale little faces up to it as if it had drawn them out of the ground. Which, in a way, I suppose it had.

I glanced over at Harry. I could see that something was worrying him and I had a pretty shrewd idea what it was. Silas Emmanuel. He'd be well within his rights to refuse to discuss Nicholas Rowland's will with us, wouldn't he? Then we would've wasted hours with nothing to show for it and nothing to tell Jonas Minnever when he wanted to know why Harry hadn't come back to Tregaron.

The sooner this damned election was over the better. Then we could just get on with our jobs without people nagging us.

Only trouble was, if Harry didn't pay any attention to the voters, we'd both have one fewer job to do.

–

When we stood in front of the premises of Emmanuel, Pask and Williams, I was even more convinced that we'd get nothing from Silas Emmanuel. The building was on the same street as the entrance to St David's College and it was a lot grander than I'd been expecting. A tall, modern affair with big windows and a little paved area in front, separated from the street by black-painted railings. Looked as if Emmanuel, Pask and Williams'd made sure that their office was ready for the important people who were part of Lampeter life now. People much more important than a cowshed schoolteacher.

But, as it turned out, Mr *Silas* Emmanuel was not the owner of the name on the plaque outside and he was nothing like as impressive as the premises he worked in. A son recently come into the business and doing his best, if I was any judge. The thought that he must've managed the solicitors' exams made me think I'd be all right. Not what you'd call an impressive intellect, Mr Silas.

We sat in his stuffy little box of an office and I watched the expressions come and go on his round, moon-ish face while Harry explained about Rowland's death and our inquiry. We'd made Silas's day – I could see that. Details of a will *he'd drafted* might lead us to a murderer! Harry didn't put it like that, of course, but you could tell that's what Silas thought. You could almost see his eyes lighting up. Motive! Murder most foul! I'd have laid good money on him having a pile of well-thumbed penny bloods somewhere in his house, trained legal man or not.

Mind, once he'd given us the substance of Rowland's will, you could see why he was so excited. There was only one main provision and it might as well have had 'motive' scrawled across it in capital letters.

Without all the legal ifs, thens and hereinafters, the will said this: if anybody was willing to take up Rowland's idea of the collegiate school in Llanddewi Brefi (subject to adherence to founding charter, appended) they were to be given access, via trustees, to all Rowland's money, worldly goods, etcetera.

'You say "all Rowland's financial resources",' Harry said. 'We found a large sum hidden in his living quarters – was there other money?'

'There was a bank account – set up in the name of the trustees of the collegiate school.'

'Might I ask who the trustees were?'

Silas Emmanuel looked a bit uncomfortable, as if he wasn't sure he should say.

'They were obviously people he trusted,' I said. 'I'm sure they'd want to help in any way they could...' I didn't say 'to catch his killer'. I most definitely did not.

'Of course,' he said, still looking uncomfortable. 'I was one...' I waited. Harry didn't interfere. This was what I was here for – seeing reactions he couldn't and making sure I didn't waste a single chance to get information. 'The others were Miss Phoebe Gwatkyn of Alltybela and Mr Daniel Owens, the Unitarian minister.'

There was more. Rowland had been nobody's fool and he'd made sure that the money wouldn't just sit there if anything happened to him. According to Silas Emmanuel, the will said that if, after the period of a year, nobody'd come forward to take over the collegiate school idea, his money, worldly goods, etcetera, were to be shared equally between Miss Anne Walters of the Three Horseshoes public house, Llanddewi Brefi, and Miss Ruth Eynon of Pantglas Farm in the same parish. *In the hope that this will enable them*, Emmanuel quoted from memory, as if it was a marvel, *in the absence of the said collegiate school, to fulfil their common wish to devote their lives to education.*

Well, well, well.

The following morning we rose early once more and, by eight o'clock, we were in Llanddewi Brefi where we had arranged to meet Miss Gwatkyn. It was another pleasant day but, despite the weather, my spirits were not buoyant. The previous evening, in the Talbot's taproom, I had been introduced by Minnever to what felt like the entire male population of the parish, an experience that had been as disturbing as it was exhausting.

I had, of necessity, become accustomed to weighing people up by means other than watching their faces but the strain of paying close attention to tone of voice, such subtleties of body posture as remained visible to me, and what might be called the animal nuances of an encounter, represented an outlay of energy unknown to the fully-sighted. And, even deploying all these means, it was impossible to gain more than the most fleeting impression of the men to whom I was introduced in an almost continuous stream.

Minnever would greet them all with variations on a theme. *My dear sir, you are sure to be a voter in the forthcoming election for coroner? Allow me to introduce Mr Henry Probert-Lloyd, acting coroner for the Teifi Valley.*

And, as instructed, at each salutation I thrust out my hand to be wrung, gripped, shaken or limply held as the mood or fervour took the recipient. I was quite certain that I had shaken more hands in the space of the two hours before dinner than I had in the whole of my life before.

Accustomed to living with the grime and soot of London, I would not have described myself as a fastidious man but, by the end of my public exhibition, I had been gripped by an almost violent need to wash my hands, filthy as they were with second-hand beer, the dirty metallic taint of other people's coinage, and the evil-smelling consequences of a day spent slapping rumps, holding up tails, opening mouths to inspect teeth and brushing marketplace ordure from trouser legs.

Despite being almost entirely at ease when examining the bodies of the dead, I found myself queasy at over-proximity with the living and excruciatingly exposed by Minnever's constant invitations to all and sundry, which included exhortations not to 'mind Mr Probert-Lloyd's gaze – he has lost some of his sight, that's all'. If there was a more uncomfortable social interaction than being scrutinised and judged by those one was unable to see, then I considered myself fortunate not to have encountered it.

–

Miss Gwatkyn, perhaps sensing my mood, initially confined herself to social pleasantries and to describing the route we would take to Aberaeron. We had just turned off the road that would have taken us down the eastern bank of the Teifi towards Lampeter – the route I, knowing no better, would have taken – and struck westwards across country when, tiring of the small talk to which my own self-absorption had confined us, I introduced the subject of our visit to Lampeter the previous day.

'I hope Mr Emmanuel was helpful?' Miss Gwatkyn asked.

'He was, thank you. Without going so far as to let us see Mr Rowland's will, he gave us ample information as to its contents.'

I hesitated, casting about for the right words with which to broach the subject at hand. 'Miss Gwatkyn, I understand your reluctance to think that Mr Rowland's death might have been anything other than accidental, but it seems to John and me that perhaps his will constitutes a motive—'

'For somebody to push him to his death and take over the establishment of the new school? I hardly think so. Nobody knew of the provisions of his will apart from the collegiate school's trustees.'

I nodded, not wanting to disagree too openly. 'I don't wish to be indelicate, but were there not other, more explicit beneficiaries? As I understand it, Mr Rowland's assistants stand to inherit a good deal of money if nobody takes up the founder's mantle.'

I had the impression that Miss Gwatkyn turned her face momentarily towards me before looking back at the road ahead. 'I advise you to put any such notion completely out of your mind, Mr Probert-Lloyd. Quite apart from the fact that I don't suppose, for a moment, that Nicholas had shared the provisions of his will with them, those young women had their hearts absolutely set on being involved with the new school. The last thing they would have wished was for any harm to come to him. And, ambition aside, they worshipped the very ground Nicholas walked on.' She sounded matter-of-fact, speaking whereof she knew.

'Do you know Anne Walters and Ruth Eynon well?' I asked.

'Nan Walters. Nobody calls her Anne. Yes, reasonably well. Nicholas initially asked if I could lend him some books for them. Then, when I showed an interest in their progress, he asked whether I might give them some tuition in history and Latin.'

'Oh. I'd understood that he was tutoring them himself.'

'He was. But he had other calls on his time and felt that they needed more than he alone could provide. Besides,' she paused fractionally, as if to signal that she was being humorous, 'my Latin was better than his.'

I did not doubt it. Phoebe Gwatkyn struck me as the kind of person who, were she to take anything up, would ensure that she did it to the best of her considerable ability. I wondered whether her pupils were cut from the same cloth. 'Were they apt students?'

'Extremely. Though in different ways. Nan is the more outgoing and enquiring of the two. Ruth is quieter – more reserved – but also more studious. She takes pains to commit lessons to memory while her friend is still asking questions.' Her tone changed slightly and I imagined a small smile. 'I think Nicholas was somewhat surprised to have found such suitable assistants here in the wilds.'

'Mattie Hughes told me that Nan's father sent her to a school in Lampeter,' John said. 'Did Ruth Eynon go there, too?'

Miss Gwatkyn turned and answered him as readily as she would me. 'No. Her father wouldn't dream of it. Pay boarding fees for a girl so she could learn to have ideas above her station?' She made a sound which conveyed her contempt for Mr Eynon's illiberal attitude. 'No, I believe one of her Sunday school teachers took an interest in Ruth. Lent her books. After all, literacy is the sole requirement of the autodidact.'

However, it was not the assistant teachers' reading habits that concerned me, so much as their writing. 'Mrs Walters mentioned that her daughter and Ruth Eynon acted as Mr Rowland's amanuenses on occasion?'

'They did. Nicholas couldn't manage a pen, so having Nan and Ruth to write his letters for him was a boon. And they appreciated being able to do something for him, I think. He would never take a penny for the tuition he gave them.'

'Will you allow Nan and Ruth to take over the cowshed academy, Miss Gwatkyn?' John asked. I was impressed at his having remembered the affectionate term Miss Gwatkyn herself had used for the schoolroom.

'For as long as they wish, certainly. Though whether others will allow them to run the school themselves I couldn't say.'

'Others?' I asked.

'Ruth's father may prove unwilling. He's a difficult man. In truth, I was surprised when he agreed to Ruth's working for Nicholas. But times are hard and I suspect that the family may be in need of the money.'

The vague sense of anxiety I had been nursing about not having spoken to Ruth Eynon's parents eased with her words. It seemed that Mr Eynon, like the entrepreneurial Morgan Walters, had a vested interest in Nicholas Rowland's continued existence and employment of his daughter.

We soon came to the point where we had to cross the Teifi and, as we trotted towards the bridge, Miss Gwatkyn announced, with as much pride as if she had engineered it herself, 'This is Pont Gogoyan.' It was a low, shallow-arched structure, quite unlike the bridges that towered above the river further downstream at Newcastle Emlyn and Cenarth, and was rather sinuous in line, tracing a graceful path across the peacefully-flowing river.

'I came across Nicholas here, one day,' Miss Gwatkyn said. 'I was going up to the site of the Roman encampment at Loventium and there he was, just standing on the bridge, watching the river flow.' She paused and I wondered whether she was remembering the conversation they had had. 'He was a great walker. Always out and about in the high summer months when the children were needed in the fields and the school was closed. Thought nothing of walking twenty miles in a day.'

'Did he share your interest in history?' John asked.

'No, not really. He was polite, of course, but Nicholas was far more interested in the future and what he could do to shape it.'

We cantered along on the sunlit valley bottom, past fields bright with the vivid gold of celandines. Cottage doors stood open to the first real warmth of the year and the people we passed at the side of the road greeted Miss Gwatkyn by name.

'Everybody seems to know you,' John said.

'I come this way often. Usually to Loventium. And, don't forget, Mr Davies, my family's been here for centuries.'

'You mentioned the Romans,' John said. 'What were they doing here?'

'What they came to Britannia to do – mine for metal ore. Gold in the Cothi Valley, lead in north Cardiganshire. And, to do it, they drove roads from the south coast up through Cardiganshire and the Beacons, all the way to the Conway estuary. Those roads have all been known by the same name since time out of mind. *Sarn Helen*. One of them runs just north of here.'

I smiled. Miss Gwatkyn's unrestrained pedagogical instincts and authoritative manner reminded me of Lydia Howell and my spirits lifted at the thought of Lydia's imminent arrival at Glanteifi.

I make no promises, she had written in a recent letter, *as I cannot foresee how much instruction and reassurance the new governess will require but, as she arrives tomorrow, I have some hopes of being able to begin my journey to Cardiganshire at the week's end.*

And, if she had set out from Ipswich on Saturday – or even on Monday – she might already have installed herself at Glanteifi and set out from there to Tregaron.

What would Mr Thomas, owner of the Talbot Inn, think of her when she arrived, a lone lady traveller? He would, no doubt, look over her shoulder for a protector or companion.

The small knot of concern that had settled somewhere below my diaphragm pulled a little tighter at the thought. I must not allow myself to be too concerned with the reactions of others to Lydia. If I were to prove unable, in person, to grant her the freedom that I had encouraged in our correspondence, her stay at Glanteifi would be short; that much had become abundantly clear when she had paid her unexpected visit, in January, to propose that she become my private secretary.

Despite the weeks of correspondence we had enjoyed before her visit, I am ashamed to say that, left to myself, it would not have occurred to me to offer Lydia employment. But she had arrived, uninvited and unexpected, into the muddle of my assuming responsibility for the estate, with the idea fully formed in her mind.

My father had still been alive at the time, but I had not consulted him. I had known perfectly well what he would say, if his apoplexy-ravaged brain proved able to marshall the necessary, outraged syllables. Instead, I had simply agreed to Lydia's proposal that I employ her for a trial period of six months.

Though his death might have spared me the need to deal with his disapproval, I knew that my father's reaction would be shared by the gentry of the lower Teifi Valley. They already thought me an odd fellow, but employing Lydia would cast me in the role of dangerous eccentric; it might even exclude me from certain houses.

The knot of tension drew tighter still as I contemplated the implications for Lydia – could she hope to enjoy any kind of society from her position at Glanteifi?

I wondered whether it might be possible to introduce her at Alltybela. Whilst not precisely a servant, she would be in paid employment, a status that rendered drawing-room introductions problematic. But Phoebe Gwatkyn was not like other Teifi Valley matrons. Indeed, had Lydia been coming to West Wales as Miss Gwatkyn's private secretary, few eyebrows would have been raised. Inevitably, some of the older generation would have considered it somewhat modern to employ a woman, but they would have smiled indulgently over their teacups and agreed amongst themselves that Miss Gwatkyn was a character.

Lydia's coming to Glanteifi to work for *me*, however, was going to cause nothing short of a minor scandal.

At a meeting of roads, Miss Gwatkyn pulled her horse up. 'If we were to follow that road to the north,' she pointed, 'in half a mile or so we would reach Loventium and the beginning of the Roman road.'

'Did you bring Nan and Ruth to see the remains?' John asked.

'Hah! I tried, Mr Davies. But the girls are far more interested in the history of these parts as it relates to the romances of the *Mabinogi*. Sarn Helen, for instance. The roads are supposedly named for Elen of Caernarfon who was married to the Emperor Magnus Maximus – the *Mabinogi*'s Macsen Wledig. The story goes that he dreamed of a beautiful maiden in a castle and sent men all over the empire to find her. Building roads as they went.'

We rode in silence for two or three miles, the terrain becoming hillier and more demanding of the horses. Amongst the tightly interwoven hills with their sudden, gorse-hung slopes and stands of trees, the sound of water was ubiquitous. Tiny streams and brooks gurgled over stone and cut channels through fields. Drainage ditches oozed and trickled. And, everywhere, water seeped slowly but inexorably through soil and peat and moss, down to the streams and thence to the Teifi which would take it to the sea. It was a sound I had been unaware of missing until my failing sight had driven me home.

On the banks of one small stream, a scatter of houses, a forge and a chapel marked a village.

'This is Capel Gartheli,' Miss Gwatkyn said. 'Saint Gartheli founded Christian settlements from one end of the country to the other during the Dark Ages, including Llanddewi Brefi. Llanddewi was only renamed after Saint David turned up at the synod of Brefi and preached so decisively against the Pelagian heresy that there was no more to be said on the matter.' She paused and, in my peripheral vision, I saw her turn her face to me once more. 'It might be worth your taking heed of Gartheli in your campaigning, Mr Probert-Lloyd. It's not always the man who does all the spadework that gets the glory. Sometimes it's the man who has the right argument at the right time.'

John

Aberaeron didn't look like a Welsh town. Or, at any rate, it didn't look like Newcastle Emlyn or Cardigan or Carmarthen. It wasn't higgledy-piggledy. It didn't have little roads and lanes going off in all directions and tiny cottages mixed in with shops and bigger houses. The houses were all the same – square-on to the road, two and three storeys high, double-fronted. Recently built and prosperous looking. Even the streets were grand – wide, well kept. And clean.

After parting from Miss Gwatkyn at the Feathers Hotel and leaving the mares in the stables there, we walked up to the quayside. It was as different as you could imagine from the little seaports I knew. Boats didn't come up on to the beach, or on to wharfs like at Cardigan. At Aberaeron the sea was tamed by high, stone harbour walls. It looked... modern. Business-like. If I hadn't already known how Aberaeron came to be, it still would've been obvious. Somebody with a lot of money had planned it and built it.

The quay was noisy after the quiet ride up – waves slapping against the harbour wall, boats nudging each other with a solid, wooden sound, iron-rimmed wheels on the cobbles as barrows and carts went to and fro. And that was before all the chattering and shouting of sailors and dockside men.

The air was thick with smells as well. That seaweed smell of the sea, the boats with their tar and fish, and a throat-catching, steamy smoke from billowing lime kilns.

The first person we asked about Rowland's chandlery told us we were in the wrong place.

'He moved – five, six years ago. He's in Ship Street now. Behind this lot.' He jerked a thumb over his shoulder at the impressive buildings that looked out over the harbour.

Ship Street turned out to be much less grand than the waterfront. It was narrower, with small commercial premises and workshops. Rowland's place wasn't hard to find. There was a sign hanging above the door – Ship's Chandlery. Flaking and faded. Didn't exactly encourage you to come here for your goods. If you were setting out on a long journey, you'd worry that your stores had been mouldering away here for months before you bought them.

The shop looked small from the outside, just a single window on one side of the door, and it wasn't any more impressive on the inside. We walked into a longish, narrow room with a flight of stairs against one wall. There was a door at the top, so Rowland probably lived over the shop.

Before I could make out much of what was in there, a woman spoke to us from behind the counter. 'Good day, gentlemen. Can I help you?'

She might've spoken in English, but her accent said she was as Welsh as I was.

'We're looking for Mr Rowland,' Harry said. 'Is he here?'

I could tell she was surprised that this gentleman in riding clothes would speak to her in Welsh but she tried not to let it fluster her. 'My husband isn't in the best of health today,' she said, carefully. 'But if there's anything you'd like to order I can note it down...?'

Did we look as if we'd come to order ship's stores? But then, I suppose she had to say something. Show willing. She looked as if she did a lot of that – her face had the kind of permanently worried look people have when they're used to being at fault. About forty, I supposed. On the thin side but nicely dressed, and not in a *betgwn* and apron. Like the town, she had a more up-to-date look. Mind, having said that, her dress was faded with washing and she wasn't any kind of needlewoman. The darns here and there were obvious.

'We're not here for supplies,' Harry said, as if he was letting her into a confidence. 'We're here to speak to Mr Rowland about his son, Nicholas.'

Her eyes widened when she heard that and one hand went up to her face.

'I don't know—'

'Please,' Harry said. 'We won't keep him long, but it is important.'

Didn't have much choice, did she? She turned away and started to climb the stairs. Slowly, dragging it out.

Harry turned to me and put his finger to his lips. I hadn't been going to say anything, anyway. I knew what these places were like – only a plank floor separating us from the room upstairs.

I looked about. I don't know what I'd expected – maybe something like a grocer's shop only more so – but, whatever was on sale, it was all packed into boxes, barrels and drawers of every size on the wall behind the counter. Biggest at the bottom – wide and deep enough to hold a small child or ten pairs of boots – smallest at the top, for papers of needles and pins and that sort of thing.

It might have been small and gloomy but the shop was tidy, cared for. The air smelled of soap and clean linen and salt. Mind you, there was a slightly less pleasant smell coming from a big barrel under the stairs. A smell I was familiar with from my old lodgings. Cheap lamp oil. We might have been having to economise at Glanteifi but Mrs Griffiths, the housekeeper, hadn't sunk to buying fish oil yet.

Mrs Rowland reached the top of the stairs and I heard her footsteps pattering across the boards. Then she stopped and spoke. Couldn't make the words out. I waited but there was no answer.

I looked at Harry. His face wasn't giving anything away.

Then there was some creaking, as if somebody was moving in an old chair whose joints were loose.

I heard Mrs Rowland speak, then came what was almost a shout. 'Let me be, woman!'

A heavy shuffling overhead, as if a hefty weight was being pushed, a bit at a time. Then Mr Rowland appeared at the top of the stairs. Bent, one hand gripping the edge of the wall. He shuffled forward again and reached out with his other hand to catch hold of the rope that was fastened to the wall. It was a thick kind of ship's rope, fed through eyelets attached to the stone. Not exactly a polished bannister rail but it did the job.

He came down, two feet to each tread. And if those feet were as knotted with arthritis as his hands were then he must've been in agony. Looked as if he'd have little more use of his fingers than his son'd had.

At the bottom of the stairs he half-turned and steadied himself on the oak post that was holding the first floor up. Head bent, he looked at me and Harry from under thick, white eyebrows. He obviously couldn't straighten up properly and I realised that the joints in his backbone must be affected as well. The man was collapsing in on himself.

'I am Caradog Rowland. What do you want with me?' He was standing in the light from the window and I could see his eyes clearly. They were forget-me-not blue and seemed to have no pupils. I'd seen eyes like that before. In a woman who'd been dosing her grief with laudanum.

Harry moved forward, as if he wanted to spare the old man the effort of speaking too loudly. 'It's about your son, Mr Rowland,' he said.

The old man kept his eyes on Harry. No matter that keeping his head in that position was causing him pain, making him shake, he didn't look away.

'I have no son.' The words came out flat. Without expression. As if he'd said them again and again till they were meaningless.

Harry cocked his head on one side as if he wasn't sure he'd heard properly. 'Nicholas Rowland wasn't your son?'

The old man didn't move, eyes pointing straight at Harry's. You could tell he would've given his right arm to stand up straight and face Harry down. 'I had a son, once. Not any more.'

I saw a movement at the top of the stairs. Mrs Rowland was standing there, her hands knitted together in front of her.

'Mr Rowland,' Harry said, 'I'm very sorry to be the bearer of bad news. But Mr Nicholas Rowland is dead. He was found on Monday morning, with a severe wound to his head, on the floor of the school where he was a teacher.'

There was a flicker of something on the old man's face. Not sadness. Not pain. If you'd put a gun to my head and told me to name the expression, I'd have had to call it relief.

His wife started down the stairs towards him. 'Caradog—'

Rowland didn't so much as look in her direction. 'Come down and mind the shop. My business here is finished.' He turned to go but Harry stepped forward.

'An inquest will be held. The day after tomorrow. In Llanddewi Brefi.'

The old man didn't turn, didn't stop. Just caught hold of the rope bannister and started pulling himself up the stairs. I could only imagine what it cost him. 'That...' his breaths were coming hard, now, 'is no... concern... of mine.'

Mrs Rowland stood aside at the top of the stairs and I saw him knock her hands away as she tried to help him. 'Let me be. Go and mind the shop.'

She came down almost as slowly as he had. When she reached the bottom, she looked from me to Harry and back again. Before she could speak, Harry inclined his head at the door and made an inviting motion with his hand. *Let's go outside where your husband won't hear.*

The sunlight was bright after the darkness inside the shop and it pinched at my eyes. Mrs Rowland put a hand up to shade her face. 'You must forgive my husband,' she begged, voice low in case he heard. 'Some days he's in such pain that he barely knows what he's saying.'

'The laudanum must help?' I said.

She looked at me, shocked. I shrugged. 'The signs are there if you've seen them before.'

'He only takes it for the pain—'

'Mrs Rowland,' Harry said, gently, 'we quite understand.'

She nodded, close to tears.

'We've been told that there was no communication between your husband and his son, Nicholas. It seems that may be true?'

Mrs Rowland dropped her eyes to the ground and laced her fingers tightly together again. 'My husband never mentions him. If I hadn't known, before I married him, that he had a son, I wouldn't know Nicholas existed.'

'What caused the rift between them?' Harry asked.

'I don't know,' she said, her face creased with all the many questions her husband'd never answered. 'He won't talk about it. Never has. I soon learned not to ask.'

I remembered that move of her hand to her face when Nicholas'd been mentioned – was it Caradog Rowland's fists that had taught her that lesson?

She was staring at Harry. Perhaps she was wondering why he was looking somewhere over her shoulder. A light breeze lifted a stray lock of hair off her temple. She might not have a single strand of grey yet, but lines of worry and tension had marked her face.

'Nobody in the family told you anything?' I asked.

'All I know,' she said, keeping her voice low and glancing up at the window above us, 'and this is from others, not from my husband, is that Nicholas was taken to a doctor after an accident and never spent another night under his father's roof.'

'An accident?' Harry asked.

'It was in the old shop. The rope for the loft's trapdoor snapped and it fell shut on Nicholas's hands. My husband was out the back doing something and it took him a while to hear the shouts. The boy's fingers were mangled beyond help, by all accounts.'

There was something in her voice – and her eyes – as she told that story. I don't think she believed it.

'And he was taken away to a doctor?' I asked.

'Yes.'

'And never came back?'

She shook her head, eyes troubled.

'When exactly did this happen?' Harry asked.

'Must be getting on for twenty years ago.'

'How long have you been married?' He'd be going on the sound of her voice which belonged to a youngish woman.

'To Caradog? Fifteen years. I was married before, but my first husband died.'

'Do you and Mr Rowland have any children?'

Such a look passed over her face then. A look full of tears and despair.

'No. I had a son from my previous husband when Caradog and I married. But he died.'

Old Man Rowland had no heir, then. Was it that, rather than age and infirmity that had brought him to cower in this backstreet?

A gull screeched overhead and I looked up. The bird's smooth underbelly was a pure white against the blue of the sky. It screamed its challenge to the air and wheeled around to join the other gulls over the harbour. One step outside the chandler's door and we were in a different world. Gloom and age and silence inside, sun and vigour and life outside.

If I'd been Mrs Rowland, I would've wanted to run and run. But then, where would she go?

'When he died,' Harry said, 'Nicholas Rowland was in possession of a large sum of cash. Is there any possibility that some of it came from his father?'

Mrs Rowland seemed to drag her thoughts from wherever they were to what Harry was saying. 'No, sir. We haven't got a penny to give away. Much less a large sum. And even if we did, his son is the last person my husband would give it to.'

'What about Mr Rowland's first wife? Does she still have family here?'

'Only me. She was my cousin. Everybody else close is gone.' She looked at Harry again. 'Everybody who might know, I mean.'

'Friends? Former neighbours?' Harry suggested.

An expression came and went, like a cloud skimming past the sun, flickering darkness, then gone. But she could wipe it off her face all she liked, I'd seen it. *If you think my husband is the sort of man who'd blab family secrets, you haven't got the sense you were born with.*

'No, sir,' she said. 'There's nobody.'

Harry chewed his lip and nodded. I could tell he hadn't expected any other kind of answer.

We thanked Mrs Rowland and left her on the doorstep. When I turned at the end of the street and looked back, she was still there. Still standing in the warm sun.

We had arranged to meet Miss Gwatkyn back at the Feathers Hotel and we walked in that direction now, past the tall, open arches of the town hall's marketplace.

The smell of the sea was less pronounced here than it had been on the harbour, almost lost in the pervasive town smells of horse dung and coal smoke. Still, there was something different in the Aberaeron air, something bracing despite the warmth of the April sun, and I could see why people had flocked to live here: elegant architecture, dignified civic buildings, a port that was attracting more industry by the month.

I was roused by a sudden outburst from John.

'Did you believe all that nonsense about an accident with a trapdoor?'

I was taken aback. 'You clearly don't.'

'Not for a second! A snapped rope? The old man conveniently out of the way? Something more deliberate happened there, take it from me. And that was the reason Nicholas never came back.'

'You think he deliberately injured his son? Why?'

'Who knows? But I don't think it was an accident any more than I think Rowland fell out of the schoolroom loft of his own accord.'

–

The Feathers Hotel, grandiose and gleaming white in the sun, was as welcoming as the Talbot Inn but far superior when it came to the appointment of its interiors and the fineness of its tableware.

When we asked for Miss Gwatkyn, we were shown to a table next to the window in a small dining room. Divested of her travelling cape, she was dressed in a simple, blue-grey riding habit and, even to me, she looked very different from the figure who spent her days at Alltybela in a woollen over-dress and the eccentric footwear John had described to me. As we joined her, she put aside the book she was reading and asked for more tea to be brought.

'How did you fare?' she asked, as we sat down.

'We were able to speak with Mr Rowland senior,' I said. 'It seems he has suffered a decline in his fortunes in recent times.'

I told her what we knew of the chandlery's move to a less prominent position and the necessity of Mrs Rowland's managing the shop. 'Her husband is a sad soul,' I concluded. 'Crippled by arthritis and all but refusing to acknowledge that he ever had a son.'

'Did you discover the cause of the rift between them?' Miss Gwatkyn asked, pouring the tea that had just arrived.

'No. Mr Rowland senior didn't wish to speak to us and his wife – who's not Nicholas Rowland's mother – seems to know nothing of why he left Aberaeron. All she knows is that he has never returned and her husband refuses to speak of him.'

I hesitated before asking the question that John's suspicions had raised; it felt indelicate. 'Did Mr Rowland ever talk to you,' I began, 'about the damage to his hands? Dr Reckitt is quite convinced that he was not born with the deformity.'

'No,' she said, 'Nicholas didn't volunteer any information on the subject and I didn't like to ask.' She paused to take a sip of her tea. 'It wasn't that he tried to hide it. For instance, when he first came to me to talk about setting up his school, he freely acknowledged that he didn't have full use of his hands and would need assistance.' She put her cup down and I felt her gaze on me.

Not wishing to try and meet her eye only to fail and induce pity, I fixed the whirlpool on the tablecloth and looked over it at the blue and white cup in front of her. 'From what we've just been told,' I said, 'it seems that whatever happened to damage his hands might be the cause of Mr Rowland's leaving Aberaeron.'

Miss Gwatkyn did not reply straight away but sipped once more at her tea. 'I see.'

Again, I hesitated before speaking. 'John thinks Mr Rowland senior might have been responsible. That what is given out as an accident with a trapdoor was actually deliberate.'

Miss Gwatkyn turned to John. 'What makes you think that?'

'The story we were told just seemed unlikely.'

At her request, John repeated Mrs Rowland's second-hand account and I was struck, as always, by his remarkable facility for remembering, verbatim, anything he had heard.

'Nicholas never spoke of his family,' Miss Gwatkyn said, when John had finished. 'I enquired after them, as one does, when we first met, only to be told that that part of his life was over. That he and his father were estranged beyond hope of reconciliation. Naturally, I did not raise the subject again.' She paused as if to illustrate her point. 'Shall we order some lunch?'

In London, a hungry man might choose between any number of dining facilities – from the stained trestle tables, uncomfortable box booths and steel-pronged cutlery of the slapdash and squalid lower end, to the pristine linen, impeccable serving men and electro-plated cutlery of the likes of Simpson's – but I had not expected much of Aberaeron. So it was a delightful surprise when a courteous young man presented us with a very creditable lunch which we consumed from fine china on a table draped in a perfectly glowing cloth. Evidently, it was not just Aberaeron's architecture that was determinedly à la mode.

Over our cold pie, cheese and piccalilli, Miss Gwatkyn steered away from the subject of Nicholas Rowland and asked whether I felt ready to speak to the electorate at the public meeting in Tregaron on Saturday. 'Presumably,' she said, without any apparent embarrassment, 'you must prepare better than your rivals as you cannot rely on notes to prompt you?'

'I'm hoping that the skills I learned as a barrister will stand me in good stead. When you're defending a man, you must have all the facts committed to memory so that you can produce the necessary one at will.'

Unlike Minnever, Miss Gwatkyn accepted that the skills of a barrister and an electioneer might be comparable, for which I was grateful. But, in truth, I had slept poorly for several nights now, as I gave speech after speech in my head, each making different points, none of which satisfied me and would not, I was quite sure, satisfy a rowdy mob.

'It's interesting to see the parties' different strategies for the meeting,' John said. 'Mr Minnever – the Liberal Party agent – is determined to introduce Harry to every voter he can lay hands on before the poll. But there's been no sign of the Tories or their candidate.'

It was true; Mr Montague Caldicot had evidently seen no need to pre-empt his first encounter with the electorate by coming to Tregaron and making himself generally agreeable and, though Minnever had poured scorn on 'poor Party strategy', it seemed to me that my rival's absence might be an indication of Tory confidence. I asked Miss Gwatkyn whether she was acquainted with Caldicot.

'No, not personally. I'm acquainted with the family, of course, but Montague I know only at second hand.'

I waited, but she said no more. 'Would it be indelicate to ask what you know of him?'

Miss Gwatkyn spent some moments folding her napkin. 'Not very much, I'm afraid. But, coincidentally, he did feature, indirectly, in the conversation we had when you came to see me at Alltybela.' She laid the folded napkin down on to the tablecloth, and let her hand remain on top of it. 'He was the Cardiganshire gentleman who suggested Llanddewi Brefi as a suitable setting for Nicholas's school.'

'Caldicot knew Rowland?' I hoped I did not sound as astonished as I felt.

'I believe they had mutual friends in London.'

What friends, I wondered, would a son of the landed gentry share with an impoverished teacher? But then I recalled that Rowland had taught at University College. The idea that

Caldicot might be interested in science or philosophy was, I must confess, a little disconcerting; it made him seem a far more formidable opponent.

'I see. In that case I should speak to him. It's possible that he might have information on Mr Rowland's connections in Cardiganshire.'

'I think that very unlikely,' Miss Gwatkyn said. 'I don't believe they were anything more than casual acquaintances.'

'They didn't maintain any association here?'

'Not to my knowledge. Mr Caldicot and his wife are only very recently returned to the family seat at Llysrheidol. Presumably to be seen to be resident in the county before the election.' She smiled, wryly.

'And, previously, they lived in London?'

'Montague certainly maintained a house there and I believe that's where his wife lived. But he had a commission in the army so he may well have been in London only sporadically, himself.'

'If he was a soldier, I assume he's not the heir? He hasn't come home to inherit?'

'No, he has an older brother. Not that there seems to be any immediate prospect of anybody inheriting. Their father's as vigorous and determined as ever.' She paused and I wondered whether she glanced in my direction. 'A man after your late father's heart, actually. A resolute agricultural improver.'

Miss Gwatkyn was, I noticed, far more comfortable talking about Caldicot senior than she was to discuss Montague.

'And my opponent?' I asked. 'What of him?'

She sighed. 'You are determined to force me into indiscretion, Mr Probert-Lloyd.'

'Not at all! I do beg your pardon.'

I thought I detected a sudden smile on her face but I was, possibly, seeing what I wished to see. 'Oh, don't mention it. It's pleasant not to be treated as if one were made of glass.' Having accepted my apology, I thought she would change the subject but she did not. 'I dare say, if he were still alive, your father would have been able to give you the information you're looking for.'

'So,' I said, carefully taking her lead, 'were my father able to pass on such information, what would he tell me?'

At the edge of the whirlpool, I watched Phoebe Gwatkyn's fingers moving restlessly on the heavy, white tablecloth. Gathering crumbs together, possibly. Though we were sitting next to the window, the room faced north and the light was not bright, making it even more difficult than usual for me to interpret small movements.

'Howell Caldicot of Llysrheidol has given everybody to understand that his son resigned his commission so that he could take up a career in politics,' she said, finally. 'But I believe it's common knowledge amongst his peers that Montague was cashiered from his regiment.'

Miss Gwatkyn might choose to believe that my father would have repeated such information, but I knew with absolute certainty that he would not. Even had he known it to be true, he would have regarded speaking of it as the most egregious discourtesy.

'May I ask whether the reason for his drumming-out is also common knowledge?'

The crumb-gathering continued unabated. 'Not to me.'

Whatever the reason, it must have been something significant; no officer was cashiered for a trifle and the loss of both money and face was considerable.

This information suggested that Caldicot's candidacy for the post of coroner, far from being a stepping stone to membership of parliament, was, in fact, a response to an urgent need for a respectable public office. And the fact that that office was here, in Cardiganshire, was all to the good. Short of crossing the Irish Sea, it was scarcely possible to be any further removed from metropolitan scrutiny.

'What *is* common knowledge,' Miss Gwatkyn added, unexpectedly, 'is that Montague's wife, Cecile, is in no way reconciled to her exile from London. She wishes to return with all possible speed.'

The picture became clearer still. Montague Caldicot would remain in the Teifi Valley only for as long as it took society's attention to move on to some other scandal, before appointing a deputy and quietly removing his establishment back to London. Deputies, and the absentees who nominated them, might be unpopular but, once elected, a coroner did not need to court public approval.

Until this afternoon, I had assumed that I would not meet Caldicot until we shared the stage in Tregaron marketplace at the weekend. However, given that he had been acquainted with Nicholas Rowland, I felt that John and I would be well advised to pay him a visit before the inquest to see whether he could shed any light on the teacher's wider circle of acquaintance. Rowland might have spent the previous three years living in a cowshed but the scant details of his life so far suggested that he had been anything but a conventional schoolmaster.

I turned back to Miss Gwatkyn. 'How long would it take to travel from Tregaron to see Caldicot at Llysrheidol?'

John

We'd been invited to stay at Alltybela that night and, by the time we'd got back and changed, there was only half an hour or so before Miss Gwatkyn joined us for dinner. That was normally the time when Harry sneaked off to write to Lydia Howell but, as she was probably already on her way here, he asked me if I'd read the newspaper to him. 'I think there's one over there,' he pointed, 'on the table where the lamp is?'

As I might've guessed, now I'd got to know Miss Gwatkyn a bit better, the newspaper was some dissenting, liberal rant-sheet. I opened it up and ran my eyes down the columns, looking for something that'd interest Harry. It wasn't half a minute before my fingers were black and I was worrying about smearing newsprint on to Miss Gwatkyn's table linen.

'There's a thing here about the census,' I told him. 'Want to know what they think?'

'Which paper is it?'

I told him and he laughed. 'Their views'll be an antidote to Reckitt's, I'm sure!'

Dr Reckitt had been all for the new, improved census. According to him, it wasn't just a tax-revenue head-counting exercise any more. Now we'd have what he called 'real data'. Well, *we* wouldn't have it, obviously. Nobody'd see his blessed data for another fifty years except the civil servants and God alone knew what they were going to do with it.

I scanned the tiny print. 'No,' I said, 'they don't agree with Reckitt in any way whatsoever. *The notion that the registration districts' chillingly-titled "enumerators" can simply deliver census forms on Saturday, expect householders to complete them on Sunday, and collect the resulting information, neatly transcribed, on Monday is simply laughable,'* I read. *'And, frankly, insulting. For the forms are all in English. A language of which upwards of fifty per cent of the working people in our county have insufficient grasp even to understand the words "head of household" or "occupation". And, even were they to understand them, are they masters of sufficient literacy to read such words or inscribe their responses correctly? Until the government sees fit to provide the whole population with a decent education at the state's expense, this intrusion should cease. No Welshman should be humiliated on his own hearth by having to ask the enumerator, a person with whom, in all likelihood, he will be acquainted, for help in recording the most intimate details of his family. The births of his children, the age of his wife, the words he must muster up to describe his own occupation, whether he and all his household were born in the county or elsewhere – all must be recorded for a government that cares not a jot for him as long as he pays his taxes and obeys the law.'*

Harry grinned. 'He's right. I don't suppose people'd be happy having to ask Simi Jones for help filling in their form, would they?'

'Nobody'd have to ask him. Thanks to Rowland, the children would've been able to fill in the forms if their parents couldn't.'

'Did you do that?' he asked. 'In the last census?'

The previous Sunday, when I'd been recording the details of the whole Glanteifi household, Harry'd asked me whether I remembered the previous census but not whether I'd had to do the writing for Dada. Had he only just remembered the kind of home I came from? Or did he think that me mentioning Llanddewi's children was an invitation to talk about it?

'My father could read and write, thank you.'

'Yes, of course. I'm sorry. I didn't mean to imply...' Harry trailed off. Of course he'd meant to *imply*. As it happened, he wasn't far off the truth. I'd exaggerated. My father could read Welsh but not English and his writing hadn't been good enough for forms. Not for anything except signing his name, truth be told.

'Mind, I wrote a nice hand, even then,' I said, to let him off the hook of his embarrassment, 'so he got me to do it.'

William Davies, 30, tenant farmer

Nancy Davies, 30

John Davies, 9

Sali-Ann Davies, 4

My parents hadn't both been thirty as a matter of fact – Dada'd been thirty-four and Mam thirty-two but you were supposed to round down to the nearest five years for everybody over fifteen. Not on the recent one, though. No females had been able to present themselves as younger than they were on that one, not when they'd had to give their actual date of birth.

I wondered if the government understood how many people didn't know the year they were born. If you didn't have a family Bible to write it in, it was easy to forget. You might remember the day, but not the year. Now, of course, the government knew. Everybody born for the last fourteen years was supposed to've had the day of their birth registered, weren't they?

Would the recording officers check, I wondered – see if the birth registers matched the census? If they checked, they'd know that some people still weren't getting round to registering their babies. How many children would there be on the census that the government knew nothing about?

Not that it'd make any difference. They weren't suddenly going to say, 'Oh dear, look at the number of children in Cardiganshire – we'd better see about some schools over there,' were they?

The government didn't care about what happened to us. As long as we paid our taxes and didn't disturb the peace. And as long as we didn't insist on speaking our barbaric, immoral language, of course.

–

We were just settling down to dinner when a maid came in. She gave Miss Gwatkyn a worried curtsey, then whispered something to the butler. He sent her away, crossed the room and bent down to murmur something in his mistress's ear.

Whatever the message was, Miss Gwatkyn was surprised, I could see that. She didn't say anything to us while dinner was being served but, once the butler and the maids were gone and we just had one footman in attendance, she took a sip of wine and looked over at me.

'Simi Jones, the *plwyfwas*, has sent word that the *ceffyl pren* is to be carried tonight in the village.'

I opened my mouth to reply but Harry got there before me. Of course, she'd really been speaking to him. 'Are you intending to stop it?'

By rights, Miss Gwatkyn should be sending a message to the magistrates because carrying the *ceffyl pren* was illegal. As far as the authorities were concerned, people gathering after dark in the open air for any purpose was an unlawful assembly and they were as hot as mustard on stopping the *ceffyl pren* being carried whenever they could. Which wasn't often to be honest. Unless the local police officers got wind of it before the procession started, there was no way they'd be there in time, or in sufficient numbers, to do anything about it.

Miss Gwatkyn cut into her fish. 'No. I make it my policy not to do that. If the people feel that they have a grievance which the law of the land cannot or will not address, then it seems to me that the *ceffyl pren* allows the boil to be lanced.'

Then why had she told us? I glanced across at the footman who was doing the see-no-evil, hear-no-evil thing that well-trained servants do. But he was listening all right. He'd be the centre of attention in the kitchen when he went back down. Everybody'd be waiting to hear the mistress's reaction.

'Is it carried here often?' Harry wanted to know.

In the area near Glanteifi, the *ceffyl pren* hadn't had an outing since the Rebecca Riots. People'd got scared of what nocturnal gatherings led to. Not to mention the fact that there were police in town now, and they wouldn't stand for it. But there was no police station in Llanddewi Brefi. People could black their faces and get a mob together to their hearts' content. Go to whomever's house they liked. Drag them out and make them face up to their wrongdoing, without fear of being arrested.

'Not often, no,' Miss Gwatkyn put her knife and fork together in the middle of her plate. How she kept body and soul together I don't know — she ate like a bird.

'Does Simi Jones know who they're going out to?' Harry asked.

'Of course.' Miss Gwatkyn played with the stem of her wine glass. 'That's why he thought I should know. It's Mattie Hughes. It seems that he's being blamed for Nicholas's death. Simi's message was that they're going to try and persuade him to confess so as to avoid an inquest.'

I looked over the starched tablecloth at Harry. Because of where the candle-tree was placed, half of his face was more or less in shadow but I could see that, as usual, he wasn't showing much expression. Only his eyes moved, constantly, to make the best use of that edge-vision of his.

'Are you confident they won't do him any harm?' he asked. 'That they won't resort to summary justice?'

She shook her head. 'Simi Jones will keep the peace.'

'Would you have any objection to our abandoning you in order to act as observers?'

Miss Gwatkyn smiled. 'If I objected to your going, Mr Probert-Lloyd, I wouldn't have told you that it was happening.'

–

'You'll need coats and hats to disguise you in case you're seen,' Miss Gwatkyn said, once we'd finished the suet pudding. 'I have a variety of appropriate items here that belonged either to my father or my husband.'

Husband?

'Miss Gwatkyn, I'm so sorry.' Harry was almost stammering. 'I didn't realise you were a widow. The people in the village referred to you as Miss Gwatkyn and I naturally assumed—'

'Mr Probert-Lloyd, please desist! I'm not a widow, as it happens. My husband is alive and well. However, as he's never taken up a position as master of Alltybela, I considered it prudent to retain the family name. So, despite the fact that I am, legally, Mrs Leonard Barton, at Alltybela I remain Miss Gwatkyn.'

Never mind what name she used – *where was her husband?*

'My husband does not enjoy robust health,' she said, as if I'd asked the question out loud. 'Sun and warmth are essential to him so, for many years now, he's lived in Italy. If he were to live here, in our cold, damp climate, I don't believe he would survive a twelvemonth.'

She might be doing a good job of hiding it but Miss Gwatkyn was embarrassed. You could tell by all the information she was giving us. More than was needed by a long way. Was she hiding something behind talk about the weather? I mean, it wasn't unheard of for people to live abroad for their health, was it? Granted, they usually took their spouse with them, but still…

'I generally spend the months of December and January with him in Naples. I don't tolerate heat well but the winter temperatures are pleasant. There's far more sunshine in winter there than here.'

'That sounds delightful.' Harry'd recovered from his stammers. 'I hope your husband's health is improving?'

Miss Gwatkyn smoothed the front of her tunic where it lay in her lap, as if it was a cat. 'Thank you, Mr Probert-Lloyd. Fortunately, his health gives very little cause for concern in that southern climate.'

She rose to her furry-booted feet. 'Shall we?'

–

After she'd found us some fusty coats and a couple of hats that made us look like our own grandfathers, we changed into our riding clothes and Miss Gwatkyn took us down to the kitchen to black our faces. Except we weren't allowed to do it ourselves. The po-faced butler got one of the footmen to do it so we didn't get our hands dirty. I stared at his face as he rubbed greasy soot around my ears and the point of my jaw but he wouldn't meet my eye. It was as bad as the business with the maids treating me as if I was invisible – I was neither fish nor fowl these days.

When I was a child, my parents and the other adults had always grumbled that we weren't people to the squires, that they treated us like animals. But, looking at the footman's face, it seemed to me that he wasn't exactly treating *me* like a person, either. To him, I was a gentleman – a job. He didn't care about my feelings or what I was going over to the village to do. He just cared about getting the greasy soot on to my face in a way that'd keep a civil tongue in the butler's head.

'Do you intend to ride or go on foot?' Miss Gwatkyn wanted to know once we were set.

I knew Harry was nervous about riding in the dark and it'd be worse, here, where he didn't know the roads. 'Probably best to walk,' I said. 'Then we won't have the horses to deal with when we get there.'

Miss Gwatkyn nodded. 'I'll get my hall-boy to take you across the fields.'

Instead of asking somebody to find him, she just opened a door and called down the hall. 'Lleu! Come here, please!' She grinned at us like a mischievous child. 'His real name's Daniel but we already had a Daniel when he arrived so I call him Lleu Llaw Gyffes because he's a handy, fair-haired boy.'

She was obviously looking for a reaction but Harry looked as blank as me. Her grin disappeared and she tutted. 'It's the curse of our nation not to value our own culture. I'm sure both of you have at least a passing acquaintance with the *Odyssey* and the *Iliad* but you've clearly never read the tales of the *Mabinogi*.'

Ah. So Lleu Llaw Gyffes was a character in the old stories. A handy, fair-haired boy, she'd said. I recognised the word *llaw* – hand – but the rest must be Old Welsh.

Miss Gwatkyn hadn't finished. 'Tell me, please, how the literature of a country a thousand miles away is of more interest or worth than our own? Do we learn more of human nature from Odysseus and Agamemnon than we do from Math and Gilfaethwy?'

I knew a rhetorical question when I heard one and so did Harry.

'Here I am, Miss Gwatkyn!' I turned and saw a boy of twelve or thirteen with a mop of straw-coloured hair and hands and feet that were too big for the rest of him. Like a cartoon in a newspaper, he was, all stick limbs and huge head.

He spoke to his mistress in Welsh, like all the servants at Alltybela did. It had almost stopped surprising me.

'Lleu, they're carrying the *ceffyl pren* down in the village tonight. I want you to take Mr Probert-Lloyd and Mr Davies over there across the fields. And, just to be clear – you're to go with them *and* come back with them. All right?'

He flashed her a grin as if she'd caught him out. His teeth were white and perfect and, if he'd had a decent suit of clothes and a haircut he'd have passed for an elegant young gent. The girls'd all be looking at him soon, doing that dance where they'd stare sideways at him then look away when he turned. Drive him mad, they would.

–

Turned out the boy was chatty, too. All the way to the village he was asking us questions and telling us things.

'What'll happen to Mattie Hughes if he confesses – will they hang him?'

'I didn't think he was so bad, Old Mattie. If you had the sense to do what you were told he was all right.'

'Have you spoken to Nan Walters and Ruth Eynon yet? Fancy themselves those two do, think they're a cut above, now they're teachers. Snooty little madams. Always on about how they were helping Mr Rowland. Helping him run the school, helping him get the money for a new one, helping him write his letters. You'd think he couldn't breathe without them blowing air into his lungs.

'What'll happen to Mr Rowland's new school now? Will they build it anyway? If they do, I'm going to go there. Miss Gwatkyn said. Says I'm intelligent.'

He didn't seem to need answers to his questions which was just as well because we were too busy trying to see where we were going. We'd decided not to bring lanterns so the dark would hide us and Harry and I were tripping over tussocks and stumbling into rabbit scrapes but Lleu seemed to be able to see his way as well in the moonlight as if it were noon. Had I been like that once? When I was a farm servant living in a hayloft, had my eyes been able to see in the dark like a cat's?

I sniffed the night air, felt the breeze cool on my face but, however hard I tried, I couldn't see where I was putting my feet. God alone knew how Harry was managing. He really *was* blind in the dark.

Lleu cut across my thoughts. 'Look! Lights.'

People going to meet the *ceffyl pren*. Had to be.

As we got nearer, we could hear voices coming out of the darkness. I shivered. What were we doing here? It was one thing going round the village during the day asking questions. But we had no business being out here in the dark. If they caught us, things might turn nasty. We'd be lucky not to get a damn good hiding before we had a chance to make anybody understand who we were.

Had Harry had the same thought? Either that or he'd slowed down because I had.

Lleu looked back at us. 'Come on or we'll have to run to catch up.'

And, as if he was in charge, we obeyed.

'Lleu,' Harry said, softly. 'Did Simi Jones say who'll be leading the procession?'

'No, but it'll be Morgan Walters. Sure to be. Thinks he's the boss of Llanddewi Brefi, that one.'

Miss Gwatkyn had told us that the *ceffyl pren* was visiting Mattie Hughes so he'd confess and there wouldn't have to be an inquest. Was that Morgan Walters's doing? Was he trying to spare his daughter from having to give evidence in front of the whole village?

'What do people think of Walters?' Harry asked. 'Do they trust him?'

'Always spoken of as a fair man,' the boy said. 'Never heard of him going back on a deal or cheating anybody. Mind, he doesn't give much away. Anybody'll tell you – he'll have the last farthing he's owed on the very day he's owed it or you'll be paying interest for the rest of your life.'

'Women?' Harry asked.

The boy might be young but he wasn't innocent. Or stupid. 'Not that I've heard. Mrs Walters'd skin him alive, anyway.'

I realised that Lleu was much the same age as Billy Walters. 'You must've been at school with his son?'

He nodded. 'Billy. Yes.'

'What did he think of his sister being a teacher?' I asked. If the other boys had shared Lleu's opinion of Nan Walters, Billy'd probably got some stick for being the brother of a stuck-up little cow.

'Pretended he didn't care. But he was jealous as hell.'

The night was quiet. Apart from our own footsteps we'd heard nothing but owls and the odd snuffle of a badger going about its business since we left the mansion. So when the noise started it sent a sliver of ice into my blood.

Wooden spoons banging on pots. Horns blowing. Fiddle strings screeching fit to grind teeth. A tuneless din that yanked me straight back to my childhood. Me on my father's shoulders, Mam at our side, shawl wrapped around her head, face blacked, wearing Dada's jacket inside out. Neighbours turned into strangers by the dark and by blackened faces. Excitement edged with fear.

The *ceffyl pren*.

Harry

We were fortunate that Mattie Hughes's cottage stood on the fraying edge of Llanddewi Brefi as it meant that there was enough open ground opposite for John and myself to stay under cover of the surrounding dark.

I had the boy, Lleu, on my left and John on my right but, still, I felt vulnerable, isolated by my inability to make out much of what surrounded me. The torches and lanterns carried by some in the crowd only hindered my attempts to see as, instead of illuminating what was around them, their light simply sequestered all my remaining vision. My only impression of the size of the crowd came from the sound of voices and movements, from which I discerned that the procession had congregated in a tight, jostling pack before Hughes's door.

'How many people do you think there are?' I asked.

'Difficult to tell,' John said. 'Fifty? Sixty maybe?'

A daunting sight to see on your threshold. So far, no move had been made to summon Hughes but he could not be unaware of the *ceffyl pren's* arrival. Though no individual voice was intelligible, the combined tone of the mob was unmistakeable: a tightly-wound anticipation with, underneath, something implacably hostile. It was no coincidence that *ceffyl pren* carryings happened at night; daylight restraints are loosened after dark, anger rises in the blood and darkness releases animal instincts.

I jumped as a ragged cheer went up and the procession's cacophony began again, its discordant clamour filling the chilly night air. The cold sky must be clear, the stars pin-prick bright.

'Looks like Morgan Walters has arrived,' John murmured at my side.

'Is he carrying the *ceffyl pren*?'

'No. He's got two men behind him with it.'

By custom, the wooden 'horse' carried in the procession was a pole with a sheet draped over it, presumably — as Miss Gwatkyn would no doubt have been able to confirm — to represent the white mare of ancient tradition. Sometimes a horse's skull was added which, though I'd never seen it myself, must have given the *ceffyl pren* a particularly sinister aspect.

'He's shutting them up,' John said, as the rough music of the crowd thudded and screeched to an uncoordinated stop. A few moments of pent-up silence followed before a voice boomed out, startling me.

'Matthew Hughes! Come out and face your neighbours like a man!'

As if it was a play and Hughes had been waiting for his cue, I heard his door unlatch and swing open.

'Here he is!' I heard a trace of the crowd's febrile exultation in John's voice. 'He's got no light though. Hasn't even lit a candle in his house from what I can see.'

'Less chance of anything getting set on fire,' I said, foreseeing the jostling and manhandling that would soon take place. 'Does he look afraid?'

'Difficult to tell. He's too far away. But he's standing straight, like a soldier. Got his crutch, too.'

'I thought you said he didn't use it indoors?'

'He said not.'

Was Hughes attempting to win the crowd's sympathy or simply arming himself in order to remain on his feet if he could?

'I don't know what you're doing here, Morgan Walters.' Hughes's voice was clear, self-assured. 'If you think I had anything to do with Nicholas Rowland's death you're wrong.'

'You hated him!' came a shout.

'Hard to love a man who takes your living away, believe me. Don't suppose you'd be any different.'

A suppressed murmur went through the crowd which Walters was quick to silence. 'Didn't just hate him, though, did you?'

'Say what you like Morgan Walters. I had nothing to do with his death.'

'Hughes is trying to go back in,' John said. 'But they're not going to let him.'

'Get your hands off my door!' Hughes might only have been a private soldier but he knew what the voice of command sounded like. 'Don't you forget – this house belongs to Miss Gwatkyn.'

'Bring him here.'

There was some scuffling and swearing as Hughes was dragged into the middle of the encircling crowd, then a shout and the hollow sound of something wooden hitting the ground.

'They've taken his crutch off him,' John said.

'On your knees!' came a voice. Not Walters this time.

'Can't, can he?' another mocked, 'He's a peg-leg!'

As if they had been waiting for the words, the crowd immediately took up a chant. *Peg-leg! Peg-leg!*

'Get it off him, then we'll have him on his knees!' It was a woman's voice and the shrillness of it seemed to further inflame the crowd who began yelling in a frenetic unison. *Off! Off! Off!*

The mood was becoming ugly. I leaned towards John. 'I think we should intervene.'

'We can't.' John sounded apprehensive.

'At this rate they'll tear him limb from limb!'

'No, they won't. This is just how it goes.'

'John, it's turning from a crowd to a mob.'

'It's been a mob since the minute they got here! This isn't a chapel outing. People think he's betrayed them. Don't you think it'd be a good idea to hear what they've got to say? See if there's any evidence for the inquest?'

I hesitated. 'Very well, but we can't stand by and see them do him real harm.'

'I know.'

From the savage cheer that went up then, I deduced that Hughes had been deprived of his wooden leg and forced to kneel.

'Now, former Private Hughes,' Walters's voice came again. 'Hear the charges laid against you.'

'Morgan Walters has given a paper to one of the other men,' John said. 'And somebody's holding a lantern for him to read it. Proper performance.'

'First charge.' The reader's voice was uncertain, either from imperfect literacy or inadequate lighting. 'That you stole coal from Nicholas Rowland so that he could not heat his school, causing him to turn children away.'

Despite the catcalls of the crowd, Hughes's response was clear. 'No. That's a lie! I did no such thing!'

'That's because you paid boys to do it!' a voice rang out.

'If any boys stole coal, it wasn't on my say-so!'

'Shut up, liar!' As the crowd rose up to dismiss Hughes's denial, I felt the mood slip another notch towards mayhem. I had never heard of a death as the result of a *ceffyl pren* carryingbut severe beatings, though not common, were known to take place.

'Carry on.' I heard Walters's voice above the crowd.

'Second charge.' The halting reader was obliged almost to shout in order to be heard. 'That you paid a boy to... per...persuade Mr Rowland's pupils to disrespect him, to refuse to do work and to... laugh at his crippled hands.'

At the crowd's renewed shouting, I gripped John's shoulder. 'We must do something! They're working themselves into a frenzy.'

'Yes, and we're hearing more evidence! I can see what's happening. Don't worry.'

Though both of us had raised our voices, nobody would hear us over the outrage that was being rained down on the accused.

Shame on you, Matthew Hughes!

Shame! Shame!

I heard the unmistakeable sound of gobs of spittle being hawked and spat.

Lleu pulled at my sleeve and I inclined my head to him. 'That's Billy Walters he was talking about. The one who persuaded the other boys to do those things. He said he wasn't going to Mr Rowland's school if his sister was going to be put over him and he went back to Mattie Hughes. And Old Mattie got him to do those things they're saying. Said they'd soon see that Rowland'd use the birch if he needed to.'

'And did he?' I asked, almost speaking into the boy's ear so as to be heard. 'Did he use the birch?'

'No. Don't think he could've handled it, to be honest.'

Possibly not. But he could certainly have instructed one of his assistants to do so on his behalf.

A voice raised itself above the cries of *Shame* and *You're nothing next to Mr Rowland*. 'Think Miss Gwatkyn's going to protect you now, do you? When she knows what kind of a man you are?'

'The pushing's started,' John said at my side.

'If they lay him out, we'll stop them. Agreed?' If Mattie Hughes ended up on the ground, I knew I would have to intervene. A man on the ground is vulnerable to boots and, in this mood, I did not doubt that the crowd would use them.

'*Enough!*' I was glad to hear Walters's voice. It implied that he was still in control of the mob. 'Go on.'

'Third charge. That you spied on Nicholas Rowland. That you watched him about his daily business and threatened him.'

'How did I threaten him?' Hughes did not sound intimidated though he cannot have been ignorant of the danger he was in. 'Who says I threatened him?'

'You were heard telling him,' Walters said, 'that you were waiting for him to put a foot wrong and then you would "have him".'

'Have him?' Hughes sounded almost amused. He waited until the publican quieted the crowd once more, then said, 'You've been misinformed, Morgan Walters. I never said I'd "have him". But I did tell Nicholas Rowland that I was watching him. I *was* waiting for him to put a foot wrong. Because I wanted Miss Gwatkyn to see him for what he was.'

'She saw him for exactly what he was,' a woman's voice shouted. 'A better man than you'll ever be.'

Loud cheers of agreement greeted her words and I felt the crowd pressing in on Hughes. I suddenly wished I had brought a walking stick or a riding whip. Anything with which I might enforce some kind of order.

'Fourth charge!' The reader had to shout over the mob. 'That you killed Nicholas Rowland!'

Now, the hollow sound of pots being struck was joined by the ominous thudding of staves on the ground.

'Silence!' Walters yelled. As soon as the crowd's noise had diminished sufficiently for him to make himself heard, he began again. 'All your schemes failed, didn't they, Matthew Hughes? Mr Rowland's school prospered. You saw that you'd lost. That he was persuading gentlemen to support his new school. So you decided to kill him!'

There was no mistaking the sound that came then. It was the baying of a pack, nostrils filled with the scent of its prey, rationality subjugated to blood lust.

'The *ceffyl pren's* coming forward,' John said. 'Walters is handling this. He'll get Hughes onto it before they can really start on him.'

Before I could respond, Lleu suddenly darted from my side into the crowd. Immediately, he was lost to me. 'John, go after him!'

John did not move. 'I can see him. He's gone straight to talk to somebody. Might be Simi Jones.' He moved aside. 'Yes. I think it is. Right, something's happening.'

'Out of my way.' I heard then. 'Let me through!'

'Well, well! Looks like the *plwyfwas* is taking charge,' John said.

Lleu reappeared at my side again and spoke into my ear. 'Miss Gwatkyn said, if things looked nasty, I should tell Simi to threaten them with the magistrates.'

'Good boy.' Instructions from his mistress or not, it had taken courage to fling himself into the crowd like that.

'If you're going to make him ride that damn thing, then get him on it and have done with it!' Simi Jones's voice cut through the crowd's complaints. 'But if you harm him, I'll have the magistrates on you, by Miss Gwatkyn's order!'

John was going to have to amend his poor opinion of Jones who, despite insults and some shoving and jostling, stood his ground.

And they did as he said. I listened to John's narration of the scene, seeing hands grabbing the old soldier, thrusting the pole of the *ceffyl pren* between his legs and hoisting it on to their shoulders. The discomfort of sitting astride a narrow pole would be the lesser of two evils for Hughes. His balance thrown off by the unequal length of his legs, his main problem would be remaining upright. John described the crowd's method of keeping him astride as they began to move up the street towards the church: rough blows from fists and staves, shoves this way and that as he almost fell to one side and was manhandled upright, only to overbalance on the other.

'Not a single door's opening to throw anything at him,' John reported. 'Everybody must be in the procession.'

Alternatively, some villagers might disapprove of Morgan Walters's resort to popular justice before the inquest's verdict.

'If nobody's watching,' I said, 'why are they bothering to parade him up the street?'

As John's face turned toward me, I saw a dull flash in my peripheral vision – a reflection of one of the crowd's torches from his spectacles. 'It's what happens, isn't it? Otherwise it's not a *ceffyl pren* procession, it's just a mob accusing a man on his doorstep.'

I wondered what Tobias Hildon's reaction would be as the mob approached his vicarage. Would he attempt to remonstrate with them or, knowing that Phoebe Gwatkyn tolerated the carrying of the *ceffyl pren*, would he stay indoors and keep his own counsel? Few in the chapel-going procession would be averse to letting Hildon understand that this was their village and they would do in it as they saw fit.

As we watched the lights jerking up the street and listened to the din of the procession's discordant circuit of the church, I gripped John's arm. 'If Simi Jones can't stop them when they pull him down, I'm stepping in. We've heard everything we're going to now, and I won't see an innocent man beaten senseless.'

'Not exactly *innocent*! He may not've killed Rowland but you heard the other charges. He tried to make Rowland's life a misery.'

'As, no doubt, Rowland's arrival had made his.'

'You're saying Rowland deserved what he got?'

'No. I'm saying that this is enough now. No more. When they get him off, we make sure he gets safely back into his house.'

The parading and manhandling of Hughes had vented the head of steam that had been building in the crowd and I could feel the reduced tension as the noisy cavalcade made its way back towards us. The shouts were accompanied by more laughter now. Somebody had managed to turn the crowd's wrath to ridicule and, though Hughes might still receive some blows as he was forcibly dismounted, I was less fearful for his safety than I had been five minutes before.

'Pull him down.' Walters's voice came when the crowd had stopped, once more, in front of Hughes's house and the banging and horn-blowing had been silenced.

'God, that must've hurt.' I heard the wince in John's voice as Hughes was pulled off the *ceffyl pren* and allowed to fall to the ground. 'He'll be lucky if he hasn't broken *his* collarbone, too.'

I almost told him not to sound so pleased but held my peace. I had no right to tell John what to think or how to react.

'Simi Jones is there,' he said. 'He's pulling him up.'

Good. The *plwyfwas* was on hand to prevent any further violence. But the work of the *ceffyl pren* was not finished. Morgan Walters had yet to issue the injunction as to future behaviour.

'Hear this, Matthew Hughes,' he called out. 'If, by noon tomorrow, you have not presented yourself to the coroner to confess that you are the murderer of Nicholas Rowland, we will come for you again. And we *will see justice done!*'

John

The next morning, we were back in Llanddewi Brefi. But, whatever people might've thought when they saw us riding over from Alltybela, we weren't there to do Morgan Walters's work for him. We stopped in front of the Three Horseshoes and I found a boy to hold the horses there, just so everybody'd know we were inside. Llanddewi Brefi needed to understand that Harry was in charge of deciding what happened to Mattie Hughes not Morgan Walters. And that included Walters himself. Harry'd taken steps the night before to make that clear.

Before we'd stumbled back to Alltybela over the fields, we'd left the *ceffyl pren* procession in front of Hughes's house and slipped away to the Three Horseshoes. Inside, right in the middle of the table furthest from the front door, we'd left a note giving notice that we'd be visiting at nine to speak to the girls. Just by being there, that note told Walters that we'd seen the carrying of the *ceffyl pren* and – if we wanted to – we could have him arrested for leading it. Harry'd never do such a thing, but Morgan Walters didn't know that. If he had any sense, he'd have made sure that his daughter was on the premises this morning, along with her friend, Ruth Eynon.

I stared at the boy holding the mares. He hadn't quite scrubbed off all of last night's soot. I could still see it around his ears and in his eyebrows.

'You can let them graze just over there.' I nodded at a patch of scuffed grass a few yards away. 'But no further. I don't want to have to come looking for you when Mr Probert-Lloyd and I are finished, all right?' Now he'd be able to tell anybody who asked who the horses belonged to.

Inside, the place had the clean smell of fresh sawdust and its owner was waiting for us. Morgan Walters had done a better job of cleaning himself up than the boy outside. His square face was clean and shaved and, if his dark eyebrows had soot in them, well, it wouldn't show, anyway, would it?

'Good day to you, gentlemen!' All cheer and welcome. Perhaps he thought his place on the local election committee gave him special privileges. He'd soon know different.

'Good morning, Mr Walters,' Harry said. 'As I mentioned in the note we left, we'd like a few words with your daughter, if we may.'

If Harry'd just kicked away any hope Walters might've had that we'd sent a boy over with the note, he didn't show it. 'Yes, yes. She's here. And Ruth. Best if you talk to them in the parlour at the back.'

Harry nodded. He didn't want anybody eavesdropping on our chat with the girls any more than Walters did.

A new fire was smoking in the little parlour but it couldn't disguise the musty smell. Walters and his family most likely spent all their time in the taproom and the kitchen, with the parlour for best. The bits of furniture stranded here and there in the room looked decent but not new. Inherited from dead relatives probably. Morgan Walters had better things to spend his money on than sofas he never sat on.

I caught a glimpse of myself in the mirror over the fireplace. Still couldn't get over how much of a gentleman I looked with my barbered hair and new clothes.

Nan and Ruth were sitting on straight-backed chairs, hands in their laps. I'd expected them to be fourteen or fifteen but they were older, more my age. Thought they were ladies, too. They might've left the best chairs for me and Harry but they didn't stand up when we came in.

I introduced us, in Welsh, and the slighter of the two replied in English. 'Good day, Mr Probert-Lloyd, Mr Davies. I'm Anne Walters and this is Ruth Eynon.'

Nan – or Anne as she was calling herself this morning – was a dark-haired slip of a thing but she had one of those faces that wanted you to know she could see right through you. Not just sharp but cutting, if you know what I mean. Ruth was softer-looking, a bit rounder, more shapely, with a dimple in her half-smile. And they might give themselves airs because Nicholas Rowland had favoured them, but they were still dressed like working women in *betgwns* and aprons. The way they'd done their hair wasn't what you'd expect, mind. Both had braids that were swirled into shapes on either side of their head. It was exactly the way Miss Gwatkyn did hers. But where, on her, it looked all of a piece with her tunic and furry boots, on these two, in their everyday clothes, it looked wrong, out of place.

'You'll be here to talk to us about Mr Rowland's death, presumably.' Nan Walters taking charge. In English. Making a point.

Billy would've laughed his head off if he'd heard her. *Presumably?*

Harry kept a straight face. 'That's correct.'

Nan's nose went even further into the air. 'Mr Jones, the parish constable, will have informed you that we were the first to see Mr Rowland's body?'

'No,' Harry said. 'We'd been given to understand that Mr Rowland's pupils had found his body. Perhaps you'd like to tell us exactly what happened? Eyewitness testimony is always to be preferred to second hand.'

Nan Walters looked pleased. Didn't know he was buttering her up.

'Ruth and I always arrived before the children. We'd go in and help Mr Rowland set things out for the morning.'

'What sort of things?' Harry asked.

'We'd make sure the slates were clean.' Ruth spoke up. 'And fill inkpots for the older ones, cut the paper into pieces for them to practise on.'

So, Rowland's school'd had ink and paper, had it? His pupils had been lucky. Learning to write by scratching on a slate is one thing but mastering pen and ink is something else altogether.

'And we'd make sure there was enough coal inside, for the stove.' Nan took over again. 'It was easier for us to do it than for Mr Rowland.'

'And sweep,' Ruth added. 'There was always mud from the children's boots.'

'Why didn't you sweep it out at the end of the day?' I asked. My mother would no more've left boot-mud on the floor for the following day than she would've left clothes there for vermin to get at.

'That was when we did our work with Mr Rowland,' Nan said. 'He didn't want us to waste the light on drudge work.'

Harry nodded. 'Can you tell us exactly what you saw when you went into the schoolroom?'

For the first time, there was a flicker of something between them, eyes moving towards each other at the same moment. They weren't quite as untroubled by what they'd seen as they were trying to pretend.

'We saw him straight away.' Something changed in Ruth Eynon's eyes and she sounded as if she'd gathered up all her courage. 'You've seen how the schoolroom's set out. The door opens so you see the right-hand side of the room and that's where he was.'

'How exactly was he lying?' Harry asked.

The girls glanced at each other again. Deciding who was going to answer? 'On his back,' Nan said. 'With the ladder on top of him.'

'Were his hands gripping the ladder?' I asked. I wanted to know if they'd really seen him, really *looked*.

Nan Walters turned to me. Her eyes were like gleaming pebbles, hard and cold. 'Mr Rowland couldn't grip the ladder, not properly. He'd sort of hook his thumbs round the edge,' she mimed with her own hands, fingers curled, thumbs catching at her palms.

'So where were his hands if they weren't holding the ladder?'

Nan's eyes shifted, looked past me, as if she was trying to see Rowland's body in her mind's eye. 'Out, like this.' She put her hands up level with her shoulders. 'As if he'd overbalanced backwards.'

'Did you move him?' Harry asked.

Both girls shook their heads.

'Did you touch him at all?'

This time there was no look, they just both went very still, like a rabbit when it sees a fox.

'Did you?' I pressed. Best if I was the harsh one, let Harry be the courteous gentleman, then they might let things slip to him. It was a game we'd played a few times when we thought people weren't telling us everything they knew.

'I did.' Ruth's voice was barely above a whisper. She swallowed and tried again. 'I touched him.'

'Why?' Harry asked. Sounded as if he was genuinely curious.

'His hair was untidy,' she said, her voice still low. 'All over the place. Mr Rowland would've hated that. He always kept it nice. He could use a comb, even with his hands.' Her voice broke again. She sounded younger and much less genteel than she was trying to pretend. 'He was very proud of his hair.'

'Thank you,' Harry said. 'That's very helpful.'

Helpful? Half of Reckitt's evidence for murder had just gone out the window. Rowland's killer hadn't rearranged the schoolteacher's hair to cover his tracks, Ruth Eynon had done it. Because she'd wanted to make him look *tidy*.

'After that,' Harry went on, 'did you let the children in when they arrived?'

'No,' Nan said. 'We kept them outside.'

'Apart from Enoch Cwmderi.' Ruth looked from her friend to us. 'He wouldn't stay outside, barged in wanting to see for himself.'

'I sent him to Simi Jones,' Nan said. 'Then Simi sent him to you.' I saw a vengeful gleam in her eye. *That'll teach him to defy me.*

Harry couldn't see her expression but, anyway, he couldn't care less about small boys being paid back for their wilfulness. 'What did you do then?'

'I told the children there'd been an accident and sent them home. Then, when Simi Jones arrived, we left matters in his hands.'

In other words, the *plwyfwas*'d packed them off just like they'd packed the children off.

There was a sudden fluttering at the window. A robin flying at the glass, pecking at its own reflection. Aggressive little sods, robins are.

Nan Walters got out of her chair. 'Go on!' she called at the bird, in Welsh. 'Get away!' I stood up and, as she flapped her hands, I saw something below the window sill. A splash of copper.

Her brother was eavesdropping outside.

Why? From what Miss Gwatkyn's Lleu had told us there was no love lost between Billy and Nan. Perhaps his mother or father had sent him to spy. If so, what did they want to know – what we asked the girls or what they said?

Before she sat down again, Nan went to the fire and stirred it up with the poker. Heavy-handed she was, too. As if it was her brother she'd really like to've taken the poker to.

Harry turned to Ruth. 'Miss Eynon, can I ask how long you'd been helping Mr Rowland with the children?'

She looked into her lap, trying to avoid his eye. Didn't know that, with his eyes pointing directly at her, she was the one thing he was guaranteed not to see. 'Right from the beginning,' she said.

But Nan Walters wasn't going to leave it at that. 'Miss Gwatkyn recommended me and I told Mr Rowland about Ruth.'

I looked her in the eye. 'Miss Gwatkyn *recommended* you, did she?'

She glared back at me. Still had to learn proper ladylike behaviour, our Nan. 'Yes, she did. Mr Barton recommended Mr Rowland to her and she recommended *us* to *him*.'

Harry stepped in. 'Excuse me, Miss Walters. Did you say that Mr Rowland had an introduction to Miss Gwatkyn from her husband?'

'Yes.' For the first time, Nan Walters looked wrong-footed. Hadn't expected that to be a surprise, I suppose. 'Mr Rowland and Mr Barton met in London.'

Hold on – London? Phoebe Gwatkyn had told us her husband lived in Italy.

'Of course.' Harry was trying to reassure Nan that she hadn't said anything out of turn. 'Mr Rowland taught at University College, didn't he?'

'Yes.' She leaned forward. 'And that's what he wanted for us, here! Right from the beginning, he said that the cowshed academy was just a start. His shop window, he said. He knew what he wanted – a collegiate school so that those who could benefit from it – boys *and* girls – could be properly educated, not just learn to read and write. He said it would change things here for ever!' Her voice broke, then, and I thought she was going to burst into tears. But she took a deep breath and pulled herself together.

Ruth caught hold of her arm. 'It *still will*!' She turned to Harry. 'Mr Rowland had already raised a lot of money. Miss Gwatkyn'll see the school built, I know she will. It's his legacy!'

Harry hesitated and I wondered if he was embarrassed by Ruth's childish faith in Miss Gwatkyn. 'Were you hoping to teach at the new school, once it was established?' he asked.

No chance of that! It would've been years before Rowland's plans came to fruition. By then, these two would've been married with children of their own who needed educating.

But they had other ideas. 'Not *hoping*,' Ruth said. 'Mr Rowland was *relying* on us. Once he'd raised sufficient funds, he wanted us to take over the running of the cowshed academy, while he concentrated on establishing the new college.'

Nan nodded. 'Then, once it was built, we were going to move over to the new school, too. All of us together.'

'I see.' Harry used that phrase an amazing amount, which was ironic when you thought about it.

'What about your husbands?' I said. 'Did you think they'd be happy to see their wives leaving their own children at home to teach other people's?'

'We don't have husbands or children.' Ruth Eynon looked at me as if she thought I was slow.

'No, but by the time the school was built you would have.'

'And what, may I ask, gives you the right to make that assumption?' That was Nan, her whole face pulled to a point.

'It's just what happens, isn't it? The way life goes.' I hated her for pulling me up. But it was true. Girls like them got married. Either that or they stayed at home to look after their parents. They didn't make lives for themselves as teachers.

Ruth shook her head, though she didn't eyeball me like Nan. 'Mr Rowland had given us his word that we'd be the first teachers appointed.'

I glanced at Harry and saw him trying not to smile. Bastard. Thought it was funny, me getting a verbal hiding.

'Perhaps,' he said, 'we could return to the matter at hand. I understand that you assisted Mr Rowland in other ways, as well as teaching?'

Ruth shot a look at her friend and Nan Walters gave Harry a thin little smile. 'Yes. Mr Rowland couldn't hold a pen to write, so we wrote all his letters for him. With my father going to and fro to the post in Tregaron every day, it was a convenient system.'

'Who was he writing to?' I asked.

Nan carried on looking at Harry, as if it was him who'd asked the question. 'Local gentry. He'd been given a list by an acquaintance of his in London. Somebody who had connections here and who'd already written to some local gentlemen on Mr Rowland's behalf, telling them about the school plans and asking them if they'd consider becoming benefactors.'

Benefactors. My goodness, these girls knew long words!

'Who was this acquaintance?' Harry asked. 'Do you know?'

They both shook their heads. 'Mr Rowland didn't say,' Ruth told him, her eyes lowered to her lap.

'But it wasn't just Cardiganshire gentlemen we wrote to,' Nan said. 'Mr Rowland sent letters all over the country – to Unitarian ministers mostly, I think. And a gentleman in London. Mr Henry Richard. There was quite a bit of correspondence back and forth with him.'

'Mr Richard is secretary of the Peace Society,' Ruth said. As if that made him more likely to donate money to a school.

'And is Mr Richard particularly interested in education?' I asked.

'I don't know,' Ruth said, with a bit more spirit than we'd seen from her before. 'But he's from Tregaron so he was very interested in having the collegiate school here.'

I'd never heard of the Peace Society but Harry obviously had. 'I knew Mr Richard was a Welshman,' he said. 'But I had no idea he was from Cardiganshire.'

Nan smiled that thin smile of hers again. 'We never think anybody important's going to come from where we live, do we?' I wondered if that was something Rowland'd said to them, encouraging them to be ambitious.

'Did Mr Richard donate any money to the school?' Harry asked.

Ruth glanced at him as if she was checking that he still couldn't see her.

'I'm not sure. We didn't read the letters Mr Rowland received; we just wrote the ones he sent.'

'But he'd usually tell us if he'd had a reply.' Nan Walters hadn't liked the sound of what Ruth had said. Made it sound as if they weren't important.

'Do you know who *was* giving money to the school?' I asked. 'Mr Rowland had a tidy sum hidden in the loft.'

I thought I saw a faint blush rise on Nan's face when I mentioned the hidden money. Hadn't they known about the linen bag in the trunk? Hearing about it from us wouldn't please these two. They'd puffed themselves up, thinking Rowland couldn't do without them.

'No,' Nan said. 'He just said our efforts were bearing fruit.'

Just then, the door opened and Mrs Walters appeared. 'Sorry to interrupt, Mr Probert-Lloyd. Mr Walters was just wondering how much longer you'll be needing Nan? There's post to deliver and the day's wearing on.'

Harry'd stood as soon as the door opened. 'Yes, I quite understand. I'm sure we can spare her now.' He turned to the girls. 'If you could compile a list of the gentlemen you remember writing to, ladies, I'd be very grateful.'

—

Morgan Walters made himself scarce with the girls but his wife was busy about the place, scrubbing the tables with a handful of hay.

'Mrs Walters, what did you and your husband think when Mr Rowland asked Nan to be an assistant teacher at his school?' I asked.

Gwenllian Walters looked at me as if she thought I was accusing her of something. 'Miss Gwatkyn'd already come to see us to talk about it. Said it was a good chance for Nan. Mr Rowland was a very respectable gentleman and he had great plans for Llanddewi Brefi.'

She didn't have to say any more. Morgan Walters, with his finger in many pies and designs on official jobs, would've done anything he could to grab on to the coat-tails of Nicholas Rowland's *great plans*.

'But were you happy about the thought of the two of them running the school on their own while Mr Rowland set up the new school?'

She looked from me to Harry and back again. Me asking the questions was worrying her. 'Why shouldn't the two of them run the school? They're educated girls. Well, my Nan is anyway and, friends as they are, she's helped Ruth a good bit. And they've both been going to Miss Gwatkyn for lessons as well.'

Nan's parents must've spent a lot of money on her education. Those ladies' boarding schools wouldn't come cheap, I was sure of that. Had Morgan Walters and his wife had their noses pushed out of joint when Ruth Eynon was put on an equal footing with Nan? Maybe Walters and Rowland had argued about it. As I'd suggested to Mattie Hughes, there was always the possibility that Rowland'd fallen out of the loft after some pushing and shoving.

'Did you and your husband see much of Mr Rowland?' I asked. 'Talk about plans for this collegiate school of his?'

She hesitated then. 'Mr Rowland came in quite a lot. A very sociable gentleman. And never gave himself airs. Beautiful manners to everybody.'

So yes, they'd seen a lot of him but, no, he'd never discussed his plans. That might've annoyed Morgan Walters, too, seeing as how Lleu the hall-boy'd told us Walters thought he was in charge of Llanddewi Brefi.

'Are you going to call us to give evidence at the inquest?' We'd made Mrs Walters nervous.

'I shall need to ask Nan or Ruth to tell the jury how they found Mr Rowland,' Harry said. 'But, at the moment, I see no need to ask you or your husband to give testimony.'

At the moment. That was a warning if ever I heard one. Morgan Walters would be well advised to behave himself from now until Friday.

–

Midday. That was the deadline Walters had given Mattie. *Come forward before noon or we'll be back for you.*

I made sure the boy holding the mares was still where we'd left him, then glanced up at the sky. We didn't want to hang about – the weather was changeable today. People were scurrying around, trying to get things done before the rain started but that didn't stop them looking sideways at us.

'Better get over to Mattie Hughes's,' I said. Miss Gwatkyn had asked us to bring Hughes to Alltybela. Didn't think it'd be safe for him in the village after the *ceffyl pren*.

When they saw us going up to Hughes's door, people stopped what they were doing and watched. Waiting to see whether we'd come to hear him confess and get the constabulary on to him.

As Harry stepped forward to knock on the door, I saw somebody familiar out of the corner of my eye. I put my hand on Harry's arm to stop him and turned around. Billy Walters was standing there, watching us. On impulse, I beckoned him over. Didn't expect him to come, if I'm honest, but he looked to right and left to see who might be watching, then strode over the road. Had some of his sister's defiance about him, Billy did. No wonder they clashed.

'Looking out for Mattie, are you, Billy?' I asked, naming him so Harry'd know who he was. Mind, with the boy's hair, he could probably see, anyway.

'They can say what they like, he didn't lay a finger on Teacher Rowland.'

'How d'you know that?'

The boy didn't miss a beat – too keen to defend Mattie Hughes to hear the suspicion in Harry's voice. 'Mr Hughes is a soldier. He knows a dozen ways to kill a man. He'd never just bash his head in!'

'We've been hearing some interesting things about you, Billy,' I said. 'How you persuaded some of the other boys to make trouble for Mr Rowland, stole his coal—'

'I never stole anything!' Redheads can't help blushing and Billy was cockscomb red to his collarbones. But I was pretty sure it was anger, not guilt.

Mattie's door swung open. 'Leave the boy alone. Anything he did, he did because I asked him. Now, come in and let's get this over with.'

Harry

I had anticipated resistance on Hughes's part to Miss Gwatkyn's offer of sanctuary but being made to ride the *ceffyl pren* seemed to have shaken him and he agreed to a few days' work at

Alltybela without fuss. A cart having been procured to take him over to the mansion, John and I headed back towards Tregaron.

Clouds had darkened the morning and now a steady rain began to fall. Soon it was running off the brim of my hat on to my coat. I lifted my eyes but, try as I might, I could not see the drops that were falling on me. In my peripheral vision, the air had a grey opacity to it but the diaphanous swags of rain that must have been blowing in ragged curtains across the valley were invisible, the hanging sweep of them confined now to my mind's eye.

I turned to John, who was hunched down into his coat and seemed to have turned the collar up to keep the rain from running down his neck. 'This associate of Rowland's in London,' I said. 'The one with the list of potential backers Nan and Ruth talked about. Given that we know Montague Caldicot suggested Llanddewi Brefi to Rowland, is it jumping to too many conclusions to think he might've provided connections here, too?'

I leaned my head in his direction to hear his answer over the pattering of rain on my hat.

'I don't know,' he said, after giving it a few seconds' thought. 'Miss Gwatkyn seemed to think he and Rowland were no more than passing acquaintances. Writing to people to ask for their support'd be a big favour to do for somebody he hardly knew.'

'Perhaps she was mistaken?' John's silence told me how unlikely he thought that was. 'Or perhaps, for some reason,' I speculated, 'Nicholas Rowland was reluctant to tell Miss Gwatkyn of their association?'

'Why would he be?' John asked. 'Unless…' I waited. 'D'you think Rowland had got wind of whatever it was that got Caldicot thrown out of his regiment?'

I nodded. It seemed perfectly possible that Nicholas Rowland might have heard rumours of a scandal brewing before he came to Cardiganshire and had chosen not to mention Caldicot's name to Miss Gwatkyn. And, if that was the case, the news of Caldicot's cashiering – by now an open secret if Phoebe Gwatkyn was to be believed – might well have brought about the loss of gentry enthusiasm for Rowland's collegiate school which she had mentioned.

It seemed a more adequate explanation than a wholesale switching of allegiance to the idea of a National School in Llanddewi Brefi, however persuasive Tobias Hildon was in its cause; if Caldicot had been disgraced, any cause he espoused would have been tainted by association with him.

'I didn't want to say anything before I'd had a chance to check,' John said, slowly. 'But I *think* I might've seen Caldicot's name on one of the banknotes in Rowland's trunk.'

A punch in the face could not have taken me more by surprise. 'You *think*? How confident are you?'

'I don't know, but when I first heard you talking about Caldicot to Miss Gwatkyn, the name rang a bell, and I'm pretty sure that was the reason.'

'Why didn't you tell me before?'

'Like I said, I wanted to check.'

'Right. We'd better go and have another look at those money bags, then,' I said, thankful that I had not allowed Tobias Hildon to browbeat me into lodging Rowland's finances with him. 'And then, if you're right, we must pay Mr Caldicot a visit.'

John

As soon as I'd changed out of my wet riding clothes and found a boy to take them to be dried, I went to Harry's room. A servant was just leaving and Harry held up a sealed letter. 'The man who came to light the fire gave me this. Said a boy brought it yesterday.'

I took it from him and unfolded it. 'It's from Llew Price – the jury foreman.' I scanned it. Short and to the point. And in English.

'*Dear Mr Probert-Lloyd,*' I read.

'*Forgive the liberty, but I wonder if you could spare a few moments to call on me at my shop? I believe I have information that will be useful to the inquest on Friday.*

Your obedient servant,

Llewelyn Price.'

I looked at Harry. 'What d'you think he wants?'

'No idea.' Harry dumped his portmanteau on the bed and took out Rowland's money bags. 'But we'll have to make time to go and see him before the inquest.'

'Fine.' I stuffed the letter into my pocket and started removing banknotes. Once I had them all, I shuffled them into a stack on my knees and quickly went through them. Had I really seen Caldicot's name? Or had it just been something *like* Caldicot? You don't generally look at anything but the amount on a banknote, do you?

Halfway down, I found what I was looking for. 'Here it is. Promises to pay M. Caldicot Esq., or bearer, ten pounds.'

'Which bank is it from?'

'Somewhere old-fashioned, if it's got the depositor's name on it.' I read the line of copperplate script at the top of the note. 'The Aberystwyth Mercantile Bank. Maybe they were using up old notes for bigger sums?'

Harry took the note from me as if he could read it. 'Aberystwyth Mercantile. I've never heard of it.'

'A shipping bank, most likely.' I went back to the pile of banknotes and found four more with Caldicot's name on them. All for ten pounds. All from the Aberystwyth Mercantile.

Harry chewed the inside of his lip as he considered the five notes. 'If Caldicot gave this money to Rowland in London, wouldn't you expect the notes to be from a London bank?'

I put the rest of the notes back into the money bag. 'He might've thought it'd be better for Rowland to be able to cash it easily back here. In case he needed to buy land or something and the seller wanted cash.'

'But Rowland wouldn't have had any problem redeeming London banknotes. He evidently went back there pretty frequently.' Harry had me in his peripheral vision again. 'Remember? Llew Price said he had his hair cut whenever he went back to London.'

'So you think Caldicot gave Rowland these notes recently – after he'd come back to Llysrheidol?'

'Yes. But why would he part with such a large sum now, when he'd come home in disgrace and had no means of supporting himself?'

'Maybe he's prudent. Maybe he's got income we don't know about—'

'Even so – now's not the time to be distributing largesse, I wouldn't have thought?'

I knew what Harry was getting at. Blackmail. But I wasn't going to encourage that type of thinking. I could just picture the Tories' reaction if they thought he was trying to blacken their boy's reputation. They'd cry 'foul' from here to Cardigan.

'I don't know,' I said. 'You could say it was *exactly* the time to be distributing largesse. Distract people from gossip about him getting thrown out of the army by giving them something *else* to talk about. Rowland's school'd be bound to get tongues wagging. Education for all – boys and girls equally – all that.'

Harry nodded, stared into space. 'Possibly. I just think I'd like to hear it from Caldicot himself.'

He wasn't going to be persuaded. But at least I could try and stop us going on a wild goose chase across half the county. 'Well, I don't think we'll need to go all the way to Llysrheidol to hear it,' I said. 'You'll be on a stage together in two days. If the Tory agent hasn't got him somewhere nearby already, he'll be arriving today for sure. All we need to do is find out where he's staying.'

–

We already knew Caldicot wasn't at the Talbot. When we'd got back from Llanddewi Brefi, Harry'd asked the landlord, Mr Thomas, whether any new guests had arrived for the public

135

meeting on Saturday. I knew he'd been asking in case Lydia Howell had turned up but Mr Thomas's 'No, none, sir,' held good both for her and for Caldicot. Most likely, our man'd be staying with a Tory family nearby. Minnever'd know. He would've made it his business to. But he was out somewhere, canvassing.

'It's probably worth our while having a look in the pubs to see if we can find Minnever,' Harry said, once we were out in the main square.

'If we do, you know he'll grab you and make you start buying drinks for people again.'

'I'll take that risk.'

'Are you going to tell him why you want to talk to Caldicot?'

That made him snort. 'No. I don't think so, do you?'

I didn't like the look on Harry's face and I didn't want him doing anything stupid. I pulled him towards the churchyard, away from flapping ears.

'Are you sure it's a good idea to try and talk to Caldicot?' He opened his mouth to protest but I cut him off. 'You've got a fight on here, with the election – you know you have. And you don't want to give Caldicot the chance to stand on that stage over there and complain that you're trying to discredit him by dragging him in to an unnecessary investigation of an accidental death.'

'Is that what you—'

'No! Of course that's not how I see it. But he could easily make *everybody else* think that!'

'You think I should hold back from asking questions just because he's standing against me?'

Obviously! 'Depends whether you want to win or not. It might be worth leaving Caldicot alone if it gives you a better chance of getting elected.'

'Even if Rowland was blackmailing him? Even if that would make him Rowland's most likely killer?'

I sighed from my boots, so he'd hear. 'There's no *evidence* for blackmail! And you're only assuming that Caldicot is strapped

136

for cash because he's been thrown out of the army. His wife might have money—'

'I don't know anything about his wife. But however you look at it, giving Rowland fifty pounds in Caldicot's current circumstances seems suspicious. *And*,' he said, before I could object, 'so far, apart from prejudice against Mattie Hughes, we've got nothing resembling a motive for Rowland's death. If we don't want the finger to stay pointed at Hughes, we need to ask more questions.'

'And Minnever'd say it's not *your* job to do that! That if the jury decides for murder – even if they name Mattie – then it's a job for the police and the assizes.'

'And how far d'you think the police would look with a plum suspect like Mattie? Do you think they'd dare go near Caldicot?'

'So you think that because *they* won't, *you* should?'

'Yes!'

I stared at him, at his eyes which were fixed on my chest so he could see my face in his peripheral vision. 'Harry, I swear, this inquest'll lose you the election if you're not careful.'

–

So off we went looking for Minnever. If we found him, he might have more luck taking Harry in hand. Somebody needed to save him from himself.

Tregaron had a lot of pubs. Most of them were simple alehouses – spare front rooms where all the drinkers were regulars and didn't want any newcomers, judging by the looks we got when we put our heads round various doors. But some were more respectable. There was the Talbot, obviously, and The King's Head, a modern-looking place with a smart sign hanging over the door. Inside it was clean and there were plenty of chairs and tables for playing cards or reading papers. I wouldn't have been surprised to see the beer pumps Harry'd talked about seeing in London. Still, the landlord wasn't a fool. He might've given the place a city-sounding name but he'd hung paintings of cows and horses on the walls so the farmers and drovers would feel at home. Displayed his pewter tankards in shiny rows on shelves above the barrels, mind. No beer-cured wooden mugs for Mr Modern.

If the election meeting on Saturday brought in the crowds Minnever was expecting, The King's Head would see its takings shoot up, so it was no surprise when the landlord greeted Harry by name. He'd have made it his business to know all the candidates, at least by sight.

'Mr Minnever?' he said, when Harry told him who we were looking for. 'He was in here earlier with a couple of other gents, chatting to people. Then they moved on. You might chance your health in The White Horse, they were going that way.'

His slanderous little dig was about right. From thatch that looked about a hundred years old to the filthy sawdust on the taproom floor, The White Horse was a dump. Minnever should've taken one look in there and backed straight out. God knows why he hadn't – I don't suppose a qualifying voter ever went near the place. But, no, there he was, sitting with two very uncomfortable-looking Liberals and three rough-looking characters.

As soon as he saw us, he jumped up and shook Harry's hand. Glad of the improvement in company.

'Could we have a brief word?' Harry asked. 'Somewhere private?'

We got some dirty looks from the locals as they watched their drinks money walking out the door but Harry couldn't see any of that so it didn't worry him. The rain had stopped now and, with the sun dancing in and out of the clouds, the ground had started to warm up. Warm earth and growing things – the smell of spring. A big relief after the bad air in the pub.

The hangers-on weren't fools. They knew they were super-fluous to requirements so they excused themselves. Minnever led the way to the churchyard and we sat on the benches in the lychgate, me and Harry on one side, Minnever on the other. All that was missing was the coffin on a trestle between us. I moved my arse about on the cracked slate slab to find a comfortable position. The whole lychgate'd seen better days and if I'd been the vicar, I'd have been getting up a public subscription for a new one. Mind, the church itself looked as if it needed a good bit of money spent on it, just like St David's in Llanddewi Brefi. Lack of congregation to fund repairs, that was the problem. Most of the parishioners in both places would be chapel-goers.

'Tomorrow, you must get down to some serious canvassing, Harry,' Minnever said. 'It's the perfect time. People will want to talk to you after the inquest.'

'I was hoping the inquest would speak for itself,' Harry said. 'Or, rather, that it'd speak for me.'

Minnever slapped his hands on to his thighs as if he wanted to get up and walk about. 'Oh, it'll definitely speak! I'm just worried about what it'll say.'

'I'm sure the jury'll make the right decision.' Harry sounded confident. 'The medical evidence is compelling.'

'I wouldn't count on that.' Minnever took his hat off and ran his hand over his head as if he was searching for his hair. 'Your medical friend was here last evening and, in his cups, he became quite inflamed on the subject of autopsy. Seemed to feel that he'd have been able to make a more definitive judgement as to the cause of death if you'd allowed him to dissect the poor chap.'

'Reckitt's back?' Harry asked, as if that was the most important bit of information he'd just heard.

'Yes. I believe he's trying to secure the support of local doctors. And, if he gets it, you could be in trouble. Doctors command a lot of respect.'

I waited for Harry to put him straight about the exact amount of respect Benton Reckitt commanded, but he didn't. Maybe it'd finally dawned on him that he'd better start listening to the advice he was given.

Perhaps Minnever thought he'd scored a point because he slapped his hands on his thighs as if to say 'right, let's move on.'

'So, what did you want to talk to me about?'

'There's a witness we haven't been able to get hold of for the inquest. We hoped you might be able to help.'

'Me? How?'

'It's Montague Caldicot,' Harry said.

Minnever jumped up, rubbing his arse. Those stone benches were cold, sucked the warmth right out of your flesh. 'No, no, no, no, no, no, no! Absolutely not! What could Caldicot *possibly* have to do with your inquest?'

'We've discovered that he knew Rowland in London,' Harry said. 'And he seems to have donated quite a sum of money to Rowland's planned school.'

'Not good enough,' Minnever said. 'Unless somebody saw him at the school on the night in question, you leave him alone. Can you *imagine* the fuss the Tories'd make if you start making accusations against their candidate?'

If he could, Harry would've stared Minnever down. 'You have your ear to the ground. Do you know where he's staying?'

'No.'

A stray raindrop blew in. The wind was getting up again and the clouds were hurrying back. The lychgate roof wasn't going to protect us if the rain came in sideways.

I watched Minnever weighing up his options. He knew as well as we did that Caldicot would be bound to come to the inquest. He'd want to see Harry at work. And, if Harry called him to give evidence, without warning, there'd be hell to pay.

'Harry, listen to me. You have to be careful here. I know what Reckitt said when we saw the body, but the man's like one of those Indian snake charmers, you can't take your eyes off him while he's speaking but when you think about it later, it all seems a tad incredible. Let's put our cards on the table, shall we? All talk of hair-partings aside, doesn't it seem more likely, to you, that the teacher's death was an accident?'

Rowland's hair. Rearranged by Ruth Eynon, not the murderer. Harry hesitated. And if I saw it, so did Minnever.

He leaned towards Harry. 'Have you considered the issue of the new school Rowland was planning?'

Harry's head came up, smartish. 'What do you mean?'

'I received a visit today, from Mr Walters of Llanddewi Brefi. He was very cross that this soldier – Hughes, is it? – had been offered shelter by Miss Gwatkyn. Felt that a confession would've been forthcoming if she'd left well alone.'

Was that what Llew Price wanted to talk to us about, I wondered.

'Morgan Walters,' Harry said, 'is trying to keep his daughter from having to give evidence at the inquest.'

Minnever shook his head, took his watch out and looked at the time.

'Maybe that's the story he's told you, but I think there's another motive at work. Money. Walters has seen the value of this school coming here and he's leading the charge for it, telling all and sundry how prosperous it'll make them, how it'll be one in the eye for Lampeter. If Hughes had confessed, that would've made a martyr of Rowland and the sympathy money would've come rolling in. But you've muddied the waters. The mob may bay for blood but those with more intelligence will weigh the evidence. They'll ask themselves who would want to kill him, if not Hughes? If somebody else wanted him dead, there has to be a reason. It'll be concluded that our Mr Rowland had secrets and the school project will fail.'

Harry waited for him to go on, but Minnever'd said his piece. 'You think I should encourage an accidental death verdict so as to promote the cause of Rowland's school?'

Minnever sucked his tongue for a second or two, eyes on Harry. 'What I think doesn't matter. But the village is all for this school. A confession from Hughes would've made Rowland into a plaster saint in a week. An accidental death verdict would be good enough – it'd make him a victim of the hardship he was prepared to endure to realise his dream. The school cause would prosper.'

I watched Harry out of the corner of my eye. I'd expected him to laugh in Minnever's face, tell him he wasn't going to steer the jury away from what he believed had happened. But he didn't. He sat, chewing his lip. And Minnever drove his advantage home.

'If you become the man who cast suspicion on their beloved Mr Rowland and deprived them of the school they've come to think of as theirs by right, you'll lose every vote in Llanddewi Brefi,' he said. 'Possibly Tregaron, too. You can't afford that, Harry.'

Harry

Minnever had shaken my confidence and, suddenly finding myself at a low ebb, I was able to offer little resistance when he suggested that I would be well advised to accept an invitation from Tregaron's Olive Leaf Circle to join them at their weekly meeting.

Having made it clear that John was not needed at the event, Minnever steered me to a substantial house on the outskirts of the town and introduced me to the Circle's hostess, a Mrs Jenkinson, who, in welcoming me, seemed to assume a proprietary right over me for the remainder of the afternoon. I was introduced to perhaps a dozen ladies and was soon drinking tea and discussing not only their work for the Peace Society – did I know that it was now led by one of Tregaron's own sons? – but also the broader cause of humanitarianism and how I might further it in my role as coroner.

Though, at any other time, I might have enjoyed the company and conversation of lively-minded women, I found myself ill at ease. My mind flitted from Caldicot's banknotes to Reckitt's suddenly less irrefutable evidence; from Llew Price's request that I speak to him to Mattie Hughes's removal to Alltybela; from the future of Rowland's school and back to my suspicions about Caldicot.

Scarcely present as anything but a social simulacrum of myself, I allowed Minnever to extol my virtues and pose questions which I might answer to my own advantage, while uncertainties stamped in determined battalions through my brain.

I nodded and smiled as my career in London was examined at length, my enforced return to Glanteifi sympathised over and my conduct of cases as acting coroner admired. And, all the while, I knew I should be elsewhere pursuing the truth.

After two hours or so, I felt I might have done my duty but, even as I was casting about for a compliment with which to take my leave, my hostess asked, 'May we hear your views on capital punishment, Mr Probert-Lloyd?'

The question prompted an outpouring from the Circle's ladies on the subject of the barbarism of the gallows, a strength of feeling which was hardly remarkable in supporters of the Peace Society but which, in my less than perfectly composed state, took me somewhat by surprise. Voices came from all directions and I felt as if I had been thrust, unwittingly, into a game of Blind Man's Bluff. Unable to see who was speaking, I found it difficult to differentiate one voice from another as all-too-palpable emotions swirled around me.

Mrs Jenkinson tapped a spoon on the side of her cup for quiet but, though the hubbub died down, my sense of disorientation and vulnerability did not. I imagined them all looking at me, seeing a man disconcerted by ten seconds' outcry from a drawing room full of polite females. How weak I must seem to them, how inadequate. A sudden premonition of an onslaught far worse than this, the following day in the market square, sent such a tremor of apprehension through me that I could hardly breathe.

With a sudden horrifying clarity, I realised that others must see me in the same way as they viewed one-legged Mattie Hughes: as diminished, existing in a category of humanity different from those with all their faculties. The same category into which my father had slipped after his stroke.

Seconds, during which I might have answered Mrs Jenkinson's question, ticked by and I saw Minnever stir in my peripheral vision.

No. I could not allow him to rescue me. The thought was intolerable. I drew in a deep breath and cleared my throat, conscious of how loud the sound was in the now silent room.

'Ladies.' My own voice sounded strange, as if I was hearing it from a distance. 'It seems, from your response to Mrs Jenkinson's question, that we are in absolute agreement.' Then, as they always had in court, cogent words started to flow. 'Though successive administrations have taken great strides towards making our legal system more humane, its continued insistence on an eye for an eye,' I had heard the phrase several times during their outrage and something in me had the wit to quote it calmly back at them, 'still marks us as a retributive rather than a humane society.'

'But what of you, personally?' a voice asked. 'The existence of capital punishment must affect you, as coroner?'

'Yes,' another voice chimed in, 'might it not hinder you in the performance of your duties?'

Politely, I turned towards the second speaker, the whirlpool blotting out the upright posture and claret-coloured dress that had been visible a moment before. 'Are you asking whether I might feel it necessary to sway a jury towards manslaughter if I felt they might be inclined to bring in a verdict of murder?'

'Yes. There must be occasions when the commission of a murder might be justified. Or,' she added hastily, as audible breaths were taken, 'at least *less culpable*, might there not? One thinks of the case of the battered wife whose son decides that if the law will not protect his mother, then he must. Or, indeed, the poor woman herself.'

I wondered whether she knew as well as I did that the courts would treat those two cases very differently. A son might expect to be treated leniently as a principled protector but no judge would countenance anything but the gallows for a woman who turned murderously on her husband, however abominable his treatment of her.

'In the kind of case to which you refer,' I said, taking great care, 'we should be very grateful that we have juries in this country. For a jury, seeing injustice in the letter of the law, will bring in a just verdict where they can.'

'And you would allow such a thing in your inquests?' another asked. 'You would neither seek to dictate to nor overrule a jury?'

I had underestimated the ladies of the Teifi Valley. I had come blithely in to Mrs Jenkinson's drawing room to make myself pleasant, but these Peace Society supporters – the wives of solicitors and ministers, grocers and drapers and bankers – had taken it upon themselves to become informed. And, now, they would go home to their husbands – qualifying voters to a man – and give them chapter and verse on my performance.

I placed my cup and saucer on the slender-legged table at my side. 'Unless I was convinced that an egregious injustice would result,' I said. 'I believe the coroner's role obliges me to allow a jury to make the decisions it sees fit. After the presentation of all relevant evidence and any necessary advice, obviously.' This careful articulation of very little drew nothing but an expectant silence, forcing me to continue. 'But I'm no absolutist. Whilst I believe the law on capital punishment should be changed, I will not object to working within it until it *is* changed.'

'But will you campaign for abolition?'

I turned in the direction of the last voice. 'I haven't the liberty of time to do so, I'm afraid. Quite apart from my current hopes of election, following my father's recent death, I have an estate to run.'

Murmurs of sympathy did not mask another challenge. 'But, as somebody who supports abolition, might your time not be better spent campaigning for the Society rather than becoming coroner?'

'I don't believe so,' I said, alarmed by the thought that the ladies might go home and persuade their husbands not to vote for me in the hope that I might turn campaigner. 'I believe I may do more good as a coroner. Not only can I put the minds of the bereaved at ease and bring to light unsuspected foul play but, in holding to account those who are responsible for accidents, I hope I can play a part in making the increasing number of mechanised workplaces safer.'

To illustrate my point, I outlined the sad case of a mill worker whose leg had been crushed in a fulling machine. Following its amputation, he had developed gangrene and died, leaving a wife and four children with no means of support. 'Had the mill owner had more care for the conditions in which his employees were forced to work, that man would not have died. As coroner, I was able to censure the owner publicly and my remarks were taken up by the press. As a consequence, he has offered a sum of money to the widow.'

A new voice came, somewhat hesitantly, from beside the drawing room's piano. 'You don't feel that, were you to sit on the bench of magistrates instead of serving as coroner, you could offer an enlightened example to your fellow justices of the peace?'

John would have laughed. That had always been his line.

'I'm afraid that my views would, indeed, be an example to them,' I said. 'Unfortunately, it would be an example of the kind of radicalism that they abhor and I fear that their own judgements would become harsher in response.'

My response had the merit of being true, though it was not the whole truth. But I could scarcely tell the ladies of the Olive Leaf Circle that I craved independent employment, that I was desperate to secure some occupation not contingent upon my position as squire to Glanteifi.

'Then we must help you become coroner,' Mrs Jenkinson spoke with the authority of somebody whose word would be the last on the matter. 'Any influence we have with our menfolk will be brought to bear, Mr Probert-Lloyd. You may depend upon that.'

'I think you might have warned me, Minnever,' I grumbled, once the front door had closed on us and we were out of earshot. 'I've seldom felt more cornered. Why didn't you tell me they'd want to ask those sorts of questions?'

'Because I didn't know. Mrs Jenkinson approached me, by letter, asking if you'd be so good as to come to their meeting this afternoon. I replied to the effect that you'd come if time allowed. Thought you'd know all about Olive Leaf Circles.'

'I do. I knew plenty of members in London. But I didn't expect to find active Peace Society campaigners in Tregaron!'

I felt Minnever looking at me askance and half-turned, keeping my eyes where I could see him. 'What?'

'I won't be the only person who's noticed your condescension towards virtually every institution that exists in the Teifi Valley. You're not going to win any elections if people suspect that you're constantly comparing Cardiganshire to London and finding it wanting!'

I felt a prickling on the nape of my neck and up my scalp. Minnever was right, I wanted London back. I wanted the freedom to be Harry Probert-Lloyd, up and coming barrister, not young Harry Glanteifi, Justice Probert-Lloyd's blind son with the odd ideas.

For once, my blindness was a refuge. To have been forced to look Minnever in the eye, both of us knowing that he had stripped me to my shivering core, would have been too much. I would have had no choice but to walk away. From the party, from the election, from everything. But blindness blotted out accusation and pity as surely and indiscriminately as it blotted out detail. I stared resolutely into the whirlpool and tried to drown myself in it.

'If you really want to be coroner, Harry, you've got to start seeing allies and equals instead of people who fall short of your ideals. You may not like it, but to get anywhere in public life there has to be reciprocity. You're not a barrister any more so stop being so combative! Believe it or not, sometimes people are actually on your side.'

I began to defend myself but he silenced me. 'You can't be defensive on the hustings, Harry – if people see that, you'll lose them. You're already at a disadvantage because of your sight – it's going to be difficult for you to read the crowd. You only need one heckler to catch the mood and then, unless you play things very carefully indeed, you may as well go home.'

The gusty breeze jostled me, combing its damp fingers through my hair, forcing any response I might have made back down my throat. I felt as if the wind had ganged up with Minnever against me, like a playground bully following hard on a teacher's heels. *Ha-ha! Harry Probert-Lloyd's not as clever as he thinks he is. Got a telling off!*

I looked about me from the corner of my eye, wondering whether people were looking, whether they had heard Minnever's words, whether they were waiting for the rest of the lecture. Instead, Minnever put his hand under my elbow. 'Come on. Let's go back to the Talbot and thrash out a strategy over a bottle of something fortifying. Then John and I can rehearse you.'

John

It was raining hard again by the time Minnever'd dragged Harry off to talk to some ladies' meeting, so I decided not to ride back down to Llanddewi Brefi to talk to Llew Price. He could wait till tomorrow morning. As long as we spoke to him before the inquest, it'd be fine. Instead, I'd stay in the warm and get down to writing a list of the questions Harry'd need to ask witnesses. That was the routine we'd got into – I'd write a list of questions then we'd spend the evening before the inquest going over them.

But when I walked into the Talbot, the landlord, Mr Thomas, was standing there talking to a tall gentleman in riding clothes, a servant hovering in the background with a couple of bags. 'Will there be anything else, Mr Caldicot?' Mr Thomas asked him.

So. This was Harry's rival. Caldicot wasn't what I'd expected. He was older, for a start – definitely over forty. And, for some reason, I'd pictured him overfed and flabby-looking. In the flesh, he was anything but. He had the kind of face you only get from sun or wind and the way he held himself showed muscle not fat.

I knew what Harry'd want me to do, so I mustered up my best English accent. 'Mr Caldicot, good day to you. I'm John Davies, Assistant Coroner.' Thought I'd better give myself a promotion, he might not speak to me otherwise.

He gave me a polite nod which I took as permission to carry on.

'As you'll probably know, Mr Probert-Lloyd is here to conduct an inquest.'

He nodded again. Not a man to waste words, Montague Caldicot.

'Were you thinking of attending?' I asked.

He didn't smile but his face changed enough to tell me he was amused by my cheek. 'You mean, am I coming to cast an eye over the opposition?'

I tried to look as if butter wouldn't melt. 'Partly that.' I was feeling my way, listening to every word in my head before I let it out. 'But also, Mr Probert-Lloyd's been given to understand that you were acquainted with the deceased. Mr Nicholas Rowland.'

Montague Caldicot frowned, very slightly. 'I think "acquainted" is overstating things. I believe Rowland and I found ourselves in the same company, once or twice, in London.'

'Ah,' I said, trying to look a bit embarrassed without over-doing it. 'In that case, perhaps our information has credited you with too much influence. We'd been led to believe that Mr Rowland's coming here was almost entirely your doing. That you'd represented Llanddewi Brefi as somewhere propitious to establish a place of learning.'

I heard myself sounding like a dictionary. *Propitious* indeed! And *place of learning* wasn't much better. But, to be fair, 'school' sounded too ordinary for what Nicholas Rowland had had in mind.

Caldicot gave me a half-smile. 'I wish that were true! I'd be delighted to wield such influence.' He turned to his servant. 'Take the bags upstairs, would you, Stephen?' Then he turned back to me. 'I was going to sit down and take a glass of something, Mr Davies. Would you care to join me?'

'I'd be delighted, thank you,' I said, trying to sound as if I sat down to drink with the likes of him every day. But then, I did, didn't I? For all his oddness, Harry was Caldicot's equal. Still, I hoped he wasn't going to offer me brandy. Couldn't stand the stuff.

Mr Thomas, who'd moved a little way off when we started speaking and made himself busy untying a parcel of printed bills, showed us into the little dining room we'd eaten in a few nights ago. He nodded wisely when Caldicot asked for a bottle of claret and left us to it.

Once we'd sat down in the two upholstered chairs that'd appeared next to the fire, Caldicot went straight back to where we'd left off, as if he owed me an explanation for some misunderstanding. 'I believe I do recall a conversation with Rowland about his school.' He stretched one leg out and rubbed at his thigh as if it pained him. 'He was introduced to me as being involved in education and the conversation moved, as it would, to the Education Commissioners' report. Rowland was quite infuriated by it, as I recall. Adamant that something must be done.'

Just as I was thinking that this was all a bit too pat, Mr Thomas came in with a decanter of claret and poured us each a glass.

Caldicot raised his. 'Your health, Mr Davies.'

'And yours.' I sat on the edge of my seat. 'Still, it's even more commendable, given your brief acquaintance, that you were kind enough to support Mr Rowland once he was here.'

Caldicot crossed his legs. The little frown was back. 'I'm not sure I follow.'

I felt my heart beating hard. Affable or not, Montague Caldicot wasn't going to take much more pushing. 'I beg your pardon, I was referring to your donation to his collegiate school fund.'

Caldicot swallowed a mouthful of wine and fixed his dark eyes on me. He might as well've said, *Listen very carefully, young man.* 'I'm afraid that, once again, you're giving me credit where none is due, Mr Davies. Laudable as I found Mr Rowland's aims, I never had occasion to donate money in support of them. I believe we met once more, fleetingly, but that was the limit of our acquaintance.'

'I do beg your pardon,' I said, again. Quite honestly, I was pleased not to have stammered and I began weighing my words very carefully, like a boy looking ahead in the Bible passage he's reading aloud for a name that might trip him up. Nebuchadnezzar. Amalekites. Onesiphorus. 'I believe we may have made an erroneous assumption,' I said. 'Some of the banknotes we found in Mr Rowland's possession – which we assumed were subscriptions to his school – had your name on them.'

The frown was still there. 'But, as we both know, Mr Davies, banknotes may change hands many times.'

'Of course. As I say, I do beg your pardon – it was a lazy assumption on our part.'

The frown left his face and he gave a single dip of the head. Apology accepted. 'Easily done. Quite honestly, I'm flattered to have been thought a benefactor. But, in this case, sadly not.'

I smiled, sipped and moved on to safer ground. 'Are you relishing the challenge of the election contest?'

He downed the rest of his claret and reached for the decanter. 'Candidly, I'd rather face an enemy armed to the teeth. At least then I'd know what to do.'

I didn't believe him. Montague Caldicot was the kind of man who'd always be prepared for whatever he was facing.

But that wasn't the only thing that didn't ring true. Those banknotes hadn't been through many hands. I'd need to double-check but I was almost certain that their serial numbers had been consecutive. So, unless all five had been passed from hand to hand together, Montague Caldicot was lying.

Harry

I slept badly. The night before an inquest was invariably a restless one, my mind going over and over facts and questions, but this was different. When I was not endlessly replaying my conversation with Minnever, I was hearing John's words again. 'Caldicot must be lying. The numbers are consecutive – three, three, five, nought to three, three, five, four. He must've gone into the Mercantile Bank and asked for fifty pounds to be drawn on his account.'

He was right, of course. And there was only one plausible reason why Caldicot should lie about the money: Rowland had been blackmailing him.

But, blackmail or not, it would do me no good to pursue him. Minnever had made it perfectly clear that I could suggest no association between Caldicot and Rowland without cast-iron evidence. Anything less would be seen as a crude attempt to call Caldicot's probity into question.

Eventually, accepting that sleep would not come, I got up and, after repeatedly thrusting a newspaper spill into the embers in the grate, managed to light the room's candles and shake the last few coals from the scuttle on to the fire.

I wanted the candles' glow not because they would allow me to see anything but to cheer me, and it was by blind touch alone that I pulled on my stockings, set the lukewarm hot-water bottle on the hearth and rested my feet on it.

Wrapped in the bedcover, I sat staring into the dark, the fire a faint red glow at the whirlpool's consuming edge.

You've got to start seeing allies and equals instead of opponents... Believe it or not, sometimes people are actually on your side.

How easy it is to see other people's mistakes, and how hard to see your own. If I had had a friend who found himself in my position, exiled from his London life, surely I would have advised him to associate himself with like-minded people, people who might suggest employment or advancement? So why had I been unable to apply the same common sense to my own situation?

Convenient though it would have been, I could not blame the shock of being told I was going blind. I had, after all, had months to come to terms with the idea. Months during which I had been forced to resort to the strongest available magnifying glass, to sitting at a window thrown open to every last speck of daylight like a medieval scribe, to employing an ever greater number of lamps once afternoon dimmed the office. My rational mind had tried to persuade me that I was simply overworking, straining my eyes but, despite days when things seemed slightly better, a more animal part of me had been undeceived and had known that I would never see properly again.

By the time I had consulted Dr Figges, an ophthalmological specialist at Moorfields hospital, I had more or less consciously been looking for an end to the torture of hope. And Figges had delivered the *coup de grâce* with pitiless compassion.

'Your condition is incurable, I'm afraid. You will, eventually, see nothing at all in that central area.'

My days in London were numbered; and that number had been distressingly small.

I had told nobody; had not been able to bring myself to do so until I knew how to convey the news with some equanimity. Until I had some kind of plan with which to ward off pity.

But no such plan had presented itself by the time penury had forced me back to Glanteifi. And – as Minnever had forced me to realise – even when the discovery of dairymaid Margaret Jones's remains had driven me to turn detective, instead of using the opportunity to forge helpful connections, my resentfulness at being forced to abandon my London life had led to unwise decisions.

Though I knew, now, that my attitude had been unjustified, at the time I had blamed my father. In my mind, he had always been a metonym for what I saw as a rigid, self-serving magistracy and, in defying him to investigate Margaret's death, I had felt myself to be defying the whole system. It would not have occurred to me to seek support from those I thought of as my father's cronies.

Subsequently, troubled by what I had discovered about my own part in Margaret's fate, instead of capitalising on my success as an investigator I had allowed myself to sink back into a species of hostile torpor. Only the request that I stand in as coroner during Leighton Bowen's last illness had roused me.

Why had that request not suggested to me that I might have allies on the bench? Though I had grasped at the post as a potential escape from the snare of filial duty, I had made no attempt to build bridges with the magistrates.

Sometimes, people are actually on your side.

If I had consulted the dying Bowen for advice, made overtures to other magistrates when my appointment as acting coroner was announced, would they still have connived at Montague Caldicot's nomination as coroner?

I had certainly given them no reason to nominate me instead.

That I should have looked for allies seemed obvious to Minnever; but I was a barrister. I had not been trained in negotiation, compromise, give-to-get. The game at the bar was winner takes all.

If I had tried to tell a magistrate, or a judge, how the accused was forced to live, how poverty had made a criminal of him or her, I should have been a laughing stock. The clergy who supported the trust for which I had done most of my work as a barrister might understand the desperate lives of the poor wretches whose cases I pleaded but magistrates and judges never would.

And how are they to know any better if nobody bothers to educate them?

Was that the voice of reason, or the voice of Lydia Howell? It was certainly the kind of riposte our correspondence had led me to expect from her.

I leaned forward and felt about on the hearth for a poker to stir the coals. With darkness pressing in as an almost tangible thing all around me, the desire to see movement, a change in the glowing light as flames flickered around the poker, was overwhelming.

Would Lydia arrive the following day, while I was conducting the inquest?

As I imagined her slipping in at the back of the schoolroom to watch the proceedings, I realised that I was both longing for her arrival and dreading the reality of it.

John

I liked the Talbot. As well as comfortable beds, they made sure that you faced the day well fed. And I preferred their cutlery to the stuff at Glanteifi. Silver spoons and forks made food taste odd to me.

We were finishing our breakfast and discussing the order we should call witnesses in, when one of the Talbot's servants brought a letter for Harry.

I recognised the handwriting straight away. Seen it often enough, hadn't I? If Harry hadn't been in the room, I would've kept it until after the inquest. As it was, I had no choice.

The note turned out to be mercifully short. Miss Howell had established herself at Glanteifi and was intending to arrive in Tregaron today. That was it.

'So she'll be here for the public meeting tomorrow,' Harry said.

I looked at him. I'd been wondering for a while what his feelings towards Lydia Howell were. Reading her letters to him might not make me blush but they were quite intimate – she addressed him as 'Harry', like a brother. Was that how they saw each other? Or was it possible that he had romantic feelings for her?

She was ten years older than him and plain, so it didn't seem likely. Not that he'd know what she looked like, of course, but he'd want a young wife, wouldn't he?

I put Lydia's note in my pocket and stood up. Time to get on with the day, take proceedings by the scruff of the neck. Harry needed this to be a well-behaved inquest. Couldn't allow it to go running off in all directions.

'Right,' I said, 'if you've finished, we should be off.'

Harry got up. 'Just let me go and write a note to leave here for Lydia.'

'Haven't you already packed your writing things for the inquest?'

'I can unpack them again. It'll only take a moment.'

'We need to be there in plenty of time, Harry! We've still got to speak to Llewelyn Price.'

I could see that he'd forgotten about Price and whatever he wanted to tell us. Unusual for him.

I hoped he wasn't going to live to regret it.

–

Harry might've decided not to hold the inquest in the Three Horseshoes, but the place was still packed as we went past. I wondered if Morgan Walters was intending to bring a barrel over to the schoolhouse on the back of a cart. He wouldn't want to see all those paying customers walking away if he could follow them and have some more of their money.

It was one of those days where the weather couldn't decide whether to cook you or drown you. Warm sun one minute, clouds racing over to rain on you the next. We'd managed to get down from Tregaron to Llanddewi without getting wet but the streets were more puddle than path and all the horseshit'd been washed into a slurry that splashed up with every step. I looked down at people picking their way through it, the hems of their *betgwns* and trousers soaked and filthy. I was glad to be in the saddle. It might make your arse sore but at least being on horseback kept you out of the muck.

The whole population of the village seemed to be turning out for the inquest. Some had put on their Sunday best, but most people'd be straight back to work after the verdict so they were in their everyday clothes. Women carrying babies in shawls shooed children in front of them and men carried little ones who didn't want to walk. You'd have sworn they were going to a fair, not to hear the details of how a man they'd all respected had died.

'Looks as if every shopkeeper and tradesman in Llanddewi's shutting up shop till the inquest's over,' I said. 'Apart from the pubs, of course.'

'Are they all doing good business?' Harry asked. 'Or is it just the Three Horseshoes?'

I looked up and down the wet street to see how many doors were open, which had people coming in and out under their sodden thatch. 'It's mostly the Three Horseshoes,' I told him. 'Wouldn't put it past Morgan Walters to've offered the jury free beer to bring the punters into his place with them. Everybody'll want to know what they're going to decide.'

Three months ago, Harry would've been horrified at the thought of a jury deciding on their verdict before the inquest. By now, he'd learned how it worked. Most jurymen relied on the view of the body and didn't bother much with the rest of the evidence. They tended to think they knew what they'd seen. I grinned to myself. It was going to be entertaining watching Benton Reckitt trying to persuade them that they didn't.

–

'Ah, Probert-Lloyd. You're here at last.'

I turned towards the voice, put my hand up to shield my eyes from the sun. It was the vicar, Tobias Hildon. He'd been waiting for us outside the schoolroom.

He ignored me and kept his eyes on Harry. 'I need to speak with you before the inquest starts.'

Harry dismounted. 'As do others, Mr Hildon. A moment, if you please.'

A pack of boys ran over to us from Morgan Walters's beer-vending cart and started clamouring to look after the mares. I chose the two who were rubbing the mares' ears instead of sticking their hands out and Harry paid them. Then he turned to the vicar. 'Now, Mr Hildon,' he said, as if the man'd been waiting patiently, instead of fuming and cuffing the boys round the ears for getting in his way. 'What was it you wanted to tell me?'

Hildon wasn't going to waste time being polite. 'I want to know who your appointed medical man is and why he's been spouting damned nonsense. It's quite obvious that this was an accident and rumours to the contrary are causing havoc in the village. There was a near riot the other night – it's unacceptable.'

'May I ask why you think it was so obviously an accident, Mr Hildon?'

If the vicar had known Harry like I did, he would've known not to trust that mild tone.

'He shouldn't have been going up and down a ladder at all times of the day and night with those useless hands of his! I don't know what Phoebe Gwatkyn was thinking, installing him in a loft.'

He had a point. Or he would have, if he'd lifted a finger to change the situation. But he'd been too busy trying to get a National School set up in competition, hadn't he?

'And, as for her conniving with him to procure those two young women as his assistants. Disgraceful!'

A small silence gathered behind Mr Hildon's words. Then Harry said, 'Disgraceful is a strong word, Mr Hildon. What exactly was it that you found so reprehensible about Mr Rowland's employment of Nan Walters and Ruth Eynon?'

'He exploited them as unpaid secretaries for that atheistic academy project of his – absolutely improper! He should have incorporated it as a proper charity and employed somebody to oversee it in the conventional manner.'

'I believe he did pay Nan Walters and Ruth Eynon,' Harry said.

'As *teachers*, yes. But only recently. And never for the other work they did.'

He seemed to know a lot more about Rowland's school than I would've expected and an image of Tobias Hildon sitting in Mattie Hughes's house came to mind. The two of them drinking tea made in that soldier's tin of his, listening to Billy Walters telling them all about what his sister was doing for Nicholas Rowland.

Shakespeare had it right. Misery acquaints a man with strange bedfellows, and anger'll do the same. Because Hildon'd been angry about Rowland coming here with his *atheistic-academy project*, hadn't he? Angry enough to start a campaign for a different kind of school entirely.

The sun was hot on my ear so I turned my head away from it and saw Billy Walters sitting amongst the celandines on a bank a little way off. Watching and listening. And, no doubt, everything he heard would go straight inside to Mattie Hughes before the inquest started. I thought of telling Harry but decided not to bother. It wasn't Harry that was letting his tongue run away with him, was it?

'Excuse me, Mr Hildon,' I said. 'Why do you call Mr Rowland's school atheistic? He was a Unitarian, wasn't he – a Christian?'

Hildon snorted. 'If Unitarianism can be considered Christian. Denying the divinity of Christ rather calls that into question, wouldn't you say?'

'Was Mr Rowland proposing a denominational affiliation for his school?' Harry asked.

'No. It was to have no religious basis whatsoever. Just like the London colleges that deny God and enthrone science. Science will be the saviour now, according to them. But it's a bleak kind of salvation that offers no hope beyond material success, wouldn't you say?'

Neither of us had any answer to that. I wondered what Lydia Howell, a Unitarian to her fingernails, would have to say on the subject. She was no God-denier.

'But none of that need concern us any more.' Hildon had reined his tone in. 'Though I wished the man no ill-will, at least his death has put an end to his pernicious scheme. Thank God.'

It was on the tip of my tongue to ask him whether he was suggesting that God had brought about Rowland's 'accident' so as to put paid to the collegiate school but common sense got the better of me and I kept my mouth shut.

'Mr Hildon,' Harry said, 'did you wish to offer any actual evidence as to the manner of Mr Rowland's death?'

Hah! That floored Mr Holier-than-the-Unitarians! Offering evidence at a public hearing? Well beneath his dignity.

'It's not *my* ability to present evidence that concerns me. It's your medical witness's. I trust that you're not going to allow him to state, unchallenged, that this was murder?'

Harry sucked in a breath and stared in Hildon's direction. 'I'm afraid you must allow me to conduct my inquest as I see fit, Mr Hildon. But I can assure you that every possible step will be taken to ensure that the jury reaches the most informed verdict possible. Now, if you'll excuse me, we are in danger of running late and I would like to make sure that everything is in order before we begin.'

Hildon put out a hand to stop him. 'Just one last thing. What became of the money you found in Rowland's quarters?'

I didn't like his tone but Harry replied as if it hadn't crossed his mind to be offended. 'It's lodged now with Miss Gwatkyn who is one of the collegiate school's trustees. Now, if you don't mind—'

–

Fair play to Rat-face Jones, he'd done what he could with the schoolroom. The benches had been pushed into rows for the spectators and, at the end of the room, two chairs and a card table were waiting for Harry and me. The furniture'd seen better days but Jones had put some thought into how he'd arranged it. We'd be sitting with our backs to the south-facing window which would put us in silhouette to the witnesses sitting opposite, while their faces would be clear as day to us. Well, to me, anyway.

The place was warmish but that was thanks to the mass of people – the stove wasn't lit. The schoolroom was already half-full of folk leaning against the walls, sitting on the low benches and perched on the big tables that'd been pushed to face the front. The nosey ones were still milling about at the door-end of the building, trying to look up into the loft.

Harry'd obviously realised what they were doing. 'Where's the loft ladder?' he asked.

'Can't see it. Looks like somebody's had the sense to take it away.'

He nodded, satisfied. 'Can you see Llew Price?'

I scanned the room. 'At the front, with the rest of the jury.'

'They're already here – good. What's the time?'

I slipped my watch out of its pocket. 'Ten minutes to.'

Harry'd got into the habit of waiting until the dot of ten, then striding up to his seat and beginning proceedings without so much as waiting for silence. It was an inquest not public entertainment. If people wanted to hear what was going on, they had to shut up quick-smart.

'Is Caldicot here?'

I hadn't seen him but I looked around the schoolroom again to make sure. Yesterday, he'd been wearing a perfectly-tailored dark suit. No lumpy home-made seams, no hairy nap to make it easy to brush dirt off. If he'd been here, wearing that suit, he'd have stood out like a raven among chickens. 'Can't see him.'

'If I were him, I'd slip in at the back as we start. He's not going to want to be stared at.'

'Well, at the moment, it's us getting stared at,' I said. 'So, what do you want to do? Are you going to try and speak to Price first?'

'I think I need to speak to the whole jury, not just Price. Hildon's obviously been making his feelings known and I want them to be sure of their rights and responsibilities. Can you ask Simi Jones to bring them out?'

Rat-face was sitting with Mattie Hughes at the front of the room on what'd been Rowland's desk. As he and the jury stood up to file out, I looked at Hughes. 'Will you be all right for a minute?'

He nodded and picked up the stick that was leaning against his wooden leg. 'Got protection, haven't I?'

The stick didn't look much and my face must've shown it because he held it out for me to take. I almost dropped it. Weighted with shot. Not something you'd want to be hit with. And if Mattie Hughes was carrying it, then he knew exactly how to use it.

Mr Hughes is a soldier. He knows a dozen ways to kill a man.

As I made my way back through the crowd, I heard bits of conversation, like you do. Mostly, people were speculating about the inquest but one sly comment caught my ear.

'What'll Miss Gwatkyn do for company now, with Mr Rowland gone?'

I stopped just behind the woman who'd spoken and pulled my watch out. While I pretended to wind it, I strained my ears back. Mrs Gossip obviously hadn't got the reaction she was after, so she tried again. 'Spent a lot of time over there, didn't he?'

One of her companions rose to the bait. 'Friend of her husband's, wasn't he?'

'So they *say*.'

I couldn't just stand there listening, people'd wonder what I was doing, so I moved on. *Had* there been something going on between Phoebe Gwatkyn and Nicholas Rowland? Was that what Tobias Hildon had been getting at when he said that Miss Gwatkyn had 'connived' with him to 'procure' the girls? The lady of Alltybela had certainly come running over to the schoolhouse when Simi Jones sent word to her about Rowland's death. And she always referred to him as Nicholas. Mind, she had odd notions about what it was appropriate to call people. Renamed her hall-boy Lleu Llaw Gyffes, hadn't she?

But, then again, she'd been pretty quiet on the subject of her husband. We hadn't even known he existed to start with.

As I looked toward the back of the room, I saw three men sitting in the middle of the last row of spectators. Busy writing in their notebooks, they were, hands flicking along the lines as they squiggled their shorthand.

I knew them from other inquests. They were from the newspapers. *The Welshman, The Cambrian* and the *Carmarthen Journal*. They'd be here for the election meeting as well as the inquest. Their editors'd be delighted – one set of travel expenses instead of two.

Before I walked back out into the sunshine, I looked around the room. Who did we know here, Harry and I? Hardly anybody. It wasn't right. If we'd been here for an inquest five or six weeks earlier – in the time before we'd even so much as heard of Jonas Minnever – I knew for a fact that I would've been able to name at least a dozen people we'd spoken to, and I'd have known a dozen more by sight. That was how Harry did things. Left no stones unturned. Asked awkward questions.

As it was, we knew Nan Walters and her family, Ruth Eynon, Tobias Hildon and Mattie Hughes.

And Miss Gwatkyn of course.

What would the newspapermen think if they knew that half the people who should've been giving evidence were just going to sit there, watching? The *Journal* would think that was quite right. As far as its editor was concerned, an inquest into the death of a teacher who taught ragged-arsed children in a cowshed had no business questioning the great and the good. But *The Welshman, The Cambrian*? They agreed with Harry. Nobody was above the law.

As I reached to pull the door open, it came towards me and I saw that the Alltybela household had arrived. I stood aside as they came in and took the places that somebody'd made sure were kept free for them. I expected Phoebe Gwatkyn to go down to the front where Minnever and Mr Hildon were sitting but she didn't. Just parked herself there, with her cook and her butler and the rest.

Outside, it was fresh and quiet after the noise and the stink of people. A mountain range of clouds was lumbering off towards the horizon leaving the sun free to flood the valley and bring out every shade of green known to creation.

I stepped out of the path of the jury who were straggling back in to the schoolroom, all except Llew Price who was hovering.

I gave Harry his cue. 'Five minutes to ten, Harry. And here's Mr Price.'

Harry turned. 'I'm sorry I've not been to see you, Mr Price. My time isn't my own, at the moment, what with the demands of the election. I believe you have some information for me?'

The grocer looked at him as if he was trying to decide whether he'd just been fobbed off or offered a genuine apology.

Then his eyes moved over to me. 'Have you spoken to Jeremiah Eynon, Ruth's father?'

I shook my head. 'As Mr Probert-Lloyd says, we've not had the time we'd have liked on this inquest.'

'Then you don't know anything about Ruth and Shoni Goch?'

Harry was too clever by far to ask who Shoni Goch was. 'Why don't you tell us what you know, Mr Price?'

The grocer shook his head. 'There isn't time to explain now. If you call Jeremiah Eynon to give testimony, I can ask the right questions.'

I could see Harry wasn't happy about that. I wasn't either, for that matter, but for a different reason. I had a feeling we'd made a terrible mistake in not making time for Llew Price. But I didn't want Harry using up the remaining minutes before ten arguing with him. I needed to tell him the gossip I'd overheard about Miss Gwatkyn.

'Thanks, Mr Price,' I said, 'we'll do that.' I put a hand on Harry's arm to keep him quiet and Llew followed the rest of the jury back inside. If Harry wanted me to be his eyes, sometimes he just had to let me do what plainly needed doing.

'There's something you need to know,' I said, before he could ask me what I thought I was up to. 'There's talk in the village about Phoebe Gwatkyn and Nicholas Rowland. Might be relevant, might not.'

I told him what the gossip-monger had said, then watched him sucking in a breath as if he was taking thoughts with it.

'There's no reason to have Phoebe Gwatkyn up to give evidence,' he said. 'It's like Minnever said about Caldicot – without an eyewitness to say they'd seen her here, I have no reason to. Besides, if there *was* anything going on between them, she wouldn't want him dead, would she?'

'Unless they argued. You know, lovers' tiff?'

'Does she strike you as the lovers' tiff type?'

What was the lovers' tiff type? And what type was Phoebe Gwatkyn, come to that?

'So you'll call Jeremiah Eynon?' I asked.

'I've no choice in the matter, have I? You told Price I would.'

'What else was I supposed to do? He's the jury foreman. He asked to see us days ago on inquest business and we didn't make time for him. I couldn't have him going around, afterwards, saying that you hadn't allowed him to bring important evidence forward, could I?'

Harry turned on his heel and walked towards the schoolhouse door.

I caught him up in three strides. He could throw a peevish fit if he liked but I wasn't going to let that stop me walking in side by side with him.

But Price's question about a man nobody else had so much as mentioned had rattled us both.

We'd never walked in to an inquest less well prepared.

Harry

We marched down to the table at the far end of the schoolroom where John opened my writing box and arranged its contents as if they were some kind of official regalia.

While John scrutinised the witnesses, I would be making notes, using what he referred to as my 'apparatus': a frame of my own design that held a sheet of paper and allowed me to keep to a line as I wrote. Knowledge of my blindness naturally led people to expect that John would record the proceedings, and my taking up my pen tended to produce a valuable degree of bewilderment.

The inquest having been called to order, I started by inviting Simi Jones to the witness's chair to explain how he had heard of Rowland's death.

Always begin with questions you know the answers to, an old barrister once told me; then, when you get to the ones you might not be so sure of, the jury will already be disposed to think you know the whole story.

Despite the presence of Minnever and Tobias Hildon, I had decided to hold the inquest in Welsh, as was my usual practice. It seemed ludicrous to me that the presence of two monoglot Englishmen should override the comfort of dozens of people who spoke only Welsh and I had arranged for proceedings to be interpreted by Ruth Eynon.

Simi Jones's uncontroversial evidence having been given, I thanked him and asked Nan Walters to come forward.

John and I had decided that, of the two girls, Nan would be the better choice to give evidence. 'She wants people to see how much she knows, how important she is,' John had said. 'If the two of them know more than they've said already, we'll get it out of her more easily than Ruth.'

In contrast to her demeanour when John and I had interviewed the two of them at the Three Horseshoes, Nan seemed subdued, even meek. The first spark of feeling she showed came not, as I might have expected, when I asked her to describe what her friend had done when she saw the disarray of Nicholas Rowland's hair, but when I asked her what kind of employer he had been.

'He wasn't our employer! We didn't work *for* him, we worked *with* him! We were his co-workers in a new educational venture.'

Welsh uses the same word for both 'venture' and 'adventure' and her use of it made their plans sound exciting, even a little daring.

'By which you mean the new school proposal?'

'No, *this* school!' She flung out an arm at the barely-converted cowshed. 'We didn't just teach the children who came here to read and write – we taught them about their place in the world! How history's brought us to this point. Where our country is situated in relation to the rest of the world. What learned men of the past can teach us about improving our own society.'

The suppressed muttering which greeted her words suggested that some of the parents who had sent their children to Rowland's school had entirely failed to grasp the scope of the education on offer.

'Yes, quite.' I made an entirely unnecessary note, in order to separate my next question from her pride at their accomplishments. 'You also helped him in a personal capacity, I believe – writing letters and so forth?'

'We did, yes.'

'And, in the course of assisting Mr Rowland, did you ever meet any of the potential donors to his collegiate school project?'

When we had asked the same question in her mother's parlour, she had denied knowing the identities of any such gentlemen. But she had not been under oath then.

I waited, hoping that John would be able to tell whether her hesitation was born of an unwillingness to name names or from a dawning awareness that Rowland's actions had not, perhaps, lived up to the fulsomeness of his words to her and Ruth.

'No,' she said, at length. 'Or, rather, nobody apart from Miss Gwatkyn. But just because Mr Rowland didn't feel able to name them didn't mean that he'd had no success. He'd already acquired the necessary land—'

'I beg your pardon,' I interrupted. 'What land?'

'Five acres on the road to Tregaron.'

Judging by the audible reaction in the room, John and I were not the only people to whom this came as a surprise.

I waited for the turning, shrugging and muttering to subside. 'I see. And how was this land acquired? Was it given to Mr Rowland or did he buy it?'

Nan hesitated. 'I don't know.'

'Perhaps Mr Rowland already owned the land when he came here?' I suggested.

'No, I remember the day he told us. He was excited.'

'But he didn't tell you how it had come into his possession?'

'No.' She bit the word off short.

Allowing her a moment to contemplate Rowland's reluctance to share important details, I dipped my pen and wrote, *Is Phoebe Gwatkyn here?* Asking questions of John audibly would make my need for assistance obvious; I hoped that writing created exactly the opposite impression.

John tapped once, softly, on the table. One tap for yes, two for no. Our other signalling system involved his posture. If he could see that a line of questioning was proving effective, he would lean forward in his chair to encourage me to push on. If he wanted me to desist and try a different tack, he would lean back.

I wiped my pen and turned to the onlookers. 'Is there anyone present who has information on how this parcel of land came to belong to Mr Rowland?'

In response, the room fell utterly silent, save for the voice of Ruth Eynon translating quietly.

I waited. Having become accustomed to seeking information from inquests' spectators, I was not deterred by the lack of any immediate reaction. Responses had to be coaxed out of a crowd; people were unwilling to put themselves forward in front of their neighbours.

'If any of you know anything,' I said, wondering whether their silence touched on Llew Price's mysterious Shoni Goch, 'it would help this inquest very much if you would speak. Mr Rowland is owed the truth, I'm sure you'd agree.'

In my peripheral vision, heads turned this way and that as neighbours passed my question from gaze to gaze, wondering how it was that not one of them knew how Mr Rowland had come by those five acres.

As far as I was concerned, if Rowland had raised the money honestly, he would have been well advised to celebrate the fact, use it as bait for more. *Look, I have this much already – you would be joining a prosperous undertaking!*

No response having been forthcoming, save some stifled coughing, I thanked Nan Walters, dismissed her and called her brother to come and give testimony. This provoked some considerable comment and Simi Jones was forced to call for order.

'You were known to hang about watching Mr Rowland's comings and goings,' I said, as soon as Billy had been sworn in. 'No, don't deny it, I'm not interested in what you did or didn't do, I'm interested in what you *saw*. Did you see anybody coming to visit Mr Rowland? Or watching him?'

When the boy did not reply, John leaned forward, urging me on.

'William Morgan! Answer my question. Mr Rowland is dead and I need to know anything you can tell me. So does the jury. When you were watching Mr Rowland's schoolhouse, *did anybody come to see him*?'

'No!' Billy sounded anxious to be believed. 'I didn't see anybody!'

John shifted his chair forward slightly. *Persist.*

'That's not true is it? Tell me the truth!'

'Nobody came to see him all the time I was watching! But he'd go out. Quite late, sometimes.'

'Where to?'

It was not necessary to see Billy any better than I could to read, in his posture, an acute reluctance to answer the question.

'Where did Mr Rowland go when he went out late?' I insisted. 'You followed him, didn't you?'

Billy, obviously deciding to make a clean breast of the spying he'd done for Mattie Hughes, gave us everything in one rushed sentence. 'Up through the village and out to where the road goes off to Pontllanio – but I couldn't follow him any further than that so I don't know where he went after, I swear!'

John

My main job during inquest hearings was to watch people. Watch the witnesses while they give their evidence. Watch the jury for signs that they didn't understand something. Watch the spectators in case trouble was brewing or somebody knew something.

Which meant that while Harry went after Billy Walters about following Rowland, I was watching the crowd. So I saw him come in. Montague Caldicot. He just opened the schoolhouse door a crack and slid in.

And, sitting right at the back where they'd see any comings and goings, the newspaper men saw him, too. They looked at each other and started writing. Knew exactly who he was, didn't they?

Miss Gwatkyn's Lleu caught me staring and swivelled his head to see who'd come in. When he saw who it was, he turned back to me and tipped his nose up with a forefinger. Bringing me down to his level, the little pup. *We both know what he is. One of the* crachach. *The gentry. The nobs who look down their noses at us.*

But Caldicot hadn't looked down his nose at me, had he? He'd treated me like someone who mattered. We'd drunk claret together and he'd laughed and joked and answered my questions as if he never doubted my right to ask them.

And then, of course, he'd lied to my face.

Eyes on Miss Gwatkyn, I watched carefully. Nothing. Neither of them turned to the other, no glances were exchanged. Either they didn't know each other or they were doing a good job of pretending they didn't.

I watched Caldicot turn to the man standing closest to him – one of the Alltybela footmen – and say something with a jerk of his head towards the front of the room. Asking who the boy giving evidence was.

Not that he had long to watch him. None the wiser about where Rowland had been going late at night, Harry dismissed Billy and called Doctor Benton Reckitt to give his testimony.

Unlike Harry and Caldicot, nobody was backing Reckitt's candidacy for the coronership and he'd had to go back to work after his brief see-how-the-land-lies trip to Tregaron at the beginning of the week. We hadn't seen him at the Talbot that morning so he'd probably come up as far as Lampeter the previous day and ridden up to Llanddewi Brefi after an early breakfast.

I wondered how Reckitt was feeling, now he knew Ruth Eynon was responsible for Rowland's tidy hair and not the teacher's murderer. I knew Harry would've told Reckitt what we'd found out from the girls if he'd been able to but, as it was, there'd been no way of getting word to him. Would he suspect that Harry'd deliberately kept Ruth's evidence quiet, to make him look like a fool on the stand? You never knew how Reckitt was going to react. Apart from his reaction to corpses. That was always the same – business-like, meticulous, diligent.

Watching him shamble down the room and lower himself on to the chair, you'd have sworn the doctor was the clumsiest person alive. But, with a scalpel in his hand, he was a different man entirely. He could lay a heart open and show you the workings of its smallest veins, then close his clever slicings up again so you'd never know he'd been in there.

The jury watched him take his seat. They didn't look very impressed. Not that that was a surprise – short of finding poison in a body, jurors didn't set much store by medical evidence, as a rule. If doctors had been better at curing people it might've been different. But, when they weren't very good at keeping sick people alive, their opinion about how somebody'd died wasn't considered to be worth much.

I flicked a glance at the newspapermen scribbling away at the back of the room. I wondered if they'd comment on Reckitt's appearance. He was one of those men who always look untidy. His body seemed the wrong shape for clothes and he made things worse by not bothering much how he wore them. His necktie was always in an untidy knot, his trousers were baggy at the knee and you could tell he expected his maid-of-all-work to do his laundry instead of sending it out because his shirts were never starched and his coat needed a damn good brushing. Still, at least he'd shaved.

Harry looked up. 'Dr Reckitt, would you be good enough to give us a description of the body as you found it and your thoughts on his injuries, please?'

Reckitt's Welsh might be good enough for his workhouse patients, but he always gave evidence at inquests in English, so Ruth Eynon swapped to Welsh to translate his testimony for the jury. It was the first time I'd heard her speaking Welsh and she seemed a different girl. More confident. Mind, some of the doctor's technical language gave her some trouble. Contusion. Dorsal. Effusion. Welsh wasn't used for autopsy reports.

While we listened to more details of Rowland's injuries than anyone strictly needed, I looked about to see how people were taking it. Every eye was on Reckitt or Ruth. Apart from one little boy on his mother's lap who was pointing at something. I followed his finger and saw a butterfly fluttering against the cracked glass of one of the windows. The warmth of the sun must've woken it up and now the spring air was calling it out. The little boy patted his hands together in that clumsy way small children have and his mother smiled down at him. Something moved in my chest, like a heartstring being plucked.

'At the jury's viewing of the body,' Harry said, 'you gave it as your opinion that Mr Rowland was the victim of foul play. Is that still your opinion?'

Reckitt hesitated. 'On balance,' he said, after a second or two, 'yes, it is still my opinion. The clavicular fracture – the broken collarbone – and the injury to the front of his head could have happened by accident; if he'd tripped over the rug in the loft, for instance. But the damage to the back of his skull definitely seems to indicate foul play. It's a very significant wound – especially when compared with the relatively minor injury to the forehead – and indicative of some force.'

'But that injury – the broken skull – could it not have been sustained by the ladder falling backwards, if Mr Rowland had tried to climb it after falling out of the loft?'

Again, Reckitt hesitated. Without the hair-combing murderer theory, he was having to re-think things. 'I think it unlikely.'

'And that injury is, in your opinion, what killed him?'

Reckitt looked at Harry as if he'd like to come over and shake him by the lapels. 'Probably. But an autopsy, which I *strongly* advised, would have allowed me to be more definitive.'

Would it? He'd only come up with the smothering theory because he thought somebody'd held Rowland by the hair and banged his head on the floor, then smothered him to make sure he was dead. If nobody'd held him by the hair then maybe nobody'd banged his head.

Harry didn't look up from his note-taking. 'Could you explain to the jury what evidence a dissection of the body would have provided?'

Other people might've thought Harry was just dotting i's and crossing t's but I knew he wasn't. He was challenging Reckitt to justify his complaint about not being allowed to open Nicholas Rowland up. He didn't want the jury or anybody else to go away thinking he should've asked Reckitt to do more. Harry knew enough had already been left undone for this inquest and he wanted to avoid awkward questions at the public meeting.

'I felt it would be prudent to look for signs that whoever was responsible for inflicting the blow to the back of Nicholas Rowland's head had finished the job by smothering him.'

'And that would, unequivocally, have proved foul play?'

'Of course.'

Harry made a note then looked up in Reckitt's direction. 'You've stated that you don't believe that the injury to the back of Mr Rowland's head is consistent with simply falling backwards from the ladder. May I ask how you came to that conclusion?'

Reckitt shook his head. 'What I actually said is that I thought it was *unlikely*. The main reason being the very different nature of the two injuries to his skull that I've already mentioned; one simply a significant contusion, the other a depressed fracture.'

Harry nodded as he wrote. 'And, finally,' he said, without looking up, 'could you tell the jury what *form* of evidence you would have looked for at autopsy to support the idea that he might have been smothered?'

Reckitt leaned forward. 'Anything in the state of the viscera that differed from normal.'

Ruth Eynon hesitated at 'viscera' and shot a glance at me. 'Insides,' I said quietly and she finished translating the sentence.

'*Anything that was different from normal?*' Harry frowned. 'Am I right in thinking that there are no published descriptions of the effects of smothering that a medical witness might refer to? Nothing, in other words, to say, "this is what a victim of smothering looks like"?'

'No. That's why we need more autopsies.'

The crowd stirred a bit, then. *More cutting people up*, I could see people thinking. *No, thank you.*

Reckitt and Harry, between them, were turning his testimony into electioneering and it wasn't going well for the doctor. Now, when he stood up the next day and spouted his nonsense about opening up every single person who'd died to see if a reason could be found for their death, people'd know that medical men weren't even sure what they were looking for.

'So,' Harry said, 'just to be completely clear for the jury. Even if you'd carried out an autopsy by dissection, you'd only have been able to say that either Mr Rowland's viscera *did* look different from what you'd expect or that they didn't. You wouldn't have been able to say, with certainty, that he'd been smothered? Not beyond doubt?'

Reckitt stared across at us. Finally, it seemed to dawn on him that he hadn't done himself any favours, here.

'Doctor?'

Reckitt stared at him. 'Not *beyond doubt*, no.'

'So, again just to be clear for the jury, in the absence of any evidence to the contrary, is it your opinion that the depressed fracture to the back of Mr Rowland's skull – however he came by it – was the most likely cause of his death?'

The doctor didn't sigh so much as deflate. 'In the absence of any other evidence, yes.'

The jurymen started muttering amongst themselves. Harry let that go on for about half a minute, while he wrote down what Reckitt had said, then he looked up.

'Gentlemen of the jury, is there anything you'd like to ask Dr Reckitt?'

All eyes turned to the foreman, Llew Price, who'd stood up. I had a pretty shrewd idea that he could speak English perfectly well – most shopkeepers could – but he asked his question in Welsh. Perhaps he wanted to be sure he'd asked exactly what he meant to. 'Dr Reckitt, are you saying it's *impossible* that Mr Rowland died from falling by accident?'

Reckitt turned to face him. Must've been unnerving for the grocer, Reckitt staring at him as if he could see his innards through his skin. I looked around the room quickly. Most people were watching the doctor but some were talking behind their hands or mouth-to-ear.

'Without clear evidence, no medical man would ever rule something out completely,' Reckitt said, finally. 'There's so much variation in what's normal that it's impossible.'

'Aye,' Llew Price interrupted before he could say any more. 'Maybe Mr Rowland had a thin skull and it was easily broken. We don't know, do we?'

'But that's something we *could* have known!' Reckitt was half out of his seat as if he wanted to go and lay hold of Llew Price, make him listen. 'Skull thickness and how it varies is a known quantity. We have data. A post-mortem would have told us whether Rowland's skull thickness was unusual in any way.'

'But knowing that he had a thin skull still wouldn't tell us whether he died by accident, would it? It would only tell us whether it was more *likely* that he *could've* died by accident.' Llew Price's voice was apologetic, as if he was having to point out something he regretted. 'It's all about *likelihood*, isn't it – all this medical knowledge?'

Likelihood. In English, he would've said 'probability', but Welsh isn't a scientific language. English is good at absolutes. Science. Welsh is better at poetry and metaphor and a different kind of truth. Not one that's clear cut and neat, like Reckitt's scalpel cuts, but messy and bloody and confusing. Like life.

'Thank you,' Harry took control once more, 'but I believe we may have wandered away from our inquest and into questions of philosophy. I think the main thing to bear in mind, from Dr Reckitt's testimony, is that he strongly believes that foul play was involved but that he cannot absolutely rule out Mr Rowland's death being an accident. Is that accurate, Dr Reckitt?'

What could Reckitt say? He might not like Harry's summary, but that was what his evidence'd said.

–

The last witness on Harry's list was Mattie Hughes. Harry didn't think Mattie had any evidence to give the inquest as to who *had* killed Rowland but he wanted to try and prove to people that Mattie *hadn't*.

The crowd watched as the old soldier hecked on to the platform with his stick. Since Rowland's death, Llanddewi Brefi'd made Mattie Hughes into a pantomime villain but now, seeing him looking tired and perhaps not in the best of health, some people had the grace to look shamefaced after what they'd done to him the other night.

I flicked a glance at Llew Price. I hadn't seen much in the way of impatience from him about Jeremiah Eynon being called. Biding his time, I supposed, listening to what everybody else had to say.

'You and I both know,' Harry began, as soon as he'd sworn Mattie in, 'that there are people in this room – many people perhaps – who think you killed Nicholas Rowland.'

Mattie didn't need to answer. The crowd did it for him. Apart from the journalists who just scribbled frantically, almost every person present turned their head to their neighbour and wondered at the coroner coming out with such a thing.

The man himself wasn't so easily shocked. Eyes front and centre, he waited for the crowd to simmer down. 'We do know that, yes,' he said, when most of them'd shut up.

'For the record, I'd like you to tell this hearing whether you did kill him.'

People who'd stopped muttering started again. They were getting good value out of this inquest.

Mattie waited, shaming them into silence. 'No,' he said, loud and clear. 'I did not.'

'Glad he's dead though, aren't you?' a voice shouted from somewhere at the back of the room.

Mattie's eyes never left Harry.

'Is that true?' Harry asked. 'Are you glad he's dead?'

'No.' Said without hesitation. 'Saw enough death fighting the Boneys to last me ten lifetimes. Did I wish him gone from here? Yes. But I never wished him dead.'

'Obviously, there are people here who might choose not to believe that,' Harry said. 'Can you give any evidence that you didn't kill him?'

Mattie glared at him. 'What happened to innocent until proven guilty?'

'The *ceffyl pren* isn't interested in that, though, is it, Mr Hughes? I'm offering you a chance, here before all your neighbours, to convince them that you didn't kill Nicholas Rowland. It's more than they offered you on Wednesday night.'

Mattie didn't move. He was already sitting as straight as he could with his peg-leg out in front of him. Looked tidy, too. Shirt a freshly-boiled white, faded red jacket brushed clean, trousers old but pressed. Did he have a smoothing iron, I wondered, or had he put them under a box?

He'd polished his one boot, too. Blacked it to a mirror shine. Not to be cowed, Mattie Hughes.

But he still hadn't said anything.

Harry and I had discussed how this would go. Hughes wouldn't want to admit that there were things he couldn't do. 'You'll have to ask him specifically,' I'd told Harry, 'make him tell you.'

'Tell me, Mr Hughes,' Harry said now, 'can you climb a ladder?'

Mattie sucked his teeth. Even to save his skin he didn't want to admit to infirmity. 'I might be able to. If it was fixed and the rungs were sturdy.'

'And if it wasn't fixed? If the rungs weren't sturdy? You wouldn't be able to do it, would you?' Harry asked.

Mattie's eyes flicked to me. He knew where these questions were coming from and his jaw worked as if he was gathering a gob on his tongue to spit at me. 'Ever tried hopping up a ladder, Mr Probert-Lloyd? Rungs are apt to give way. Found that out, to my cost, as a much younger man.'

'Very well. You couldn't have climbed into the loft over there and pushed Mr Rowland out. But let's assume, for the sake of argument, that you just happened to be down here, in the schoolroom, when Nicholas Rowland fell. You could have killed him then – just as Dr Reckitt suggested – couldn't you?'

'I could if I'd been here. But I wasn't. And I didn't.'

'I've heard it said that you know a dozen ways to kill a man. Is that true?'

If Harry was trying to make Mattie Hughes angry, it was working. And it was getting the crowd going as well. The comments around the room were loud enough to hear and some were along the lines of *see, even the coroner thinks he did it.* But Harry knew what he was doing.

'No,' Mattie said, in a voice loud enough to shut people up. 'I'll admit to knowing a few. Every soldier does. Nothing like a dozen though.' He leaned forward and began to stab the air between him and Harry with a finger. 'But I learned to kill for King and country. Enemies. I didn't learn how to kill people so I could come home and do it. Anybody who says that is insulting my regiment and insulting the crown!'

A certain amount of shouting broke out then, telling Mattie to mind who he accused. The little boy who'd clapped his hands at the butterfly looked frightened by all the shouting and his mother held his face to hers, stroking his hair.

'I'll tell you something else as well,' Mattie said, as Simi Jones shouted for quiet. 'I've only been in this school building once before today. And it nearly killed me.'

That shut people up more effectively than the *plwyfwas*.

Harry waited for absolute silence. 'Can you explain, please, Mr Hughes?'

'Just after Nicholas Rowland set up the school here, I came to see him. Couldn't get a lift so I walked. With my crutch.' He stopped, eyes on Harry, trying to pretend there was nobody else here. 'It's not comfortable, using a crutch. It rubs against you, here.' He lifted his arm and slapped his hand onto the red material where his ribs went up into his armpit.

'Here and back from my house is almost a mile. Nothing to you but it's ten times what I normally walk. Rubbed the skin clean off. Red raw. Then it festered. Had a fever for a week. Had to have the doctor at the finish. Ask him if you don't believe me.'

Harry didn't need to ask. A respectable-looking man sitting near the front stood up. 'It's true,' he said. 'I treated him.'

Harry asked for his name and, while he was writing it down, Mattie Hughes sat, back straight, glaring at the two of us. Knew he wasn't done with, yet.

'So, Mr Hughes, from that compelling piece of evidence, we can infer that, if you'd walked here less than a week ago, your ribs would, once more, be rubbed raw.'

'Correct.'

Harry turned to the doctor. 'That's right, is it?'

'It is.'

Quick note made, Harry turned back to Mattie. 'May we see your ribs, please?'

Mattie's face turned red. From anger, not embarrassment. 'Will people believe me if they see them?'

'Have you other means of transporting yourself?'

'You know I haven't.'

Harry turned his gaze to the rest of the room. A hundred pairs of eyes looked back at him, waiting. He'd feel them even if he couldn't see them. 'Did anybody here provide transport for Matthew Hughes last Sunday?' he asked.

I ran my eyes from face to face, looking for any flicker of guilt or recognition, before I settled on Phoebe Gwatkyn. If anybody was going to've taken pity on Mattie Hughes, it was her. She had a guilty conscience about him. But, apart from looking over at her stableyard servants who all shook their heads, her response was the same as everybody else's. No.

'Did anybody see any strangers in the village on Sunday, then?' Harry asked. 'Anybody who might have offered Mr Hughes a lift?'

People looked about, wanting somebody to say that they'd seen a cart passing through, but all they got was their neighbours looking back at them, shaking their heads, pursing up their lips like cats' arses.

'So, without any form of transport, to have reached the school, you would have to have walked. I ask again, please will you remove your coat?'

For a second, I thought Mattie'd refuse. But he knew that, if he did, he'd be a dead man. Harry'd made the case for his innocence, now it was his job to prove it.

Finally, his hands went up and, eyes still fixed on us, he undid the buttons down the short front of his jacket. Then he stood up but, before he could shrug himself out of the jacket, Billy Walters ran up on to the platform and helped him take it off. It was an act of pure kindness, to save Mattie from the humiliation of losing his balance, and I knew Billy'd suffer for it. At home if not in the village.

I looked over at Morgan Walters. His face was blank but he was staring at Mattie and his son. Perhaps the *ceffyl pren* outing hadn't just been to save Nan from giving evidence. Selling beer and keeping a post office was never going to compete with war stories, but with Mattie blamed for Rowland's death, he wouldn't have been able to fill Billy's head with notions of running away to be a soldier, would he?

The boy held Mattie's coat while the man himself stumped forward to stand in front of me. 'No point showing Mr Probert-Lloyd,' he said, loud enough for everybody to hear. 'Getting his own back.'

He lifted his shirt and unbuttoned the front of his underwear for me to see where the wound was. Fair play, the man was clean. I looked past the grey hair on his chest and round to the side, under his arm. There was a big patch of shiny pink scar-skin. It'd healed but it still didn't look right and I could believe that it'd festered badly. But as for recent rubbing or scabbing, there was no sign of anything like that.

'Look on the other side, just in case people decide to start wondering,' Mattie said in the same, loud voice. He might be standing in front of me and Harry, but this spectacle was for the crowd's benefit.

I looked. Nothing.

Harry nodded. 'Thank you, Mr Hughes.' Then, while Billy helped him back into his jacket, Harry said, 'I have only one more question. Why did you come to see Mr Rowland on that one occasion you mentioned?'

'Why do you want to know?'

Harry looked at him. 'If people don't know, they'll invent answers which might be to your disadvantage.'

Mattie nodded. 'Fair enough.' He finished buttoning his jacket and sat down. 'I wanted to ask him if he'd leave the little ones to me and just take the bigger ones who could already read and write.'

'And he said no, presumably?'

'He did.'

'Did he give a reason?'

'Made some excuse. But excuses don't put bread on the table.'

Mattie thanked and dismissed, Harry turned his seat to face the crowd.

'This isn't a trial. It's an inquest. The job of the jury is to say how Nicholas Rowland died. If – and I emphasise that "if" – the jury decides that he was unlawfully killed, it is for the law – the magistrates and the police force – to apprehend and try the guilty party. I hope it has been clearly demonstrated here, today, that Matthew Hughes had no part in Nicholas Rowland's death. I know the *ceffyl pren* was carried to his house this week. People were angry and they were looking for a scapegoat. You may have thought Matthew Hughes had reason to want Mr Rowland dead. But he did not kill him. He couldn't have. So let that be an end to it.'

At the back of the hall, the newspapermen's hands must've been cramping. They'd want that little speech verbatim, for sure.

I glanced sideways at Harry. Had he forgotten about Llew Price, or did he just think the jury'd heard enough to come to a verdict? Either way, I could've sworn he was about to give the jury their instructions. He turned to them and began. 'Gentlemen of the jury, you've heard from all the witnesses that I am going to call—'

Llew Price stood up as if he was on a spring. 'Excuse me, Mr Probert-Lloyd.'

Harry sighed. 'Sit down, Mr Price. I'm getting there.' Llew sat and Harry carried on. 'As I was saying, you've heard from all the witnesses that I had meant to call. But this has been an unusual inquest for me. The forthcoming election has left me insufficient time to prepare as I would have liked and I have been forced to rely – more than usual – on the support of my jury. I now call Mr Jeremiah Eynon to give evidence. But it is not I who will be asking questions of him but the jury's foreman, Mr Price.'

The man I took to be Jeremiah Eynon began to make his way along the row where he was sitting and I felt a cold dread creep over my scalp at what might be about to emerge.

Sitting there, having ceded control of my own inquest, my negligence was plain for all to see. I had been all too ready to believe that Ruth's financial contribution to the Pantglas household would obviate any objection her father might have to her working for Rowland. I should have acted as soon as I realised that Ruth had not simply been Rowland's assistant, nor even simply a teacher but some kind of protégé.

Even before Rowland had arrived in Llanddewi Brefi, Nan Walters had been sharing her Lampeter ladies' school education with her friend, and Phoebe Gwatkyn had taken both girls under her wing when Rowland had asked for her assistance. It was entirely possible that Jeremiah Eynon had resented this multiple annexation of his daughter and I should have gone to see him, questioned him. But I had been preoccupied with too many other things.

Sunday shoes squeaking with each step, Eynon strode down the length of the schoolroom. Unlike most farmers of his age, his back was straight and his movements had a sureness which spoke of joints as yet untroubled by arthritis.

I confirmed his identity, swore him in and turned to the jury. 'Mr Price?'

As Llew Price rose from the jury benches, Ruth Eynon also stood up and almost ran to where Nan Walters was sitting with her family. A brief but inaudible conversation ensued and Nan made her way to the front to take her friend's place. Evidently, Ruth did not wish to translate her father's evidence.

Llew Price waited for Nan to take her place then began. His voice was clear and confident, that of a man whose moment had come.

'Your cousin – the sailor, Shoni Goch – was staying with you at Pantglas until recently, wasn't he?'

'Yes.' Eynon's voice was cold, flat.

'Did he go to chapel with you the day Mr Rowland died?'

'Yes.'

'And did he go home with you?'

'Yes.'

'All the way home?'

When Eynon failed to respond immediately, Price did not wait. 'He didn't walk all the way home with you, did he? He wanted to talk to Ruth so the two of them set off back to Pantglas together. But they argued and, when she got home, Ruth was by herself.'

Llew Price had missed his vocation: he should have been a barrister. His tone brooked no contradiction. 'That's true, isn't it?'

The question was met with another silence from Eynon which I decided not to tolerate. Best to remind people that Price might be asking the questions but this was still my inquest. 'Mr Eynon?' His face turned towards me. 'Did your daughter arrive home alone?'

For a moment, I thought Jeremiah Eynon would defy me but then his answer came, clipped and tight. 'Yes.'

Llew Price waited a moment to see whether I would ask another question and, when I did not, he set about Eynon once more. 'Word in the village is that Shoni Goch wanted to marry your Ruth and he wasn't very happy about her working with Mr Rowland.'

Finally, Jeremiah Eynon managed more than a resentful affirmative. 'What do you mean "word in the village"? Who's saying that?'

'I can ask any number of people to come and swear to that if I need to. Answer the question please.'

'You didn't ask a question, Llewelyn Price!'

'Did your cousin, Shoni Goch, want to marry your daughter, Ruth?'

'He's always been fond of her—'

'Was she engaged to be married to him?'

After a brief silence, Eynon said, 'There's an understanding. Has been for years.'

It was quite clear, now, why Nan had replaced Ruth as interpreter.

'So, if there was an *understanding*,' Llew Price's tone slid from assured towards self-righteous, 'if Shoni Goch had told Ruth that he didn't want her teaching at the school any more, she'd have given it up, would she?'

'Nobody was asking her to give up teaching, Llewelyn Price.'

'So what did they argue about?'

'It's only you that *says* they argued.'

'No. It's not only me that says it. As it happens, I didn't see the argument but I've been told about it by more than one person. They thought I should know.'

A tense silence followed Price's words. Why would he say that people thought he should know of this argument? Because he was the jury foreman?

Before I could give the question any thought, Price began again. 'When did Shoni Goch get back to your house?'

'I don't know. I didn't take my watch out and make a note. We don't all keep records of every going out and coming in like you do, Llewelyn Price.'

Was Eynon belittling assiduous stock-taking or insinuating that Price spied on people? A shop which sold everything from salt to lamp wicks would be an ideal vantage point.

'I'm not asking you to name the minute, Jeremiah Eynon! I'm asking you to give us some idea of when your cousin came back to Pantglas. Was it ten minutes after Ruth? An hour? Was he away the rest of the afternoon?'

In the silence that followed, everybody in the room heard a little voice ask, 'Mami, where's the butterfly gone?' but such was the tension that nobody laughed and the only answer was a self-conscious shushing from the child's mother.

'Well?'

Even without Eynon's barb about note-taking, the animosity between the two men was obvious. I wondered what the cause of their antagonism was and whether it might be relevant.

'I don't know when he came back,' Eynon said. 'We went out to chapel again in the afternoon, then there was a *cymanfa ganu*. He was there when we got home.'

'He wasn't with you at the *cymanfa*?'

'No. Wouldn't expect him to be. Everybody knows he can't sing a note.'

I watched Llew Price pull himself up to his full height in my peripheral vision. Did I see him shake his head slightly? And, if so, was he signalling denial or disbelief? Price would know as well as anybody in the room that a *cymanfa ganu* – a gathering to sing – was as much a social event as it was a musical one. If Shoni Goch was home from the sea, everyone would have expected to see him there, even if he spent more time outside with the men smoking a Sunday ration of tobacco than inside with the singers.

Finally, Price spoke again. 'Very well then. After arguing with your daughter, Ruth—'

Eynon began to object but Price raised a hand. 'Let me finish then you can have your say. After arguing with Ruth, your cousin, Shoni Goch, wasn't seen again for several hours – that's true, isn't it?'

'You're still talking about an argument that didn't happen—'

'They did argue. I can ask—'

'—and just because *we* didn't see him till later doesn't mean nobody did.'

Eynon and Price spoke over each other, each attempting to drown the other out and I feared that proceedings were in danger of deteriorating into a public quarrel. I had heard tales of fisticuffs at inquests and I did not intend to preside over anything of that kind.

'If I may intervene?' I looked out into the schoolroom, featureless faces crowding in around the whirlpool. Not a single person would I be able to identify and yet every eye was fixed on me; it was an unpleasantly exposing feeling, as if I had appeared before them in my underlinen. 'Did anyone see Mr Rowland after he left the Unitarian chapel on Sunday last?'

A voice was raised to say that its owner had passed the time of day with him on the way home. One or two others said they had done the same.

'And about what time of the afternoon would that have been?'

'About one o'clock,' the first voice said, to general agreement.

'Did anybody here see Mr Rowland after one o'clock in the afternoon?' I asked.

At my side, I knew John's gaze would be combing through the whole crowd from the darkest corner of the room to the most sunlit. A general restlessness amongst the spectators told me that they, too, were looking to each other for evidence that Rowland had survived the afternoon. But if he had, then it had been an afternoon passed without the company of anyone from Llanddewi Brefi, for nobody admitted to having seen him.

Before Llew Price could say anything that might prejudice the rest of the jury, I asked another question. 'Did anyone here see Mr Rowland in the company of this man, Shoni Goch, at any point after he left the chapel?'

No one spoke. I counted a full minute while I waited but, if anybody had seen Eynon's cousin with the teacher, they were not going to tell me so.

'Did anyone see Shoni Goch approaching this school?' I sensed a shiver of something go around the room at this more fraught question; heads turned to share wordless speculation with neighbours, bodies shifted uncomfortably on benches and against walls.

'Can anyone here shed any light at all,' I asked, finally, 'on where Shoni Goch spent the afternoon and early evening?'

I was aware of deviating uncomfortably from normal inquest procedure but I did not want suspicion simply transferred from Mattie Hughes to the absent Shoni Goch without good cause. When nobody offered any information, I turned back to Jeremiah Eynon. 'Mr Eynon, what time did you get home and find your cousin there?'

'At about ten o'clock.'

'And did he go out again after that – after the rest of the family had gone to bed, perhaps?'

'No.'

'You're quite sure?'

'He couldn't have gone out without us knowing.'

'Very well. And what was his demeanour when you got home – did he speak to you about Ruth?'

'No.'

'Not at all?' That seemed unlikely, given his argument with the girl.

After a short silence, Eynon said, 'He was drunk.'

Presumably, as nobody had seen him in Llanddewi Brefi, he had walked to Tregaron and relative anonymity to drown his sorrows.

'Did you speak to Ruth about what had happened?' I asked.

'She wasn't there.'

'Where was she?'

'Went off with Nan Walters after the *cymanfa ganu*.'

So as not to have to face Shoni Goch and an inevitable argument with her father, presumably. 'Before you went back for the *cymanfa*,' I asked, 'did Ruth say anything, then, about what had passed between her and your cousin?'

The silence that greeted this question had a teeth-grinding quality. 'Told her mother that Shoni'd want to speak to me later. Nothing else.'

I took my time over writing this down then turned my gaze back to Eynon, positioning the whirlpool so that he appeared in my peripheral vision.

'Mr Price said that your cousin *had been* staying at your house recently. I assume that means he's no longer at Pantglas?'

'No.'

'Where is he?'

'Gone back to sea.'

'And when did he leave?'

Eynon hesitated. 'First thing on Monday morning. But he'd always been going to leave then,' he added, quickly.

I noted Eynon's answer and asked the jury whether they had any more to ask him. A man rose from the bench.

'Mr Probert-Lloyd doesn't know Shoni Goch like we do, here,' he said. 'So I think you'd better tell him why your cousin went away to sea.'

'Same reason most young men go to sea. Because there was no room for him on the farm.'

His words were greeted with forced, incredulous laughter and scattered cries of 'Shame' and 'Tell the truth, Jeremiah Eynon.'

'Not because he half-killed a man in a fight, then?'

'It was a fair fight!' Eynon had to raise his voice above the crowd. 'And he didn't half-kill anybody.'

'Don't lie, man! It took four men to drag him off! If they hadn't pulled your cousin away, he'd've killed him. Everybody knows that. Including you.' Shouts from the floor immediately corroborated this claim.

'I don't know any such thing!' Eynon was on his feet, now, and shouting to be heard. 'That story's grown in the telling so much I don't even recognise it any more! And the only reason it grew is because the man he knocked down went round for months accusing Shoni of trying to kill him.'

'I was *there*,' the questioner spat, jabbing at the air with a finger. 'And you can tell your lies till Judgement Day but I know what I saw. Shoni Goch's got a nasty, violent temper on him. Once his dander's up, he can't rule himself!'

Shoni Goch's violent nature having been established to the juryman's satisfaction, amidst a hubbub of speculation from the crowd, I dismissed Jeremiah Eynon and called his daughter to come and give evidence.

Our encounter in the Walters's parlour had left me with the impression that playing second fiddle to Nan was Ruth's choice, not a result of any feeling of inferiority on her part. Cautious where her friend was impulsive, she would weigh her answers carefully and any suggestion that I was trying to force her into an admission would only work against me.

'Miss Eynon,' I said, once she had given her oath, 'can you tell me which chapel you attend?'

'The Methodist chapel in Llanddewi.'

'You don't share Mr Rowland's religious convictions, then?'

'We're a Methodist family.'

I made a note of that before asking, 'Did you ever discuss religion with Mr Rowland?'

Ruth hesitated. 'Mr Rowland didn't speak a great deal about religion.'

Perhaps Hildon's complaint of atheist sympathies had not been so wide of the mark. 'Did his beliefs – religious or political – cause friction with anybody in the village?' I asked.

Did she shake her head? Visible to me only in my imperfect peripheral vision, Ruth Eynon seemed almost unnaturally still, as if she was determined to make no movement of which she was not wholly in control. 'I don't think he ever spoke about politics in the village. He didn't like to upset people. Didn't like arguments.'

'Would you say he kept himself to himself, then?'

'No. Not particularly. I believe he spent time in the Three Horseshoes like other men. He liked company. He just didn't like to argue.'

A wise man.

'Miss Eynon, I know that you and Miss Walters wrote Mr Rowland's correspondence for him. Did you send any letters to arrange meetings with anybody?'

When we had spoken to Nan and Ruth earlier in the week, both girls had denied knowing anything about any arrangements to meet with potential donors. But, now, Ruth Eynon was under oath.

Still, she was positive. 'No. But I couldn't say whether he *received* any letters of that kind.'

'You don't know, then, who Mr Rowland might have been going to see when he went off up the Pontllanio road, as we heard in Billy Walters's testimony?'

This time, her answer was accompanied by a visible head shake. 'No. But that's in the direction of the Unitarian chapel, isn't it?'

I turned to the spectators. 'Is the Unitarian minister here?'

The absence of response indicated that he was not. In all likelihood, he would be preparing for Rowland's funeral which was due to take place as soon as the mourners could make their way from the inquest to his chapel.

I addressed myself to Ruth again. 'When we first met, I asked if you could remember the names of any of the gentlemen to whom you and Nan wrote on Mr Rowland's behalf. Have you managed to bring any to mind?'

Before she could answer, my attention was distracted. The door to the schoolhouse opened and I looked around, trying to see what was happening.

John leaned towards me. 'Montague Caldicot's just left.'

Had Caldicot simply felt that he had observed my approach for long enough, or, seeing that I had no qualms about asking witnesses to come forward *ad hoc*, had he feared that he might find himself under oath?

Ruth rose and approached our table. 'Nan and I made a list of all the names we could remember. We wrote them down for you.' She gave her slip of paper to John and returned to her seat.

The crowd became restive as John scanned the list. After hearing details of Shoni Goch's motive and character, the people of Llanddewi Brefi could not see what relevance these charitable gentlemen's names could have. It was clear from audible mutterings that many felt we should move swiftly to a conclusion.

I turned my head towards John. 'Is he on the list?' I asked, voice low.

'Caldicot? No.'

Ruth had taken her seat once more.

'Miss Eynon, we've heard how your family attended chapel as usual on Sunday last. Do you happen to remember what text the minister preached on?'

I was hoping that if I could walk alongside her, in her mind, from the chapel to Pantglas, she might speak more freely about what had happened between her and Shoni Goch than if I simply asked her outright.

'He was preaching on the raising of Lazarus.'

'And did you discuss it with your cousin, Shoni Goch, on the way home?'

There was a brief silence. She seemed to be staring at me and John but, perhaps, her mind's eye was seeing the walk home from chapel.

'No.'

I waited but she offered nothing more. 'Will you be so good as to tell us, please, what you and your kinsman did speak about on the way back from chapel that day?'

But, instead of answering, to my horror, Ruth Eynon began to cry.

John

When Llew Price started questioning Jeremiah Eynon, you could see that most of the jury thought this was just Llew on a hobby horse. They swapped glances, rolled their eyes, shook their heads.

They had another look on their faces altogether by the time Eynon went back to his seat. And they were agog when Harry called Ruth. They couldn't wait to see her father's reaction when he heard what'd gone on between her and Shoni Goch.

Of course, to start with, you could tell they didn't know what Harry was up to, asking questions about the sermon at chapel. I don't know why, mind. The farmers on the jury should've spotted his game straight away. It was no different to letting a skittish filly come and sniff you, see you're nothing to be afraid of, so you can get a halter on her.

But then Harry asked about the argument and the weeping started. You'd have thought people'd be sympathetic but maybe Billy Walters wasn't the only one who thought Ruth and his sister had made too much of their position with Nicholas Rowland.

'Come on, girl,' somebody shouted. 'Don't keep the coroner waiting!'

I watched Jeremiah Eynon. His eyes were fixed on his daughter, the way a cat pins its prey with a stare before pouncing.

Finally, Ruth took her hands away from her running, red eyes and looked at Harry. She swallowed and wiped her eyes with a sleeve, like a child.

'It's like Mr Price said,' she sobbed. 'He wanted me to be his wife.' And she broke down again.

'But you didn't want to marry him?'

A shake of the head while she smeared the tears from her cheeks. '*No.*'

'So did you argue, like Mr Price said?'

She nodded. I was afraid she'd take fright if I told her to speak so that Harry could hear her, so I tapped the table once for 'yes'.

'Your father told this hearing that there was an understanding between you and Shoni Goch that you were to be married – is that not true?'

Ruth did that thing girls do where they sob and hiccup at the same time and shook her head again.

Harry'd seen. 'Not ever? No previous fondness that you might have grown out of?'

'*No!* It was *them* who had the understanding – my father and Shoni Goch. Not me. They never asked me.' She sounded like a child who'd been accused of something she didn't do.

'I see.'

We all saw. For whatever reason, Jeremiah Eynon had decided that his daughter should marry his cousin.

'Miss Eynon,' Harry said, quietly, 'I'm sorry to have to ask you this, but we've heard that Shoni Goch has a temper. Did he offer you violence?'

Could everybody else see that Ruth had started to shake, or were they too far away? Made me uncomfortable, if I'm honest, but we had to get at the truth, didn't we?

'No. He just shouted.' Her voice was small again. Frightened.

'Did he blame Mr Rowland – for you not wanting to marry him?'

I could hear her quick breaths, as if her lungs were full of fear and she could only use the tiniest part of them for breathing. She was panting through her nose, nostrils flaring in and out like a hare on its form, twitching at the scent of a hunter.

'Miss Eynon?'

She nodded.

I leaned forward, urging Harry to go on.

'Did Shoni Goch threaten Mr Rowland?' he asked.

Ruth's eyes shut and she started to rock herself in tight little jerks, as if she wanted to run away but was pulling herself back, again and again.

'Miss Eynon?'

She looked up at Harry. 'He said Mr Rowland needed teaching a lesson. That he'd turned me against him.'

'And had he?' Harry asked. 'Had Nicholas Rowland turned you against the idea of marrying your father's cousin?'

'No! No! No!' Her hands flew apart and her little fists drummed on her thighs. 'I never wanted to marry him! Ever!' The snot that comes when you cry was running out of her now and spit flew out of her mouth as she shouted.

'That's enough!' Jeremiah Eynon was on his feet but Simi Jones and Harry spoke simultaneously.

'Sit down, Jeremiah Eynon!'

'Be quiet, please, Mr Eynon.'

Instead of shutting her up, her father's words seemed to unstop Ruth.

'I told him I couldn't marry him! That I was promised to somebody else!' She didn't sound scared any more. Perhaps it was easier to defy her father in front of a crowd, where he couldn't touch her.

Eynon was on his feet again. 'Don't talk nonsense, girl! You weren't promised to anybody.'

He was having to shout to make himself heard again. This was more entertainment than the crowd could've hoped for and they were making the most of it.

Ruth was on her feet now, facing her father.

'Yes, I was! Mr Rowland had asked me to marry him and I'd said yes! We were going to wait till I was of age then get married!'

There was uproar then. People started gabbling at their neighbours, craning their necks to see what people behind them thought, leaning forward to share astonishment with the people in front of them.

Too late, I realised that I should've looked over to see Nan Walters's reaction. By the time I'd scraped my wits back together enough to see whether the news had come as a surprise to her, too, Nan's face was in her hands.

Jeremiah Eynon was a different matter. He looked as if his daughter'd just grabbed him by the balls. Luckily for him, the shock stunned him long enough for him to get a grip on his rage. Otherwise, I'm pretty sure Ruth would've been getting a hiding there and then.

She knew it, too. Or maybe the wave of voices had over-powered her. Either way, she collapsed back onto the chair and began to sob, hands over her face.

Harry leaned towards me. 'Can you translate for Minnever and Hildon while I sum up?'

I got to my feet and listened to Harry telling the jury what they had to do. Didn't know why he was bothering. Llew Price and Ruth Eynon, between them, had just handed the jury its verdict on a plate.

Harry

Though I spoke at length to the jury, sailing as close as I dared to telling them what verdict they should bring in, I was unable to prevent the naming of Jonathan Eynon – alias Shoni Goch – as the person responsible for the death of Nicholas Rowland.

'Begging your pardon, sir,' one juror said, in response to my argument that 'unlawful killing by persons unknown' would suffice, 'but if Llew hadn't called Jeremiah Eynon to tell us about his cousin, and Ruth hadn't said what she did, I believe we'd have found for misadventure. Wouldn't we?'

He had obviously looked to his fellow jurymen for corroboration as a scattered mumble comprising varying degrees of agreement was punctuated, finally, by a more definitive statement.

'From what we've heard, here today, it's Shoni Goch that's killed him. No doubt at all!'

So, having charged Simi Jones with the task of conveying the jury's verdict to the magistrates, who would now be obliged to send police officers to Aberaeron in the slender hope that Shoni Goch had not yet taken ship, I spent most of the ride back to Tregaron answering Minnever's questions. It is a measure of how dismayed I was by the whole inquest that I would rather have been discussing election strategy.

Even more depressing was the knowledge that it was all my own fault. By failing to look conscientiously into the circumstances of those most closely associated with Rowland, I had allowed Llew Price to take control of the inquest and produce a culprit entirely unknown to me. And been made a laughing stock in the process.

Minnever, however, chose to see things otherwise.

'I believe this inquest will bolster your chances at the election, Harry. Yes, I really do!'

I did not ask him to explain; I knew he would be unable to restrain himself.

'One of the criticisms of you as coroner,' he went on, 'is that you've spent too much time and money in conducting your inquests. That you've not relied enough on local officers who are already paid for their efforts. But, here, you relied almost entirely on the parish officer to bring forward witnesses. And you gave the jury its head, proving your respect for an ancient institution and bowing to its judgement even when you'd rather it had been otherwise. That will sit very nicely with the voters of Llanddewi Brefi and Tregaron.'

Dear God! If Minnever was offered a turd he would look for the clean end by which he might receive it.

'If you say so.'

'I do!'

I did not know how to respond to his optimism but, as so often, he did not require a response.

'The point is, Harry, voters are easily swayed. And that's why, tomorrow, we must ensure that you speak last. Yours must be the words that everybody takes away from the meeting, the words they remember.'

'But what if I speak last and still can't convince people? Or if Caldicot's an orator of the first order and it's his words they can't forget?'

Minnever didn't miss a beat. 'That's when we'll depend upon two things – party allegiance and your popularity as a candidate. Why do you think I've been trying to get you to speak affably to people? They need to know that you're an approachable man, a man who doesn't turn his nose up at a drink after a hard day's work. A man they could come to with news of a death that troubles them without fear of being sent away with a haughty flea in their ear.'

Which meant that, once back in Tregaron, we would make straight for the public houses of the town to discuss the inquest with anybody who wished to do so. And I would not even have John by my side as I had asked him to represent me at Rowland's funeral.

I groaned inwardly.

John

I was glad Harry'd asked me to go to Rowland's funeral. Hanging around with him while he canvassed made me feel about as useful as a wether at tupping time and Minnever was getting on my nerves.

What I wasn't so happy about was the reason he'd asked me to go.

'I want you to see who's there,' he'd said.

'You mean Caldicot? You think he's going to be there?'

Harry shook his head. 'Given that he's determined to deny any association with Rowland, I doubt that very much. But others might be. If Rowland did have influential supporters we need to know—'

'We? *We* don't need to know, Harry. *We've* held our inquest. The verdict's in. That's the end of it for us.'

'As coroner, maybe. But not as citizens of the Teifi Valley. Rowland's school idea was ambitious and it might not survive without his vision. If there's money in the kitty for it, I think we need to know who supported him, who might want to take the idea and see it through.'

I stared at him. That was a load of what Mr Schofield would've called *post hoc* justification and my mam would've called pitiful excuses.

Harry saw my silence for the argument it was and started trying to justify himself. 'The will says that if somebody can be found to carry on the school idea, they can have access to all

Rowland's funds. But, unless they know that, supporters might not come forward.'

'Tell Silas Emmanuel to put out a public notice, then. Put it in the paper.'

Harry sighed and turned his face up to the sky as if he was looking for another way to persuade me. 'Do you think the jury's right, John? About Shoni Goch?'

What was I supposed to say? What answer would stop him picking at this like a scab?

'More than likely,' I said. 'And I think the only reason you *don't* is because all that stuff about him and Ruth came out of the blue. If somebody'd told us about him before – especially how he'd been here and then left, *conveniently*, the day after Rowland died – we'd have been up to Pantglas, quick-smart, to talk to Jeremiah Eynon, wouldn't we?'

I could butter him up all I liked but Harry knew as well as I did that somebody *had* tried to tell us. We'd got Llew Price's note days before the hearing but we'd been too busy with the election to go and see him. And too busy wasting time thinking suspicious thoughts about Montague Caldicot.

The *Carmarthen Journal* was going to have a field day.

–

I rode to the funeral alongside Miss Gwatkyn, with Alltybela's *gambo* trundling along behind two sturdy cobs, carrying the household. Miss Gwatkyn was quiet, hadn't spoken a word since we left the schoolhouse. Not like her servants. They were in high spirits, funeral or not. I wondered how much of Morgan Walters's beer had gone down their throats.

The young people sat side-on to the flat bed of the cart, legs dangling in between the uprights, with the older people sitting on a bench in the middle. It wasn't very stable but, with half a dozen backsides on it, the bench stayed put. To be honest, I was more worried about the wheels. A *gambo* like that's only really meant for the fields and, from the look of it, the wheel strakes were old and likely to spring on the stony road.

Still, that wasn't my problem, was it? Mind, I did wonder about the man whose problem it was. Where was Phoebe Gwatkyn's steward? With her husband elsewhere, I would've expected him to be at her side for an occasion like this. But then, knowing Miss Gwatkyn, perhaps she did without a steward and ran the estate by herself. It wasn't difficult to picture her going out to collect rents – or, more likely, people coming to the old hall in Alltybela on quarter days, their scraped-up shillings warm and grimy in their hands. Not that I'd have put it past her to let half of them pay in the old way. People'd got used to cash rents but that was mostly because of absentee landlords who had no use for butter and chickens and hay where they lived. They wanted cash. That was why they'd bought estates, to make money. Well, that and to look like the genuine article, like the old families.

But then, even the old families – like the one Harry's father'd married into – needed cash, didn't they? Especially when they'd taken out mortgages to improve their tenants' houses and hold-ings. The figures Mr Ormiston had shown me came into my head along with a dull, nagging feeling that I should be there, at Glanteifi, with him now, doing something about the state of things, learning all the tricks I could. To be honest, in my less optimistic moments, I wasn't sure I was up to managing the estate if Mr Ormiston decided to retire sooner rather than later. Not with the finances as they were.

To distract myself, I turned my eyes to the chattering Allty-bela household. They looked a lot like the Glanteifi servants. Not well dressed. All a bit down at heel, really. But well fed. Healthy. The boy, Lleu, was sitting at the back of the *gambo*, dragging a stick along the ground to make the end into a sharp point. He'd be lucky. The horse needed to be going at least at a trot for that to work. I knew, I'd done it myself as a boy. At a walking pace all you got was a stick with a muddy end.

Suddenly, Miss Gwatkyn turned to me. 'If somebody gives false testimony at an inquest and that comes to light, would the coroner be obliged to hold another inquest?'

I stared at her. Was *that* what she'd been thinking about, all this time? 'You can re-open an inquest,' I said. 'But only if there's new evidence which throws doubt on the verdict,' I said. 'Do you think somebody lied to the jury?'

She turned to me. Her solemn face looked out of place under her jaunty little felt hat. 'I strongly suspect so. I don't think the lie affected the verdict but Nicholas Rowland might have died because of it, if the same lie had been told before.'

I didn't ask her who she suspected of lying. The more she told me, the more pressure I'd feel to tell Harry. And I didn't want to give him any encouragement to carry on poking about into this case. It was best left to the police and the magistrates now.

Not that that stopped me wondering. In fact, I only stopped picking away at that question when we got to the Unitarian chapel and I saw somebody whose presence there was such a surprise it drove everything else out of my head.

Lydia Howell.

I'd never been to a Unitarian funeral before and it was different from what happened at other chapels. Mind, that might have had nothing to do with the denomination – it might've just been to do with Rowland's circumstances. There was no widow to collect for, no orphans who'd need supporting, so the usual offerings stayed in people's pockets and nobody was quite sure what to do instead.

Inside, the chapel was squarish in shape and full of light from the long windows in every wall. And very symmetrical. The only thing that threw the balance out was the pulpit which stood to one side at the front, high up, with a steep staircase curving round it.

Everybody was here. Even people I was pretty sure I hadn't seen at the inquest.

Like Lydia. She was sitting in the front row of the chapel's pews as if she was family, busy chatting with another woman. I didn't go up to her. Plenty of time for that later. But that didn't stop me wondering what on earth she was doing here.

I looked around. Coming straight from the inquest, the congregation wasn't in what you might call a funeral mood, and instead of a chapel full of respectful, sad-faced murmuring all you could hear was gossip about Shoni Goch and the Eynons. People couldn't wait to pass on the news to friends who hadn't been at the inquest.

You'll never guess who was secretly engaged to Mr Rowland? That fancy little piece Ruth Eynon! Yes, Eynon Pantglas's girl. And without her father's permission, too. Happy about it? About as happy as a man bitten by his own dog.

Conversations about Ruth and Rowland were going on all around the place. You could tell from the way eyes searched out Jeremiah Eynon and his family. The Eynons themselves weren't doing any talking. Just sitting there, stiff as stooks.

Ruth was with Nan Walters. And, if she had any sense, that's where she'd stay until her father calmed down. Or died. The sister who must've been nearest to her in age kept darting glances at her but Ruth huddled between Nan and Gwenllian Walters and kept her eyes down. Much good that'd do her if her father decided she was going home with him. Or would Miss Gwatkyn intervene?

The lady of Alltybela herself had been greeted by the minister as soon as we'd walked in. Was she a Unitarian herself? I wouldn't have put it past her and she certainly looked at home, chatting with him. Her household weren't sitting together like they had been at the inquest but were all scattered about the place, chatting to people as if they were here every week.

Soon, the ground floor was packed and people were starting to make their way up the spiral staircases at the back on to the balconies. Young people were turfed out of their seats and shooed upstairs so that grandparents who couldn't manage the steps could sit in their places and there was a certain amount of to-ing and fro-ing as people swapped seats to be near friends or relatives.

Was the turnout so big because there hadn't been a *gwylnos* – a vigil? Even if Phoebe Gwatkyn had held one – and maybe she had, who was I to say she hadn't sat up all night with the body before coming to the inquest? – I couldn't see the people of Llanddewi thinking it was their place to go and sit with her. It just wouldn't have felt right, would it, eating the *gwylnos* cake and drinking tea with Miss Gwatkyn? That was what ordinary people did – the gentry had their own traditions, no doubt, and the two shouldn't be mixed.

I tried to imagine Miss Gwatkyn in her blue tunic and furry boots, wrapped in a blanket against the cold of the small hours, keeping Rowland company on his last night above ground.

I'd only been to one *gwylnos*, myself. My grandmother's, when I was seven years old. To my childish mind, the coffin had seemed too large for such a small woman. Huge, it'd looked, sitting there in our house on trestles borrowed from the chapel.

Had Phoebe Gwatkyn put candles at Rowland's head and feet, like Mam did for Mamgu? Had she hung evergreen branches over the door?

My grandmother's *gwylnos* had been a quiet affair, only a few of her old friends and us family. It'd been strange – being up all night, keeping the fire burning bright instead of banking it down, making tea, watching the candles burn down through hours when we'd normally have been fast asleep. The quiet talk of the old men and women, remembering a time long before I was born. I remembered falling asleep listening to stories of a mischievous girl with pigtails the exact colour of a blackbird's wing. Somebody they'd known and I never had.

There was nobody in Llanddewi Brefi who could've talked about Nicholas Rowland like that. No family or friends of his youth. Had there been friends in London? If so, he'd left them behind just as surely as he'd left his family behind when he ran away from Aberaeron. Nobody, here, had known him as anything but the teacher who'd come to them with an ambitious idea.

I was just thinking about that when I heard a question behind me that made me sit up and take notice.

'What I don't understand,' a woman said, not bothering to keep her voice down, 'is why her father was trying to marry her off to somebody like his cousin?'

'Ah, well now...' a voice next to her replied. 'Too young to remember, aren't you?'

'Remember what?'

'Yes... you'd only have been four or five, I suppose.'

'What are you talking about?'

'Same thing, wasn't it? Father wanted one thing; girl wanted another.' The second woman waited for a question but none came so she had to go on of her own accord or leave the story dangling. I pictured the two of them in my head. With at least one of them too old for heads-together whispering, they'd be sitting six inches apart, each queen of her two feet of pew.

'Mari Eynon – Ruth's mother – was promised to the son of the farm next door. From the cradle, just about. You know how it goes – two small farms into one big one for the next generation.'

'So who was the man she'd been promised to?'

'Jeremiah Eynon.'

'But that's who she's married to now!'

'I know. But Mari wanted somebody else. She'd started *courting* somebody else, if you please, without her father knowing.'

'Who?'

'Llew Price. The grocer.'

'So what happened?'

'Begged and pleaded with her father, Mari did. Said she loved Llew and wanted to marry him. Might as well've tried to stop the wind with a sieve. An only child, wasn't she? No brothers to take the farm over. Llew'd never make a farmer and her father didn't want to see all his work go to somebody outside the family when he was gone, did he?'

'That doesn't explain why Jeremiah Eynon's making his daughter marry his cousin.'

'Yes, it does.' Dramatic pause. 'Because she's *not his daughter*.'

'Never! Llew's then, is she?'

'Yes. Thought they'd force her father's hand, Mari and Llew did. So she went to him and said she was carrying Llew's child. Thought that'd be the end of the matter.'

'But he made her marry Jeremiah anyway?'

'He did.'

'Did Jeremiah know?'

At first, there was no answer. Or maybe there was one of those shrugs that tells you more than a hundred words. 'He will've done soon enough, even if he didn't know before the wedding. And everybody else knew, too, when the baby came. Been counting, hadn't they? You can put it about that a child's come before its time till everybody's deaf from hearing it, but... everybody knew. And Jeremiah Eynon knew they knew. Hates the sight of Ruth, he does. Treats her no better than a skivvy.'

'Wicked.'

'That's the Eynons for you, isn't it? Always been a strange lot. Hard. Eye for an eye, they want.'

There was silence behind me, then, and I pictured the two women staring at the Eynons.

'I'll tell you one thing,' the older one said, after a bit. 'I wouldn't be Ruth when he gets her home.'

–

All through the service, I couldn't stop looking over at Lydia Howell and wondering why she was here. Had the note Harry'd left for her at the Talbot asked her to come?

I stood for the hymns and sat for the readings and the eulogy like everybody else but I couldn't get the thought out of my head that Harry might've asked Miss Howell to come here. Didn't he think I'd be a good enough representative for Glanteifi? Or was this about her being a Unitarian? Perhaps he thought she'd be able to get some information from the minister.

The last hymn done and the blessing given, we all trooped out to watch Rowland put in the ground.

Afterwards, I made my way towards Lydia Howell and waited till the woman she was chatting to left with a friendly touch on her arm and a quiet, 'I hope it all goes well for you, my dear.'

'Good afternoon, Miss Howell,' I said. 'I'm surprised to see you here.'

She smiled. No, she *grinned*. 'Good afternoon, Mr Davies. I must admit, I hadn't expected to find myself at a funeral.'

Mr Davies. She'd often referred to me as John in her letters to Harry but I was glad she didn't assume she could call me by my given name. And, if she hadn't known there was going to be a funeral, Harry couldn't have asked her to come. Good.

'We'd expected to see you later, at the Talbot,' I said.

'Waiting for the pair of you?' That grin was waiting to come out again. 'The note Harry left for me said you'd be busy most of the day with the inquest,' she said. 'So I decided to come and talk to Mr Owens.'

I blinked. Mr Owens was the Unitarian minister. 'Are you acquainted?'

'No. He wasn't here when—' She hesitated. 'When Nathaniel was at Treforgan.'

She could see I wanted an explanation.

'Unitarians are few in number compared to Methodists and Baptists,' she said. 'We tend to know each other and news travels quickly from one to all the others. I knew that if I came and introduced myself here, word would go to Treforgan ahead of me. Now, I'll be less of a wonder than if I'd suddenly appeared unannounced.'

Treforgan had been Nathaniel Howell's chapel, a short walk from Glanteifi's mansion.

'The longer something stays unknown,' she said, when I didn't reply, 'the more it's talked into being a mystery. If I can make myself known as Nathaniel's sister, and prove myself to be quite ordinary, rumour and gossip are less likely to fester.'

Which just went to show that she wasn't as clever as she thought she was.

—

People weren't quite sure what to do once the earth was being shovelled over Rowland's coffin. They hung about in dribs and drabs, gossiping, enjoying the sunshine, waiting to see what everybody else was going to do. And whether Miss Gwatkyn was going to propose anything.

Meanwhile, Phoebe Gwatkyn spoke to a lot of the mourners, getting curtsies from the women and respectful hat-holding from the men. But talk was all she did. And, in all fairness, why should she do more? She'd given his body house-room when nobody else knew where to put it and she'd had a very decent coffin knocked together for him. Anything more would've claimed kinship. Or given the parish something to gossip about.

Gave the funeral meal for him, she did, as if she was his sister.
Or his wife…

I watched as her servants gathered around her like chicks to a mother hen, then made my way over to the paved path where she was standing. I hadn't intended introducing Lydia but when Miss Gwatkyn's eyes looked past me I had no choice.

'Miss Gwatkyn, may I present Miss Lydia Howell.'

'Delighted to make your acquaintance, Miss Howell.'

'And yours, Miss Gwatkyn.' Lydia gave that angled nod of the head that ladies use instead of a bow. Then she gave that grin again. 'Mr Davies is being delicate in neglecting to tell you why I'm here. I'm Mr Probert-Lloyd's new private secretary.'

Miss Gwatkyn's face changed entirely when she smiled. 'Are you indeed? How marvellous! You'll have to get Harry to bring you over to Alltybela for tea tomorrow.'

'If I'm invited, I'm quite happy to bring myself, Miss Gwatkyn. I have no need of being squired about the countryside.'

Miss Gwatkyn smiled a different smile, then. 'No,' she said. 'I see that you haven't. I shall look forward to seeing you. Shall we say three o'clock?'

Before she could bid us goodbye, I quickly made arrangements for Mattie Hughes, as per Harry's instructions. He thought it'd be better for Mattie to stay out of the way for a while.

'It'll be no trouble accommodating him,' Miss Gwatkyn said. 'We've tools in need of new handles and it turns out he's a dab hand at that, so he'll earn his keep. I know he won't stay otherwise.' She glanced off to one side, looking back towards the grey chapel where the Walters family was standing, Ruth Eynon still with them. 'Alltybela is quite the home for waifs and strays at the moment. Ruth Eynon has asked if she might stay with me for a little while.' She looked back at me but, when our eyes met, I didn't see what I expected to there. No resentment of the girl, no ill-feeling. 'Given the circumstances,' she said, 'it seems the best course.'

'You think Jeremiah Eynon'll stand for it?'

She looked me squarely in the eye. 'I've asked it of him as a favour to me. Let him, and others, make of that what they will.'

She knew what people thought, then. Knew and took no steps whatsoever to make them think otherwise. But then, that's the privilege of rank, isn't it? To do as you want and to hell with what people think.

Once she'd set off with her *gambo* full of servants behind her, I turned to Lydia Howell and asked how she'd got to the chapel.

'I walked.'

'Three miles?'

'Yes. Three, not thirty.' Again, that little grin. It was getting annoying. As if she knew things I didn't.

'I rode over,' I said. 'The mare can take us both on the way back.'

'I don't think that would be suitable, Mr Davies.'

'Then you have her and I'll walk.'

'That's very noble of you but, as you can see,' she gestured at her clothes, 'I'm not equipped to ride astride.' She was wearing a high-collared blouse and what my mother would have called a working skirt, made from a sensible brown material whose hem wouldn't show the dirt. She had a coat, too. One Harry'd approve of. It wasn't a Mackintosh but it was obviously designed for use not ornament. Except that it had a lot of fiddly little buttons down the front. The sun meant that she hadn't bothered doing those up.

'Very well then,' I said, 'I'll walk with you.' I knew Harry would've insisted, so, with him not being here, it felt like my job.

I expected her to tell me there was no need. That she didn't need 'squiring about'. But she didn't. She smiled – a proper smile, not a social one. Or that grin. 'That would be very pleasant, thank you.'

It felt odd, walking along that unfamiliar road with the mare on one side of me and Lydia Howell on the other. High up on one side of the valley, it felt as if we were raised up above the rest of the world, removed from everything. The sun was hot and there was almost no wind, just a little stir of the air now and again. With nobody else on the road, our solitude pressed in on me like an accusation. There wasn't a cloud in the sky and, if I'd been by myself, I'd have taken my jacket off but that didn't feel right with Lydia Howell at my elbow.

I wasn't used to walking anywhere with a woman. Such company as I'd kept with females had been indoors – at chapel meetings, or at Mr Schofield's house when he was having a social occasion and needed numbers making up. I'd never got to the walking-out stage.

But Lydia Howell didn't seem to be finding it uncomfortable. She strode out, legs swinging under her skirt. Not like the ladies of Newcastle Emlyn who walked as if their knees were tied together.

We matched our steps, stride for stride, up a long, slow incline with the hills on the other side of the Teifi away to our right.

I tried to keep my eyes ahead but ignoring Lydia Howell's presence next to me seemed as bad as looking at her. I tried to tell myself that it was all right, the two of us walking alone together; she was old enough to be my mother. Was that right? She must be about the age my mother'd been when she died, eight years ago. Thirty-five. Fifteen or sixteen years older than me.

I tried to remember my mother's face. For years, I hadn't been able to. Not properly. Only the odd expression. A quirk of her mouth. One eyebrow rising, as much as to say 'You're not telling me the truth, are you?' The way her hair always fell out of its pins and she'd hook it behind her ear as she worked. But I couldn't see her whole face. Couldn't see a picture of her in my mind, just looking at me.

Still, I was pretty sure that her face had been more lined than Lydia Howell's. Being a governess wasn't the hard work that farming was.

Had Miss Howell seen me glancing at her? I hoped not. Didn't want her to think my mind was on her. I tried to fix my thoughts on something else. Anything. How far we'd walked. What I had to tell Harry when we got back to Tregaron.

I turned to bother with the mare, talked nonsense to her.

But it was no good. The longer we walked, the more awkward the silence between me and Lydia Howell felt.

Harry wouldn't have been at a loss for conversation. He would've said something interesting, she'd have responded and off they'd have gone. Chatter, chatter, chatter.

Perhaps Miss Howell could see how uncomfortable I was, because she turned to me. 'I suppose the late Mr Probert-Lloyd's funeral was a little different from that one?'

I was so grateful to have something to say that I gave her chapter and verse – who'd been there, the formality of the occasion compared to Rowland's funeral, the eulogy by the vicar which had made Harry so pensive, the fact that Mr Probert-Lloyd'd been buried with his second wife, not his first wife and eldest son.

She listened as if it all really mattered. Then, when I'd finished, she said, 'In one of his letters, Harry told me that Dr Reckitt wanted to dissect his father's brain. But Harry couldn't bear the thought.'

He hadn't told me that. 'I think he's gone off the idea of dissection,' I said. 'He didn't even let Reckitt do a proper autopsy examination on the teacher.'

She nodded. Looked as if Harry'd told her that, too.

'They had a bit of a disagreement about it at the inquest,' I said. At least that was something I knew and she didn't.

'Yes, the inquest. Will you tell me about it?'

So I did. And telling her must've slowed my walking because, by the time I'd finished, she wasn't striding along, just keeping a slower pace with me and we were crossing the bridge over the Teifi that would take us on down towards Tregaron.

Harry

The following morning, after a convivial breakfast during which Lydia tried to distract me from my nerves by relating the tall tale she'd heard from our landlord of the circus elephant that had died in Tregaron and been buried in the Talbot's garden, our little election party made its way out into the crowds already gathering in the square.

Minnever had been outraged, the previous day, to find that Caldicot's agent, not content with buying up the town's entire stock of Tory-red ribbon with which to festoon the stage and make rosettes to distribute amongst his candidate's supporters, had also found a way to corner the market in blue ribbon so as to prevent our acquiring any.

'Damn it, it's underhand!' he raged. 'Having no Liberal colours about the place makes us look friendless and penniless.'

To my surprise, Lydia had suggested a solution. 'I'm sure the Olive Leaf Circle you mentioned would help. If you give me a name and address, I'll write a note, now.'

I hoped that this would soften Minnever's attitude to Lydia. He had been lukewarm in his reception of her when I had introduced them and, when Lydia had retired to bed, he had taken me to task.

'What are you thinking of, Harry?' he'd asked. 'The only acceptable female companion for a candidate is his wife!'

'She is my private secretary—'

'Yes, and I'll thank you to keep that nonsensical notion to yourself as well! If people get wind of that kind of eccentricity you can kiss goodbye to any chance of being elected. The best thing you can do with Miss Howell is send her back to Glanteifi tomorrow and ask her to keep within doors until the election is done!'

Shaking hands and responding to greetings as we went, Minnever, John and I made our way through the crowds to the election platform. Still fragrant with resin from its freshly-cut boards, it was in the process of being draped with ribbons of a quite startling blue by various ladies who had gathered in answer to Lydia's call.

Reckitt and the Tories were already in their seats and they rose courteously as we climbed the short flight of wooden steps on to the platform to take our places.

Lowering myself carefully on to a chair whose dimensions and stability I could estimate only imperfectly, I found that I was trembling at the prospect of the ordeal to come. Minnever had assured me that he would see to it that I delivered my speech last so that I might leave a favourable impression on the minds of those inclined to believe the last thing they had heard, but he had not made it clear how he was going to manage this. Now, he began his manoeuvre.

Drawing the town clerk to one side, he pitched his voice so that only our little party could hear his words. 'Mr Pritchard, may I make a suggestion? As something of an outside bet in the competition, perhaps Dr Reckitt should speak first, leaving Mr Probert-Lloyd and Mr Caldicot to speak once the crowd has its listening ears on, as it were?'

He did not specify whether Caldicot or I should follow Reckitt but I could only trust that he knew what he was about.

Pritchard having seen nothing to object to in the suggestion, Reckitt was invited to come forward and, having pulled his notes from a pocket, began with a strident declaration. 'Citizens of Tregaron, I am the only candidate before you who does not have a party to please before he pleases the voters!'

The resounding cheers that greeted this statement did nothing to lessen my apprehension; I had not expected such a tactical opening from Reckitt. But worse was to come.

'Everybody knows that Mr Montague Caldicot has been whisked down from London to stand in this election and that he'll probably spend all of five minutes in Cardiganshire if he is elected before appointing a proxy and returning to the capital.'

Jeers and catcalls ensued and I wondered if the hecklers noticed my discomfiture. For Reckitt had just reiterated something I had said at dinner the previous evening.

'As for Mr Henry Probert-Lloyd.' I felt a visceral response go through me as Reckitt spoke my name. 'He will tell you that he is an independent man and will represent your interests over and above those of the magistrates and the police force. And yet,' Reckitt's voice rose, 'here he is today, not standing before you as an independent candidate, but as the Liberals' darling. Their agent has been parading him all over the parish this last week. Indeed, he has even been to woo the ladies of Tregaron. He represents the Liberals' interests, not yours!'

I felt a knot develop in the region of my diaphragm. This identification of me with the party had been exactly what I had feared when Minnever approached me.

'You cannot trust men whose primary allegiance is not to seeing justice done but to their party. I have no party allegiance. I stand before you as nothing more than a medical man who wishes to improve public health.'

Fortunately for me, that statement proved Reckitt's undoing. Had he gone on in his previous, critical vein, I believe the crowd would have rallied to his cause, for who does not love to see brickbats thrown at politicians? Instead, he began to enumerate the qualities which made him a superior candidate, and he had not progressed far from his experience of surgery and medicine into his views on the coroner's responsibilities to society when the heckling commenced.

Once begun, the jeers and catcalls only gathered momentum and soon, seizing on Reckitt's own use of the word 'quack', the crowd began quacking derisively.

I sat, a mocking crowd before me that I could not scrutinise, my stomach churning at the thought that I might be treated in the same way. How many people were here? More than a hundred but less than a hundred and fifty, I guessed. A good crowd from a small town in a sparsely-populated district. I wondered how many of the assembled men were eligible to vote. A good deal fewer than half, in all probability. But people came to these meetings to be entertained as much as to allow their opinions to be formed.

The quacking was getting louder now and I doubted that a single word Reckitt said could be heard. Sitting behind him, acutely aware that I, too, was being watched and judged, but unable to meet a single eye, I suddenly felt as if my head was covered in a sack. I could not see, could not gauge reactions or adjust my speech accordingly. I might as well have been sitting behind a screen with a light and making shadows upon it with my hands.

Look! A rabbit! A swan! An elephant!

A blind coroner!

Apprehension rising within me, I turned to Minnever. 'How exactly are you going to make sure they don't haul me up next?'

I was able to see a smile if it was broad and close to me but could not hope to tell whether it was genuine. Was Minnever amused by his own initiative or did he simply wish to reassure me?

'By the helpful intervention of your friend, Miss Gwatkyn.'

'What do you mean?'

'You'll see.'

Reckitt ground on, though his voice had lost some of its assurance, and I imagined a look of pained incomprehension on a face that John had once described as 'pale and doughy'.

Abruptly, without waiting for Reckitt to finish, Minnever turned away from me to speak to the town clerk. 'Mr Pritchard, Miss Gwatkyn from Alltybela has not yet arrived,' I heard him say above the crowd's clamour. 'She's been tremendously supportive of Mr Probert-Lloyd and I know she wishes to hear him speak.' He paused, delicately, to give Pritchard the opportunity to offer the favour without being asked. But Tregaron's administrator was shrewder than he was obliging. He knew as well as Minnever that, if a favour is sought, then one is also owed.

Minnever was not a fool and did not prolong his silence. 'I wonder if I could ask that Mr Caldicot speak first?' he said. 'So as to allow time for Miss Gwatkyn to arrive?'

Pritchard, a portly man sporting a moustache that would, had he been taking part in a play, immediately have identified him as a foreigner, raised a hand to smooth his whiskers. 'Definitely coming, is she?'

'Oh, yes, I'm quite sure of that.'

Minnever's certainty, I very much suspected, arose from the fact that he would have a boy stationed in the crowd ready to alert Miss Gwatkyn as soon as it was safe to enter the square. That is to say, as soon as Caldicot rose to his feet to speak.

I could feel Pritchard staring at Minnever, making him wait. 'Very well, then. As a favour to Miss Gwatkyn, mind.'

'Of course.' Minnever knew that both he and Miss Gwatkyn would soon be making a donation to whatever municipal facilities the town clerk was currently seeking subscriptions for.

Reckitt having been persuaded to sit down and end his own humiliation, Caldicot was duly called to speak. Did he cast a baleful look in our direction? His head certainly turned towards us when Pritchard invited him to come to the podium but he said nothing, simply pulled down his waistcoat as he rose and marched to the front of the stage.

He proved to be an effective speaker. He began by refuting Reckitt's suggestion that he would not remain in the county, then went on to present himself as a plain man, a soldier who knew nothing of politics. 'I'm accustomed to taking orders as well as giving them,' he said. 'And, unlike Mr Probert-Lloyd, *I* will be content to submit myself to the magistrates.'

I felt those words as his first palpable hit and, as the cluster of bright blue ribbon on my lapel fluttered in the light breeze, I put my hand to it lest it unravel.

But Caldicot was not to have it all his own way. 'You got thrown out of the army!' a heckler shouted. 'You're not a suitable person to be coroner!'

'Yes,' another responded, 'tell us why they threw you out!'

The crowd found its tongue again and the air filled with shouts. 'Shame, shame!' went up in one quarter, though it was not clear whether this was directed at Caldicot or the heckler. 'Tell us, tell us!' others shouted.

Minnever leaned towards me. 'This is all staged.'

'By you?'

'No! The Tories. They know his cashiering is common gossip and they want to give him a chance to say his piece without bringing it up himself.'

Caldicot left the lectern and his notes and moved towards the edge of the platform.

'You'll forgive me,' he said, 'if I don't speak, publicly, about matters that are between me and my regiment. You would, I know, want a coroner who knows how to keep private matters private. But I will promise you this,' he said, his voice rising above the jeering provoked by his refusal to satisfy their curiosity. 'I am a man who understands what it is to have to face up to his mistakes. My own troubles have given me a lesson – it's not always easy to do what's right.' He paused slightly, no doubt to look around the crowd, meeting an eye here, nodding man-to-man there. 'If you elect me, you will not find me harsh and unwilling to listen. I am a man humbled by experience.'

Having abandoned his notes, Caldicot did not move back to the lectern but remained at the front of the stage. 'Since somebody has seen fit to bring up past scandals.' He turned his head, implying that I, or perhaps Minnever, was the culprit. 'I might just ask you to think about the conduct of Mr Henry Probert-Lloyd.'

I had known this attack might come but, now that it had, I could not muster the detachment with which I had hoped to greet it. I felt as if my very life was threatened. My pulse raced and my palms were sweaty.

'Last autumn,' Caldicot went on, 'having insisted that an inquest be held on human remains known intimately to him, Mr Probert-Lloyd sat, watching proceedings, *and never spoke a word*.' A brief pause allowed the audience to take this in. 'He bore witness to nothing of what he knew of dairymaid Margaret Jones's last days. As the son of a county magistrate, he knew he would not be compelled to do so. So there he sat, protected and complacent.'

Caldicot was a soldier. He knew how to wield power. And he knew how to manage men. He allowed the crowd to bay their disapproval of my supposed refusal to give evidence for a few moments, then raised his hands to call for calm.

'But, worse than that, when the verdict was delivered, he refused to accept it. A jury, composed of men like you, had its verdict rejected as unworthy! And off he went to investigate on his own behalf. Without so much as a nod to the constabulary or the magistrates, he went about the countryside interrogating people, bullying them into giving up evidence, while he hid his own part in proceedings to the last.'

At that, as if he could impose upon them no longer, he threw up his hands and the crowd exploded into outrage and condemnation.

It was masterly. Because, on the face of it, everything he said was true. I had not given evidence at the inquest into Margaret Jones's death. But only because my father had refused to sanction an inquest until I had given him my word that I would not attempt to speak during the proceedings. And I had not involved the constabulary or the magistrates because it had been made abundantly clear to me that officialdom wanted no part in any investigation. As far as the magistrates had been concerned, the sleeping dogs of the Rebecca Riots, however much they might intimidate a jury, should be left to lie undisturbed, lest the whole rebellious business be re-ignited.

Fleetingly, it occurred to me to retaliate. To stand and accuse Caldicot of lying about his association with Nicholas Rowland. To ask him, outright, how consecutively-numbered banknotes with his name on them came to be in the teacher's possession when Caldicot claimed never to have given him money. To suggest that, though he might respectfully decline to speak of the reason for his leaving his regiment, it seemed that Nicholas Rowland might have been aware of it and used the knowledge for his own ends.

Fortunately, however, wisdom prevailed and I held my peace.

But I would have my questions about that money answered, one way or another. By God, I would!

My legs were beginning to shake with the prospect of standing to deliver my speech when I became aware of a stir in the crowd. Something away from the stage had caught their attention.

'A policeman's just come marching into the square,' John said, into my ear.

The hum of the crowd's diverted interest felt like balm after their angry shouts of a few moments before and, as Pritchard stood to greet the officer, I also rose to my feet, pleased to note that my knees were no longer trembling.

'I've come to see Mr Probert-Lloyd, the coroner,' the face beneath the tall hat said.

I identified myself and the constable marched up to position himself below me in front of the stage. 'I've been sent to inform you that Jonathan Eynon, also known as Shoni Goch, has been apprehended in Aberaeron. He is being taken to Cardigan to await a hearing before the magistrates' court.'

The Talbot Inn
Sunday

My dear Miss Gwatkyn,

I could not leave, this morning, without scribbling a brief note to thank you for your kindness in welcoming me at Alltybela yesterday. It is a great comfort to know that I may claim at least one friend here in Cardiganshire.

It is strange, don't you think, that it is possible to know some people for years and never be more than familiar acquaintances whilst, with others — as in our case — mere hours suffice to make intimate friends?

I hope you will not feel that I am trespassing on such a new friendship when I say that, though my opinion has not altered about the wisdom of attempting to re-open the inquest at this stage, I do feel that, perhaps if any new information were to come to light regarding Mr Rowland, it should be communicated to Mr Probert-Lloyd? Having discussed the case at length with him last evening, I know both that he has misgivings about the general assumption of Jonathan Eynon's guilt and concerns about the future of Mr Rowland's proposed school. He will, I know, do whatever he can to ensure that neither cause is forgotten.

As to the other matter, I wonder whether it might need to be made public in the event that the magistrates decide to commit J. Eynon to trial? If he is able to provide witnesses to attest to his whereabouts during the afternoon he may be exonerated. However, if he cannot produce such testimony and he is committed to trial, any evidence that there might be other parties who had reason to wish Mr Rowland ill should, surely, be brought forward – do you not agree? I understand how delicate this matter is but I am confident that your conscience will guide you in the right path.

I hope we may meet again – soon! – but, in the meantime, I remain

Your friend,
Lydia Howell

Part Two

With Shoni Goch being marched down to Cardigan gaol, I knew Harry'd want to stay in Tregaron to try and find out the truth. But he couldn't. For one thing, the inquest was over and it wasn't his job to ask any more questions. And, for another, Minnever'd got the next week mapped out for him. After what'd happened at Tregaron, he reckoned Harry needed a lot of coaching before his next public meeting in ten days or so.

So, on Sunday, we packed up and went back to Glanteifi.

At least Harry was down to a single opponent now. Dr Reckitt had decided not to stand. One crowd quacking at him'd been quite enough.

Harry was pleased. Reckitt's withdrawal had mended what could have become a rift between them.

'I was badly advised,' he'd said to Harry when he came to apologise. 'Led to believe that it was common practice to undermine the other candidates. It was only when I saw you refuse to rise to Caldicot's taunts, that I realised it was not.'

And refuse to rise was exactly what Harry'd done. When he'd stood up to speak to the crowd after the news of Shoni Goch's arrest, he hadn't tried to put up any defence against the things Caldicot'd accused him of, nor thrown any of his own accusations about. No, he just talked about some of the inquests he'd held. Told the crowd that the job of the coroner wasn't just to find out how somebody'd died, it was also to take care of those they'd left behind.

His speech had been dignified, respectful. It'd spoken well of him.

Trouble was, it'd spoken too quietly to do him any good. The crowd in Tregaron market square had heard insults and accusations from Reckitt and Caldicot and they'd wanted more of the same from Harry. They hadn't come for reasonableness or humility.

And the hustings in Cardigan and Newcastle Emlyn would probably be no different. Caldicot or his agent would pay somebody to ask what'd got him thrown out of his regiment, he'd give his 'I've learned my lesson' speech and then accuse Harry of being a hypocrite.

If Harry couldn't find a better way of getting voters on to his side, he was going to lose the election.

–

For that first week back, I was no help to him. A whole pack of new tenancy agreements'd been signed on Lady Day and Mr Ormiston and I were already a long way behind where we should've been with our visits to the various farms. Not to mention seeing late payers who'd begged another few weeks to find the money for the quarter's rent. Those were hard visits, especially the ones to tenants who still didn't have the money and who, in all likelihood, would soon need to be given notice to quit.

The following Monday, I came back to the mansion at dusk to find Minnever blessedly absent for once and Harry in the library with Lydia Howell. They'd obviously been discussing Rowland's inquest because, once he'd greeted me, Harry turned back to the long windows and stood, peering out into the last of the daylight. 'When I go to Cardigan tomorrow, I'm going to go to the gaol,' he said. 'To see Jonathan Eynon.'

I looked over at Lydia Howell but got no reaction. Up to me, then.

'Minnever won't like that,' I said, warming my hands by the fire and wondering whether I'd have time for a bath before dinner. It'd been a long day in the saddle and I was sore and stiff. And, to be honest, I still hadn't got over the novelty of being able to have a bath whenever I felt like it.

'I don't give a damn what Minnever says.' Harry's voice was flat, quiet. 'It's because of him that I didn't pay enough

224

attention to the hearing. I'm not going to let ~~Eynon hang for~~ my negligence.'

'For all you know, he's guilty,' I said. 'Might've confessed by now.'

'Or been induced to confess.' Harry was set on blaming himself for anything that happened to Shoni Goch.

I was saved from having to say anything else when the door opened and Glanteifi's housekeeper, Isabel Griffiths, came in with a letter.

'Twm's just brought this back from town.' She held it up. 'Who should I...?'

Lydia got there first. 'Please, give it to Mr Davies. I know he usually reads Mr Probert-Lloyd's letters to him.'

'I have done in the past,' I said. 'But you're his private secretary now. That's the sort of thing you should be doing, isn't it?'

Harry lost patience with us. 'For goodness' sake, does it matter? Will one of you just read it to me, please?'

Lydia took the letter and Mrs Griffiths left. But not before I'd caught a backward glance from her. She had her eye on things. On me as well as Lydia.

The light was better by the window so we all moved to the other end of the room.

'It's from Miss Gwatkyn,' Lydia said. 'Informing you that Nicholas Rowland's will is being read next Saturday, in case it's still of interest to you. And inviting you to stay at Alltybela.' She read on. 'And she's enclosed another letter. As his executor, she's directed that all his mail should come to her and she thinks you should see this one.'

'Who's it from?' Harry asked.

With a bit of luck, it'd be a note from somebody who'd seen Shoni Goch coming out of the schoolhouse on Sunday afternoon looking furtive. That'd put an end to all this nonsense about Harry going to Cardigan. And, as for him going to hear the will read on Saturday, that was nonsense, too. Saturday was nomination day – the day polling would start in the election.

But Lydia took the second letter out of an envelope and my hopes faded. It was unlikely to be from an eyewitness. Cardiganshire folk generally couldn't see the point of buying something to wrap their letters in when just folding and sealing them did the job perfectly well.

'It's from a bookseller,' she said. 'The address is Holywell Street in London. *Dear Mr Rowland. I beg to inform you that your complimentary author copies and payment, as usual, await collection. I remain, etcetera.* It's signed by a W. Gordon.'

'Copies?' Harry was bemused.

Lydia went back to the other letter. 'Miss Gwatkyn's no better informed than you. Rowland apparently never mentioned being the author of anything.' She turned the letter over and read the back. 'She wonders whether this is to do with his connections at University College.'

'Payment *as usual*,' I said. 'Sounds like he'd been busy. Maybe that's where some of the money in his trunk came from.'

'Yes.' Looked as if Harry wasn't so much agreeing with me as adding things up in his head.

'I suppose we'd better write back to this Mr Gordon,' I said, not knowing whether I should be talking to Harry or Lydia. 'Ask him to send the books and the money to Miss Gwatkyn?'

Lydia held Phoebe Gwatkyn's letter up to me. 'Actually, as one of the trustees of the collegiate school charity, Miss Gwatkyn feels that it might be as well to clarify what's owed by – or to – this printer before the will is read, so that Rowland's assets and liabilities are clear to anybody who might want to continue plans for the school.'

She began reading again. '*Perhaps it might be in order for one of Mr Rowland's executors to travel to London in order to speak to Mr Gordon and put all Mr Rowland's London affairs in order.*'

She looked up at Harry, who was chewing his lip. Thinking.

'I agree,' he said. 'If this W. Gordon receives a letter telling him that Rowland's dead and asking him to send the payments due, what's to stop him shaving a good slice off?'

'So shall I write back to her to that effect?' Lydia asked.

More lip chewing.

'It seems to me,' Harry said, staring hard at the carpet he couldn't see, 'that there are two imperatives here. Firstly, to ensure that all the monies owed to Nicholas Rowland come into his estate. The larger the fund, the more likely it is that somebody will come forward to establish the school as he'd planned.' He looked up and fixed his eyes somewhere in the air between me and Lydia where he could see us both. 'Which I imagine we all agree would be a good thing. Secondly, to ensure that we acquaint ourselves with all the circumstances which might have had a bearing on Rowland's death. Especially if it bears on Jonathan Eynon's guilt or innocence.'

I looked at him. He could talk about imperatives all he liked but I knew what he really meant. 'Executors be blowed,' I said. 'You want to go to London, yourself, don't you?'

–

Except, he couldn't, could he? He was speaking at a public meeting in Cardigan in two days' time. Unless he sprouted wings, London was out of the question.

So I went instead.

Harry

The following day, with John already on his way to London, I packed a bag, told Mrs Griffiths that, if necessary, I could be contacted at the Black Lion Hotel in Cardigan, and went out to the stableyard.

I found Lydia waiting for me.

'Did you want to speak to me before I go?'

'No. I'm coming with you.'

'That won't be necessary. I don't need you.'

'Then on what basis have you employed me?'

227

'I mean I don't need you in Cardigan. There'll be no corre-spondence, no paperwork.'

'I thought I'd made it clear that I wasn't accepting a post as a clerk.'

Conscious that the stableyard had become unnaturally still, I drew Lydia aside to a spot where we might less easily be overheard. 'What I mean is that there is no Glanteifi business to transact. Everything I do in Cardigan will be as candidate for coroner.'

'So I'm private secretary to Glanteifi, not to Harry Probert-Lloyd?'

'You're my private secretary not assistant coroner.'

'Thank you. I understand that perfectly well. But the assistant coroner isn't here. If I were a man, we wouldn't be arguing. You'd have assumed I would come in John's place.'

That pulled me up short. She was right.

'Despite your protestations of egalitarianism, when it comes to suiting the action to the word, you can't accept the assistance of a woman.'

'It's nothing to do with your being a woman.'

'What *is* your objection, then?'

I knew that, in our correspondence, I would have answered her question without a second thought. Face to face, however – even though I could not see her – I found the whole thing humiliating.

'The truth is,' I said, attempting to keep my tone matter-of-fact, 'that I'm still not entirely reconciled to the notion of needing help from anybody.'

There was a pause as if she was weighing up my words. 'I hadn't envisaged being at your elbow the whole time. I know you're not incapable. But surely I could be of some help in Cardigan? While you're at the gaol with Jonathan Eynon, I could talk to shopkeepers and their customers, for instance, canvass opinion about the election.'

Belatedly, I realised that this was as much about Lydia's needs as mine. I should have forseen that being left behind at Glanteifi without employment would be both humiliating and frustrating for her.

And her proposal did seem sensible. No doubt Minnever had his spies amongst the populace, but women would be less guarded about their opinions if Lydia were to engage them in conversation while out shopping.

'What would you do while I'm dining with Minnever and the magistrates this evening?'

'What I'd do if I was here. Read. Write letters.'

I bent to pick up our bags. 'In that case, I'll ask Twm to get the carriage ready.'

—

Following the inauspicious start to our journey, I sat opposite Lydia in what I still thought of as my father's carriage, wishing that we could have brought the box cart instead. But that had been out of the question. Minnever had made it quite clear that I could not appear alone in public with Lydia and I could only imagine the fury with which hè would greet the idea that she and I had ridden all the way to Cardigan together in the open air, visible to everyone we passed.

Though I knew I should say something to smooth things over between us, the right words eluded me and it was Lydia who took the bull by the horns.

'We're in an odd position, you and I,' she said. 'Having exchanged letters for months we know each other both very well and hardly at all. It's only to be expected that it will take a while for us to find a comfortable *modus vivendi*.'

I nodded. With my gaze somewhere in the vicinity of her knees, Lydia's face was visible to me above the whirlpool.

'I suspect,' she went on, 'that we're both wondering whether the compatibility of thought we discovered in writing to each other is robust enough to survive day-to-day commerce. So I suggest that we simply try and say exactly what we would have written.'

'That's not possible, surely?' I said, more abruptly than I had intended. 'Physical presence affects things too much.'

'Only if we allow it to, Harry.'

A jolt like a mis-step off a kerb went through me at her use of my given name, entirely giving the lie to what she had just said. Until now, I realised, she had avoided addressing me by name and, despite hearing '*Dear Harry*' for weeks in John's reading of her letters to me, her use of it now, alone with me, felt shockingly intimate.

'Very well,' I managed. 'I'm willing to try if you are.'

'Is it so difficult? From your letters, it's obvious that you had occasion to meet with women on equal terms in London.'

It was true. Until failing sight had tethered me to my lodgings, wary of people's curiosity or pity, I had attended talks and debates where equality of expression was championed and where, in the main, a tolerable attempt at practising it had been made. 'But, in those circumstances,' I pointed out, 'one was always surrounded by other people.'

'Conveniently chaperoning everybody present without the word ever having to be uttered.' She sounded half amused, half exasperated and I was afraid I had disappointed her already.

Distracted from my discomfort by the sound of a cuckoo's call through the carriage's open window, I laughed. 'That's what I feel like. A cuckoo. A London cuckoo in a Cardiganshire nest. As if I have to fight for all I'm worth to survive and not be caught out for the imposter I am.'

I wondered if she felt the same. She certainly had as much cause as I did, more, perhaps. 'And you?' I asked. 'How is it, being back? Does it feel odd?'

She sighed as if a tension had been broken and I felt my own shoulders ease a little. Outside, the horses' pace slowed as they approached a steep hill and their hoof beats slowed to a walk.

'The smell of the air is the smell of home,' she said, her head turning to the open window. 'And speaking our own language again—' She shook her head as if she could scarcely find the words. 'But I find I'm wary,' she went on. 'Afraid of being recognised – my previous life revealed.'

'Yes, I see.' And I did, for her situation was something of a mirror-image to my own. I was always at a disadvantage when I went out amongst people, for they always knew me before I knew them. Lydia would know people but would have to pretend ignorance, for she had no right to be acquainted with anybody in Cardiganshire. Not as Miss Lydia Howell. It must have been a strain, constantly watching for a spark of recognition, of suspicion, and having always to be vigilant lest her reactions should suggest familiarity with people who should be strangers.

'Poor Nathaniel,' she said. 'I miss him.'

There was much that I could have asked in response to Lydia's wistful comment but discretion kept me silent. It was not yet time for such questions. And she, perhaps feeling that we had made progress enough, changed the subject.

–

Taking Lydia at her word, I left her at the Black Lion to make arrangements for us while I made my way to the police station. If I wished to see Jonathan Eynon, it would be necessary, first, to pay a visit to Inspector William Bellis.

To say that I did not enjoy a cordial relationship with the constabulary's senior representative in Cardigan would be to understate matters. We had got off on the wrong foot from the very beginning of my first inquest as Coroner Bowen's locum, and had remained there ever since.

A former soldier, Bellis was a man who enjoyed the exercise of power and, unlike inspectors elsewhere, often exercised that power personally, taking to the streets with his men at the merest suggestion of a threat to the town's peace and shouting, *Go about your business!*

Much mocked for this, he had quickly become known in Cardigan as Billy Go-About and I repeated the belittling nickname silently to myself as I walked, like a protective charm. Without John at my side I felt vulnerable and shifted my unfocused gaze constantly. It had been market day the day before and, though the streets were relatively quiet today, they were also more than usually foul with the droppings of livestock. I tried my best to skirt the more obvious piles and slicks that remained, but I knew that the first thing I must do on arriving at the police station would be to locate the boot scraper. It would not be wise to give Inspector Bellis further cause to dislike me.

Locating the police station both from memory and its lack of large shop-front windows, I opened the door and walked in. At least, having been there before, I knew the layout of the place and could look directly at the constable who had risen to his feet.

'Mr Probert-Lloyd, sir!'

Thankfully, the voice was familiar. 'Good morning, Constable Morgan.' I knew Morgan to be an overweight sluggard who rarely went out on patrol, preferring to act as Bellis's general factotum and guard dog. He aped his superior's attitude towards me and could not resist a sly dig.

'I'm sorry. Mr Caldicot's beaten you to it, sir.'

Just for a second, I wondered why Caldicot had come to ask about the case against Jonathan Eynon, but reason swiftly reasserted itself and I understood that my rival was here to canvass Bellis. 'I see.'

'Been in with the inspector for a while, he has. Would you like me to tell Mr Bellis you're here?'

I hesitated. On the one hand I did not wish to stand about in public, unannounced but, on the other, Bellis might just prolong his conversation with Caldicot if he knew I was waiting to see him. Fortunately, the decision was made for me when the door to the inspector's office opened and Montague Caldicot strode out. At least, I inferred that it was Caldicot since the figure was not in police uniform but wore a long jacket with a patterned waistcoat beneath.

'Probert-Lloyd! I thought I heard Morgan utter your name.' Caldicot closed the door behind him as if I could have no possible business with the inspector. 'The assistant coroner not with you today?' He emphasised the title just enough to let me know that he did not approve of John's appropriation of it.

'No. He's travelling up to London.'

'London?'

His tone implied that he could imagine no earthly reason why John might have business there and it riled me into an injudicious reply. 'Indeed. I've sent him to bring back information which may lead to my re-opening the inquest into Nicholas Rowland's death.'

'What do events in London have to do with a death in Llanddewi Brefi?'

'That's what John has gone to find out.' I did not wish to continue this conversation beneath the gaze of the torpid Morgan. Nor within earshot of Bellis, whose ill-fitting office door offered him privacy from the public gaze whilst allowing him to hear everything that was said beyond it. 'Caldicot, I'd value a few moments of your time, actually. In private?'

'I'm afraid I have a meeting in…' He took his watch out and consulted it. 'Ten minutes.'

'This will take no more than two, I assure you.'

'Very well.'

Outside, I drew him away from the police station into a quieter side street.

'Reckitt has withdrawn his candidacy,' I said. 'It will be a straight fight between you and me.'

He did not respond. With my gaze offset, I tried to get an impression of him in my peripheral vision but could see nothing more than the shape of his face and his dark hair. John had described him as stiff-countenanced. As an army officer, he must have become used to keeping his reactions well guarded.

'Given that,' I went on, 'is it possible that you and I might agree to conduct the remaining public meetings in a civilised fashion and allow the voters to decide which of us would be the better coroner, rather than which of us is the greater hypocrite?'

Caldicot betrayed no reaction to this directness; not so much as a shift in position or an intake of breath. 'You don't think hypocrisy is a topic that should be addressed when considering fitness for public office?'

'I don't think it's as important as other things.'

'I disagree. Your assistant's trip to London provides an excellent example. In your remarks after the verdict on Rowland's death, you made great play of the fact that the jury had exercised its right to bring forward evidence as well as to decide on the ultimate verdict. It was the coroner's job, I believe you said, to respect that decision.' Caldicot leaned toward me, emphasising his height advantage. 'But, in actual fact, you have no respect whatsoever for that decision. You've sent John Davies to London to find evidence with which to overturn the jury's verdict because you don't agree with it.'

'If new information comes to light, it's my duty to pursue it.'

'No.' Previously he might have been speaking to a subaltern; now he was barking as if at a private soldier. 'That is the job of the police. They must now make a case against Jonathan Eynon. If there is evidence that somebody else is guilty then so be it, but finding that evidence is *not* the coroner's responsibility. Not once the inquest jury has given its verdict.'

He straightened up once more and I felt his eyes fixed on me. 'If you want me to stop calling you a hypocrite, give me an assurance, now, that the verdict on Nicholas Rowland's death will stand and you will stop interfering in this case.'

If I did not agree, I might as well join Reckitt in withdrawing my candidacy. I had seen the effect of Caldicot's words at Tregaron and they were unlikely to produce a different effect elsewhere. But I could not do as he wished. The jury at Rowland's inquest had not heard all the facts. More than that, if Miss Gwatkyn was to be believed, some of the evidence they had heard might have been untrue. Did Nicholas Rowland not deserve better?

'I cannot give you that assurance,' I said. 'Because I'm not *interfering*. I'm doing my duty.'

'Then the scope of the coroner's duty is another thing on which we will be seen to disagree, and on which the electorate may judge us.' He took his watch from his pocket again. 'And now, if I'm not to be late for my meeting, I must take my leave.'

'Wait. A moment, please.' I held out a hand as if to restrain him but did not touch his arm. 'Quite apart from the inquest's verdict, there is the fate of Rowland's new school to consider. He'd already secured a parcel of land and accumulated not inconsiderable funds – the project might still attract a sponsor and come to fruition. It's been brought to my attention that he'd been writing books for which he was owed money. Money that rightly belongs to the school fund. Would you have me simply ignore it?'

There was a pause before he answered. A pause filled – I would have sworn it – with deep discomfort on Caldicot's part. 'It's not the coroner's duty to pursue monies owed.'

'Possibly not. But this bookseller may also have information which helps us better understand Nicholas Rowland and suggest a different motive for his murder. The police, as I'm sure you're aware, wouldn't dream of going to London in pursuit of evidence.'

I willed Caldicot to reply but to no avail. The news that John had gone to London to see Mr Gordon had obviously disconcerted him. Why?

I tried to fix my eyes somewhere near his face. I could not look him in the eye, but that would have to do. 'I know you told John that you were barely acquainted with Nicholas Rowland but I wonder whether, perhaps, you had reason to keep any association to yourself? If so, it would be better to tell me now, man to man.'

Still, he said nothing.

'God knows, Caldicot, I am no friend to the county magistrates but even I can see that they would be put in a very unenviable position if some scandal should suddenly attach itself to one of their coroners—'

'How dare you threaten me?' Caldicot's tone was such that I took a step back.

'I assure you, I was not—'

'Enough! I will not allow you to delay me any further. I shall see you at the meeting, tomorrow.'

And, with that, he turned and was gone.

—

When I returned to the police station, Morgan announced my presence and was instructed to show me in.

'Good morning, Acting Coroner,' Bellis greeted me without rising from his seat. 'Though you will be burdened with that temporary title for less than a week, now, I'm pleased to say.'

He had phrased it carefully but my temper had already been roused by Caldicot's accusation. 'Yes,' I said, sitting down uninvited. 'By next Tuesday evening, the Teifi Valley will see its coroner duly elected once more. But that's not why I'm here.'

'Oh? You don't believe in seeking the support of men of influence?'

His mocking tone set my teeth on edge. 'Mr Bellis, let's not pretend that my asking for your support would be anything other than a waste of both our time. I'm here to see Jonathan Eynon.'

His posture changed abruptly as if to exaggerate his surprise, a gesture largely wasted on me. 'Why? Eynon's no longer any concern of yours. The magistrates have heard his story and seen fit to commit him for trial. You've absolutely no reason to see him.'

I fought down a very real urge to leap to my feet and punch Bellis, concentrating on what he had not said rather than what he had. 'He hasn't confessed then?'

'He might as well have done.'

'Meaning?'

'He has no alibi. We have witnesses who'll testify that he left Tregaron at no later than six o'clock. Time a-plenty to walk back to Llanddewi Brefi and kill the teacher.' Bellis leaned back in his chair as if the argument was over. 'You don't know men like Eynon,' he said. 'But I do. The army's full of them. Illiterate, violent, ruled by animal instincts. Jilted like that, by a chit of a girl, a man like him wouldn't have stood for it. The jury'll see it straight away. When we've put our case, they'll find him guilty in a minute.'

He folded his hands over his midriff, the picture of complacency. 'Go home, Acting Coroner, and leave this to men who know what they're doing.'

I once heard that a man's senses are sharpened in battle, that he becomes aware of things that might pass unnoticed in a less exigent state. When I had walked in to Bellis's office I had been aware of only one dominant smell – the beeswax and turpentine polish that had been used on the huge desk behind which he sat. But, now, I became aware of other smells. The filth that remained on my boots despite my best efforts at the scraper. The rubberised coating of my coat, warmed by my leaning back against it. And the smell of hair oil. I wore none, therefore it was Bellis's.

As the perfume of it turned in my nostrils and became distasteful, I knew that I would never again smell it without thinking of this moment of clarity. Bellis was my adversary, not my ally. There was no point in arguing that we both worked in the cause of justice; he despised me and would frustrate me if he could, and I would not ask for his assistance unless compelled to do so.

I stood and pointed my gaze down at him. 'New information has come to light which may lead to my re-opening the inquest into Nicholas Rowland's death. As we speak, John Davies is on his way to London to gather evidence.'

There was a silence during which Bellis rose, slowly, to his feet. 'If *you* intend to re-open the inquest,' he said, finally, 'then you'll need to hurry, won't you? You may soon find it's not your *job* to do so.'

He was going to try and deny me access to Shoni Goch. I sniffed the air like a hound taking scent of the fox, breathing in Bellis's oily stink, feeding my detestation of the man. 'That's why I'm keen to see Jonathan Eynon today, Inspector.'

'And if I refuse to allow it?'

'You and I both know that you cannot refuse. But if you make it difficult, then I will go to a magistrate.' I allowed the whirlpool to settle directly over Bellis's face and glared into it. 'It would be unfortunate if I was obliged to report that you had been less than helpful. I know how much you value being on good terms with the bench.'

The struggle for dominance could not have been more obvious if we had opened our trousers and started pissing up the wall.

'I'm very busy at present. If you come back tomorrow, there will be a letter waiting for you.'

'And, as you know, *I* am busy tomorrow.'

'Indeed. And yet, here you are, insisting on doing my job instead of doing what you can to retain the one you *temporarily* have.'

I had had enough. The overpowering smell of his hair oil was beginning to make me feel sick. 'Inspector, either you provide me with a letter now, or I go to the nearest magistrate.'

Several silent seconds dragged by and I began to fear that he would call my bluff. Then, abruptly, he bellowed, 'Morgan!' The constable put his head around the door. 'Write a note to the governor of the prison asking that Jonathan Eynon be produced for the *acting* coroner. When it's done, bring it here and I will sign it.'

I turned to pluck my coat from the back of the chair. 'I'll wait outside.'

Bellis stood in silence and watched me go. I hoped I would not live to regret my small victory.

John

I'd been to London before with Harry, so I wasn't as nervous setting out on the coach for Carmarthen on Tuesday morning as I might've been. Plus, I had money in my pocket and a tongue in my head. One or the other'd get me out of any difficulties there might be.

The steamer across the Bristol Channel was just as unpleasant as I'd remembered, with its shifting deck and drifts of coal smoke and staggering passengers but I managed not to be sick and, once I was on land again in Bristol, I found a bed for the night near the railway station.

But then, with nothing definite to do, time dragged.

I ate the dinner which came with the room I'd paid for. I drank a pint of beer I didn't really want. And I watched the other two people sitting in the grubby little parlour. A man and a young woman. He was old enough to be her father but any fool could see that that wasn't the relationship there.

I started out for a walk to kill a bit more time but, after ten minutes of looking over my shoulder every time I heard footsteps behind me, I went back to the boarding house.

When I asked for a light to take upstairs, the harassed-looking woman who seemed to be in charge of everything, from cooking to making sure the street drunks didn't stumble in over the threshold, offered me a candle. I smiled nicely and said I had work to do and could she let me have a lamp instead. She said she'd have to add the cost of it to my bill. Didn't care whether I lived or died, that much was clear, as long as I paid for everything I got. If I died in my rented bed, she'd probably strip me and sell my clothes.

I shook the lamp when she handed it over to make sure she wasn't going to charge me for putting oil in it as well.

The room I'd paid for was a garret at the front of the house. The stairs were worn and, as I climbed up, the lamp showed greasy stains on the wall from steadying hands. When I got up to the second landing, I could hear noises through the door next to mine. My trousers went tight as I realised what was going on in there. *You can have cheap or you can have respectable*, my old landlady used to say, *but not both*. She ran a respectable house, of course.

The room was just as depressing as when I'd come up to dump my bag, earlier. The rug rucked up when you opened the door. The narrow bed sat against the partition that divided this room from the knocking-shop on the other side. There was a tiny washstand under the window, and a rickety chair in the corner.

I tried looking out of the grimy window but all I could see were roofs under a dark sky. Carefully, I sat on the bed. It was a slat-frame and the mattress was thin enough for me to feel the slats through it. Maybe it'd be too thin to have many bugs.

At least the linen looked clean enough. I'm not saying it was changed after every lodger but at least it didn't look as if it'd been on there for months. I remembered what my mother used to do to make sheets go longer between washes and whipped the blankets off to see if the sheets'd been top-to-toed. Didn't look as if they had – when I pulled them untucked, they were still in clean creases under the mattress. So I put them back on the other way up and turned the pillow over.

Then I turned it back again. It'd been clean side up already.

I took my boots off and sat with my back against the chimney breast. There was no fireplace in the room but the wall was warm. I reached into my bag for the book I'd brought with me.

The third volume of the *Mabinogi*. Translated by Lady Charlotte Guest. Miss Gwatkyn had sent all three volumes to Glanteifi with Lydia Howell, along with instructions to encourage Harry and me to read them.

'She said it would open your minds,' Lydia Howell'd told us.

Turned out she was right. What she didn't know was what it was going to open my mind *to*.

Harry

When my father first arrived in Cardiganshire, at the turn of the century, Cardigan gaol was a brand-new building, designed by John Nash who cut his architectural teeth on prisons and mansions in Wales before moving on to much grander things in London and Bath. Now, Nash had been dead more than a decade and his prison was in a shoddy state of repair. I had heard the magistrates' concerns often enough from my father: leaky roofs, lack of a proper water supply, the poor state of the courtyards where the prisoners were supposed to exercise.

I was, therefore, expecting to find Jonathan Eynon in no great state either of comfort or health but, when he was brought to me in the spartan dayroom, his greatest complaint proved to be the solitude in which he was kept.

'I'm used to close quarters below decks,' he told me. 'In a space the size of my cell, there'd have been half a dozen men and I'm going half-mad with my own company. Get them to move me to a cell with another man, will you?'

Awaiting trial, Eynon was kept apart from the prisoners sentenced to hard labour but that seemed a dubious privilege. Only during the short time each day allowed for prisoners' exercise did he enjoy the company of other men.

'I'll speak to the governor,' I promised. 'But, meanwhile, are you well cared for? Do you have enough to eat? Is your bedding clean and dry?'

He had resolutely refused to answer me in Welsh so I had switched to English but I was curious about his reticence. Had he lived among English folk for so long that Welsh no longer came easily to him, or was he keeping a distance between us?

'No complaints on that score. I'm not used to comfort or high living. Sailors' rations wouldn't put fat on a rat. As for my bed, it's a luxury to stretch out. In a hammock you sleep like a child in the womb, curled in on yourself. Some mornings I can barely stand when I put foot to the deck.'

I shifted my own feet on the bare floor of the small dayroom. Eynon had declined the chair offered to him and stood at the window, looking out. I thought of those sailors – whippet-thin from poor rations, folded like unhatched chicks into their hammocks. It was a life that was unlikely to suit any but wiry specimens like Jonathan Eynon.

'You've been questioned by the police, I believe?'

'Twice,' he said without turning to face me. 'Once when they brought me down from Aberaeron. Then again when they'd spoken to my cousin.'

His tone gave nothing away. He might have been speaking about gossip after church, not evidence which Bellis might use to have him hanged. He leaned against the wall, hands in his pockets, staring out over the courtyard of the prison.

'Were you offered any violence?'

'A few slaps. Any wharfside molly could've done me more damage than those constables. Soft, the lot of 'em.'

That had not been my impression of the Cardiganshire constabulary. Clearly the mollies who frequented the docks were tougher than the painted boys – some tricked out as women, some as dandies – who walked the seedier streets of London.

'Did they tell you what Ruth Eynon had said?'

Still, he did not look round. 'Had a lot to say for herself, 'parently.'

'She accused you of making threats against Nicholas Rowland.'

'That teacher she was s'posed to be marrying?'

'Yes.'

Eynon grunted.

'She told the inquest that you'd said he needed teaching a lesson.'

Finally, he turned to look at me. 'Believed her, did you?' His tone was flat, as if he expected little of me. When I made no reply, he continued in the same vein. ''Spect she cried. Seen her do that often enough to get out of trouble with her father. Convincing, she is mind. Very.'

John had used the same word. He had told me that Ruth Eynon's crying fit at the inquest had seemed completely genuine.

'Doesn't matter what you think, though, does it?' Eynon said. 'You won't be on the jury. Will *they* believe her, that's the question.' He raised a hand to his nose, turned his head and blew a plug of snot on to the floor. The intensity of daylight through the window altered as, beyond the grim precincts of the gaol, the sun broke free of the clouds. In the sudden flood of light, the red hair that had given Shoni Goch his nickname was very conspicuous, though I imagined it had been brighter still when he was a boy. Like that of Billy Walters.

Red hair was not common in Cardiganshire and two people in the same parish with that colouring might well be related. 'Are you kin to Morgan Walters?' I asked.

He sucked his teeth. 'His wife. Second cousins. Same as me and Jeremiah. All had the same great-grandfather.' He turned to the window again and seemed to be looking up at the sky. The craning of his neck affected his voice. 'Nasty piece of work, if you believe the family tales. Same as my grandfather. And Jeremiah's father. Got a temper, the men in our family have.'

'Including you, from what I've heard.'

He made a dismissive sound. 'Told you about the fight that got me sent away to sea, did they?'

'Is it true? Did you try to kill the man you were fighting with?'

Shoni Goch jammed his hands into his pockets again. 'Ever been in a fight, have you? A real fight, not boys' stuff?'

Boys' stuff. I was suddenly assailed by unpleasant memories of my schooldays. Did he think that boys' fights were never

243

real, never potentially deadly? Nevertheless, I shook my head, fearing, as I did so, that he would think me soft, not a real man.

'Then you won't know what it's like. You're not always master of yourself. After a certain point, you're not thinking any more. You just punch till they stop moving.'

There was something percussive about the way he uttered the word 'punch' that made me flinch. I was in a room, alone, with a violent man whom I could not adequately see. If he wanted to, he would be able to do me serious harm before the warder outside could respond to any cries for help.

'Is that why Ruth didn't want to marry you?' I asked. 'Because she was afraid of your violence?'

'Hah! After what she said to me that day, I wouldn't've married her if you'd paid me! It wasn't *her* that was afraid of *me*, I can tell you that. That boot was on the other bloody foot and no mistake!'

There was something in his voice – a kind of grudging vehemence. How could a girl like Ruth Eynon have struck fear into the heart of a man who dismissed a police beating as 'a few slaps'?

'So? Are you going to tell me what she said?' I prompted when he said no more.

Shoni Goch shouldered himself away from the wall and came to stand at the table before me. 'What difference would it make?'

'I won't know till you've told me.'

'You won't get me off. The police've decided I did it and that's that.'

Unexpectedly, he drew out the chair opposite me and sat down. 'Look. I went to Pantglas because there was a letter waiting for me at the post office when my ship docked in Aberaeron. From Jeremiah. I got our mate to read it – he's not too bad with his letters. It was from Jeremiah saying it was time for me and Ruth to marry.'

It was them who had the understanding – my father and Shoni Goch. Not me. They never asked me.

244

'You thought that was what Ruth wanted?' I asked.

'Yes. Taken a fancy to her, I had, when I was home three or four years ago. Jeremiah was all for it. When she was more grown-up, like. So, when I got the letter, I went straight to Pantglas. Jeremiah told me it was time. That she'd got too hoity-toity to help around the farm. Wanted to be mistress in her own house.'

'And you didn't mind her being hoity-toity?'

I was watching him carefully over the whirlpool so I saw him grin. 'I like a woman with a bit of spirit. Mind, there's spirit and there's madness.' The approval had disappeared from his voice.

'Madness?' Not a word I would have associated with Ruth Eynon in any context. 'What do you mean?'

He drew in an audible breath then huffed it out as if he was expelling something. 'Look, I believed what her father said, right? That she wanted to be married to me. And soon.'

There seemed no reason to challenge him with Ruth's version so I simply nodded.

'But when I raised it with her, that Sunday after chapel, she was all quiet, wouldn't say anything. Wouldn't give me an answer. Wouldn't even look me in the eye. Well,' he shifted in his chair, 'that got my temper up a bit. No, no—' He was quick to correct the assumption he saw I had made. 'I didn't lay a finger on her. Just said her father'd told me she *wanted* to marry me. And, as soon as I said that, she just turned on me.'

'Turned on you?'

Eynon did not reply. Simply pushed his chair back and stood. I knew that if I did not press him now, whatever he had meant to tell me would be battened down again. 'Mr Eynon – how did she turn on you?'

He stopped and glanced over his shoulder at me. 'No point me saying. You wouldn't believe me.' The words might almost have been muttered for his own ears only for I barely heard them.

'You don't know me, Shoni Goch,' I said, switching to Welsh and roughening my voice. 'You don't know what I've been called on to believe in my time.'

Unable to see his reaction, all I could do was wait for a response. When he spoke, finally, he too had slipped into Welsh.

'Well, *I* wouldn't've believed it. Not of Ruth. But I heard it with my own ears.'

I stood and moved to where I could more easily see him. 'Why don't you tell me what she said and then we'll see, won't we?'

Eynon hawked and spat on the floor.

'Whatever she said,' I pushed, 'if it meant that you didn't want to marry her then you had no motive to kill Rowland. You need to tell me.'

'All right.' He took half a pace forward. 'I told her that her father'd said that's what she wanted – to marry me. And she said—' He pulled himself up. 'No, she *screamed in my face*, that, if her father forced her to marry me – *forced*, mind – she'd wait till I'd had enough to drink one night, then, when I was asleep and snoring, *she'd come for me with a butchering knife.*'

I tried to imagine Ruth Eynon's carefully cultured voice saying such a thing. Perhaps it had been easier to say in Welsh, but to ask him what language they had been speaking would have been a distraction.

'She threatened to killyou?' I asked, matter-of-fact.

From a slight movement of his head, I got the impression that his eyes had moved away from my face. He rolled his shoulders. 'No. Not to kill me.'

'What then, man?'

'She said she'd cut my cock off.'

'She'd—'

'I told you you wouldn't believe me.'

'No, I do.' It seemed too outlandish a threat for him to have made up. 'But—'

'Why would she say such a thing?'

'Yes.'

Jonathan Eynon's shoulders slumped. His whole demeanour had changed, as if, in telling me of Ruth's threat, he'd crossed a line he had not meant even to approach. Now, his voice was different, but in a way that was hard to identify; it gave me pause.

'There are things you don't know,' he said.

The light in the room changed as clouds covered the sun and the sudden gloom mirrored the darkening atmosphere in the little room.

'So, tell me.'

For a long while Eynon seemed stranded there, neither moving nor responding. Then, he turned and resumed his seat at the table. I did likewise, locating the chair carefully so as not to knock it awry, wary of breaking the charged silence between us.

Opposite me, Eynon ran a hand over his face and I heard rope-thickened skin rasping against stubble. 'I believed Jeremiah when he said Ruth wanted to marry me,' he said, at last, 'because she had reason to want to get away from Pantglas.' He put both hands to his head and scrubbed at his hair as if lice were plaguing him. 'Was Mari – Jeremiah's wife – at the inquest?' he asked.

'I was told he had his whole family there with him.'

'And were you *told* that Mari had bruises on her face?' I did not reply which was clearly answer enough. 'Never forgiven her, has he?'

'For not wanting to marry him?' I asked, cautiously.

'For coming to the marriage bed with Llew Price's bastard in her belly.'

Outside the window I could hear a blackbird singing and wondered at such a hedgerow sound within the bare stone precincts of the prison. There must have been a garden tucked away somewhere within the walls.

'Would Ruth not have wanted to stay at home to protect her mother?' I asked.

He grunted. 'Not just Mari he took it out on, was it?'

I moved my eyes a fraction, tried as hard as I was able to read something, anything, from his posture besides an acute reluctance to tell me what he knew.

'Mr Eynon. What are you trying to tell me?'

'Things weren't right in that house,' he said, from between gritted teeth.

'Go on.'

Again, his hand rasped over his face. 'Jeremiah's one to hold grudges,' he said, laying words down as carefully as he might have coiled a rope on the deck. 'Nurses 'em like *swci* lambs. And he's been nursing a grudge against Mari ever since his wedding night.'

Was he watching my face as he spoke, trying to see what I knew, what I understood? In the perfect silence of the small room, I heard him swallowing.

'When he'd had a skinful, he'd get nasty, see? And he'd say he'd been cheated. Told me once that he was owed—' Another swallow, as if he was taking Dutch courage. 'That he was owed a maidenhead.'

I unclenched my jaw, appalled. 'Ruth?'

At the edge of the whirlpool, I saw him nod. 'Like I say, things weren't right in that house. Whether she threatened *him* with a knife, at the finish, I don't know. But take it from me, whatever Ruth wanted, it wasn't me.'

John

I'll be honest – I was about as enthusiastic about reading that volume of the *Mabinogi* as I would've been if you'd suggested I read some Greek, but Miss Gwatkyn's comment about knowing Homer better than the legends of my own country had provoked me. It was as if she thought I'd *chosen* the *Iliad* and the *Odyssey* in preference to the *Mabinogi*.

So, to make sure I'd read at least some of it, it was the only book I'd brought with me. And I needed to read something to take my mind off the sounds of what was going on – again and again – next door.

Lydia Howell'd told me that the four most famous stories were in the third volume of the translation from Middle Welsh, so that's the one I'd brought. I suppose I shouldn't have been surprised that she knew all about the *Mabinogi*. Cut from the same cloth, weren't they, Lydia Howell and Phoebe Gwatkyn?

The first story was about a prince – Pwyll Pendefig Dyfed – and, right from the beginning, I recognised places I knew. Homer's stories had been about Troy, somewhere long forgotten, if it ever existed, but Pwyll had a palace in Narberth – a town you could still go to now – and his favourite hunting grounds were in Glyn Cych, a couple of miles over the river from Glanteifi. It was odd to think that the people who'd made these stories up, centuries and centuries ago, had known the land where I lived now – the valleys, the rivers, the mountains. Even Miss Gwatkyn's Sarn Helen and her Roman remains, probably.

When we'd read the *Odyssey* and the *Iliad* at Mr Davies's school in Adpar, he'd explained the difference between fairy stories and legends. Fairy stories, he'd told us, were morality tales. They held messages, warnings about things to avoid. Of course, they were entertaining – they had to be if people were going to pay attention to them – but they were made up. Just stories.

Legends, on the other hand, were what Mr Davies called 'folk memories'. They were about people and events that had been real, once upon a time. All sorts of exaggerations and extra elements might've been added to make them more colourful but they had a basis in fact.

So I found myself wondering which the tales in the *Mabinogi* were – fairy stories or legends?

Like fairy stories, there was an awful lot of magic in them. And actual fairies. Or, at least, people who were half-fairy. But then, there were gods in the *Odyssey* and the *Iliad*, weren't there? Presumably, when the *Mabinogi*'s stories'd first been told, people had still believed in magic. Mind, if we were talking about fairies, there were plenty of uneducated people who still believed. You met old people who were superstitious like that everywhere in Cardiganshire.

But the real places in the *Mabinogi* made me wonder whether the people might have been real, once, too. Trouble was, they were all fairy-story types – kings and princes, fairies and magicians, warriors and beautiful maidens. But that was true of the Greek legends, too, and I knew Miss Gwatkyn'd tell me I should be comparing the *Mabinogi* with them, not with the penny bloods I used to read before law books and monographs on agricultural improvement started taking up all my reading time.

The further I got into Miss Guest's translation, the less I understood why somebody like Phoebe Gwatkyn thought so highly of these stories. Because, to be honest, some of what I was reading was quite disturbing.

Killers hidden in leather bags having their skulls crushed. Branwen being forced into marriage with an Irish prince and taken over the sea to his court where she was beaten and humiliated. King Math's nephews, Gilfaethwy and Gwydion, starting a war so that Gilfaethwy could rape Goewin, his uncle's virgin foot-holder, while Math was away fighting. Math transforming the treacherous brothers into beasts who then mated with each other and produced offspring.

What on earth did Miss Gwatkyn find to admire so much in stories full of treachery, rape, murder and incest? Or Lydia Howell, come to that. Mind, Miss Howell'd have more sympathy than most with the *Mabinogi*'s shape-shifting characters and their secrets, wouldn't she?

I read on, my fingers in my ears against the sounds coming through the lath and plaster, and found the story of Lleu Llaw

Gyffes – the character Phoebe Gwatkyn had named her hall-boy after. When his mother cursed him never to have a human wife, Lleu's magician uncles conjured one up for him out of flowers. In a fairy story that would've been the happy-ever-after ending. But not in these stories. In the *Mabinogi*, the flower-wife, Blodeuwedd, fell in love with somebody else and the two of them plotted to kill Lleu.

Making a woman out of flowers was about as fairy-storyish as you could get but Blodeuwedd wanting to make up her own mind about who to be married to felt very real. Because that was exactly the situation Ruth Eynon'd found herself in, wasn't it?

I sat there, my arse numb, my back warm against the chimney breast, my toes freezing out of my boots, and tried to think.

Look beyond the story to what Homer's trying to tell you, boys, Mr Davies used to say. *Look at the characters and the virtues they embody.*

I remembered how he'd had us comparing Achilles, the warrior, the man of action, with Odysseus, the thinker, the user of words as weapons. Like the magicians in the *Mabinogi*, Odysseus had used words to get what he wanted, to make the world into the shape he'd wanted it to be.

The state of his hands meant that Nicholas Rowland'd had no choice but to be more of an Odysseus than an Achilles. Words and learning had been his weapons. But, for all his thinking and talking and persuading, some Achilles'd come along and pushed him out of the loft, hadn't they?

So who was our Achilles?

Shoni Goch? He was a man of action. A fighter.

But then there was Montague Caldicot, too. A fighter of a different kind. More noble. More Ajax. In the *Mabinogi*, he'd have been a warrior forced to return to the court of his father in disgrace and magicked out of his true shape for a while until he repented, like Gwydion and Gilfaethwy. But what was he supposed to be repenting of? What had got him thrown out of the army? And, whatever it was, had Nicholas Rowland been misusing his powers of persuasion to blackmail him?

Caldicot hadn't been on the list of Cardiganshire gentlemen Nan and Ruth had given to Harry, which meant that Rowland hadn't written to him to ask for money or support. But, if Miss Gwatkyn was right and it was Caldicot who'd suggested that Rowland should set up his school in Llanddewi Brefi, you'd have expected Caldicot to be at the top of the list. So why wasn't he? And, if Rowland hadn't written to him, where had the fifty pounds in banknotes come from?

I thought of Nan and Ruth, sitting in the gloomy cowshed schoolroom, writing those letters. In a story like the *Mabinogi*, Rowland would've been a magician and the girls his captive fairy servants, writing magical spells that he dictated to trick people into giving him the things he coveted, the things that'd make him more powerful.

But that was me getting fanciful. The only young girls I'd come across in the *Mabinogi* were the maidens at the court of King Math. His virgin foot-holders. Objects of men's lust.

The thought made the hairs on the back of my neck stand up. Was *that* what had happened? Had Rowland—?

No. That was just a disgusting suspicion brought on by reading Gwydion and Gilfaethwy's plot to rape Goewin. And by the grunts and moans on the other side of the wall. We'd heard not a whisper of anything like that about Rowland. And, anyway, Nan and Ruth had always been together when they were with him, hadn't they? Protection for each other.

But then, Goewin had always been with the other maidens of the court, too, until she'd been lured away.

I pictured Nan Walters and Ruth Eynon, demure and prim in the parlour of the Three Horseshoes. Young women. Virgins.

Objects of men's lust.

Was that how it had been?

Back at the Black Lion, I told Lydia what I had learned from Shoni Eynon. I had repeated his words to myself over and over, so that she might not find me lacking in my desire to treat her as my equal. Was she shocked by the sailor's revelations? Given her history she must have heard similar things but, still, my face burned beneath my beard and I felt like a degenerate for saying such words in front of her.

'Hmmm,' she said, when I had finished. 'So there is more to Ruth than the studious, diligent young woman she presented to Nicholas Rowland and Miss Gwatkyn. But, if what Jonathan Eynon says is true, her accomplishments are all the more remarkable, don't you think?'

'Making her the kind of woman Nicholas Rowland might very well wish to marry,' I agreed. 'But we saw none of the resilience she must possess when she gave evidence at the inquest.'

Far from it. She had simply broken down when questioned too hard. But were her quick tears not now called into question?

'Spect she cried. Jonathan Eynon had said. *Seen her do that often enough to get out of trouble with her father.*

If that was the case, it seemed entirely possible that, in making the startling declaration that she and Nicholas Rowland had been engaged and then breaking down emotionally, Ruth Eynon had contrived both to set the cat among the pigeons and to see to it that the cat went entirely unchallenged.

'I've been a fool,' I said. 'And I've relied on John's opinion too much. When all's said and done, he's only just turned twenty. What does he know of the ways in which people deceive each other?'

'Hindsight is a wonderful thing,' Lydia said. 'But you shouldn't blame yourself. You had no reason, then, to doubt the girl's word, did you?'

'But I should have had reason, shouldn't I? I should have done my job properly. Spoken to Llew Price sooner. Gone to see Jeremiah Eynon.'

My self-recriminations were interrupted by the arrival of a coach party keen to be fed and watered before the next leg of their journey. They swarmed in, thrusting cold hands towards the fire, exclaiming how good it was to be out of the bouncing coach, and effectively ended our conversation.

A minute later, Minnever arrived and squeezed himself into the corner where we were sitting. I listened to his civil but profoundly unenthusiastic 'Good morning' to Lydia and knew that he was displeased to find her here. Still, there was nothing I could do about that now.

'I have good news,' he said, not needing to keep his voice low due to the surrounding hubbub. 'I believe we can persuade Caldicot to step down. Withdraw from the election.'

'Withdraw?' I repeated, assuming that he would take back such a wild claim in favour of something more realistic.

'Yes. I've found out why he was cashiered.'

'How?' Had he sent spies to London to prise the secret from somebody in Caldicot's regiment?

He leaned towards me. 'I told you I'd do my utmost to win this, Harry.'

Was he calling my own commitment into question or was the coldness in his tone explained by Lydia's presence? 'You did,' I said. 'And I'm very grateful. Now, please, tell us what you've discovered.'

There was a pause, then Lydia rose to her feet.

'If you'll excuse me, gentlemen, I have things to attend to.'

I stood up. Minnever had obviously signalled his unwillingness to speak in front of her. 'Lydia, stay—'

'It would be best if this were for your ears only, Harry,' Minnever objected.

'Nevertheless, I would prefer—'

Lydia put a hand on my arm. 'Harry, please. As I said, I have business to attend to. You may tell me whatever you wish later.'

Belatedly, I realised that Lydia was trying to absolve me of the need to stand up for her against my election agent and, as the door closed behind her, I sat down and waited to hear Minnever's news.

He wasted no time in taking the seat that Lydia had vacated and inclining his head towards me. 'Major Caldicot was cashiered for failing to report a capital offence. To wit: buggery. He caught two private soldiers at it. Didn't have them taken into custody. Didn't report them to his colonel.'

My mind started racing. 'I see.'

How did this tie in with anything we currently knew of Caldicot?

'And that's not all,' Minnever continued. 'Seems he allowed the men to escape. To desert, I should say. When the subaltern who'd been with him realised that Caldicot'd failed to do his duty, it was too late to have the soldiers taken into custody. They were gone.'

So Montague Caldicot was not as wedded to the letter of the law as he might like to pretend. But was it significant that his dereliction of duty should involve this particular crime?

'He'll have to stand down, of course.' Minnever's confident assertion broke into my thoughts. 'If I can discover the truth, so can others. He'd be vulnerable to blackmail and the corruption of his office.'

'Indeed,' I said. 'And, if Nicholas Rowland had found out, it gives Caldicot an excellent motive for murder.'

Minnever swivelled to face me. 'No, Harry. We're not going down that road. There's absolutely *no* reason to think that Rowland had—'

'You've just said yourself, if you can find out—'

'I meant anybody else who was digging about! It's nonsensical to imagine that the teacher might've stumbled across information like that. He was here, days' travel away from rumours and news.'

'He still had friends in London. A letter could have—'

'No, Harry! This is not a line of enquiry. This is our way to dispose of Caldicot and have you stand, unopposed, on Saturday.'

Minnever was not to be contradicted on this, that much was clear; I would have to keep my suspicions to myself.

'It's perfect,' he said. 'You needn't be involved. I'll ask to see Caldicot, in private. Lay the situation out. Tell him that, if he doesn't withdraw, I'll have no choice but to go to the Tory agent and tell him what I know. There'd be absolutely no question of his continuing as the Tories' candidate if they knew. Even if they could stomach it themselves, they wouldn't want to risk that kind of news being made public.'

I knew he was right and I did not try to argue against his plan. But it was not the thought that I might go to the nomination meeting at the end of the week unopposed that kept me awake half that night. My thoughts were consumed by the notion that Caldicot was not the man he seemed, and that, whatever Minnever said, the possibility that Rowland might have got wind of his dereliction of duty gave my opponent a compelling motive to have wished the schoolteacher ill.

John

Before I left Glanteifi, we'd worked out that I wouldn't get to London till late on Wednesday afternoon. Too late to go searching about for hansoms to take me to Holywell Street to collect Rowland's 'copies' and whatever money he was due. Mr Gordon, the bookseller, wouldn't thank me for keeping him talking when he was trying to shut up shop and get home for his dinner. Better to leave it till the following day.

So, my plan was to go straight to Gus Gelyot's house. Mr Gelyot was an old friend of Harry's who I'd met when we'd been travelling through London the previous autumn, on the way to see Nathaniel Howell. It was hard to believe it'd only been a few months ago. My life'd changed so much in that time that it seemed more like years.

The first time I'd seen Mr Gelyot's house I'd been getting out of a hansom cab with Harry, surrounded by thick, smoky fog – what they call a London Particular. Everything about London had been strange and foreign to me then, and the Gelyots' house'd been no exception. Because I knew Mr Gelyot's family was wealthy, I'd expected a grand house set in its own grounds, but I soon realised that London houses weren't like that. Not the modern ones, anyway. The Gelyots' house had turned out to be one of a long, shallow crescent of tall brick houses, each with its own pillared entrance porch.

On that first visit, everything'd been a surprise. The peculiar construction of the houses in the crescent, with their lower storeys below ground. The strange new colour of the Gelyots' wallpaper – *turquoise*. The bright, hissing light of the house's gas lamps. Even the surprisingly small entrance hall.

This time, of course, I knew what to expect as the door was opened for me and I went in. In London, the size of the entrance hall didn't tell you much. It was just the introduction to a house, a way of getting to the rooms. Not like the halls in the old gentry mansions which were bigger than some of the rooms and had fireplaces and furniture. But it wouldn't do to confuse narrowness with meanness – you could tell the money that'd gone into this place from the patterned floor tiles and the stained-glass fanlight over the door, as well as the polished wood of the staircase with its new runner. Harry'd told me that Mrs Gelyot insisted on changing the runner every season so that it never looked worn.

After a footman'd taken my coat and bag, the butler led me up to the drawing room.

I'll be honest. I'd been worried about what kind of greeting I'd get from Gus Gelyot. Last time I'd been here, there'd been an argument when he'd tried to put me in the servants' quarters and Harry'd objected. I didn't want things to be difficult.

Turned out I'd underestimated Harry. And Gus Gelyot, too, come to that. Letters'd obviously gone to and fro between the two of them where they'd talked about me. Letters Harry must've asked Mrs Griffiths to read. Which was just as well because, when it came down to it, I wasn't sure I would've wanted to read whatever Gus Gelyot had to say about me. It's like my mother always used to say, eavesdroppers never hear good things of themselves.

'So,' Mr Gelyot said, after the butler had left us, 'I gather you're Glanteifi's under-steward now?'

'I am.'

He waved at a brightly-upholstered chair and I sat down, remembering to pull the knees of my trousers up so they didn't bag. Baggy knees are for working men, not gents, and the maids at Glanteifi wouldn't thank me for making it more difficult than it already was to keep my clothes looking smart.

'And set to be a solicitor into the bargain?'

I smiled nervously at his use of the word. A bargain was what it was. I was taking a risk on Harry and Glanteifi and he was trying to make sure that I wouldn't lose by it.

'What brings you to the capital? The note I got from Harry this morning was nicely vague – just said you were coming up on coroner's business and he'd be obliged if I offered whatever assistance seemed necessary.'

It took longer than I would've guessed to tell him all about the case. He didn't say much, just asked the kind of questions you'd expect from a barrister and let me get on with it.

'Well,' he said, when I'd finished. 'That's quite the tale.' He was looking at me as if I was a witness in the dock. A witness whose story he only half-believed. 'And what's your opinion, Mr Davies? Why do *you* think this schoolteacher was done to death?'

I shifted in my seat. Not that it was uncomfortable – far from it. It was the way Mr Gelyot was looking at me that was making me feel uneasy. Perhaps I'd got too used to Harry not being able to look at me at all. To tell the truth, what I thought was that the inquest hadn't been handled properly. But I wasn't going to tell Gus Gelyot that.

He was still looking at me, waiting. And I knew, from our previous meeting, that he was a man who didn't try and smooth over what he thought for the sake of politeness.

'I don't think we got to the bottom of who might've killed Rowland,' I told him. 'Not by a long shot. We probably should have postponed the inquest until after the public meeting. It's difficult to run an inquest and an election at the same time.'

He sighed. 'Yes. The election. How's Harry faring? I don't imagine having to bow to this agent suits him at all?'

I grinned. It was odd talking to somebody who knew Harry even better than I did. 'Not especially, no.'

He gave a little smile and crossed one leg over the other. Gus Gelyot was one of those tall, slender men who look as if the main point of them is to wear expensive clothes. The poised way he sat showed the perfect cut of his waistcoat, the way his dove-grey jacket lay flat and trim over it. He was wearing one of those fashionable starched collars and a gold-coloured necktie that would have raised eyebrows anywhere west of Merthyr Tydfil. At home, neckwear was white if you were old-fashioned and black if you were up-to-the-minute. Bright colours were for women. Or flowers.

'Is he going to win, do you think?'

I shifted again. If anybody'd been watching us, I'd have seemed like a fidgety schoolboy compared to Mr Gelyot. Composed, that was the word for him. In both senses.

'If you were a betting man, I'd advise you not to put your shirt on him,' I said.

'Should've nobbled this Caldicot when he had the chance, shouldn't he?' He laughed. 'Don't look so shocked, Mr Davies. I'm only joking. Even in London it's not done to implicate one's rival in a murder investigation.'

He stood up and tugged his waistcoat down a whole eighth of an inch. 'Time for some refreshment, I think, before dinner.'

He pulled at a length of fabric that dangled next to the gilt-framed mirror over the fireplace and a footman appeared. Evidently, they didn't have hall-boys in London. 'Could you bring us two cobblers, please, Timothy?'

Right then. A cobbler must be London slang for some kind of drink. I just hoped it wasn't brandy.

Gus Gelyot wandered over to the long window that looked out on the well-swept street below and the trees and grass of a little park opposite. 'What will Harry do if he doesn't win the election?'

I'd been giving that some thought, myself.

'Before the magistrates asked him to stand in for Leighton Bowen, he was thinking of becoming a solicitor,' I said. 'We could set up in practice together.'

If we could run Glanteifi while doing the coroner's job between us, I was damn sure we could run a solicitor's practice.

'What, and have him even more at loggerheads with the magistrates? D'you really think that's a good idea?'

His question made me feel like a girl who's been hugging some stupid, romantic dream. He was right, Harry'd never be able to stick to wills and land agreements. He'd be interfering in cases brought before the bench and getting in the way of the police before anybody knew what was happening.

'What would you suggest?' I asked.

'Since you ask, I'd suggest he tried a bit harder not to lose the election. And you can tell him that from me.' He turned and gave me a grin that said, *But we both know what Harry's like, don't we?*

'Maybe, if I can find something while I'm here – something to re-open the inquest – that'd help. And there's Mr Rowland's collegiate school. If people think Harry's doing what he can to make sure that still gets established, I think they might vote for him.'

'Yes.' Gus Gelyot drew the word out until it had three syllables, not one.

'What?'

He looked away, picked up a glass ornament and stared at it. 'Has Harry given you any indication of what you might find in Holywell Street?'

Before I could reply, the footman came in carrying a silver tray with two glasses on it. Not ordinary glasses with a stem – tall beakers filled with a brown drink with what looked like ice floating in it. Slices of orange cut across the round were wedged into the tops of the glasses and there were long, slender sticks poking up out of the liquid.

'Here.' Gus Gelyot took the glasses off the tray and handed one to me. 'Try this.'

He took hold of the stick in his glass and, instead of stirring the drink, put it in his mouth. It was a reed made of paper.

I sucked up a sip of the liquid. It was only sherry. Sweetened and with orange in it, but sherry. Why anybody'd take it into their head to name it after a shoe-mender, I couldn't tell you. But then, that was rich people for you, wasn't it? Wouldn't know real life if it hit them over the head with a pin-hammer.

Gus Gelyot was watching me, waiting for my verdict. I nodded. 'Very pleasant.'

He laughed. 'You'll go far, Mr Davies. You've got more *savoir-faire* than Harry's ever had. He could learn a lot from you.'

Harry

Minnever already having left to confront Caldicot by the time I rose in the morning, I breakfasted with Lydia then made my way, obediently alone, to the middle of town where the stage from which we were to give our speeches stood in front of Cardigan's grammar school.

The previous day, while chatting to ladies in shops, Lydia had learned that there had been considerable debate as to where our public election meeting should be held. The borough magistrates had favoured the Corn Market at Shire Hall lest it should rain, while the businessmen of the town preferred somewhere in the open where a bigger crowd might gather. The likely weather notwithstanding, the latter view had prevailed.

Though it was an hour and more before the public meeting was due to begin, a decent crowd had already gathered, determined, no doubt, to be in the front row when the entertainment started. The *Carmarthen Journal* had described Caldicot's criticism of me on the platform at Tregaron in unremitting detail and people had undoubtedly come to Cardigan expecting more of the same.

The day seemed set to remain fine with the sky an almost cloudless blue and the breeze from the estuary light and warm. I walked towards the blue- and red-decked platform (Minnever had clearly learned his lesson where ribbons were concerned) searching my peripheral vision for the agent's short figure and bald pate. Could he still be with Caldicot? It seemed unlikely: ultimata are apt to cut conversations short.

If Minnever persuaded my rival to withdraw from the contest, this morning's public meeting would be rendered redundant, but I did not need an agent to tell me that I would be well advised, opposed or not, to make a speech. Giving the people of Cardigan a reason to grumble against me before I was officially confirmed as coroner would be unwise.

I looked about but Minnever's tall hat was not to be seen. Still, it did not matter whether he was here yet or not, did it? The likelihood was that the contest was over and that I would speak unopposed.

And yet, I felt an unease building inexplicably at the back of my mind.

Seeking distraction, I turned away from the crowd. Behind the stage, the grammar school's windows glinted in the early sun and I imagined the scholars, bent industriously over their lessons. Would they be allowed out to watch the meeting? Their master might find it difficult to keep them at their studies if the crowd was as voluble as the one in Tregaron had been.

Minutes ticked by, still Minnever did not appear, and I devoutly wished that John were with me. Without him, I could not tell whether I was the object of avid scrutiny or collective indifference. Feeling the gathering crowd's eyes on me, I tried to reassure myself that nobody was, in fact, staring. Given that Minnever had not paraded me around the streets of Cardigan in the way that he had insisted on at Tregaron, I must surely have been a stranger to these people.

'It's a different crowd, here,' Minnever had told me the previous day, when I made a joke about his failure to drag me to every inn and alehouse in the town. 'The people we really need to talk to will be at the dinner this evening.'

He had organised the dinner in question 'to build some bridges' as he had put it, and the invitees had included a number of the town's businessmen as well as every single one of Cardigan's borough magistrates. Quite how he had persuaded them all to a Liberal-sponsored dinner on the night before the hustings, when the Tories must also have been angling for a meeting with their candidate, I had no idea; but, after my experience with the ladies of the Olive Leaf Circle, the pressure I had felt to overcome the feelings of isolation my blindness provoked and present myself in a way Minnever would approve of had resulted in a manner so resolutely hail-fellow-well-met that I had heartily detested myself. The sooner the election was over and I could distance myself from the dishonesty of politics, the better.

However, participating in an evening of vacuous insincerity was scarcely the only cause I had for self-reproach, nor even the most pressing one. For days, I had allowed Minnever to whore me through the streets of Tregaron mouthing platitudes and insincerities to everybody I met; and, as a consequence, I had conducted Rowland's inquest so badly that a man I believed to be innocent was awaiting trial for murder. Not only that but, *at that very moment*, my election agent was seeking out Montague Caldicot to present him with unsubstantiated gossip, for the express purpose of forcing him to withdraw his candidacy for the coronership.

How had I allowed myself to behave so entirely unlike the man I believed myself to be?

Needing to escape as much from my own thoughts as from the crowd's unseen eyes, I turned and would have made for the safety of the Black Lion once more had I not heard my name being called.

I turned. Minnever. His bald head was hatless and he was unmistakeable.

'Have you seen Caldicot anywhere?' He sounded agitated.

'What? No!' My voice felt tight in my throat. I swallowed and tried again. 'Why? What's going on? Did he say something about me when you met?'

'We didn't meet. I've just seen one of the Tory committee. According to him, Caldicot hasn't been seen since yesterday. He was supposed to have dinner with the Tory committee last night but he didn't turn up. Nobody knows where he is.'

John

After breakfast, I'd expected Mr Gelyot to tell me where I could get a hansom cab to take me to Holywell Street but he surprised me. Said he'd walk me there.

'I'll show you a bit of London on the way. There's no better way to see this city than on foot.' He looked sideways at me. 'Don't tell Harry I said that. He likes to dismiss me as a lazy Londoner who thinks the only use for his legs is to get into a carriage.' I laughed. I could hear Harry saying that. 'But it's a lovely morning – it'd be a shame to spend it in a smelly hansom.'

We set off in hazy sunshine. I wasn't really sure whether the haze was cloud, or smoke from the city's chimneys, but at least it wasn't raining.

We'd not had time to talk much more the evening before. Mr Gelyot senior had arrived with Mrs Gelyot while we were drinking our cobblers, and dinner had been taken up with talk of all sorts of things other than our inquest.

Now, as we strode along, dodging on and off the pavement, in and out of the muck of the road, Gus Gelyot said, 'You provided an excellent summary of the inquest, yesterday, but I didn't get much of an impression of the victim. What kind of a man was your Mr Rowland?'

I looked sideways at him, wondering why he wanted to know, but his face gave nothing away. 'A radical – certainly as far as education was concerned. Somebody who'd moved up in the world a bit – when he was in London, at any rate. Why d'you ask?'

'Just wondering what kind of literature we're likely to find waiting for us.'

There was something behind his words but I was prevented from asking because we'd reached a wide crossroads and I had to pay attention to make sure I wasn't run over by a large carriage pulled by three horses. Through the window, I could see eight or ten ordinary people – not gentry – sitting on benches inside.

Mr Gelyot must've seen my face. 'That's a horse-bus. Or omnibus, I should say. More expensive than walking but a lot cheaper than a hackney.'

And the 'bus' wasn't the only sight to be seen – there was something new and different on every side. I did my best to stop my head going this way and that as if it was on a swivel; I might not be dressed in London fashion but I didn't have to behave as if I was just up from the country.

Most of the time, Mr Gelyot left me alone to take it all in. The huge, impressive buildings of three, four, five storeys. The carriages jammed up against each other, here and there, like branches in floodwater after a storm. The street sellers shouting their wares – everything from coffee and muffins to pies and eels. The different fashions of rich and poor. Those in the middle trying to pretend they were nearer rich than poor. But, now and then, he'd name the street we were on or tell me something. 'That's Regent Street, which tells you when all those classical-looking buildings went up,' or, 'This is Oxford Street. It's supposed to be a Roman road – straight enough, don't you think?'

I looked behind me. Mr Gelyot was right – you could see half a mile in either direction which was a real rarity in London. Odd to think of the Romans building this and Miss Gwatkyn's Roman road in a time when London and Cardiganshire weren't in England and Wales, just Brittania. Britain. The land of the *Mabinogi*.

'This way!'

I dodged around a huge pile of horseshit and scurried after Mr Gelyot down a road at right angles to Oxford Street.

'This'll take us to Drury Lane and then we can cut through to where you need to be.'

Drury Lane was a lot less respectable-looking than Oxford Street so I wasn't surprised when Mr Gelyot pointed out a boxy modern building on the other side of the road with an ugly kind of porch supported on square columns. 'That's the theatre where all the real actors perform. None of your suspect musical entertainment there. Drury Lane theatricals are almost members of respectable society.'

I glanced at his face. I didn't know him well enough to be able to tell whether he was joking or serious so I just gave him a half-smile that'd do for either and carried on walking.

Whatever else you might say about London, you couldn't say it was all the same. Adjoining streets were as different from each other as a field of barley and a stand of gorse. But everybody seemed to know where they should be. You didn't see well-dressed people in the dark, narrow, little streets and any poor people on the bigger, wider roads kept out of the way of their betters. Apart from the urchins – they darted about like ragged magpies, swooping on things that'd been dropped, and shoving their hands out with a 'spare a ha'penny, gov'nor?' to any well-dressed person who looked in their direction.

So it was a surprise when Mr Gelyot stopped at the junction with a street which seemed to be mostly full of the middling class of folk, and announced, 'This is Wych Street. I'd advise you to keep a hand on your watch and your wallet. The place is full of pickpockets who'll relieve you of either without you knowing they've gone.'

My watch was actually Harry's, and if I lost my wallet I'd be stuck for a way of getting home, so I took both out and put them in my bag. Safe.

Wych Street was narrow but, even if it'd been wide enough, it wasn't the sort of street where carriages'd go. The shops on either side were small and mean and their wares were spilling out on to the street from almost every door. Half of them seemed to be selling second-hand clothes and, from the smell, some of them hadn't been brushed or washed before going on sale. Coats with frayed cuffs and collars, trousers with shiny seats, shirts worn thin and boiled till they were almost white again, shoes and boots polished up to hide the wear and the cracks – all under the eye of shopkeepers with folded arms and hard eyes who watched people picking over what was there. Looking into one shop, I caught the eye of a rough-looking man standing outside.

'Whassamarrer wiv you?' he wanted to know.

I shook my head and looked away, straight into another shop window. My legs stopped moving. The window was full of naked women. Photographs of naked women. Sitting with one leg crossed over the other. Looking over their shoulders. Some had corsets on, some had hats with feathers. But, mostly, they had very little on. Or nothing.

Mr Gelyot was watching me. 'That's what Wych Street's famous for. That and seditious literature.' He moved on to the next shop and waved a hand at the window. I looked in. No photographs this time, just books, open to show title pages which had words I'm not even going to write down. The kind of words you'd never expect to see in print. Language boys use when they're trying to sound like men. I couldn't look at Mr Gelyot. Just hoped he thought I'd seen it all before. But he wasn't fooled.

'Some people call it erotic literature,' he said. 'Others call it pornography. You've studied some Greek so you'll recognise the root. Pornographos – Prostitute writing.' He pointed at one large book whose title wasn't as scandalous as the rest. *Fanny Hill or The Memoirs of a Woman of Pleasure*. 'The most famous of them all and the book most of the rest are trying to be.'

My face was burning and I had to move my bag in front of me so nobody could see what was happening in my trousers but I couldn't see anybody else who looked even the smallest bit uncomfortable. The men who were going in and out of the shops looked about as guilty as if they'd gone in for an ounce of tobacco or a pair of bootlaces.

The shops themselves were just as brazen. Not one of them made any attempt to hide what they were selling – the books spilled out on to the street, stacked on packing-boxes, just like the clothes from the second-hand sellers.

'This is why I wondered what sort of book you'd come to collect,' Mr Gelyot said. 'Holywell Street is a little less lurid than this, these days, but not much.'

We walked to the end of Wych Street, where it widened out as it joined an open area with a large church in the middle. Mr Gelyot nodded towards it. 'St Clement Danes. Don't ask me why it's called that, or whether it's got anything to do with the Danish.'

But, instead of walking towards the church, he turned back, almost the way we'd come, and went down another street parallel to Wych Street. I looked up at the corner and saw the sign.

Holywell Street.

If Wych Street was a warning, what was I going to see in Mr W. Gordon's bookshop?

At the advertised hour of eleven o'clock, Minnever and I, in the company of several members of Cardigan's Liberal organising committee, sat on the stage in front of the grammar school, waiting for the Tories to make an appearance. In front of us, an ever-increasing number of people gathered in Cardigan's high street; beside us, on the platform, sat the town clerk and borough magistrates.

'If he doesn't turn up,' Minnever murmured, his head turning this way and that as he scanned the crowd for any sight of our opponents, 'his agent may try and persuade us to postpone the meeting.'

'Should we agree?' I asked.

'Absolutely not!'

The words had scarcely left his mouth when, to my left, somebody said, 'There's Tom Elias.'

'But no Caldicot,' Minnever said, as what was evidently the Tory contingent finally pushed through the crowd towards us, heckled and catcalled on their way by the Liberal-voting populace.

We stood as they climbed the steps on to the stage.

'You've not found your candidate, I see, Crowther.' Minnever's tone suggested that he was relishing our opponents' predicament.

'Good morning, Minnever,' Caldicot's agent replied.

'Good morning be damned! Will he appear and address the electorate or will he not?'

Before Mr Crowther could reply, a large man wearing a suit in an unfortunate shade of green stepped forward. 'Perhaps your candidate can shed some light on that. He was seen, yesterday, speaking to Mr Caldicot in a very underhand manner.' The man turned his face to me. 'I don't know what you said to him but, whatever it was, you had no right to approach him in such a way. In a back alley!' Evidently, that last comment had been made to his companions. 'I've a mind to speak to the magistrates!'

'And say what, Elias?' Minnever was, I realised, acquainted with all our opponents. 'That our candidate had a quiet chat with yours? I can't imagine what you'd expect the magistrates to do with that information.'

'A quiet chat? It was nothing of the sort! Your candidate was *threatening* Mr Caldicot!'

A figure moved to my side. 'Gentlemen, please!' This was Cardigan's town clerk, Mr Lewis. We had met the previous evening and I recognised his very upright stance and pleasant baritone. 'I'm sure there's no need for accusations. Our only concern must be to find Mr Caldicot and ensure his wellbeing.'

'It's not *we* who are threatening his wellbeing.' Thomas Elias was not going to give up his bone of contention simply for the asking. 'Ask this gentleman what he said to Caldicot yesterday!'

Lewis turned to me, his unflamboyant competence and natural authority offering a welcome corrective to Elias's bluster. 'Mr Probert-Lloyd, I'm quite sure that nothing unto-ward took place between you and Mr Caldicot yesterday, but perhaps you'd be so good as to tell us anything you know? Anything that might help us understand why he's not here?'

By now, the crowd had grasped that something was afoot and had begun to press in around the stage, booing and jeering.

'I have no idea why Mr Caldicot isn't here,' I said, conscious that, in raising my voice above the din of the crowd, I might make our conversation audible to those below the stage. 'And, I assure you, I did not threaten Montague Caldicot in any way.' I turned to the harrumphing Elias. 'What do you imagine I might threaten him *with*?'

'Threats apart,' Crowther said, 'Mr Caldicot's failure to appear for dinner with the election committee last night and now, again, today, is a cause for concern. If he'd merely been detained, I'm sure he would have sent a note.'

Sidelong, I observed the man. He was a slighter, less bombastic figure than Thomas Elias and his dark suit and sober demeanour brought undertakers to mind.

'Mr Caldicot and I met yesterday, by chance, when we both found ourselves at the police station to speak to Inspector Bellis,' I told him. 'I asked for a few moments of his time to speak in private – which, incidentally,' I turned my head to Elias, 'is the only reason why our meeting took place in a "back alley". I suggested that it might be better for all concerned if we were to address the public in a civilised fashion and refrain from casting aspersions on each other's integrity. Mr Caldicot, on the other hand, issued me with an ultimatum.'

That silenced them.

'Are you prepared to tell us the nature of this ultimatum?' Crowther asked.

'Perfectly. He said that unless I ceased all further investigations into the death of Nicholas Rowland and assured him that I would not attempt to re-open the inquest, he would continue to call me a liar and a hypocrite at every public meeting we addressed.'

I heard a sound which might have indicated distaste. Then, with a polite, 'If you'll excuse us for a moment, gentlemen,' Crowther moved the Tories to one side.

Two could play that game, so I took Minnever's arm and led him to the back of the stage, leaving the rest of the Liberal retinue to resume their seats.

'I didn't threaten Caldicot,' I told him, keeping my voice low lest the scholars sitting beneath the nearest grammar school window should be listening, 'but it's possible that he *felt* threatened when I told him John had gone to London.'

'Why should he?'

'This is what I was trying to tell you yesterday, Minnever. I think he was afraid that John would discover that he knew Nicholas Rowland far better than he's been prepared to admit. John has believed, all along, that Caldicot was lying when he claimed he barely knew Rowland. I think it's possible Rowland was blackmailing him.'

Minnever's sudden stillness suggested that he was digesting this. When he spoke again, his tone was unusually cautious.

'Taking into consideration what we know about why Caldicot was forced to leave the army, do you think there's any possibility that he might be... involved... with the sort of crime he chose to ignore?'

'Involved?'

'You know what I'm saying, Harry.'

I sighed. 'I have no idea what – or who – Caldicot is or has been involved with. But there must be a reason he's not here.'

We made our way back towards the Tories. They were still without a candidate and Crowther had no suggestions to offer but that we 'wait a while'.

'I think not.' Minnever clasped his hands together as if only a significant exercise of will had prevented him breaking into gleeful applause. 'The voters need to be presented with *something* to reward their patience, so I suggest that Harry speaks to them while you decide what to do about your side of things.'

Caldicot's entourage could hardly complain, so everybody sat down, once more, save Mr Lewis who stepped up to the lectern at the front of the stage to introduce me.

As the crowd began to cheer the fact that something was happening at last, I leaned towards Minnever. 'D'you think one of the Tories will say something on behalf of Caldicot?'

He grunted. 'More likely they'll just pray that he actually turns up.'

While I hoped, fervently, that he would not.

John

The bookshop wasn't difficult to find. I'd memorised the number and, anyway, its owner advertised his name and business on the front. I looked at the books in the window of Wm. Gordon Bookseller & Publisher, almost dreading what I'd see. But I needn't have worried. Most of the titles seemed to be to do with politics and government. I let out a breath I hadn't known I was holding.

One of the books particularly caught my eye. Like the others, it was propped up and open at the title page so you could see all the details. *Thoughts on the Education of Daughters* was its main title and, underneath, *With Reflections on Female Conduct in the More Important Duties of Life*. Its author was Mary Wollstonecraft and she'd written it – I worked the date out from the Roman numerals at the bottom of the page – in 1787.

Were we here to collect something similar? Had Rowland written a book arguing for free education for everybody who could benefit from it? Miss Gwatkyn'd told us that he'd been outraged by the Education Report and determined to do something. I could see Nan Walters and Ruth Eynon being keen to help him with a project like that.

'Ah,' Mr Gelyot said from behind me. 'A Chartist establishment. Providing egalitarian literature and raising money for the cause.'

I thought he meant that Gordon the bookseller was raising money by selling this 'egalitarian literature', but then I looked at where he was pointing. The shop had two windows – one on either side of the door – and the second was full of the kind of thing we'd seen in Wych Street. I looked back at the window advertising radical literature. How could a man who believed in a better society sell – what was the word Gus Gelyot had used? – *erotic* literature alongside books like Mary Wollstonecraft's?

Mr Gelyot obviously saw the question written on my face. 'The fight for the vote is hungry for cash,' he said. 'And there are plenty of Londoners who are equally hungry for this sort of thing.'

He pushed the door open and the spring-bell brought a man into the shop from a dark room beyond. I noticed that he shut the door carefully behind him. What on earth did he think he should be hiding if he was prepared to display the books he had in his shop window?

'How can I help you, gentlemen?'

I glanced over at Mr Gelyot but he was looking around the place as if he hadn't heard a word. Letting me get on with it.

'I'm here on behalf of Mr Nicholas Rowland, in Cardigan-shire,' I said. I didn't want this man thinking I'd come in here for anything he had for sale. 'You sent him a letter, saying that his copies and payment were ready. As usual.'

He looked me up and down. 'Sounds as if you've come from all the way over there yourself.'

He had a rich, cultured voice and his clothes definitely hadn't come from any of the Wych Street shops. I didn't know what to make of him. Was this kind of thing acceptable in London? I couldn't think of anywhere in the Teifi Valley where people'd be prepared to admit to selling what he had in his window. Even the Chartist stuff would've made booksellers a bit wary. Fair enough, the Newport Rising might've been a few years ago now, but convictions for high treason tend to stick in people's memory. I could still see my father's face when he told my mother that the Chartist leaders'd been sentenced to be hung, drawn and quartered. 'What century do the judges think they're living in?' he'd asked her.

Luckily for the Newport men, some people in government'd had more sense than to make martyrs of them and they'd been transported to Australia instead. But if the executions'd gone ahead, there'd most likely have been risings all over the country and we might all have had the vote by now. Made you think.

I hadn't answered the bookseller's question about whether I'd come from Cardiganshire but that didn't seem to have both-ered him. 'Normally,' he said, 'if Mr Rowland isn't coming to London, the other gentleman calls in for the goods. I trust your being here indicates nothing untoward?'

I wasn't going to lie to him but I wasn't going to tell him Rowland was dead, either. 'This other gentleman, that would be…?'

William Gordon looked at me as if he knew exactly what my game was. 'I don't believe we were ever introduced.'

I took a gamble based on nothing but suspicion. 'A tall, upright kind of man with dark hair?' I suggested. 'About forty, well dressed in London fashions?'

Gordon's eyes never left mine. 'Possibly. I don't have a terribly reliable memory for people's appearance. My life is dedicated to words. I tend to remember people by what they say.'

I nodded as if he'd given me all the information I wanted. And he had, really. *If people don't answer the question you've actually asked*, Harry'd told me once, *the more they try and tell you, the less you should believe.* 'That'll be Mr Caldicot,' I said. 'He's no longer living in London.' I raised Mr Gordon's letter between us. 'May I have the goods and the money owed to Mr Rowland, then?'

'Might I just see that, please?'

I handed his letter over and Mr Gelyot spoke up. 'Just for your information,' he said, 'as neither Mr Rowland nor his usual proxy were available on this occasion, that letter has been copied and the copy notarised as an exact reproduction by an attorney.'

It was a barefaced lie but it sounded so much like the truth that even I believed it for a second or two.

Gordon looked at him. 'My dear sir, I do hope you're not implying that I might, in some way, attempt to evade paying what I owe? I assure you that you will find neither printer nor customer in the whole of London who will tell you that William Gordon has *ever* been anything but scrupulously honest.'

He sounded genuinely offended and Mr Gelyot bowed his head courteously. 'I apologise if I've given offence. I merely wished to make the situation quite clear.'

Gordon's feathers unruffled a bit. 'Very well. Please bear with me for a moment.'

He closed the dark door into the back room behind him, leaving us to look at the stock he was prepared to leave on the open shelves. I'd assumed that London bookshops would be stuffed, like the library at Glanteifi. But no. These shelves were no fuller than the bookshop in Cardigan. Obviously, it worked the same here as at home – you asked for the book you wanted, the bookseller told you whether he had it and, if he didn't, whether he could order it in. Half the bookshops we'd seen in Wych Street and Holywell Street claimed to be publishers as well, so a lot of the time they must be trying to pass their own books off as something similar to what was wanted. I could just picture Gordon with a new customer. *Ah, I know just the volume to which you are referring. That, of course, is published by Messrs What-d'you-call and What's-his-name but we happen to have a volume similar in subject matter but infinitely superior in style.*

One of the titles I'd seen in Gordon's window was *The Amorous Adventures of a Thousand Arabian Nights* by *A Sloe-Eyed Seductress* which, though it was a lot more tasteful than some of the titles in Wych Street, was very similar to several of them.

I looked at Mr Gelyot who raised his eyebrows. 'Quick thinking of you to try and identify your Mr Caldicot.'

'Thank you.'

Before he or I could say anything else, Gordon was back with a newsprint-wrapped parcel big enough to hold several smallish books or two large ones. 'The remuneration is contained within,' he said, handing me the parcel by its string. I noticed there was a label stuck on addressed simply to *Nicholas Rowland Esq.*

'Do you, by any chance, have copies of Mr Rowland's previous work?' Mr Gelyot asked. 'I've not yet had the pleasure of reading any of it.'

Gordon stared at him for a moment or two then turned back to his stock room. When he came back, he had three slim volumes in his hand.

'These are all I have at present.' He handed them to Mr Gelyot in return for his card so that he knew where to send the invoice, then turned to me. 'Please encourage Mr Rowland to send me the next manuscript at his earliest convenience. His work is popular, which is helpful to both our causes.'

As Mr Lewis, the town clerk, made his opening remarks to the crowd, I tried to estimate how many people were standing in Cardigan's high street, waiting to hear what I had to say. More than in Tregaron, I thought, despite its being a normal working day. Cardigan, as the bigger town, had more voters, of course, and the bright sun had, no doubt, persuaded those who were out and about to linger where they might otherwise have hurried on with their day.

'So now, without further ado,' Mr Lewis said, 'I invite Mr Henry Probert-Lloyd to speak to us.'

I rose to my feet, heart racing and stomach full of frantic butterflies. But, before I could reach the lectern which would protect me, somewhat, from the public gaze, there was a stirring in the crowd. A voice repeated, 'excuse me, excuse me', in Welsh as the speaker pushed his way toward the stage and came to a halt at the foot of the steps. I was able to make out a man in shirtsleeves and waistcoat, as if he had been interrupted at his work and sent here. 'Message, Mr Lewis. For Mr Probert-Lloyd.'

The note was passed to Minnever who opened it.

He read in a voice designed not to carry beyond the stage. 'Regrettably, I must leave it to you, Probert-Lloyd. Sincerely, M. Caldicot.' The hand holding the note dropped to his side. 'What the devil does he mean by that?'

I shook my head. I had no idea. What was Caldicot leaving to me? Today's meeting? The coronership? Discovering the truth about Rowland's death?

Mr Lewis approached me. 'Are you happy to continue, Mr Probert-Lloyd?'

I pulled myself together. 'Perfectly.'

Minnever took his seat once more and I stepped forward to the lectern, gathering my thoughts and looking for a way to align myself with the mood of the crowd. Caldicot's absence from the stage was on everybody's lips, so I began with it.

'I know you've come to see a contest today – to see me and Mr Montague Caldicot slugging it out as to who deserves your vote more. But, as you'll have noticed – because, unlike mine, your sight is probably perfectly good – I've just received a message. Unfortunately, Mr Caldicot's unable to be here.'

That garnered groans and cries of 'Shame' and 'Aren't we good enough?'

I grinned. 'So, because he's not here, I'm going to talk about him!'

As I had hoped, that got a few cheers and some laughter.

'No Dr Reckitt, no Mr Caldicot,' a wag shouted. 'Are you making work for yourself and killing off the opposition?'

I laughed along with the audience but the thought of a dead Caldicot sent a chill through me. *Regrettably, I must leave you to it.*

If Montague Caldicot were to kill himself, any scandal in which he had been involved would be likely to die with him, sparing his family any further embarrassment. Was that the path he had chosen? And, if that proved to be the case, how would this crowd remember what I had said to them, in the light of his death? Which of my words would come to their minds as they murmured to friends and family, 'and all the time he was speaking, poor Mr Caldicot was lying, dead'?

Without Caldicot, there was no competition. I needed neither to set up an impregnable position before he could speak, nor rush to my own defence following his prior attack.

So, when the humorous comments had petered out and the crowd was quiet again, I spoke of Montague Caldicot and what I had learned from him. That there was a time for standing in opposition to things and a time to ally oneself. That one had to recognise one's own shortcomings and not deny them but see them for what they were and try to do better.

'I can't promise you that I will never make mistakes if I become coroner,' I said. 'Only a fool would tell you that. Or a politician.' I waited for the laughter, which duly came, and persuaded myself that there was affection in it. 'But I can promise you that I will listen. To medical evidence. To common sense. And to the people who knew the person whose death I am investigating. Because, as much as the relatives of the dead need peace of mind, the dead themselves need the truth of their death to be told if they are to rest in peace.'

It was not what they had anticipated, not what they had come for, but, from the enthusiasm of the applause, my speech seemed to have found favour with the crowd. There were, of course, many questions, some frivolous and some to the point, all of which I answered as best I could. Then a voice somewhere to the side of the crowd shouted, 'You and Montague Caldicot are both recently back from London. What's to stop either of you finding a deputy and going back there? Then we'd have somebody we've never voted for, wouldn't we?'

I nodded. 'It happens, doesn't it?' I paused. 'I can't speak for Mr Caldicot, of course, but I can promise you that *I* won't be going anywhere. I have Glanteifi to run and I mean to do it myself, with the help of John Davies who, as well as being coroner's officer, is also under-steward to the estate. I'm a Cardi,' I said, switching to Welsh to prove the point. Minnever wouldn't like it and neither would the Tory worthies but I was willing to bet that the majority of the electors in town were more comfortable in Welsh. 'I was born in the Teifi Valley, my mother was a solicitor's daughter from here, in Cardigan. I grew up with Welsh as my first language. I am *not* an English squire. I'm grateful to the English side of my family for sending my father here as a young man, but I don't know them very well and I feel no real connection to them or to their lands in Worcestershire. All my loyalty is to you and to Glanteifi. England was a foreign country to me, growing up. I know I lived in London for a time, but that was because I was a bit of a prodigal son – I didn't want to stay home on the farm, I wanted a more exciting life. But this is where my mother's family is. This is where my heart is. And I won't be going anywhere.'

As I listened to their cheers, I wondered whether it was true. Would I have come back, had blindness not forced my hand? It seemed unlikely. I would, in all probability, have pursued a career at the bar and done exactly as they had suggested – found a proxy to run Glanteifi's affairs. And yet, since I had returned, something of the feeling for the land that had grown in me from infant to boy to young man had reawakened and, speaking the language of my youth, I had discovered my younger self again.

But, more than that, as acting coroner, I had discovered a vocation. What had begun as a convenient excuse to cultivate a life away from the estate and from my father's oversight had become an occupation to which I felt peculiarly suited.

A calling I was determined to heed.

John

Nicholas Rowland hadn't been writing radical works on education. He'd been writing erotic literature. I didn't need to open the parcel of books I'd come for to know that. The three that William Gordon had put in Mr Gelyot's hand were more than enough. One would've been plenty.

They were in my bag now, stuffed in along with the parcel. Having them there, I felt as if I was carrying a burning coal about. As if the books'd burn through my bag any minute and fall out for everybody in Drury Lane to see.

When Mr Gelyot'd given them to me, I'd flicked the top one open expecting to see a title that had something to do with Chartism, or education. Instead, what I saw was:

What the Girls Found

or

A Tale of a Naughty Teacher and His Two Naughty Pupils

by

Nicky Revell

Nicky Revell, not Nicholas Rowland. Had there been a mistake?

No. I'd come for Nicholas Rowland's books and that's what William Gordon had given me. I hadn't told him Rowland was dead so, as far as he was concerned, I was going back to Llanddewi Brefi to congratulate the man on his latest work.

They must be his.

But Nicholas Rowland couldn't hold a pen. If he'd written these books, he'd had help. And if it'd come from his two 'Naughty Pupils' perhaps Ruth'd been telling the truth about him asking her to marry him.

I didn't want to look at those books. I really didn't. I knew what effect the photographs in Wych Street'd had on me and I was disgusted at how my body'd responded to pictures of naked strangers. Women who were nothing to do with me and never would be. What would any sweetheart or wife I had in future say if she knew I'd looked at things like that? Not just looked at them but been excited by them.

That kind of reaction was supposed to be for real live girls, girls you knew, girls you fancied. Girls you wanted to walk out with, kiss, lie with, marry even. Not strangers posing next to potted plants and waving ostrich-feather fans. Strangers making eyes at you over their shoulders.

But I didn't have any choice – I'd have to read the books. If I didn't, Harry'd think I was a know-nothing boy who blushed even to think about what was between those covers. The kind of boy who might be passed over for a woman of the world like Lydia Howell when it came to investigating deaths. Because, if Harry could invite her to Glanteifi to be his private secretary, what was to stop him asking her to stand in as coroner's officer if he thought I was too busy with the estate? And if she stood in once—

No. I had to show Harry that I was a man not a boy. When I got back to Glanteifi, I had to be able to tell him exactly what Rowland had been up to.

Back on Oxford Street we had to dodge through increasing numbers of people and traffic and I tried to keep my mind on where I was putting my feet. Gus Gelyot kept pace with me but said nothing. He hadn't been surprised when he saw what the books were. I'd watched his face carefully as he took them from Mr Gordon and I could tell. I think he'd known from the beginning what we were going to find waiting for us in Holywell Street.

That still didn't mean he *understood*. 'Naughty, as the title suggests,' he'd said, watching me flip the books open before I stuffed them in my bag. 'But hardly the sort of thing that gets a man murdered.'

'Maybe not here.'

'Really? You think this might be a motive?'

'If the Two Naughty Pupils are those young women I told you about, and either of their fathers found out about this, then yes.'

'Wouldn't they simply have carried out one of your nocturnal processions? Humiliated him? Warned him off?'

'No. Because everybody knew the girls worked with him. There'd never have been an end to the gossip and rumours.'

Mr Gelyot had nodded. 'Still, I suppose this puts paid to your blackmail idea. Whatever Rowland knew about this Caldicot, he couldn't have been blackmailing him if Caldicot knew about this, surely?'

I thought about that as I waited on the platform at Paddington Station. If the 'other gentleman' was Caldicot then he and Rowland must've known each other well. Been friends, even. Which explained the fifty pounds in the school fund. Caldicot had good reason to deny any friendship once Rowland was dead, though, didn't he? If what was in my bag had become public knowledge, he'd have wanted to make sure he wasn't associated with it in any way.

But he was associated with it. So, as far as I could see, his campaign to be coroner was over. All Harry had to do was show Caldicot these books and tell him that Mr Gordon had recognised my description of him. Being a party to this sort of thing – especially as it'd involved Nan and Ruth – wasn't compatible with holding public office.

Harry

Try as he might, Minnever could not persuade the Tory camp that Caldicot's cryptic note represented a withdrawal from the election; they insisted that, unless and until he formally withdrew his candidacy, Caldicot's name would go to the nomination meeting.

Minnever, inevitably, took this as our cue to get down to some serious canvassing and I am certain that he would have displayed me on the streets of Cardigan until nightfall, had Lydia not sought me out.

'Twm's come from Glanteifi to take us back,' she said. 'Phoebe Gwatkyn's there and she's keen to see you urgently.'

–

The homeward journey was a good deal less awkward than the outward one as Phoebe Gwatkyn's unexpected arrival at the mansion freed us into speculation, and both Lydia and I arrived at Glanteifi in good spirits.

We found the lady of Alltybela in the drawing room with my housekeeper, Mrs Griffiths. I scarcely had enough time to wonder how the two women came to be sitting by the fire like boon companions, before Mrs Griffiths rose from her chair.

'Mr Probert-Lloyd, you're back!'

I knew that she would not dream of calling me Harry in front of a guest so I bore her formality with the best smile I could muster.

'I'll go and have some tea and *bara brith* sent up,' she said. 'You must both be hungry after that drive home.'

As she made for the door, Miss Gwatkyn said, in Welsh, 'Thank you so much for indulging me, Mrs Griffiths. It's been delightful talking to you about the history of the house.'

The door closed behind Isabel Griffiths and apprehension pulled at me: had they been discussing Glanteifi's history or mine? Mrs Griffiths would have found it far easier to maintain the proprieties had they been speaking in English; in Welsh they could easily have been two middle-aged women talking about a boy they were both fond of.

Phoebe Gwatkyn and Lydia began talking like old friends and I found myself having to stifle the feeling that my home had been annexed by women. However, once our tea and cake had been put on a small table before the fire, and the quality of both *bara brith* and butter had been complimented, Phoebe Gwatkyn came to the point and I was the coroner once more.

'As I believe you know, Ruth Eynon has been staying with me since the funeral. She and Nan Walters have begun teaching the children again but I've still had ample opportunity to speak to her.' Miss Gwatkyn's pause had the quality of a well-directed stare. 'I'm quite sure that her claim to have been engaged to be married to Nicholas Rowland is a fabrication.'

I waited for her to elaborate but Lydia, seeing perhaps that Miss Gwatkyn required some prompting, asked, 'Can you tell us why?'

Miss Gwatkyn placed her cup and saucer on the occasional table at her elbow. 'There are several reasons, some of which have nothing to do with Ruth Eynon, but her own account of their supposed courtship has reinforced my suspicions. She described numerous occasions when she and Nicholas were together – alone – during which their fondness developed. What she does not know is that Nicholas was in London – occasionally accompanying me – on many of the occasions she claims for herself.' There was a brief pause during which something seemed to pass between her and Lydia. 'High days and holidays and so forth. Added to which, Nicholas and I had agreed that he would never allow himself to be alone with either Nan or Ruth. Both he and I had far too much consideration for their reputation to allow such a thing. They were educated young women; they could expect to make advantageous marriages and I was keen to ensure that nothing stood in the way of that.'

'But, from what they told John and me when we interviewed them, neither girl aspired to marriage. They had their minds set on independence as teachers.'

'They are, as yet, very young.'

Miss Gwatkyn's somewhat repressive tone surprised me; I would have expected her to support Nan and Ruth's ambitions unequivocally.

'But it's not simply that,' she said, her voice softening and becoming more hesitant. 'There is another reason why I felt, from the beginning, that Ruth's claim was false.'

She reached for her teacup once more, and, as she took a sip, I saw Lydia put a hand out to her as if to offer reassurance.

'I'm aware of the rumours that circulated about Nicholas and me,' Miss Gwatkyn went on. 'But they demonstrate that, even though people are apt to allow their imaginations to run unchecked, they are, in other ways, almost entirely unimaginative.'

I said nothing, simply waited for the explanation she was edging towards.

'I knew, from the first time I met him, what kind of man Nicholas Rowland was. In fact, I suspected it before I met him.' There was a tremor in Phoebe Gwatkyn's voice. 'Because he came to Llanddewi Brefi on my husband's recommendation. And I know what kind of man my husband is.'

I stared at her. I could not help myself. Though she instantly disappeared into the oblivion of the whirlpool, my eyes instinctively sought out her face because I realised what she meant and, suddenly, many of the things we had learned slipped into place like the pieces of a Chinese puzzle.

'He's a man who prefers the physical attentions of other men to those of women,' I said. 'Isn't he?'

John

On the train, an hour went by before I could bring myself to open my bag and take one of the books out. And I wouldn't have done it then if any of the other people in the carriage had been close enough to see what I was reading. I felt as if I had a stray cat on my knees. It might lie there quietly before I touched it but, when I did, I feared what it might do to me.

What the Girls Found was the thickest of the three books. The other two – *Tales from the Western Shore, or a Young Man's Awakening* and *Two Rollicking Lads, Scenes of London Life* looked as if they'd be easier to get through. At least as far as the number of pages was concerned.

I'd had enough of London for now, so I opened *Tales from the Western Shore* and – though I started it with one eye closed, so to speak – within a minute, I was as absorbed as if I'd been reading a penny blood. It might be 'erotic' but it was also the story of a young man and I found myself pulled in by it.

Every now and then I'd look up and be surprised to see fields and countryside outside the train. The small port in *Tales from the Western Shore* – which was never given a name but was Aberaeron to a 't' – was described in such lifelike detail that I was there.

The ship's chandlery featured, too, as a trysting place. Amorous adventures took place by moonlight among the barrels of slippery fish oil and boxes of stiff white candles. But the 'awakenings' weren't confined to the shop. They took place in gently tossing boats; on warm, yielding sand; in the unexplored crevices of dark and dripping caves – there seemed to be nowhere within a day's walk of Aberaeron where the Young Man hadn't had some adventure or another. With girls and boys.

An hour later, I'd finished the book and a lot of things had become clear. The young man of the western shore was obviously Nicholas Rowland, and now I knew why he'd been estranged from his father. The old man'd deliberately dropped a loaded crate on Nicholas's hands after seeing them wrapped around another boy's cock. Rowland junior had left and never once looked back.

Of course, after reading *Tales from the Western Shore*, I knew what to expect when I opened the *Rollicking Lads*. The plot, such as it was, was a bit different and all the 'scenes' happened in London – sometimes spied on by the Lads and sometimes involving them – but, just like the characters in the *Western Shore*, everybody seemed to be having a high old time.

By the time we reached Bristol, I'd finished the adventures of the rollicking lads and started on *What the Girls Found*, where I read how the Naughty Pupils – Nan and Ruth, renamed Bess and Mary – had gone up to their teacher's loft one summer's day while they were waiting for him to come and tutor them.

Curious as to the literature with which their beloved mentor beguiles his leisure hours, our heroines lightly peruse the small store of books to be found in his poor bookcase.

I remembered that bookcase. Built out of books and a plank. And, of course, the titles hadn't meant anything to me at the time. But Gus Gelyot'd pointed one of them out to me in Wych Street. *Fanny Hill*. Of course, that was all that'd been written on the spine and, when I saw the book in Rowland's loft, I'd passed over it. Thought it was just another one of the Jane Eyre and Mary Barton brigade. It was only when I'd seen its title page spread wide in the Wych Street window that I'd realised it was *The Memoirs of a Woman of Pleasure.*

If that subtitle'd appeared on the spine as well as inside, our investigation into Nicholas Rowland's death would've been very different. We'd have asked a lot more questions about Mr Wonderful Rowland. And perhaps we'd have been a bit quicker to listen to Llew Price, too.

But the naughty girls had been more curious than me.

'Fanny Hill,' cried Bess, 'I once had a friend called Fanny!' And she slipped the book from amongst its fellows and opened it at the first narrative page.'

Before I got off the train, I'd read enough of *What the Girls Found* to start to worry that the suspicions the *Mabinogi* had raised might not've been so fanciful after all. What exactly had happened to Nan Walters and Ruth Eynon in that loft? Where did real life end, in this book, and fantasy begin? Because, if Rowland and the girls had got up to all the things described, then Ruth Eynon very definitely had a claim on a marriage contract from him. Come to that, so did Nan Walters. Mind, whether either of them would've wanted him, given what the girls in the book'd spied their teacher doing with another man, was another matter. And the same could be said of *their* marriageability; I'd never be able to hear the term 'intimate friends' again without blushing.

In my mind, there couldn't be much doubt that the girls'd been responsible for writing the books with Nicholas Rowland. Who else could've done it? There was weeks and months of work here in these books and there'd been nobody else who could've helped him – his friend Caldicot had only recently come back from London. So, even if Nan and Ruth'd just written what he dictated and had no part in the actual invention, they weren't the good little girls they pretended to be, were they?

–

That night, back in the same Bristol garret, I lit the same lamp at the same ridiculous extra price and sat down on the bed with the parcel containing Nicky Revell's latest work.

I cut the string with my penknife and unfolded the paper to find three books and an envelope containing banknotes. The books were identical. All three were bound in green leather embossed in gold, just like Miss Guest's *Mabinogi*; much more handsome than the other erotic books which'd been pretty cheaply produced.

The gold lettering on the front read *Amorous Celtic Tales of Long Ago*. And, when I flipped the book open and looked at the title page, there was the sub-title: *The Ancient Tales of the Mabinogi Re-told for Cosmopolitan Gentlemen*. It reminded me of the book in Gordon's window – *The Amorous Adventures of a Thousand Arabian Nights by A Sloe-Eyed Seductress*. I'd never read the original *Arabian Nights* stories but I was pretty sure they weren't considered to be erotic literature. Presumably, using old tales and adding elements that would appeal to 'cosmopolitan gentlemen' was easier than making up your own.

I stared at the *Amorous Celtic Tales*. I didn't want to read it. Because, now I knew what erotic literature was, I could imagine how the tales of the *Mabinogi* would be re-told.

The people in Nicky Revell's other books had all been willing – no, *eager* – participants in the goings-on. But that wasn't the case in the *Mabinogi*, was it? There were forced marriages, rape, incest. I didn't want to read about those. Especially not in the kind of anatomical detail that Nicky Revell was fond of.

But, however much I disliked the prospect, I couldn't go home and admit to Harry that I hadn't even opened it. I wanted to be able to look him in the eye – even if he couldn't see me doing it – and tell him exactly what use Rowland'd made of the tales Miss Gwatkyn set so much store by. Exactly how much of a motive these books represented for anybody who cared about the girls.

I wasn't going to have Harry think that I was too weak, too – what was the word Mr Schofield'd been so fond of? – *pusillanimous* to do what needed to be done by a coroner's officer.

Putting the moment off, I looked around the dismal little room. The window in the eaves caught the lamplight and I saw my own dim reflection. My specs magnified my eyes and made them look huge. Like a calf's. Or a girl's.

Nan Walters and Ruth Eynon had written the words in this book. If they could do that, I could read it.

Harry

'Leo was my art master,' Miss Gwatkyn said. 'My father had undertaken most of my education himself but he was sufficiently concerned about my place in society to understand that I needed the accomplishments of a lady. So he employed a music master who tutored me at the piano and, once I had mastered that, an art master.' She sighed. 'We got on famously.'

Having been educated at home and denied much experience of the world, it was, perhaps, not surprising that the youthful Phoebe Gwatkyn had fallen in love with the first eligible man to pay her any attention.

'My father was away a great deal and, though he might have realised that I needed to learn the arts of refinement, he failed to remember that I might also need chaperoning and Leo and I were left alone a good deal. He always behaved like a perfect gentleman but I was not to be refused. I told him that I wanted to marry him, however much he was 'not the marrying kind'. I didn't know what he meant, of course, and, at first, he was too careful of my tender sensibilities to tell me. I thought that, if I showered enough love upon him, he would see that he *was* the marrying kind. At least where I was concerned.

Eventually, he was forced to tell me the truth in the hope that I would desist. But even that could not make me stop loving him. I told him that I just wanted to be with him and that, if he married me, he could leave off being a tutor and paint as he wanted to. That we could move to London.'

'So his illness – Italy – is a necessary fiction?' I asked.

'No! Not at all. He is ill – or at least, he *was* when we lived in London. Not at first. At the beginning, we managed to be happy together. He did love me, in his way, and did his best to fulfil his end of the bargain. We had a child – a son – Justin.

I called him Iestyn. Leo *adored* him. Couldn't believe that he'd had a part in creating such a beautiful child. We were happy,' she repeated.

'But he betrayed you?' I said.

Miss Gwatkyn sighed. 'Leo couldn't betray me. I knew from the beginning what he was, what he would do. It was understood between us. Accepted. He would love me as best he could but—'

I saw her hands clasp in her lap, as if she were looking for comfort and had nobody but herself to provide it.

'No, the thing that destroyed our marriage was the death of our son.'

At four years old, little Justin had fallen ill. A sudden, unexplained fatigue and sickness had been swiftly followed by convulsions, unconsciousness and death.

'The doctors could do nothing. We had to watch as he slipped away from us.'

Despite all the deaths I had recently investigated, I had never heard a person sound so utterly desolate and I wondered if Miss Gwatkyn's profound sadness – only now revealed to me – was written on her face, plain for those with sight to see.

'My heart was broken. First by my son's death and then by Leo's decision to move to Italy. He had begun to cough before, but grief accelerated his illness. He said he couldn't stay in London, couldn't stay with me, that everything in our life together reminded him of Justin.'

She sat there, at the very edge of my vision, a small figure in a plain gown, a shawl about her shoulders. I wondered if her furred boots hid beneath the blanket which Mrs Griffiths had put over her guest's lap to keep out the drawing room's draughts.

'My father had recently died so, as Lady of Alltybela, I could leave London and come home without attracting too much comment. And, being ill, it struck nobody as odd that Leo would go to Italy for his health.

'So the die was cast. And thus it has remained for almost twenty years. I go to Italy to see Leo every winter. We are careful with each other. We talk about our son, the man he would be now. We cry. We walk about Naples. And I come home. Leo comes to London when he has paintings to sell and sometimes we see each other then, too. We remain married and neither of us wishes it otherwise. I have Alltybela and its people. He has Naples and his painting and such companionship as he chooses.'

I sat, watching the small, still figure, unable to think of a single thing to say.

Lydia, of course, spoke the words that should have come from me. 'Miss Gwatkyn, I am so very sorry.'

'Thank you, my dear. They say that time heals, but some things do not and should not heal. The extremity of grief for a child fades, of course. But the wound caused by such a death never truly heals. If it did, it would be to deny his place in my heart.'

'It hardly seems appropriate,' Lydia continued, 'after such a sad story, to ask you about Nicholas Rowland...'

Phoebe Gwatkyn unclasped her hands and laid them flat on her lap as if preparing to rise. 'Not at all. I came to try and help. Please ask whatever you like and I will answer if I can.'

'You said that Nicholas Rowland came here at your husband's recommendation,' Lydia began. 'Did they know each other well?'

Did a look pass between the two women as an acknowledgement of the delicacy of this question?

'I believe they had known each other some while,' Miss Gwatkyn replied. 'There is a club, in London, to which both Leo and Nicholas belonged.'

She paused and I felt an acute discomfort. Was she looking at me, waiting for some sign?

'Was the school Rowland's idea?' I asked, my voice creaky with embarrassment. 'Or your husband's?'

Miss Gwatkyn drew in an audible breath, as if she had a long story to tell.

'Leo wrote to me after the publication of the Commissioners' Report. He told me that his friend, Nicholas Rowland, was incensed to the point of fury by it. That he wanted to do something to counter the prejudice and calumnies it contained. To establish a school that would act as a beacon for Welsh education.' She broke off to raise what must surely, by now, have been a cup of stone-cold tea to her lips. 'Leo knew that the Unitarians had a strong presence in the area and that, as a denomination, they take a great interest in education. So he suggested that Nicholas consider setting his school in Llanddewi Brefi. When Nicholas heard about the history of education in the area, he decided that it was the perfect spot.'

'Who did he hear that history from?' I asked. 'Was it from your husband, or did Montague Caldicot tell him?'

Miss Gwatkyn's teacup rattled as she replaced it on its saucer, betraying feelings to me which must already have been quite evident to Lydia. 'Nicholas was always very discreet. He told me that a gentleman with family in Cardiganshire supported the idea and had written letters of introduction for him, in the hope that other county families would support the school. But he never mentioned the gentleman by name.'

Given the action for which Caldicot had been cashiered, surely the club Nicholas Rowland and Leo Barton had belonged to must also be the link between Rowland and Caldicot?

'But I think you must be right,' Phoebe Gwatkyn continued, 'about Montague Caldicot's support. A few months ago, Nicholas confided in me that, after an encouraging start, enthusiasm for the collegiate school had begun to dwindle amongst the gentry. I assumed it was because of Tobias Hildon's campaign for a National School and Nicholas did not contradict me. But now that their association is clear, I do wonder whether, in fact, Montague's disgrace might have been the reason. You can appreciate that families might not want to be associated with something he championed.'

There was a knock at the door, followed by the scurrying figure of one of our maids, Elsie. Offering entirely superfluous apologies, she took one of the spills of tightly-rolled newspaper from the pot on the mantelpiece and proceeded to light the lamps. Lydia, seeing what she was about, lifted a lamp glass to raise the wick and check the oil. She would soon learn that Mrs Griffiths insisted on the lamps being seen to every morning, when the fires were laid.

'You don't need to get your hands dirty, Miss Howell,' Elsie said, an edge of reproach in her voice. 'That's my job.'

I waited for Lydia to argue but she simply said, 'I'm sorry, Elsie. You're quite right, of course.'

The room lit, the girl left, but the lighting of the lamps was a reminder that, before long, we would be called in to dinner. I wished to finish this conversation before we were interrupted.

'You won't yet be aware, Miss Gwatkyn,' I began, 'but Montague Caldicot absented himself from the public meeting in Cardigan today, having sent me a note regretting that he must *leave it to me*. Nobody knows where he is.'

'Leave it to you? What did he mean by that?'

'I don't know. He might have meant the meeting. Or the whole campaign.' I paused in case she wished to respond but she said nothing. 'His agent, of course, is refusing to see it in those terms. He's insisting that the election proceeds towards the nomination meeting on Saturday.'

'But you don't think Montague will be back?'

I hesitated. The conversation had already taken turns I could not have foreseen and I was loath to push it still further beyond the bounds of decency. And yet… Miss Gwatkyn had come to see me of her own free will and had volunteered the information about her husband and her marriage in the same spirit. 'His disappearance came,' I said, feeling my way, 'after I told him that John Davies had gone to London in search of information that might see Rowland's inquest re-opened.'

In my peripheral vision, Phoebe Gwatkyn did not move. She simply sat, her back straight, a now redundant cup and saucer clasped in her lap, waiting for me to continue. Did she know what I was going to ask her next?

'I believe that Mr Caldicot knew – or feared – what John might find when he went to London. That whatever it was would destroy his reputation.'

'And, as a consequence, he would be forced to withdraw from the election?'

'At least that. Alternatively, that facts might come to light which, were they to be made public, would ensure that he had no future here.' *Or, perhaps, no future in the world at all.*

'What facts?' For the first time, Miss Gwatkyn sounded troubled. 'Do you believe that Montague Caldicot had something to do with Nicholas's death?'

I shifted in my chair, profoundly wishing that I could ask my next question of anybody but this small, extraordinary woman.

'As you know,' I began, 'the inquest heard that Mr Rowland had been observed going out, quite often, after dark. We can only assume that he was meeting somebody. Given certain other information I have received, together with what you have told us about Mr Rowland's—' I hesitated. '*Preferences*, it may be that he was meeting Montague Caldicot. Do you have any reason to believe that might be true?'

Miss Gwatkyn shifted slightly and something about her posture seemed stiffer, less at ease. In the lengthening silence, I had the impression that she was ordering her thoughts, perhaps understanding certain things for the first time.

'Nicholas had been more cheerful of late,' she ventured, finally. 'Despite the falling-away of support for his school. Despite Tobias Hildon's increasingly vociferous opposition to it. When I commented on it, he told me that plans were afoot to secure the school's future and that all would be well.' She paused and, when she spoke again, it was as if she had allowed Nicholas Rowland to redirect her thoughts. 'I know Montague Caldicot's wife is wealthy. Do you think he had promised significant sums to Nicholas's school?'

I would have given a week of my life to be able to exchange a look with Lydia, to have seen, in her eyes, a reflection of my own suspicions.

No. That is not what I think at all. Whatever the relationship between Montague Caldicot and Nicholas Rowland might have been, I think Caldicot panicked at what your friend knew and what it could do to his political career and murdered him.

John

All the way home – on the steamer to Carmarthen and on the road to Glanteifi – I found myself thinking about the *Amorous Celtic Tales*. The *Mabinogi* but very definitely *not* the *Mabinogi* at the same time.

Same events, same people. But in Nicky Revell's hands they'd become something very different. And I don't just mean more explicit about the intimate goings-on.

It was as if somebody with Harry's views about equality and a taste for very florid erotic descriptions had written the *Amorous Celtic Tales*. In this version, the women of the *Mabinogi* had stepped out of the shadows cast by the men, grabbed hold of the stories by the scruff of the neck and shaken them into a different shape. The women weren't just characters in the stories any more, they'd taken charge. They weren't pushed into marriages. They weren't mistreated or raped. They were powerful creatures who took their pleasure where they chose and did as they wished. They were equal – if not superior – to the men.

As I walked up from Carmarthen docks to the livery stable in town, I thought how even the servant-girl Goewin – King Math's virgin foot-holder – had been transformed. In Nicky Revell's version, instead of being raped by Gilfaethwy after he'd started a war in Dyfed to occupy his uncle and leave her defenceless, Goewin commanded Gilfaethwy to start the war, as a test. If he was determined and ruthless enough to do that, then she'd allow him into her bed. According to the *Amorous Tales*, Goewin was no virgin and it hadn't been King Math's feet she'd been holding.

But, when I thought about it, the original stories hadn't had to be changed all that much to put the women in charge. Hardly at all, in fact.

Branwen and Goewin might've been badly treated but Rhiannon, Blodeuwedd and Arianrhod had all turned difficult circumstances to their own advantage and done more or less as they wanted.

Rowland and the girls had seen what I'd been too blinded by rape and incest and treachery to see — that the tales of the *Mabinogi* were full of women who were powerful and resourceful and clever.

They were the Odysseus of the tales while the men were more or less all Achilles. The women did the thinking and manipulating and the men did the acting.

Was that why Miss Gwatkyn was so fond of them — because she'd seen the women's hidden power?

The *Amorous Celtic Tales* had given the women of the *Mabinogi* the only thing they lacked — authority over men. Well, that and utter shamelessness when it came to taking their pleasure.

I thought about what the Naughty Pupils had got up to. About Goewin stripping Gilfaethwy of his war-gear until he stood before her, cock-standing nakedness revealed. Was that what women were really like?

I thought again about the photographs I'd seen in Wych Street. Much as they'd disgusted me, they were only showing the truth. Because that *was* what women — young, beautiful women, at any rate — looked like under their clothes, wasn't it?

So were the *Amorous Tales* also telling the truth — did women manage to wield power even when they had no authority?

As soon as I asked the question, I realised that, of course, some obviously did. Like Mrs Parry, the shipbuilder of Tresaith who we'd tangled with when we were investigating the death of her business partner, Jenkyn Hughes. And Miss Gwatkyn, obviously, though she was in a man's position, as squire. But then there were the ladies like the Olive Leaf Circle in Tregaron. I remembered what Harry'd said after he'd come back from his meeting with them – that they might not have the vote but the ladies made it their business to be informed, so that they could influence the way their husbands voted. And, in the end, who was more powerful, the informed one or the one who put his mark on the voting paper?

What about Nan and Ruth? Were they just the lucky girls everybody painted them – girls fortunate to have been recommended to Nicholas Rowland by Miss Gwatkyn – or had they been as resourceful as the women in the *Mabinogi* and done everything they could to make sure they were the obvious choices? Maybe they'd even put the idea of recommending them into Miss Gwatkyn's head without her knowing it.

In *What the Girls Saw*, Bess and Mary had been intrigued and excited by what they'd read in *Fanny Hill* and wanted to try it out themselves. But what had really happened when Ruth and Nan discovered the book on Rowland's bookshelf? Whose idea had it been to write the books in my bag – Nicholas Rowland's or the girls'?

My bet was on the girls but I knew what Harry'd say. He'd say that Rowland had corrupted them, that it would never've occurred to Nan and Ruth to do such a thing unless Rowland had manipulated them into it. He'd say they'd only gone along with it because money'd stopped coming in for their collegiate school and they were so desperate to see it a reality.

But that was Harry and his tendency to see women through rose-coloured specs. The truth of the matter was that those girls might choose to speak English and give themselves airs but they weren't ladies and they hadn't had the upbringing of innocents.

Ruth was a farm girl. She'd grown up surrounded by animals – she knew exactly what Gilfaethwy and his brother had been forced to do by their animal natures when Math had cursed them to be deer, then swine, then wolves. And, on a farm big enough to have a few male and female servants, she'd more than likely have observed other things, too. The Rollicking Lads weren't the only ones who could hide in dark corners and spy on courting couples.

And what Nan Walters might've seen and heard in the lane at the back of the Three Horseshoes was anybody's guess. Llanddewi Brefi might be a small village but the oldest profession's plied everywhere.

What if Nan and Ruth had got fed up with being Rowland's assistants, with being the neat writers of letters and manuscripts that everybody thought were from him? What if they'd got tired of being overlooked and decided to claim some power for themselves?

If they'd decided to do that, maybe they'd also decided that they didn't need Nicholas Rowland any more.

Harry

On Friday morning, I met with Minnever at his hotel in Newcastle Emlyn over breakfast and told him I would not be available for canvassing after the public meeting in town.

'I'm afraid it can't be helped,' I said, in response to his inevitable protestations. 'I know we'd agreed to ride to Lampeter together tomorrow morning but my plans have changed and I must go there today.'

'Listen to me, Harry. If there's the slightest chance that whatever it is will prevent you being at the nomination meeting *on the dot* of midday tomorrow, you'd better change your plans back again. I'm not having a Caldicot on my hands!'

I shook my head. I had not wished to tell him as I knew what his reaction would be but there was little point trying to keep the truth from him – he would find out the following day, anyway.

'Nicholas Rowland's will is being read at ten.'

'Harry, we *agreed*!' Minnever's agitation propelled him to his feet. 'The inquest is done! You have to let the police make their case at trial.'

'Which will either result in an acquittal and the case being abandoned or in Jonathan Eynon being hanged for something he didn't do,' I said, striving for a calm I did not feel. 'Either way, the real killer is left at large.'

Minnever was still on his feet, looking down at me. 'You don't know Eynon's not the killer.'

'All the evidence points elsewhere.'

'It's still not your responsibility!'

But it was. It was my responsibility because I had failed to conduct a competent inquest.

Minnever sighed heavily and sat down once more, pushing his breakfast plate away, the meal unfinished.

'I assume there's no news of Caldicot?' I asked.

Minnever called to a servant and ordered coffee for us both before responding. 'No. None whatsoever.'

Though I had been plagued by fears for Caldicot's safety since receiving his 'I must leave it to you' note, I could not deny that I felt a little cheered by the thought that I would not have to contend with his opposition this morning.

'What did Crowther say when you told him you knew why Caldicot'd been cashiered?' I waited. 'Minnever?'

'I didn't tell him.'

'Why not?'

Minnever pulled his watch out of his pocket, consulted it, then replaced it. Given his air of distraction, I would have been ready to offer a considerable sum against anybody who thought he now knew the time.

'Two reasons,' he said, finally. 'Firstly,' he leaned over the table so that I could hear his lowered voice, 'there's a significant chance that Caldicot has taken himself off somewhere and put a bullet in his brain and if I started slinging mud about it could look very distasteful.' He leaned back, slightly, as if he was relieved to have got that off his chest. 'And, secondly, it occurred to me that the Tories might be playing a clever game and keeping him out of the public eye.'

'To what end?'

Minnever leaned forward once more, submerging himself completely in the whirlpool. 'What if they already know why he was cashiered and were planning to call our bluff if we found out?'

'In what way *could* they call our bluff?'

'By having Caldicot stand on the hustings, admit his *act of omission* and dare you to say that you'd have behaved differently.'

I leaned back and moved my eyes to one side, but I could still see nothing of Minnever, his outline was simply silhouetted against the window behind him.

'If he stood there and faced you down, could you honestly claim that you'd have marched those men straight to the authorities?'

I had hoped for a supportive crowd in my home town and the people of Newcastle Emlyn did not disappoint me. As I walked to the stage – placed in front of the church so as to be well out of the way of the market which, as always on a Friday, was taking place in the main square – I was cheered to the echo; and my speech – in which, once again, I referred to Caldicot's absence and resisted the temptation to speak ill of him – could not have been better received had I been coached by Cicero.

Deputising for his candidate, the Tory agent spoke briefly, suggesting that the proof of the matter was not in fine words but in votes cast at the poll.

'Oh, it's easy to be here, today,' he sneered in the face of the crowd's taunts, 'when you've come to town for the market anyway and somebody's shoved a blue ribbon into your hand or a young lady's pinned it to your lapel, but what about tomorrow when you've got to turn out again to actually vote? That's when the men'll be separated from the boys. That's when the Tories'll come out. Because they understand duty!'

To me, it seemed an irascible and ill-judged speech; a challenge to the voters to turn out for me.

'Just shows how rattled they are,' Minnever said, when I shared my thoughts with him.

I hoped he was right.

–

Having submitted myself to an hour or so of glad-handing with voters to pacify Minnever, I quit the crowded high street and went to collect my little mare from the stables at the Emlyn Arms hotel.

I smiled and waved at the crowds whose faces I could not see, then, as soon as I was over the bridge and alone, I exhaled the breath I seemed to have been holding all morning and allowed myself to slump in the saddle. I felt utterly drained. My face was cramped from maintaining a smile, and the effort of keeping people in my peripheral vision while trying not to walk into pigs and sheep had given me a headache.

Letting the little mare find her own pace, I breathed in the warm spring air and enjoyed the peace and quiet of the Llandyfriog road until I reached the point where Lydia was waiting with the box cart. Though propriety had to be observed until the election was over, we had agreed that taking the carriage all the way to Lampeter would be both uncomfortable and a waste of Twm's time.

I dismounted, tied Seren to the back of the cart and climbed up next to Lydia. The road ran very near to the Teifi at that point and the river's quiet flow, just down the willow-hung bank, was like balm to my battered senses. There is something infinitely soothing about the slow, stately progress of a river, something simultaneously ageless and constantly renewed that calms the soul.

'That's a very splendid rosette,' Lydia remarked as I took my seat.

'Minnever insists,' I said, unpinning it from my lapel and stuffing it into my pocket.

She laughed softly at my discomfiture. 'He'd be negligent if he didn't.'

'I know. And he's been very assiduous, I can't say otherwise. But I think even he's realised that there are limits to what it's appropriate to do or say.'

As we set off, I told her about Minnever's reservations about confronting the Tories, given Caldicot's continued absence.

'I thought your tone had something of the eulogy when you spoke about him,' she said. 'But don't you think we'd have heard if anything had happened to him?'

Splashes of colour appeared in the trailing edge of my peripheral vision as we jogged past violet- and primrose-filled hedges. 'Not if he's drowned himself.'

'A soldier? Throw himself into the river like a ruined house-maid?'

'Drownings can always be written off as misadventure. It would spare his family the scandal.'

'Which scandal are you referring to?' she asked, turning to look at me. 'Suicide, his possible implication in Rowland's death or his sexual inclinations?'

She spoke the words as if they were part of everyday conversation and I tried to respond in the same manner. 'Any or all of the above.'

Lydia did not reply, simply turned her gaze back to the road. From what I could see, she held the reins easily and the horse trotted along without fuss.

'Do you really think he would have killed Rowland if there was a tenderness between them?' she asked.

'*Tenderness?*'

She made an impatient noise as if I had said something facile. 'You think men like that – like Rowland and Leo Barton – are merely indulging a physical appetite? That two men couldn't possibly feel, for each other, the tenderness that you felt for Margaret Jones?' She was not asking; she was correcting me. 'Judgement is easy. But walk a mile in a man's shoes before you condemn him, Harry. Don't judge him for being unable to wear yours.'

Thus chastised, I could think of no response and we continued in silence. But my mind was busy. Exactly what did Lydia know of such things? Had her dead brother confided in her? Or had the life she lived before our meeting in Ipswich informed her in ways I could only imagine?

As we bowled along, the horses' hoof beats unhurried in the warm air, I tried to put aside my instinctive reactions and confront Lydia's question with an open mind. Could one man feel for another what I had felt for Margaret? The sticking point, I found, was the word Lydia had used. Tenderness. Lust, I could imagine. Desire, even. But the feeling of protective fondness I had felt for Margaret, that simultaneous, adolescent desire to possess her and to die for her if necessary? Both flesh and feeling rebelled against the idea that I might feel such emotions for someone of my own sex.

'I know you don't believe in Jonathan Eynon's guilt,' Lydia said. 'But have you considered his likely reaction if, somehow, he'd got wind of how things stood between Rowland and Caldicot?'

'We don't know, definitively, that there *was* anything between them.'

'Rowland was meeting somebody under cover of darkness,' she said. 'We know that from Billy Walters's testimony. And Caldicot had written introductory letters for him and given him a substantial sum of money. Yet, he denies anything more than a slight acquaintance with Rowland. He's hiding something.' She paused. 'And, if there was nothing between them, why did Caldicot slip in to the inquest?'

'To observe me.'

'Do you really believe that? Or are you simply struggling to believe that one man might love another?'

Not wishing to be thought either vain or narrow-minded, I did not reply.

'If Jonathan Eynon – a man known to have an uncontrollable temper – heard that he was being thrown over in favour of a man who couldn't even be a proper husband to the girl he'd expected to marry, don't you think he might have reacted violently?'

The horse between the shafts slowed to a walk on a sharp incline and the sudden loss of speed made me feel unaccountably cautious.

'Eynon told me about the fight that got him his reputation for a violent temper,' I said. 'He wanted me to believe that, by the time he was pulled away from the man he was beating, he didn't know what he was doing any more.' I watched her out of the corner of my eye. 'If that's true, d'you think it would excuse him if the man'd died?'

Lydia responded without hesitation and I knew that I had succeeded in moving us from the uncertainties of desire to solid philosophical ground.

'Always assuming that Eynon was telling truth, I suppose it would depend on whether that was the first time it'd happened. If he'd never experienced such an animal rage before, then he might be less culpable because he couldn't have predicted his loss of self-control.'

'Then, using that logic, if he'd confronted Rowland and lost his temper, he'd have had no excuse because he would've known exactly what might happen.'

'Exactly.'

I nodded. 'So, to turn your question back on you, is that what you think happened? Or are you just struggling to accept that a man who loved another man might kill him?'

As I had hoped, she laughed. 'Touché, Harry! Touché.'

After all the travelling and strange beds, back at Glanteifi I slept like a puppy and I was up and about in the greyish half-light before sunrise to follow Harry and Lydia to Lampeter.

Somebody'd taken the dirty linen out of my bag while I ate dinner the evening before, so I repacked, had as much breakfast as could be got ready for me in ten minutes and went out into the stableyard. I'd asked Twm which horse'd be the best to take me twenty miles in a hurry and the big gelding that'd been old Mr Probert-Lloyd's favourite was saddled and waiting for me.

If you wanted the perfect day for people to come out and vote, this was it. The sky got bluer and bluer as we cantered up the Teifi Valley and the breeze lost its chilly early-morning edge and warmed up nicely. Voters would be setting their sons and servants to work and trotting off down to Lampeter to cast their vote in droves.

—

Lampeter was already a hive of greetings and gossip, chatter and excitement by the time I arrived, even though it was only just gone ten o'clock. People were coming from all directions, like bees to a clover field, ribbons and rosettes on almost every breast. The party committees'd obviously been busy. And, in the middle of the town, on the square where the Newcastle Emlyn and Tregaron roads met, the hustings platform was draped in what looked like furlongs of red and blue cloth.

Minnever saw me and darted over. 'John! Thank God!'

He'd never been that pleased to see me before. Something wasn't right. He looked tired and I wondered if he'd been up even earlier than me. Gingerly, I dismounted to put me on the same level as him. 'Where's Harry?' I asked, trying to ignore the horrible aching in my legs and backside. 'Has he gone to the will reading?'

'Yes, damn it, he has! It seemed harmless enough to let him go because Caldicot still hadn't turned up, but things've changed in the last half an hour. I need you to go and fetch him.'

'Why?' As I asked the question, I looked about for a boy to take my horse to the livery stable, only half-listening for Minnever's answer. But, when it came, it got my attention like a bucket of cold water.

'The Tories are putting up another candidate.'

I forgot about livery. '*What?* Why?' Had the Tories got wind of what I'd discovered in London? But no, that wasn't it at all.

'Caldicot's disappeared. Hasn't appeared at the last two election meetings. The Tories are panicking.'

'But can they just decide to put someone else up, just like that?'

'Of course they can! This is the nomination meeting.' He waved a hand in the direction of the platform. 'Caldicot may have absented himself but that doesn't mean the Tories are going to throw the whole contest into Harry's lap. I need you to—'

'Hold on a minute, who's the new candidate?'

Minnever shook his head as if he'd rather be shaking me. 'He's some nonentity. Name of Verwick. That's all I know at the moment.'

I didn't recognise the name. But then I didn't exactly mix in those circles. Especially not in Lampeter. 'Then does it matter?' I asked. 'I mean, nobody's going to vote for somebody they don't know, are they?'

'The Tories aren't stupid!' Minnever was almost stamping his foot now. 'They'll have made sure he's somebody people *do* know! Here, at least. They've probably promised him that he can name a deputy as soon as he likes and fob all the work off on to him!' He stopped, pulled himself together. 'The truth is, they've got wind that Harry's in town for this will and they'll have written this Verwick's speech for him so he can go for Harry with all guns blazing. They'll say he's looking for a reason to re-open the inquest. That he's trying to undermine the inquest jury's decision – just like Caldicot said in Tregaron. And you know what?' His eyes started sifting through the crowd as if he was hunting for Tories. 'Men with the vote are the same men as those who get called on to sit on a jury. They'll be outraged at the thought that their decisions can be disregarded.'

He was right. We'd both seen the crowd's reaction when Caldicot had criticised Harry's response to Margaret Jones's inquest jury. We didn't want a repetition of that here.

'We can't wait till Harry's finished with this will,' Minnever said. 'We need him here *now*, talking to people, getting them on his side. I was going to go to the solicitor's office myself but he'll listen to you more than me.'

–

So Minnever went off to do whatever he had to do and, after collaring a boy and sending him off to the livery stables with a note for the ostler and a penny for him, I hurried up the street towards Silas Emmanuel's office. I wasn't intimidated by the grandness of it this time and I was about to march straight up to the door and get the knocker going when I spotted Billy Walters on the other side of the road.

Something about the way the boy was just standing there pulled me up and I went over to him. 'Waiting for your sister, are you?'

He nodded and his eyes flicked to me then back to the door across the street.

'Your father and mother in there with her?'

He gave me another quick glance. 'Just Dada. Mam's shopping.' The look he gave me told me he thought it was none of my business but he kept the words behind his teeth.

'How long've they been in there?'

He shrugged. 'How long does it take to read a will, anyway?'

'Longer than you'd think.' I'd been present at any number of will readings and I knew that there was no end to the questions people asked. Nor to the arguments they were prepared to have in front of a solicitor, come to that.

Plus, Harry'd be wanting to ask some questions of his own. About contracts with publishers and the sums accrued in different bank accounts. Not to mention what guidance might've been given about who could be entrusted with the money raised for the collegiate school.

Billy might have to cool his heels a while yet.

I was just on the point of leaving him to his sulk when he spoke up.

'My sister says she's getting money out of this will. Is that right?'

I couldn't tell what was behind his question. Did he think he'd be in line for some of the money himself? What with Nan still living in her father's house, Morgan Walters'd be the one deciding what happened to any money she got.

'I don't know,' I lied. 'Where'd she get that idea from?'

He glanced at me, then away. 'Says Teacher Rowland promised it to them.'

'That may be the case', I said, 'but I don't think they'll get any money to start with. I think it'll be a case of waiting to see whether anybody takes over Mr Rowland's idea for the collegiate school.'

'What if *they* do? Her and Ruth?'

'You think they'd try and put themselves in charge of such a big project?'

Billy shrugged. Trying to pretend he didn't care either way. But he did, I could see right through him. What I wasn't sure about was whether he really *wanted* to see it happen or really *didn't*.

'I don't know what Mr Rowland would've thought of that,' I said, watching him. 'From what I understand, he'd only thought of them being teachers at his school, not running it.'

Two men walked past us. Gave us a proper look up and down, too, but Billy spoke as if he hadn't seen them. 'Think that'd stop my sister and Ruth Eynon?'

I thought of the books I'd brought back from London, hidden under my mattress so the maids didn't find them. He was right. Not much would stop the Two Naughty Pupils.

As if he could see into my mind, Billy asked, 'Will it be enough? The money Rowland's left? Enough to start the school without—' He pulled himself up. 'Without raising any more?'

I stared at him. Did he mean what I thought he meant? *Without writing any more of those books?*

I thought of Billy listening under the window when we were interviewing his sister and Ruth, spying on Nicholas Rowland for Mattie Hughes, following the teacher after dark as he walked up to the Pontllanio road.

Had Billy snooped around the cowshed academy when Rowland was supposed to be tutoring Nan and Ruth? Had he heard what they were really doing?

'You spied on them, didn't you?' I said, trying to get Billy to look me in the eye. 'On Rowland and the girls.'

'I didn't spy—'

'It's all right! I understand. I've got a sister, too.' It didn't matter whether Sali-Ann was dead or alive. I *did* understand. As only a brother could. Your sister might drive you to taunts and blows but she's still your flesh and blood and nobody else is allowed to say a word against her or lay a finger on her. 'You were making sure nothing happened to her, weren't you? Because she's not always the wisest, is she, Nan? Bit hot-headed. Bit strong-willed.'

He shrugged, shoved his hands in his pockets.

'You watch out for her, don't you – keep an eye on what's going on?'

He flicked a glance at me.

'And you never trusted Nicholas Rowland, I suppose?' I was guessing, but maybe Nan's bossing him at school hadn't been the only reason Billy'd stuck with Mattie Hughes.

The boy shrugged again but his eyes told me I was right.

I looked away from him, turned my face up to the sun, as if I was just enjoying the warmth. As if I wasn't a breath away from the question that'd change everything.

'Did you know?' I asked. 'What Rowland and the girls were up to – writing those stories?'

His head whipped round and I caught the look of horror on his face but, just as I was about to press him, the door of Silas Emmanuel's office opened and Miss Gwatkyn stepped out.

Billy pushed himself away from the wall and ran across the road. If I didn't get the truth out of him now, I probably never would, so I jumped up and followed him.

'Billy!'

He spun round. 'Doesn't matter now, does it? He's dead. It's finished.'

I grabbed his arm. Everything had suddenly fallen into place in my mind. As if you'd thrown a handful of dice on the ground and they'd arranged themselves in a perfect sequence. One to six. I could see it all. Clear as day.

'Ruth came to your house that afternoon, didn't she? In a state about her and Shoni Goch. Did you spy on them? Were they both crying?'

I didn't need an answer. His face told me I was right.

They were all out in the street, now. The girls'd come out after Miss Gwatkyn, with Lydia, Harry and Morgan Walters following behind. And Montague Caldicot. Not missing after all.

I still had hold of Billy and I shook him to make him pay attention to me, not to the people on the solicitor's steps. 'You'd had enough of it, hadn't you? You went to confront Nicholas Rowland. You argued, got into a fight, pushed him out of the loft.' Billy's eyes went huge and his mouth gaped as if he was struggling for air but he didn't make a sound. 'But he got up off the ground, didn't he? Struggled up towards you. One arm hanging loose, maybe he was limping as well. Groggy from where his head'd hit the ground. He came towards you, hooking himself up the ladder—' I mimed the gesture with my left hand and saw the horrified look on Billy's face. 'You must've been scared out of your wits! What was he going to do to you? What was he going to say to your father? That you'd tried to kill him?'

Billy tried to pull his arm free and run away but I had him with both hands now.

'You pushed the ladder backwards, didn't you? As hard as you could.'

I could see it in my mind's eye. The boy scrabbling back from the edge of the loft, terrified of what would happen when Rowland got to the top. Terrified of what his own actions'd brought about. I could see him kicking the ladder backwards with all the strength that terror gives you. I'd been a boy like him. A man had come for me with murder in his eyes and I'd used that strength not to fight but to run. But if I'd had nowhere to run to and the presence of mind to push…

'Over he went,' I said, 'back, back. His head hit the ground with a hell of a smash, didn't it, Billy? Because you'd pushed that ladder as hard as you could. You all but threw him on to those flagstones. No wonder he didn't get up again. His head was cracked open.'

'No!' I could see the terror and rage of a cornered animal in Billy. 'No, I didn't!' He stopped trying to pull away from me and looked wildly around at the small, horrified knot of people standing a dozen feet away. 'Tell him! Tell him it's not true. Tell him that's not what happened!'

I looked at Ruth and Nan, standing slightly to one side of Phoebe Gwatkyn. Both of them looked frozen with shock.

Nan put a hand out to grasp Ruth's arm, shaking her head at Billy.

'That's *not what happened*!' Billy yelled. He was panicking. He'd lost all control. Soon I wasn't going to be able to hold him. Morgan Walters saw the situation and stepped forward.

'Billy!'

His son stopped struggling and swung around. Walters put a hand on each of Billy's shoulders. 'Enough, now, son. We'll sort this out.'

But, if there was any sorting out to be done, Harry was going to be the one doing it. 'The street is not the place for this,' he said. 'Mr Emmanuel, may we use your office for a few moments?'

Everybody else was watching Harry and Silas Emmanuel, who'd come out when he heard Billy's screaming. But I had my eyes on Nan Walters and Ruth Eynon. Nan still had hold of Ruth's arm and the grip looked to be painful. Ruth's face hinted that, any moment, she might collapse from shock but it wasn't Billy her horrified eyes were fixed on, it was her friend.

Harry

As we all made our way back into the offices of Emmanuel, Pask and Williams, John took me by the arm and held me back. 'Did you hear all of that?'

'Enough to know that you think the boy might've killed Rowland. And that he's terrified.'

'There's something I need to tell you. What I found out in London.'

I looked around. Caldicot's unmistakeable figure was on the steps behind us. 'I can guess,' I muttered. 'Holywell Street is notorious.'

The fact that John said no more was enough to confirm my suspicions: Rowland had been in the pornography business. That explained his nocturnal sorties; as he could not hold a pen, he would have needed to work with somebody and he could not risk a stranger being seen near the schoolroom. But who?

I had thought Silas Emmanuel's office somewhat small for the number of people involved in the will-reading but the addition of Billy, Morgan Walters and John made it distinctly crowded.

Emmanuel arranged chairs behind his desk for the ladies, as if he felt a physical barrier was required to protect them from Billy, then he and Caldicot positioned themselves at either side of the desk. I placed Billy with his back to the assembled company, facing me, his father no more than an arm's length away at his side.

John was leaning on the windowsill, a position from which he would be able to see everybody. I did not know what to make of his sudden, unexpected accusation of Billy Walters. Had he discovered some other evidence, in the last three days, that implicated the boy? I did not think so. If it had been crucial, he would have detained me so that we could confer.

He had, however, sounded very sure of himself and, try as I might to keep an open mind, I must take such certainty into account.

'Right, Billy,' I said, locating the whirlpool over his midriff so that his face appeared in my peripheral vision. With only six feet or so separating us, I might observe something, however indistinct. 'I'd like you to tell us what happened the night Mr Rowland died. Did you go to the schoolroom?'

There was no answer from the boy and something about his breathing made me wonder whether he was fighting off tears.

'Billy,' Morgan Walters said, 'tell Mr Probert-Lloyd what he wants to know. Did you go to the school that night?'

'Yes!' The boy's voice was strained, as if his throat was constricted. 'But it's not like he said!'

'He', I realised, referred to John.

'Tell us what happened, then, son.'

Billy ran a hand under his nose. Tears might not have been running down his cheeks but they were, it appeared, finding their way out nonetheless. '*They* went over there, Nan and Ruth—' He half-turned towards where the women were sitting.

The fairer of the two girls, Ruth Eynon, sprang up from her chair as if propelled by a hidden spring. 'How *dare* you, Billy Walters?'

314

I opened my mouth to silence her but, before I could speak, Nan took her hand and pulled her into her seat again. 'Let him be, Ruth. He'll say whatever he wants, like he always does. It doesn't mean anybody will believe him.'

Billy spun around. 'They *will* believe me, because it's the truth!'

This was rapidly descending into a sibling spat.

'That's enough!' I said, in a tone that I hoped would bring both of them to heel. 'This is not a schoolyard. A serious allegation has been made against Billy and I would like to hear what he has to say in his defence. Uninterrupted. Now, carry on, Billy.'

The boy hesitated, presumably gathering thoughts that had been scattered by Ruth Eynon's interruption. 'They thought they were being quiet, the pair of them, but I heard them go out. So I went after them. Nan isn't supposed to go out of the house after dark.'

Despite his self-justifying caveat, I wondered if, in fact, he had been snooping on them all evening. The boy seemed to be something of an habitual spy.

'They didn't have a lamp so they weren't going very fast. It was easy to follow them. And I knew where they were going anyway.'

'You followed them to the schoolhouse?'

'Yes. They thought they'd just be able to walk in but the door was barred.'

That was interesting. In a community where doors were rarely locked, I wondered why Rowland had felt it necessary.

'They had to knock and shout for a long time before he came to the door. Then, as soon as he opened it, they pushed in. Ruth said she had to talk to him. Urgently.'

I saw the scene in my mind's eye. Nicholas Rowland at the door, his face lit by the lamp he was carrying. The two young women pushing past him, unexpected, uninvited.

Rowland had not been wearing his jacket when he died but, otherwise, he had been fully dressed. If Billy was telling the truth about the delay before Rowland had come to the door, the knocking and shouting must have forced him out of bed and into sufficient clothes to make him decent.

John's train of thought had obviously gone in the same direction. 'What time of night was this?' he asked.

Billy's face turned towards John but he didn't answer.

'Billy?' I prompted.

'Just after ten. Mam and Dad were busy in the taproom. People drink late when there's no work the next day.'

I nodded but, as I waited to see whether John would ask anything else, I wondered whether Nan and Ruth could have crept out of a crowded pub without anybody seeing them? I had not formed a clear picture of the layout of the Three Horseshoes and could not remember whether the main staircase came down into the taproom.

John did not ask another question, simply inclined his body away from the wall. *Go on.*

'What happened then?'

'I went up to the door to listen.' Evidently, Billy had understood that being accused of spying on his sister was, now, the least of his worries. 'I could hear Ruth talking. Wanting to know if Mr Rowland'd seen Shoni Goch, if he'd come to the school. I don't think he knew what she was talking about and she started shouting. About Shoni Goch and her father. She was *hysterical*.'

The word sounded oddly out of place but Welsh does not have a word for the condition.

'Mr Rowland said he wasn't going to stand in the schoolroom having this conversation, they should come up to the loft so he could light some candles and they could sit down and talk sensibly. So up they all went.'

Sit down and talk sensibly. That was, surely, exactly what a teacher might say to an overwrought girl.

'Did you follow them in?'

'When they'd all gone up the ladder. Went in and hid where they wouldn't see me.'

Which, presumably, meant that he would not have been able to see them, either.

'And, when they were in the loft, what did you hear?' I asked.

Billy shifted his feet, jammed his hands in his pockets. 'Mr Rowland said something like "well, what's all this about?" and then she was off. Ruth. But she wasn't raving any more, just angry.'

'What did she say?'

'Told him she'd just found out that her father had promised her in marriage to his cousin. Which was a lie,' Billy said, his voice rising and his fists coming out of his pockets. 'Because – *weeks* ago – I heard her telling Nan that Shoni Goch was coming and he'd want to marry her and she wasn't going to. My sister told her to say that, if they made her, she'd cut his cock off.' He clapped his hand to his mouth and turned to look at the women. 'Sorry—'

Over his shoulder, I saw Miss Gwatkyn raise a hand as if she was offering a blessing. Next to her, Nan and Ruth seemed to be sitting close enough together to prop each other up. I would have given a year of my life to be able to see their faces, gauge the effect Billy's words were having.

'Then Ruth started going on about how Mr Rowland had to say he'd proposed to her – that he had to tell her father that, otherwise she'd have to marry Shoni Goch and she said she'd rather die than marry him, then she started crying—'

Ruth made a sound and tried to rise from her seat once more but Miss Gwatkyn restrained her.

'And what did Mr Rowland say?' I asked.

'He didn't say anything. But I could hear him pacing about. Then Ruth started shouting again – shouting that he'd promised to look after them, promised that they could be part of the new school. She kept saying the same thing. "You said to come to you if we needed help. You said. *You said*."' He fell silent and I wondered who he was looking at.

317

'Mr Rowland surely must have given some response to that?'

'Yes. He started on about investors and what they'd think. And Ruth said he didn't really have to marry her, just tell her father that they were betrothed. That's all. But he still didn't say yes and Ruth started on with her "You said" again and then…'

'Then what?'

'Then Nan said… She told Ruth that he was just like all the rest. "Tell you anything to keep you sweet and then break their promises when it suits them," she said.' He spun around to look at his father. 'But what does she know about anything like that? She's never had a sweetheart, has she, doesn't know what she's talking about!' He was trying to sound dismissive but there was something desperate in his voice.

Morgan Walters did not reply and I wondered what was going through his mind. Did it occur to him simply to take his children home and challenge us to send the police to the Three Horseshoes? Llanddewi Brefi considered him to be a forceful man, a leader, but he was not in Llanddewi Brefi now. He was surrounded by people who knew the law better than him.

Billy seemed deflated by his father's silence; when he turned back to me, his tone was more subdued.

'Then she went on about how Ruth couldn't trust anybody apart from her. Said the only people they could rely on were each other – like as if they'd sworn an oath or something. But Ruth wasn't listening to her. She shouted at Mr Rowland. She said—' He took a shuddering breath, like a child who's recovering from a crying fit. 'She said if he didn't do what she wanted, she'd tell everybody what they'd been doing with him.'

What they'd been *doing with him*? I felt as if I'd been upended, as if the ground I'd taken for granted as solid had suddenly fallen away beneath me. Was my confusion visible to everybody? Every invisible gaze in the room seemed to pull at me physically.

And then John spoke. 'It's not what you think, Harry. I'll explain afterwards.'

I turned and looked right at him. Stared stupidly into the whirlpool as if my absolute need to see him would dispel the grey blindness.

'I can't tell you, now,' he said. 'It's not appropriate. Let the boy go on.'

Not appropriate – why? Because of who was in the room? I bit down on my frustration.

'Go on, Billy,' John said. 'You were saying Ruth threatened to tell her father what the three of them'd been doing.'

Out of the corner of my eye, I saw Caldicot move, just slightly. I knew that I could not prevent him if he tried to leave.

Billy cleared his throat. 'Yes. Then Mr Rowland said that she couldn't tell. It'd be the end of everything – the school, their reputation, everything. But Ruth said she didn't care. Anything was better than marrying Shoni Goch. She said she'd tell people Mr Rowland'd made them do it. That they'd been afraid to say no.'

The boy stopped and I wondered whether he was looking to his father for reassurance.

'Then he laughed. Mr Rowland did. He laughed and said nobody'd believe that. Then I heard footsteps on the floorboards so he must've gone over to Ruth. It sounded as if his face was up against hers like this—' Billy raised his hand and held it in front of his own face. 'And he said to her...' His voice changed as he hissed Rowland's words. '"You *wanted* to do it, Ruth Eynon. You *know* you wanted to." And then there was a noise – a kind of scream – and I heard a scuffle and a shout from Mr Rowland – "Ruth!"' I flinched at the sudden vehemence he put into the name. 'And, next thing, he was falling down out of the loft.'

John

Knowing what I did, it all sounded completely believable, but Nan wasn't having any of it.

She was on her feet and yelling at her brother before anybody could stop her. 'You disgusting liar!' Lydia Howell and Ruth both tried to pull her into her seat again but she tore herself free, pushed past Silas Emmanuel and went for Billy. '*Liar!*'

I don't think she'd expected any opposition from Harry but he had her by the shoulders before she could lay a finger on her brother. 'Miss Walters—'

Nan carried on screaming as if Harry didn't have hold of her. As if he wasn't there. 'How *dare* you tell lies about me and Ruth? This isn't one of your horrible penny books! This is real life – you can't just make things up about people—'

'*I'm not!*'

'Yes, you *are!*' Without looking away from her brother, Nan tried to struggle free of Harry. 'You're trying to protect Shoni Goch. But he's not one of your made-up heroes – he's *real*. And he's a dangerous man. Just because he wears a uniform—'

'Don't be stupid!' Now that he was speaking to his sister rather than to Harry, Billy was losing the tight grip he'd had on himself. 'Shoni Goch's a merchant sailor. He doesn't *wear* a uniform. And what does that matter anyway—?'

'Because you think everybody in uniform's a hero! Like bloody Mattie Hughes!'

I saw Silas Emmanuel flinch at the profanity. He'd faint clean away if he knew what Nan'd been up to with Rowland.

'I'm *not lying!*' Billy moved half a step forward, fists clenched at his sides. Even from where I was standing, I could see he was shaking. 'Ruth pushed Mr Rowland out of the loft and *you know she did!*'

In the light from the window, the boy was pale as chalk. Every freckle on his face stood out as if it'd been put there with a finger dipped in clay.

'No.' Nan had stopped shouting now, got a hold of herself. She pulled herself up straight so she could just about look down on him. 'She did *not* do that. You're making it all up. It's what you always do when you don't like the truth. Like when Mr Rowland found out it was you stealing the coal—'

'*Shut up! You don't know what you're talking about!*' Billy's voice was almost hoarse he shouted so loud.

Harry'd let go of Nan by now. 'Miss Walters,' he said, 'would you mind sitting down again for a few moments while I finish with your brother?'

For a second, she looked at him as if he'd spoken Mandarin. But she'd been properly schooled at her Lampeter ladies' establishment. 'Of course, Mr Probert-Lloyd, if that's what you'd prefer.'

I watched her go back and sit next to Ruth. Her friend stared at her and reached for her hand. They looked into each other's eyes, as if they were passing secret messages from mind to mind. I thought about the things the Two Naughty Pupils'd got up to together and I felt a heat rise in me. *Had* they – Nan and Ruth – in real life?

'Billy,' Harry said, pulling my attention back to him. 'I just need to ask you a few more questions. Are you all right to do that?'

Billy nodded. He was trying hard not to cry. His eyes were bright and he swallowed again and again, as if he was trying his best to get rid of the Adam's apple that was just starting to show in his throat. Thirteen feels grown-up when everything's going your way. But when things start to go wrong, you're Mammy's little boy again shamefully quickly.

'What happened after Mr Rowland had fallen?' Harry asked. 'Did Nan and Ruth come down to see whether he was badly hurt?'

Billy shook his head. He couldn't hold the tears back any more and they started spilling out and rolling down his cheeks. He bent his head to one side then the other, wiping them off on the shoulders of his jacket the way a man might have wiped sweat. Then he turned to me. 'It was like you said,' he managed. 'Outside.'

'Can you tell us?' I didn't move from the windowsill, didn't want to frighten him.

'I thought he was dead.' Billy swiped a forearm across his face. 'He was just lying there. I didn't know what to do. Just waited for the girls to come down. But they didn't!'

After everything I'd accused him of outside, he was desperate for me to believe him. I nodded. 'But then he started to stir, didn't he, Billy?'

The boy's eyes went wide again, remembering. 'He made this sound. It was—' He struggled to find a word to describe what he'd heard, the effect it'd had on him. 'Then he tried to get up. He wasn't right, you could see that. He was all over to one side—' Billy drooped one arm and bent his leg on the same side as if it wouldn't take his weight. His eyes were fixed and I knew all he could see was Nicholas Rowland dragging himself up from the flagstones. 'And he was making this noise. Like panting and moaning.'

The boy looked terrified and I knew why. Nan had just told me. Those *horrible penny books* of his. Penny bloods were full of half-human monsters who made animal noises and moved as if their limbs didn't belong to them. Dead bodies scrabbling up through soil and crawling out of graves. Dark beasts dragging themselves out of caves and cellars on deformed limbs. Billy must've been terrified when Rowland turned into one of them.

'Then he *looked at me*—'

Of course. Billy'd been hiding, but only where he couldn't be seen from above. Once Rowland hit the ground, he'd been on the same level as the boy.

I could imagine that moment, feel in my own guts the terror of those eyes meeting mine.

'He started coming towards me—'

I could barely make out what Billy was saying now, he was crying so hard.

'Did you go to help him?' I asked.

Billy shook his head, screwed his eyes tight shut, then covered his face with his hands.

I waited till he'd finished sobbing and was smearing the tears off his face.

'That's when you hid your eyes, wasn't it?' I asked. 'Like this?' I folded my arms around my head, blocking out everything in front of me. I daresay Billy curled up tight, too, but I wasn't going to mime that in front of everybody.

The boy didn't have to answer. The fact that he'd started crying again told us all it was true.

How often had he gone over this in his head? As often as I'd gone over and over what I'd done when Margaret Jones's murderer had come for me. I knew what something like that could do to you. You tried to tell yourself you hadn't been a coward, that you hadn't had any choice. It never worked.

'And then?' I asked, gently. 'Did you hear anything?'

Billy pulled himself together. 'I heard him going up the ladder...'

'Anything else?'

'The ladder falling. I mean, him falling – a thud and a crack and—' Billy was panting. 'The ladder clattering.'

In perfect silence, every eye in the room was fixed on him.

'And then?' I asked.

The boy stared into the air between us. 'A scream,' he said, eyes focused on the scene in his mind. Him, hiding, eyes tight shut behind his arms. Sounds happening outside the little protective bundle he'd made of himself.

'Was the scream from Mr Rowland?' Harry asked.

Billy spun round, as if Harry'd sneaked up on him. 'No.'

'One of the girls, then.'

Billy nodded.

'Did you hear anything else?' Harry asked. 'Did Ruth or your sister say anything?'

'They were whispering – while he was climbing up the ladder – but I couldn't hear what they were saying.'

'And after Mr Rowland had fallen – did they say anything then?'

Billy swallowed. Shook his head. 'I don't know.'

'You'd covered your ears after the scream, hadn't you?' I said.

He stared at me, not answering, but it was the only explanation. He must have been a gibbering wreck. How had the girls not seen him when they'd come down out of the loft? They must've been in a state, too, and the only thing they could think about was Rowland.

'You heard nothing else?' Harry asked.

'Only some bumps.' He hesitated. 'Must've been Nan and Ruth jumping down. The ladder'd gone, they had to come down without it.'

I imagined the two girls sitting on the edge of the loft, nerving themselves for the seven- or eight-foot fall. Or had they turned around and lowered themselves down on their arms for a shorter drop? That's what boys would've done. But boys have stronger shoulders than girls.

Bumps when they hit the flagstones. Had there been a third when one of them banged Nicholas Rowland's head on the floor, like Reckitt had said?

'How many bumps?' I asked. 'Two, three, four?'

He shook his head, not looking at me. 'I don't know. Just bumps.'

To be fair, he probably hadn't been in a fit state to count. 'When did you look up again?'

Billy looked to his father, as if he wanted to ask why he wasn't protecting him from questions he didn't want to answer, when they could go home. 'Go on, son,' Morgan Walters said. 'Answer Mr Davies.'

The boy swallowed, hard. 'I didn't hear anything for a long time. When I looked up, they were both kneeling over him.'

'What were they doing?'

'I don't know. They had their backs to me.'

Had they been just trying to help Rowland? Or, as Reckitt had suspected all along, had they been making sure he was good and dead?

324

No sooner had I released Billy to his father than John was at my side. 'Harry, we need to go now. Minnever's going to be going spare. He sent me here half an hour ago to tell you that the Tories are putting up another candidate.'

It was an effort to fix my thoughts on the election rather than on what we had just heard but, once I was able to concentrate, I realised that the Tories' decision was hardly surprising. With Caldicot having disappeared, it was the obvious course. Nevertheless, it was a risky strategy. The moment when candidates were nominated couldn't be more than an hour away.

I wondered if the Tory contingent was aware that Caldicot had re-surfaced, that he was here in Lampeter.

John grabbed my arm. 'Harry! Now!'

'We can't just let Nan and Ruth go. I'll need to talk to them.'

I turned my attention towards the ladies who were in audible discussion with Morgan Walters. 'I'm sorry Mr Walters but I can't allow you to take your daughter home just yet. Miss Gwatkyn, Miss Howell, would you be so good as to take Miss Walters and Miss Eynon to the Black Lion, please? There is evidently more that we need to discuss but I must attend to the election first.'

As Miss Gwatkyn addressed the girls, I drew Lydia aside. 'Use one of the rooms we've taken and, if you wouldn't mind, please stay with them. I don't want them conferring. I'll come and speak to them as soon as I may.'

The words were barely out of my mouth before John began to hustle me from the room but, as we left the building, he suddenly stopped at the top of the steps.

'Caldicot's not going towards the hustings. He's leaving.'

I could tell from his voice that he felt uneasy. He turned back to me. 'He knew about the erotic literature. Was involved, even—'

'Yes, he must've been Rowland's scribe at the very least—'

'No. That was the girls.'

'What? No, that's—'

'Harry, trust me. I've read the books. It was them.'

I felt everything shift, like the image in a kaleidoscope when the barrel is turned.

'I'll go after him,' John said. 'You go on to Minnever. He's down by the election platform.'

With that, he left and I stepped out into the street to join the general flow of people towards the square, my mind scrambling to see the new picture John's words had created. If Nan and Ruth had been complicit with Rowland in producing the kind of book sold in Holywell Street, surely Billy's story was more likely to be true? If his sister and Ruth Eynon had stepped so far beyond what any right-thinking person—

I pulled myself up, disconcerted by my own thoughts. Writing pornography might be scandalous – might be seen, even in free-thinking circles, as decadent, if not exactly as degenerate – but it was not illegal. And being a party to it did not inevitably lead to pushing a man out of his own loft or banging his head on the flagstones of his own schoolroom until he was dead.

Snatches of conversation intruded on my thoughts and I looked about me. Minnever's cohorts had exerted themselves to great effect. Blue rosettes were being sported by a significant number of my fellow-pedestrians and I was passed by a cart swathed in blue and carrying a dozen or more Liberal supporters in high spirits.

But the election could not hold my thoughts. I needed at least half my attention for not tripping over or bumping into people and the other half was fixed on what I had just learned. If Nan and Ruth's collaboration with Rowland had become common knowledge, their reputations would have been ruined and any chance of them remaining as teachers forfeit. Which meant that Ruth must have been desperate not to be married to Shoni Goch if she had truly been prepared to make good on her threat to tell the whole parish that not only had Rowland been a purveyor of pornography but that he had coerced them into helping him.

In my mind's eye, I saw the scene Billy had described. Ruth pleading, threatening. Rowland laughing, dismissing her.

It sounded as if his face was up against hers like this, Billy had said. *You wanted to do it, Ruth Eynon, he said. You know you wanted to.*

Abruptly, in another turn of the kaleidoscope, the dayroom in Cardigan gaol appeared in my mind. *Her father'd told me she wanted me*, Shoni Goch had said. But, when he had put that suggestion to Ruth in so many words, she had screamed at him like a banshee and issued blood-chilling threats.

Rowland had accused Ruth of wanting to write pornography with him and, a few seconds later, Billy had heard a scream and Rowland had fallen from the loft after what seemed to have been a scuffle. Was it the injustice of his accusation that had led Ruth to turn on him, too, or simply the way he had phrased it?

You wanted to do it. Had those words been Nicholas Rowland's death warrant?

—

Minnever saw me as I pushed my way clumsily through the crowds that were steadily packing the square around the stage.

'Harry!' He took me by the arm to steady me. 'Finally!'

'What's this about the Tories putting up another candidate?' I almost had to shout over the general din. 'Caldicot's *here*. In Lampeter. He was at the will reading.'

'What?' Minnever stopped in his tracks. 'Where is he now?'

'Last seen walking up the Tregaron Road. John's gone after him.'

'The Tories are billeted on that road. If Caldicot's going to talk to them, we need to be there, too. We can't let them nominate him.' And he set off again, my arm still in his grasp.

'Who is this new candidate?' I said, as we fought our way clear of a group of newcomers jostling their way nearer to the stage.

'One of the election committee. Old buffer by the name of Verwick. Has a house in the county but spends most of his time in London. Ridiculous choice. The Tories are panicking.'

'Then shouldn't we just let them?'

'If Caldicot's not headed to parley with the party now.' Minnever elbowed his way through a thicket of young men already audibly the worse for drink. 'We run the risk of a public confrontation if he turns up on the stage and demands to be reinstated. We both know that he can't stand. But there'd be a riot if people thought we'd nobbled him in front of the whole town. We've got to tell the Tories what we know *now*. Stop Caldicot getting anywhere near the nomination.'

Two minutes later, we were being shown into the drawing room of a substantial, stuccoed house.

'Crowther!' Minnever marched up to the Tory agent. 'Ten minutes ago, Montague Caldicot was seen in Lampeter, fit and well. What the devil is going on?'

In the ensuing confusion of questions and bluster, it became clear that George Verwick had allowed his name to be put forward by the town's Tory supporters but had not yet been formally adopted as the new candidate. The committee's preference was that Caldicot remain as their nominee and they were, naturally, encouraged by the news that he had reappeared.

Minnever drew the Tory agent aside. 'Is there somewhere we can speak in private?'

Crowther led us to a small but well-furnished study. The fire was lit and the smell that hung in the warm air suggested the frequent smoking of cigars. Crowther ignored both armchairs and sofa and we all remained standing.

'Well?' he demanded. 'Say your piece, Minnever.'

As far as I could tell, Minnever was not remotely intimidated by this *de haut en bas* manner. 'Are you aware of the reason for Montague Caldicot's departure from the army?' he asked.

'He wanted a more settled life. He's relatively recently married and the army's not conducive to domestic harmony.'

'So goes the fig-leaf. But do you know what hangs behind it?'

Did Crowther glance at me? Did he glare at Minnever, defying him to breathe a single scandalous word? Or did he know that the game was up?

He took a step backwards and perched on the desk behind him. 'You're obviously under the impression that you do.'

'I do. And I want to know whether you put him up for election despite knowing, or whether you were sold a pup.'

Crowther rose to his feet again. 'Now, look here, Minnever—'

'Spare me the display of Tory rectitude! Did you or did you not know that Montague Caldicot failed to report a capital crime to his commanding officer? *And* that his failure to do so allowed the perpetrators to desert from their regiment?'

Sometimes, in the wake of a gunshot, there is a silence so complete that the explosion seems to have obliterated all ambient sound. Minnever's words produced the same effect.

When Crowther finally found his voice he did not prevaricate. 'No,' he said, carefully, 'as it happens, I was not aware.' He hesitated. 'What was the crime?'

'Does it matter?'

'It might.'

The two men were standing far enough apart for me to be able to keep both in the extremities of my peripheral vision. While Crowther now stood unnaturally still, as if any movement might grant us some advantage over him, Minnever was characteristically twitchy, clasping and unclasping his hands behind his back. 'Buggery,' he said, after a few moments.

Crowther made no response and, if his demeanour betrayed any emotion, the change was so slight as to be invisible to me.

'The point being,' Minnever went on, 'if I can come by this knowledge, so can anybody.'

'Meaning you'll make it public?'

'*Meaning* that it shouldn't have come to this! With that sitting in his recent past like a turd on a drawing-room carpet, he shouldn't even be contemplating public office!'

'But he is. So I'll ask you again. Will you make it public if he is nominated as our candidate?'

'I think the wisest course of action is to withdraw. As I say, if I can discover the truth, so can anybody. And it would be very embarrassing for your party if that happened. Especially as Caldicot has made so much of knowing his duty.'

Crowther sighed but anything he might have said was interrupted by a knock, followed, without invitation, by the appearance of a head and shoulders in the half-opened doorway. 'Crowther, time's marching on. We need a decision.'

John

As I hurried along the street after Montague Caldicot, a group of young people flaunting blue rosettes and ribbons tried to turn me around and take me with them. 'You're going the wrong way!' they laughed. 'The election's this way!'

I ignored them, pushed their hands away. 'Mr Caldicot!'

I'd expected him to pretend not to hear me. But he stopped and turned. 'Mr Davies.' He looked me up and down as if I was on the parade ground and didn't quite pass muster. 'How was your visit to London?'

That surprised me. How did he know? 'Enlightening, thank you.'

He eyeballed me as if I couldn't possibly have discovered anything that would trouble him.

'Nicholas Rowland and those assistant teachers of his were writing erotic fiction,' I said. 'But you already know that. Because you fetched and carried for him.'

Caldicot didn't look away but something in his eyes changed. He waited to hear what I'd say next.

'As they were keen to tell me,' I said, jerking my thumb over my shoulder at the blue-ribboned crowd who were calling out to bystanders to come along with them, 'the hustings are that way.'

'Which is why I'm going the other way.'

'Have you told them you're withdrawing?' I asked. 'The Tories?'

There was a flash of the soldier then, a flash of *How dare you, private?* And then it was gone. He shook his head as if it didn't matter.

'Until today,' I said, 'I thought you'd killed him. Rowland. I'm sorry.'

Why had I said that? I wasn't usually one to fill a silence with babble. But Caldicot's silence was more than just a lack of words. It was as if something had gone out inside him.

'Those girls,' he said, eventually. 'They'll claim he corrupted them. But the books were their idea. When support for his school began to fall away.' Montague Caldicot seemed to be looking through me, now. 'They enjoyed it. Making Nicholas say the words. Humiliating him. They enjoyed the transgression.' He drew out the last word, as if Nan Walters and Ruth Eynon were some kind of wonder to him.

'This'll be enough for Harry to re-open the inquest—'

'Nicholas Rowland is dead! What difference will it make?'

'Shoni Goch isn't dead. Would you let him hang?'

'Tell Probert-Lloyd to go to the police.' He turned to walk away.

'D'you know what Harry did at the meeting in Newcastle Emlyn?' I asked. 'One of the grooms at Glanteifi told me all about it. He praised you. Made excuses for you not being there. Said he was sure you had good reason. Said he'd learned things from you. Things he'd have to bear in mind if he became coroner.'

Caldicot looked away, a look on his face as if what I'd said had caused him actual pain. Behind him, I could see a crowd of people coming down the street – a whole village-worth, it looked like, having a day out at the election. They'd be on us in a minute and Caldicot might easily use the bustling about to escape.

'We all know what this contest is really about,' I said. 'Next year's election. If you stand in front of people and tell them that... tell them that you don't want politics to be involved with things it shouldn't concern itself with, that Harry's obviously the better candidate for coroner—'

'Is he? Despite his antipathy towards the magistrates and the police?'

'Yes, he is. You know he is. He risked losing this election because he was so determined to find out the truth about Rowland's death. He sent me to London at his own expense—' I cut myself off. Harry wouldn't thank me for advertising Glanteifi's financial state. 'I truly believe that, if he's elected, he'll try and work with the magistrates and the police force. He knows he can't go on the way he has. But he's not going to roll over and just do whatever they say. They're going to have to reckon with him and his tenacity.' Desperate as I was to convince him, I was pleased with *tenacity*. So much better than *stubbornness*. 'Harry cares about people. About the truth. About what's said of the dead.'

I waited for a response but Caldicot just stared at me.

I took Harry's watch from my pocket. 'It's five minutes to midday. We're running out of time.'

The younger villagers at the front of the crowd broke into a trot. One of them must've had a watch as well.

'I had a subaltern like you, once,' Caldicot said, looking me right in the eye. 'Smart as a whip. Wasted in the army.'

'I was wasted as a solicitor's clerk. But not as assistant coroner.'

Montague Caldicot stared at me for a few seconds longer. Then he nodded.

Once we'd left Crowther's house, instead of marching towards the waiting crowds as I had expected, Minnever stopped and took a flask from his pocket.

'Snifter?'

I took it from him and swallowed a single mouthful. On an empty stomach it would have an immediate effect and I did not want to appear drunk on the election platform.

'What do you think they'll do?' I asked, returning the flask.

Minnever drank no more deeply than I, then slipped the flask back into his pocket. 'They can't put Caldicot up. Not now. It's just a question of whether they decide to do the sensible thing and let you go forward uncontested.' He took my elbow. 'Come on. Let's bear ourselves in a calm and collected manner. It'll contrast nicely with the Tories' hectic disarray.'

On the way back to the election platform I allowed my hand to be wrung, received good wishes, smiled in a fashion that I hoped would seem humble-yet-competent and generally behaved exactly as Minnever wished until we climbed the steps up to the stage. Aided and abetted by the Liberal cohorts, news of Caldicot's absence from both Cardigan and Newcastle Emlyn had gone far and wide, and speculation as to whether he would appear today was rife in the crowd awaiting us.

We greeted the town worthies, Minnever regretfully denied any knowledge of when the 'other party' would be pleased to present themselves and we sat down. 'We shall sit here and look prepared,' he murmured. 'As, indeed, we are.'

I hoped his confidence was not misplaced. Verwick, as a local man, might reasonably anticipate a significant number of votes.

Suddenly, I was aware of somebody pushing through the crowd and bounding up the steps on to the stage. John.

'Harry. You've got to come with me.'

'What? It's about to start.'

'The Tories aren't here yet. And Montague Caldicot wants to speak to you.' I did not move. 'Come on, Harry!'

'Why should I speak to Caldicot?'

'Because he can give you the coronership.'

I felt a rush that was half excitement, half apprehension. Was that within his power? I stood up. 'Where is he?'

'Harry, you can't walk off the stage!' Minnever hissed.

'I have to.'

'Then I'll come with you.'

'No. You stay here. Unruffle any affronted Tory feathers.' Minnever's presence would, inevitably, confine any conversation between Caldicot and me to matters electoral and this might be my only chance to force information from him about Nicholas Rowland.

I followed John down from the stage, trying to ignore the jeering that our departure provoked.

Was I being foolish in chasing off after Caldicot? Could this be a ruse on his part to make me seem as dilatory as he was?

'He's just this way,' John said, leading me through the crowds.

We found Caldicot standing a few yards back from the street, beneath the bare branches of a substantial tree.

'I appreciate your coming, Probert-Lloyd.'

'Whatever you have to say, be quick. We have very little time.'

Did he glance over at John? Or was he staring at me, appraising me for weakness? 'I have a proposal,' he said. 'I will make a speech in which I will both renounce my own candidacy and make it clear that you are the only man for the job. In return, you will see to it that nobody stands trial for Nicholas Rowland's murder.'

Whatever I had expected, it was not that. 'I can't possibly—'

'It's clear that one of those girls pushed Nicholas to his death but if they come to trial, there will be a scandal. Nicholas's reputation will be ruined and any prospect of the collegiate school's coming to fruition will be destroyed.'

'And how do you imagine I would prevent a trial?'

'By obtaining a confession and having the culprit committed to an asylum. Not a mad-doctor in the country would quibble.'

He was right. Men who write erotic literature might be considered rakish and their acceptability in polite circles questionable but women are held to a different standard; any female found writing erotica would be considered morally insane. But his plan was unconscionable.

'That's absolutely out of the question. I'll do my best to obtain a confession and avoid a trial but I will not conceal those young women's actions by having either of them quietly shut away.'

'And if there's no confession? If it all comes out? Are you prepared to see plans for Nicholas's school perish on the altar of your self-righteousness?'

'Not on any altar of mine, Caldicot.' I kept a tight hold on my temper despite the insult. I could not be seen in a public argument with him; not today of all days. 'If it perishes, it does so because Rowland could not live up to the values he supposedly wished to inculcate.'

There was a pause, then Caldicot sighed. 'Very well. So be it.'

John

'Harry, I didn't know that's what he was going to say, I promise you!' We'd barely stepped away from Montague Caldicot but I didn't care if he heard me.

'He said he could make sure you got the coronership but he wanted to talk to you first.'

Harry waved my apology away, already heading back towards the stage. 'He's desperate to keep it all quiet. I think it was him that Rowland was meeting when he went walking at night.'

I thought of the *Young Man's Awakening* and the *Two Rollicking Lads* and I knew what he meant.

'He and Rowland belonged to a club in London,' Harry said, staring straight ahead so that he could see where he was putting his feet. 'A club for men with particular tastes.'

'For sex with other men.'

He stopped in his tracks and his head whipped round.

'One of the books I brought back is about a young man and what he gets up to.'

'You've read them?'

'Yes.'

A few yards ahead of us, I spotted Mr Crowther and the Tory committee. I grabbed Harry's arm. 'Come on. If we hurry, we can get back on to the stage before the Tories.'

I used my shoulder to make a path for us and one of the people I shifted out of the way turned to push me back but stopped when he saw Harry. 'Oh, here's Mr Probert-Lloyd back again!' he shouted out. 'Hasn't run away after all.'

There was a bit of mock-cheering then and a few people threw rolled-up ribbons so that they unravelled in the air and draped themselves over Harry. I could see that the policemen at the front of the stage weren't too keen on that so I turned around and held my hands up. 'Thank you but we haven't won yet! Save your ribbons, ladies and gentlemen!'

We got to the steps just ahead of the Tories and there was more cheering and jeering as we climbed up. Once we were in our seats, I scanned the crowd for Caldicot. At first, I couldn't see him, then I realised that he was climbing up on to the side of the stage to cut the Tory committee off before they could sit down.

'Stand down your new candidate, Crowther,' he said. 'I'll address the meeting.'

'Indeed you will not.' The Tory agent's teeth were clenched so hard that his voice barely escaped from his mouth. 'You're no longer the party's nominee.'

'Nevertheless, I wish to speak.'

Mr Crowther seemed to gain another inch in height and six in girth. 'Out of the question. Your abominable behaviour has forfeited any right—'

'I don't wish to speak on your behalf but on my own.'

'Then you may speak on your own time. After the nomination.'

Caldicot took half a step toward his agent. 'Do you want a riot?' he asked. 'These people have come for a contest. If you send me away now, they won't be best pleased.'

He was right. And Mr Crowther knew it. The crowd was here for a contest. Keeping Caldicot quiet would be a big mistake.

If either of them could hear that the crowd had fallen silent, they gave no sign. They just stood there, less than a yard apart, eye to eye, neither wanting to be the one who backed down. 'Let me speak,' Caldicot said, 'then you can proceed with the nomination.'

Mr Crowther seemed to be working hard to unclench his jaw. 'Sit down and we'll proceed with the nomination. *Then* you may speak.'

'No. I must speak first.' What was Caldicot going to demand next? Mr Crowther on all fours so he could stand on his back? 'Don't think I won't tell them that you're trying to silence me.' Caldicot gestured at the crowd, eyes fixed on Mr Crowther.

The agent turned, just for a second, to look at Harry, as if he thought he might be in on this. Then he went back to giving Caldicot the beady eye. 'Very well. In the interests of preventing a riot. But this is the end for you. Do not imagine that you'll be able to count on the party's support again.'

'I assure you, Crowther, henceforth Tory support or the lack of it will be wholly irrelevant to me.'

And that was that. Mr Crowther went and took his seat, shaking his head at all the stares and questions he got from the other Tories. *It's finished. He's taken things out of our hands now.*

Caldicot walked to the front of the stage and, slowly, swept his eyes around the crowd.

'I'm sure some of you were at Tregaron when Mr Probert-Lloyd and I spoke,' he said. 'And all of you, whether you were there or not, will have a pretty good idea of what was said by both of us. The *Carmarthen Journal* was very generous with its quotations.'

He smiled and a few titters went round, but I don't think people were really sure whether they were supposed to be laughing or not. This wasn't what they were expecting.

'I told no lies at Tregaron,' he said, 'but the way I used the truth was dishonest. I criticised Mr Probert-Lloyd for refusing to accept the verdict of a legally-constituted jury. I accused him of being a hypocrite.'

He stopped and looked around at the crowd, drawing them all in. Every face was turned up to him, every eye on him.

'And the reason I did that was because I wanted to stop him from refusing to recognise the verdict of another jury. A more recent one. The jury that sat at the inquest into Mr Nicholas Rowland's death.' He stopped for a moment and I saw frowns and heads turned to neighbours. *What's he saying?*

'I knew Mr Probert-Lloyd felt that the jury had made a mistake and I did not want him to continue to investigate.' He paused again. 'You're wondering why.'

Nobody said a word, not even the drunks. This was the kind of speech you didn't heckle. No more than you'd interrupt a eulogy to speak ill of the dead.

'I wanted to stop him,' Caldicot said, 'because I feared that he would discover information that would not be to my advantage.'

A murmur went round then, but it didn't rise to anything more than that. Just a murmur of surprise and uneasiness.

'I'm not going to talk about what that information was. All you need to know is that I didn't want it to be made public. But, you see...' He held his empty hands out – no secrets! 'The thing about the truth is that it *needs* to be made known.'

Again, I saw his head move as he looked around, drawing every one of them in to this almost-telling of secrets.

338

'Hidden truths are dangerous. People who want to keep them hidden do desperate things. And the more damaging to them the truth might be, the more violent and drastic are the steps they have to take. It's only by letting the truth come out that violence can be prevented.'

I saw looks exchanged here and there. Didn't matter whether people were wearing blue ribbons or red, none of them knew what they were supposed to make of this.

'Mr Probert-Lloyd knows the value of the truth. He knows it's the only way to stop the poison spreading. The truth isn't always easy. Sometimes it's hard, painful. It feels as if it might kill us. But it is *necessary*.'

I'd never heard a crowd stay so silent for so long. But then, this wasn't just a speech, was it? It was a confession.

'Harry Probert-Lloyd isn't a man to give up when the search for the truth gets difficult. He won't give up when magistrates tell him he can't have the money he needs to pursue it. He won't give up when the Cardiganshire constabulary's decided that it already knows who the guilty party is. He won't give up in the face of threats, bribes or embarrassment. He's shown you that already and he's been acting coroner for less than four months.'

In the Tory camp, an argument was going on in whispers and mutters. An argument where at least one person had to be asking why Mr Crowther wasn't stopping this. But it would've been a brave man who'd stood up and tried to silence Montague Caldicot now.

'I failed to turn up at the last two hustings,' he said. 'And, as a result, I suspect that the Tories have found an alternative candidate.' He turned, as if he wanted an answer from Crowther, but all he got was a face like a block of wood. 'However, the best candidate for the coronership is already doing the job.' He turned and held his hand out to Harry. 'I give you Mr Harry Probert-Lloyd.'

I rose in response to Caldicot's speech and shook his hand while the crowd celebrated as if I had ordered a public holiday and a pound sterling for each person present. And, bowing to manifest public opinion, the Tories capitulated.

Thus elected unopposed, I made a brief speech, thanked all concerned, and – as swiftly as decorum would allow – left Minnever and the Liberal contingent to celebrate on my behalf while I returned to the job in hand. Elation would come later; for now, I felt only relief.

–

On the way back to the Black Lion, at my request, John outlined exactly what kind of books Rowland had involved the two young women in writing.

'According to Caldicot, it was the girls' idea,' he finished. 'They'd discovered Rowland's copy of *Fanny Hill* and, if what happens in the *Two Naughty Pupils* book is what happened in real life, they took it away from the loft to read it in private. They must have decided they could make money by doing the same. If not better. I mean, with the *Amorous Celtic Tales* I think they might've thought they were doing something a bit superior.'

We arrived at the Black Lion to find it teeming. Excusing our way through the crowds in the coachyard, we made our way up the outside staircase which gave access to the upper floors. Lydia opened the door to her chamber as if she had been standing with her hand on the latch, waiting for us.

'I was watching for you out of the window,' she said, joining us on the balustraded gallery and closing the door behind her. 'We've tried to speak to them,' she said, keeping her voice low lest people in the courtyard below overhear. 'But, despite our best attempts, they're choosing to say nothing about that night.'

'Nothing at all?'

'Nothing.'

'What's your opinion – both of you?' I asked looking from her to John. 'Do you think Billy was telling the truth?'

There was clearly some silent communication while they decided who should answer first, then John said, 'I do believe him, yes. But, from what he told us, there's nothing to say it wasn't an accident, more or less – so why would they refuse to speak?'

'You don't think Ruth pushed him deliberately?' I asked.

'If Billy's description is any guide,' Lydia said, 'Rowland had become confrontational. Perhaps Ruth simply pushed him away from her, not realising how close he was to the edge of the loft?'

The suggestion seemed plausible. 'Let's put it to her, shall we?' I opened the door and we filed in.

The room was not large and the small window, set low in the wall, let in relatively little light. Nan Walters and Ruth Eynon were sitting side by side near the foot of the high-framed bed while Phoebe Gwatkyn occupied the room's only chair. She rose as we entered the room but the two young women remained seated.

'Ladies,' I greeted them. They responded in kind but did not move from their position on the bed. As I could not observe their facial expressions, I decided that I might as well make use of my blindness to put them at a disadvantage so I crossed the room and sat on the low windowsill. With my back to the light, they would be unable to see me well. Still, I paid a price in discomfort as I was obliged to stretch my legs out in front of me without anything to lean back on.

'I'd like to ask you about Billy's account of what happened in the schoolroom on the night of Mr Rowland's death.'

Neither of them stirred and I had the impression that they were holding themselves firmly in check lest they unintentionally reveal something.

'You both accused Billy of lying,' I proceeded. 'But perhaps he simply didn't understand what he'd heard. It seems to me that perhaps an accident took place?' I paused, waiting for one of them to take the bait, and realised that I was holding my breath as I tried to wring every modicum of information I could from what remained of my vision. As far as I could tell, neither of them so much as twitched. I tried again. 'Would you like to tell us, in your own words, what actually happened that night?'

'I don't think so, thank you, Mr Probert-Lloyd.' Nan Walters spoke for both of them, her voice clear and decisive. 'You may choose to believe Billy if that's what you wish. Ruth and I have nothing to say on the matter.'

'You don't want to tell us what actually happened?'

'It's your prerogative to believe what Billy said or not as you see fit. We have nothing to say.'

'But you don't deny you were there?'

I was almost certain that Ruth Eynon drew breath to answer me but Nan Walters put a hand on her friend's arm and nothing was said.

I allowed a silence to develop. Nan Walters remained true to her intention to say nothing more and Ruth Eynon followed suit; she had, I suspected, become accustomed, long ago, to bearing uncomfortable silences in her father's house. However, I did not think she was as determined as her friend so I decided to test her resolve.

'Ruth Eynon,' I snapped, 'did you or did you not go to the schoolroom on the night Mr Rowland died?'

Before Ruth could respond, Nan put out a hand once more, this time clasping Ruth's in her own. 'Mr Probert-Lloyd, you can bully Ruth and me if you like. You might even make us cry. But we shall still have nothing to say.'

'We know all about Nicky Revell,' John said. 'The Naughty Teacher and his Two Naughty Pupils.'

If he had hoped to shock them into a reaction, he was disappointed. Nevertheless, he persisted. 'Was Mr Rowland right? *Did* you enjoy writing those books with him?'

Acutely uncomfortable to find myself discussing Rowland's pornography in front of Miss Gwatkyn, who knew nothing of it, I stood up once more and addressed her and Lydia. 'Ladies, perhaps you might like to go downstairs and take some refreshment while John and I speak to Miss Walters and Miss Eynon?'

'Don't send them away on our account,' Nan said. 'Only you can embarrass the ladies. We shall be saying nothing to you on that subject, or any other. Nothing at all.'

Despite myself, I felt a rising irritation at her composure, her defiance.

'You do understand that a failure to offer any explanation in your own defence will be seen as damning when it comes to court?'

It was a risk on my part. In actual fact, I had no small degree of apprehension about taking Billy's story to the police, but Nan Walters was not to know that.

She stood as, perforce, did Ruth Walters, their hands still joined. 'I think we would like to go home, now, if you don't mind.'

'I can't allow that.'

'But I don't think you can prevent it, Mr Probert-Lloyd. Not unless you're going to have us arrested?'

She was calling my bluff.

'Not at this time, no. I need to speak to the inspector in charge of the case first. It is he who will authorise any arrest.' My stomach clenched at the thought of how keenly Bellis would relish such an opportunity to thwart and humiliate me.

'Then we shall go home.' Nan moved towards the door but was stopped by a word from Phoebe Gwatkyn.

'A moment, if you please, Nan! In the circumstances, perhaps it would be best if you did not – I foresee only strife between you and your brother, and that can be good for nobody. But I would be more than happy if you were to join Ruth in staying at Alltybela with me for a little while. If that would be acceptable to you, Mr Probert-Lloyd?'

It was kind of her to allow me the dignity of approving her suggestion; in truth, I had no jurisdiction in the matter beyond that bestowed by deference. 'That's most kind of you, Miss Gwatkyn.'

'Very well then. I will go and make arrangements.'

I followed Phoebe Gwatkyn from the room and escorted her down the staircase into the coachyard. 'Thank you, Miss Gwatkyn,' I said. 'Your offer has saved me from a great deal of embarrassment.'

'A happy corollary only, I confess. My intention was to keep her and Ruth under my roof in the hope that I might be able to persuade them to speak more freely.'

I left her to make the necessary arrangements for her return to Alltybela with the two young women and climbed back up the staircase. I found John and Lydia outside on the gallery, waiting for me.

'I was just asking John who Nicky Revell is?' Lydia said. 'But perhaps you'd like to tell me, Harry?'

John

Letting the two of them stay together'd been a mistake, that much was clear. And Harry'd been far too soft with them as well. All right, he'd barked a bit at Ruth Eynon but he hadn't gone far enough. We needed to separate them. Then Nan wouldn't be able to keep Ruth quiet.

So, when Harry'd finished explaining to Lydia Howell who Nicky Revell was, I put my two penn'orth in.

'While Nan's doing the talking for both of them, we'll get nothing out of Ruth,' I said. 'We need to get her by herself.'

Harry might not like me saying what I thought in front of Lydia Howell but he was just going to have to learn to live with it. I wasn't going to hold my tongue every time she was about.

As it turned out, she wasn't holding her tongue, either. 'I agree. If I take Nan into town to find something to eat, you two can talk to Ruth.'

344

'You think they'll allow themselves to be separated?' Harry obviously didn't think so.

Lydia Howell rubbed her chin with the tips of her fingers. A thinking-aid, I supposed, like Harry's trick of chewing his lip. 'Ask Nan to come with me,' she said to Harry. 'Then, if she doesn't agree, let me try and persuade her, will you?'

Harry hesitated and I could see he wished he'd come up with a better idea. But he hadn't, and I had no idea how to part the two of them, either. Not without picking Nan up and carrying her off, which we couldn't do. Not unless we wanted her screaming the place down. So he just had to agree.

And back in we went.

This time, both the girls stood up. 'We'd like to leave, now, please,' Nan said.

'If you'd just be so good as to wait a few more minutes,' Harry said. 'Miss Gwatkyn has arrangements to make. But if you'd go with Miss Howell, Miss Walters—'

'We can go to the bakers and get something for us all to eat before we leave for home,' Lydia Howell said, not missing a beat. 'You must be hungry, I know I am.'

'Why can't we both go?' Nan wanted to know.

'Because Mr Probert-Lloyd would like to speak to Ruth.'

'But she doesn't want to speak to him, do you, Ruth? I've said all either of us want to say.'

Her friend shook her head. *What's the matter*, I wanted to say, *cat got your tongue*? But I knew the answer. It wasn't the cat; it was Nan Walters.

Lydia Howell nodded but her eyes were on Ruth, not Nan. 'I thought you were equals, Miss Eynon? Mr Probert-Lloyd would like to hear what you have to say rather than taking Miss Walters's word for it.'

'She'll say the same as me,' Nan insisted. 'Nothing.' She turned to Ruth. 'Won't you?'

Ruth nodded.

'Why won't you let your friend speak?' Lydia Howell asked. 'Don't you trust her?'

'Of course I trust her! But neither of us has got anything to say about my brother's foolish story.'

Lydia Howell turned so that her shoulder was facing Nan, getting into the space between the two of them without seeming to move. 'Is that right, Ruth? Because it sounds to me as if Nan wants to stop you saying anything she doesn't approve of.'

'That's not true!'

Lydia turned right round. Now, her back was to Ruth but the two of them were still separated. 'Isn't it, Nan? And yet, here you are, answering a question I was asking Ruth.'

Nan Walters tried to reach out, past Lydia, to Ruth. 'She's trying to trick you—' But Ruth drew back, just enough so that Nan's fingertips didn't touch her, and I saw something in her change. It was as if her face became firmer, harder – turned from soft and anxious to something more resolute. More like the Ruth we'd seen in the Walters's parlour the first time we met them. A girl who modelled herself on Phoebe Gwatkyn, right down to her hair arrangement.

Ruth breathed in, deeply, as if she was stiffening her backbone. Squared her shoulders. 'It's all right, Nan,' she said, in that cultured English that'd also come from Miss Gwatkyn if I was any judge. 'You go. I'll be fine with Mr Probert-Lloyd.'

They gazed at each other over Lydia Howell's shoulder, Nan's eyes searching Ruth's face. She wasn't happy about this but she couldn't say anything, not without proving Miss Howell right.

In the end, she nodded and turned away. I caught Lydia Howell's eye as she opened the door, and she inclined her head towards me slightly. *And that's how it's done.*

Once they were gone, Harry turned to Ruth Eynon. 'Would you like to sit, Miss Eynon?' He gestured towards the one chair in the room, a dainty affair with scrolled legs and worn velvet upholstery which looked as if it'd started life in a lady's parlour.

'Thank you.' She sat down gracefully, as if she was done up in an evening gown instead of her best *betgwn* and apron. This wasn't little Ruth Pantglas, Jeremiah's skivvy. This was Miss Eynon, prospective collegiate schoolteacher.

I thought Harry'd sit on the windowsill again but, instead, he sat on the bed. From where I was standing, I couldn't see Ruth Eynon's face very well so I moved slowly along the wall until I had a better view. She saw me move, glanced at me, then fixed her attention back on Harry. Compared to him, I wasn't important.

'Miss Eynon, can you tell us what happened on the night you went to see Mr Rowland at the schoolhouse, please?'

Ruth's chin went up. 'There's nothing to tell, Mr Probert-Lloyd. It's all Billy Walters's stories.'

Harry didn't so much as raise an eyebrow. 'So you didn't go to the school? Billy didn't follow you?'

'Billy Walters may have followed *somebody* – he's good at sneaking about after people.' She sighed, clasped her hands in her lap, her fingers loose, relaxed. 'I was exhausted, Mr Probert-Lloyd. It had been a trying day. All I wanted to do was sleep so I could put Jonathan Eynon and his presumption out of my mind.'

Presumption! Fair play, she was good. You'd have sworn that every word coming out of her mouth was the gospel truth.

'So who do you think Billy Walters might have been following?'

Ruth shook her head. 'You'd have to ask him. You're the coroner. You must be able to tell when people are lying to you and when they're telling the truth?'

Harry nodded. 'Yes. I believe I can. And I think Billy Walters was telling me the truth in Mr Emmanuel's office.'

Ruth unlaced her fingers and began smoothing her apron out over her knees, aligning the stripes just so. Even though I was watching her carefully I couldn't see any of the trembling I'd seen when she was giving evidence at the inquest.

'He's sly, that boy,' she said. 'Knows how to say things to get other people into trouble. He did it all the time when he

347

was coming to Mr Rowland's school, before he ran off back to Matthew Hughes.'

Harry leaned forward slightly. 'Just to avoid any misunderstanding, Miss Eynon, can you tell me exactly what lies Billy Walters has told me to get you into trouble?'

She didn't hesitate for a second, either in her apron-smoothing or her answer. 'All of it.'

'Everything he said in Mr Emmanuel's office?'

'Yes.'

This wasn't getting us anywhere. Ruth Eynon might be talking now but she wasn't saying anything, was she? Nothing to the point, anyway.

'Oh, come on now, Ruth,' I said in Welsh. 'Let's have the truth, shall we?' I pushed myself away from the wall and stepped forward, keeping my hands in my pockets and a sneer on my face. 'I've just come back from London. From a visit to William Gordon, the bookseller. And I've read the books you wrote with your precious Mr Rowland. Books he was selling in that disgusting shop of his. Books full of filth – behaviour a nice girl would be ashamed to even hear about!'

She stood up so quickly the chair almost fell over. It lay back, balanced on one leg, the opposite one caught up in her skirt. 'Shut your mouth! You're just an ignorant boy. You don't know what you're talking about!' She shouted at me in Welsh, which was exactly what I'd been aiming for with my disrespectful provocation. Not so easy to keep up the innocent young lady act in the language we'd both learned crawling around farmhouse kitchens.

I stepped forward and put my face close to hers, like a brother or a cousin.

'You and I both know *exactly* what I'm talking about, Ruth Eynon. You and Nan were the Two Naughty Pupils. You wrote smutty books with Nicholas Rowland—'

'They're *not smutty*,' she shouted. 'They're honest and truthful!'

I ignored her, talked over her. 'And then, when he wouldn't do what you wanted and say he'd asked you to be his wife, you pushed him out of the loft and killed him. Never mind *naughty*, you're as bad as they come!'

'No!' she wailed. 'No. No. No.' She started pulling at her hair, moaning. 'I'm not bad. I'm not! I'm a good girl. You're telling lies about me!'

The plait-swirls were down now and she didn't look much like Phoebe Gwatkyn any more.

All at once, she crumpled on to the floor and the chair landed with a crash behind her.

'Everybody tells lies about me.' Her voice was high, now, shrill with tears, just like she'd sounded at the inquest when her father had shouted at her. 'Why?' she wailed. 'Why won't they leave me be? I'm a good girl—' She covered her face with her apron and started to sob.

I wasn't having that. I crouched in front of her and pulled her apron down. But, instead of the dry, calculating eyes I'd expected to see, they were already red and overflowing.

'John—' Harry said from behind me. But he didn't seem to know what to say next.

Ruth stared at me through her tears. 'Why are you shouting at me? I do what I'm told. I keep quiet. I do my work.'

The hairs on the back of my neck went up. If you'd told me Ruth Eynon would start speaking in a little girl's voice I'd have laughed and said that'd do her about as much good as crying – that it wouldn't fool me. Well, I'd have been wrong. Except it didn't feel as if I was being fooled. Evidence of my own eyes or not, it felt as if what was cowering in front of me was a frightened, bewildered child.

I turned around and looked at Harry. He was looking off to one side so he could see Ruth and I could see him chewing his lip. He stood up.

'Miss Eynon, I'm sorry we've upset you. Please, the floor's no place for a young lady.' He was back to English. Fair enough, my effort hadn't got us far.

She looked up at him but, when he stretched out a hand to help her up, she flinched and protected her face with her forearm as if he'd tried to hit her.

'Miss Eynon, nobody's going to hurt you. Please, let me help you.'

She stared at him for several seconds as if she hadn't understood a word he said. Then she lowered her arm and gave him her hand.

Once she was on her feet again, she seemed to notice the state of her hair and, as quick as you like, she'd gathered it up and twisted it together into a knot at the back of her head. She took a handkerchief from the sleeve of her *betgwn* and wiped her face as she sat down.

She'd got hold of herself again. The frightened child was gone but there was something different about her. Something half-threatening, half-fearful, like a cornered cat, claws ready, eyes wide and black.

'You're cleverer than your friend, aren't you?' Harry said. 'She might be the one that went away to school but you're the one with the brains.'

What did he mean – did he think she'd deliberately broken down in tears like a child to fool us? Maybe he did but then, he couldn't see her.

Ruth glanced at him, then away. Said nothing.

'You realised that you'd have to go and see Nicholas Rowland that night, didn't you? You'd have to get him to back up your story to Shoni Goch or there'd be trouble from your father.'

I jumped a foot in the air when, without any warning, Ruth leaped out of the chair and threw herself at Harry. He couldn't see what was happening properly so he flinched back, elbows on the bed. Ruth leaned over him until her face was no more than a handspan from his. 'He is *not – my – father*!'

If ever three words held a whole bookful of meaning, it was those three.

'I'm sorry. Of course he's not.' Harry sounded genuinely contrite. 'Please, accept my apologies.'

He waited a few seconds. Ruth stood up straight so she wasn't spitting in his face any more but she didn't sit down. 'Anyway, you're wrong,' she said. 'Nan's the one with the brains. Always has been.'

Then she turned around, knelt in front of the window and acted as if we weren't there. Just stared into the street, waiting for her friend to come back.

Harry

The following morning I should have risen with a song in my heart and a smile on my lips: I was the coroner for the Teifi Valley, no longer a temporarily employed, barely officially-tolerated stop-gap. Nobody could take the post away from me now.

But, when I was woken from what seemed like little more than minutes' sleep by the arrival of a servant with warm washing-water, I found myself in very low spirits. I might have been duly elected, but nothing else had changed. Jonathan Eynon was still in Cardigan gaol, and I found myself obligated to reconvene the bungled inquest that had put him there.

My mood was only slightly improved when I finally came down in search of coffee – the concept of breakfast was quite beyond me after a celebratory dinner accompanied by alto-gether too much wine – to find Lydia waiting for me. As she had returned to Alltybela with Phoebe Gwatkyn and the two young women the previous afternoon, I had not anticipated her return much before mid-morning, yet here she was, sitting before the fireplace in the Black Lion's main room, drinking tea and eating toast.

'Good morning!' she enthused.

'Good morning. You're here early.'

'I didn't want to keep you waiting.'

Her voice was as lively as her manner and it made my head hurt. Was she mocking my fragile state?

'How did you get here so quickly?'

She had, it seemed, ridden over from Alltybela in the company of one of the grooms, wearing a borrowed pair of trousers so that she might ride astride.

'Don't worry,' she reassured me. 'We parted company outside town and I walked in. No early risers were scandalised at the sight of me in male attire.'

Perhaps it was my low mood, but I found her insouciance irritating. Fortunately for me, John appeared at that point and conversation turned to whether tea or coffee was more efficacious in alleviating the effects of over-indulgence.

–

Despite the warm sun of a clear spring day, my mood lifted only fractionally as we headed for home and, once we were on the open road, I nudged my little mare into a trot, leaving Lydia at the reins of the box cart, with John on my father's old gelding, alongside.

Soon, snatches of conversation behind me suggested that they were trying to lure me out of my doldrums and I imagined the two of them shooting glances at me as they spoke, troubled by my silence. But I had no appetite for chit-chat; my thoughts were occupied by the previous day's conflicting testimonies.

When John and I had picked over our interviews with Nan and Ruth before dinner the previous evening, we had agreed that, though Nan's refusal to answer questions was easily explained as an unwillingness to incriminate herself, Ruth's disturbingly changeable demeanour was far more difficult to rationalise.

'It's as if, whenever she feels she's under attack, she forgets how to be an adult and becomes a child again,' John said. 'A little frightened child who doesn't know how to save herself.'

'Save herself from what?'

'Anger?'

But, if Billy Walters's account of what had taken place in the loft was to be believed, Nicholas Rowland's anger had not turned Ruth into a frightened child; his accusation that she had been a willing participant in their pornographic writings had turned her into a furious, screaming woman.

I had lain awake for hours fretting at the conundrum of Ruth Eynon's behaviour. And, in the smallest watches of the night, when all manner of darkness creeps through a man's soul, I had confronted the implications of Shoni Goch's words about his cousin.

He said he was owed a maidenhead.

Had Jeremiah Eynon persuaded himself that his stepdaughter desired him, so that he could take what his twisted soul felt he was owed without guilt? Had he accused her of *wanting* him?

Such a violation of trust, of all that was expected of a father, made me almost physically sick but it might explain Ruth's extreme response to both Jonathan Eynon and Nicholas Rowland when they had suggested that she wanted something which she perceived as being forced upon her. It also gave rise to a question which would have to be addressed at the re-opened inquest: if Ruth had pushed Rowland away in disgust or terror, could she be charged with manslaughter, or would it be more just to see his fall from the loft as a tragic accident?

A sympathetic jury might bring in a verdict of misadventure but sympathy could hardly be expected once a jury had heard evidence that would include the writing of erotic fiction.

Even if I were to take matters into my own hands and simply rule on a new cause of death *ex cathedra* instead of holding a second inquest – something I was extremely loath to do as it would imply an entitlement I did not feel – I must still find a way to persuade the Cardiganshire constabulary to withdraw the charges against Jonathan Eynon.

But the Cardiganshire constabulary meant Inspector Bellis, and he was convinced that Eynon was his man.

I know men like him. Illiterate, violent, ruled by animal instincts. The jury'll find him guilty in a minute.

I could not allow that to happen.

Harry

On Monday morning, despite John and Lydia's combined and considerable efforts to make me reconsider, I set out, alone, for Cardigan. Ormiston had made it quite clear that he would need John all week on estate business, and Lydia would be busy arranging matters in Llanddewi Brefi on my behalf.

'As I'm sure you'll be writing to Miss Gwatkyn in any case, to let her know what I'm planning,' I said, 'will you be so kind as to ask her whether she'd mind accommodating Nan and Ruth until after the new inquest, please?'

I knew I sounded officious but I had been unexpectedly hurt by Lydia's joining forces with John to try and dissuade me from speaking to Bellis. So much so that it had been on the tip of my tongue to suggest that Nathaniel Howell would never have allowed Jonathan Eynon to languish in gaol for a crime he had not committed. Fortunately, though two nights' near-total insomnia had lent my thoughts a regrettable degree of self-pity, they had not impaired my judgement quite so disastrously.

–

St Mary's Church clock was striking ten as I rode past the entrance to Priory House, on the outskirts of town, and onwards to Cardigan's high street.

Outside the police station I dismounted and chose at random from the boys who came rushing to take charge of my little mare. Then, my palms suddenly sweaty and my heart beating perceptibly faster, I opened the door and walked in to Bellis's domain.

354

The smell of beeswax-and-turpentine polish reminded me forcefully of my last visit and, as the torpid Morgan lumbered to his feet to offer me good day and congratulations on my election, I took a deep breath. 'Thank you, constable. Would you ask the inspector if I might have a few minutes of his time?'

'He's not here, sir. Went out ten minutes since. Said not to expect him back for the rest of the day.'

I felt a rush of both intense relief and unreasonable antagonism. How dare he not be here when I had spent sleepless hours rehearsing what I would say to him?

'I need to see him urgently. Do you know where he is?'

'No, sir, I don't.'

I did not entirely believe him; I could almost hear Bellis giving instructions that his whereabouts should not be revealed 'to all and sundry'.

'It's in connection with the case against Jonathan Eynon,' I pressed. 'I have new evidence.'

'But no evidence will be needed now, sir. Eynon's confessed.'

'*What?*'

'Yes, sir. Called for somebody to go up and see him yesterday.'

'And what exactly has he confessed *to*?'

'Manslaughter, sir.'

–

On the short ride up to Cardigan Gaol, worried that the warden might refuse to let me see Eynon, I considered various lines of argument. However, having been admitted on the same errand before, I was granted entry to the gaol without demur and, having exchanged tedious but necessary pleasantries with the warden, I soon found myself being escorted to the dayroom.

'Must admit,' my guide volunteered, 'I didn't think he'd confess. Not the type, if you know what I mean.'

'He certainly didn't seem so.'

'But there's always something, isn't there?' the warder said, apparently taking my response as evidence that I was keen to discuss Eynon's change of heart. 'Something that'll push a man to do the right thing?'

My mind on my interview with Eynon, I made a sound that might as well have been dissent as agreement.

'I think he realised the game was up when his cousin's husband came to see him. Even a man like him wouldn't want the blame falling on an innocent young woman.'

I stumbled as his words almost stopped me in my tracks.

His cousin's husband.

Morgan Walters.

He must have come down from Llanddewi Brefi the previous day.

Eynon did not acknowledge me as I entered the dayroom, simply stood, motionless, in front of the window.

'What did Morgan Walters say to you?' I demanded as soon as the door had closed behind me. 'It must have been something very persuasive to get you to confess to a crime you didn't commit.'

Eynon's stance shifted as he folded his arms, but he did not turn to face me. 'None of your business, Coroner.'

'It is my business. Because it was my inquest that got you arrested. But now there's going to be a second inquest. Because I'm not even sure there *was* a crime.'

Eynon had his window, so I stationed myself at the only table, a little island of furniture in the bare room. I did not sit, simply stood there as if I was at the lawyers' table in the Old Bailey.

'Nan and Ruth clearly had some kind of altercation with Rowland,' I said. 'And he fell out of the loft. It might've been an accident. Or they might've pushed him.'

Still he did not turn around. 'Never was an *altercation*. Billy Walters invented all the nonsense he told you to get his sister into trouble.'

I forced a mirthless laugh. 'That's his father's game, is it? He's going to force the boy to perjure himself?'

'Won't come to that. There won't be a trial. Not if I plead guilty.'

He seemed very sure of himself. 'Who told you that?'

'The police inspector.'

So Bellis himself had been here.

'So.' I pulled one of the battered chairs from under the table and sat down. 'The constable at the police station said you'd confessed to manslaughter. How's that then?'

Still Eynon stood with his face to the window. 'Didn't mean to kill him, did I?'

I waited to see if he would say anything more and he obliged. 'Inspector said if a death happens in a fight and it couldn't've been foreseen, then it's manslaughter not murder.'

'Hah!' I rested my booted feet on one of the other chairs. 'Any judge worth his salt'll look at your record and conclude that Rowland's death was *perfectly* foreseeable!'

Finally, Jonathan Eynon turned to face me. 'Haven't got a police record, have I?'

Was it wishful thinking on my part or was there a sliver of doubt in his voice? I smiled. 'Not on paper, perhaps. But do you seriously think that Inspector Bellis doesn't know why you ran away to sea? After you were arrested, he sent constables up to Llanddewi Brefi and Tregaron to ask around—'

'Yes, about where I'd been and who'd seen me. They got nothing out of anybody.'

I leaned back in the chair so that it was standing on its back legs. 'Come on, Shoni! You know how people are. They like to be the ones who *know*, don't they? The ones who've got the juicy bits of gossip.'

He shook his head. 'No. People wouldn't tell the police. They don't trust them.'

'Not even the relatives of the man you half-killed?'

He knew as well as I did that where excessive violence was concerned people tended to have long memories and a limited

357

capacity for forgiveness. 'And don't you think it'll seem damned odd to the judge if you claim that Rowland fell out of the loft during a fight, when he didn't have a mark on him other than the ones he got from falling? Where's your evidence for this fight?'

'Never got to lay a fist on him. Went to hit him and he dodged me.' Eynon was definitely rattled, now. 'Lost his balance, didn't he? Fell.'

I swung my feet off the chair in front of me and let the front legs of the one I was sitting on hit the ground with a thud. Then I leaned forward over the table, my stare fixed determinedly in Eynon's direction. 'I don't believe you.'

'I don't—'

'Even if you went there, Rowland would never have let you in, never mind let you go up into the loft.'

In two paces, Eynon was at the table, looming over me. 'He didn't *let me in*. I just opened the door and—'

I stood up suddenly, cutting him off and making him straighten up. 'You're telling me he left the key in the lock?'

'No. The door was open—'

'So you just turned the handle and in you went?'

'Yes.'

'And the handle turned nicely, you didn't have to force it – you didn't break in?'

'No!'

Keen to avoid being charged with another crime, he had fallen right into my trap.

'You're a liar, Shoni Goch!' As I spoke, I hit the table with the side of my fist and he jerked back. 'There was no handle on that door! Just a thumb latch. And there was no key or lock, just a bar on the inside—'

'Handle, latch, it doesn't matter! I just got the door open and went in—'

'Stop lying to me! Do you really expect me to believe that Nicholas Rowland just watched you come up the ladder at him?

A stranger, in the dark? He'd have pushed the ladder over and you with it before you could get halfway up to him.' The blood was racing through my veins and I glared into the whirlpool. Though it meant I could not see him, I hoped Eynon might be unnerved by my blind stare.

'He was in bed. I surprised him—'

'He wasn't in bed. He had his overcoat on!' If I could trip him up again, he might just stop lying to me.

'It was cold, most likely went to bed in his clothes and just put his coat on when I came in—'

'*More lies!*' I slapped my palms down on the scarred table top. 'You've no idea what he was wearing! Morgan Walters has let you down – he should've given you a better idea of the details—'

'Says the blind man!'

I leaned over the table at him, recklessly putting my face within range of his fists. '*Yes*, says the blind man! Because the blind man has an assistant who sees and notes everything. Because that's what inquests need. Thoroughness.'

Eynon made a sound that was half derision, half amusement.

'Oh yes, you were so thorough you'd never heard of me before Fatty Price stood up and pissed all over your inquest! The only reason you don't want me to confess is because you don't want to look a fool!'

It was as if he'd thrown a bucket of dirty water over me. I straightened up, suddenly aware that I was panting slightly, my hands shaking.

Morgan Walters had been very shrewd. He might not have provided enough corroborating detail to withstand cross-examination but he had pre-empted all the arguments I might use to get Jonathan Eynon to withdraw his confession.

But second guessing was a game two could play.

'Morgan Walters probably told you that you'd only get a few months for manslaughter,' I said. 'But, take it from me, the Cardiganshire Constabulary will be having a word in the judge's ear before you're sentenced. And, whatever he might've told *you*, Inspector Bellis had you down as a murderer before you'd even left Aberaeron.' I let him think about that for a moment. 'He's going to want to see you hanged, Shoni.'

He stepped around the table and came towards me, the intensity of his stare a physical thing. Good sense told me to move, put the table between us again; pride told me to stand toe to toe with him. I did not budge.

'I know what that teacher had Ruth and her friend doing,' he spat. 'You want to bring all that out, do you? Tell everybody? Make sure no decent man ever wants to marry them?'

My blindness trained on his face, I saw his feet shuffle forwards. He was no more than half a pace away from me, now.

'This isn't about what I'm going to do. It's about what you're going to do. Are you really going to hang for those girls, when this is none of your doing?'

With a bellow like a wounded bull, Eynon laid hold of the table and swung it across the room. 'Nobody's getting hanged!' he yelled, as chairs crashed to the floor and the table hit the wall.

The door to the dayroom was flung open with plaster-denting force and the warder ran in. Despite the fact that my pulse was racing from Eynon's unexpected violence, I held up a hand and the warder stopped in his tracks.

Stranded in the middle of the room, at a loss as to what I should say or do next, I just waited, heart thudding, knees trembling. Eynon seemed similarly bewildered and simply stood there, breathing heavily. Then, as if responding to an order only he had heard, he turned and dragged the table back to the middle of the room, putting a barrier between us once more.

'Ruth needs to get out of Jeremiah's house,' he said, his voice trembling with suppressed violence. 'And now she can, 'cos there's money coming to them, isn't there? Morgan said. For a school.'

I stood there, my fear of him hardly diminished by the warder's presence, my mind sluggish.

Morgan Walters thinks he's the boss of Llanddewi Brefi. That was what the boy, Lleu, had said on the night when the *ceffyl pren* had been carried to Mattie Hughes's house. Walters was a man who knew how to make things happen, how to manipulate people so that they thought they were acting in pursuit of justice when, in fact, they were serving his purposes.

Eynon leaned over the table at me, both hands planted, palm down. 'So, Mr Coroner, if you come to the court and try to interfere, I'll stand there in the dock – with all the newspaper men listening – and I'll tell the judge that you came here today and tried to bribe me to withdraw my confession.' He leaned closer still, until I could smell his breath, feel it on my skin. 'How long d'you think you'll last as coroner then?'

John

I never thought I'd hear myself saying this, but thank God for Lydia Howell.

Harry'd gone off to Cardigan, confident that she'd follow his instructions and get on with the business of arranging Rowland's reconvened inquest. Specifically, that she would write a letter to Morgan Walters asking him for the use of the Three Horseshoes on Friday at midday; a letter to Simi Jones giving him instructions about finding a jury and producing them at the specified time and place; and a letter to Miss Gwatkyn asking her to put up with Nan and Ruth for a bit longer and then, if she'd be so good, to put us up at Alltybela when we came up for the inquest.

But no. Lydia Howell had decided not to do any of that.

'Harry, I'm your secretary, not your slave,' she told him, calmly, when he demanded to know why she'd gone against his express wishes. 'Which I take to mean that I must act in your best interests rather than simply on your instructions. And, if that's not the case, then it would be best for all concerned if we proceeded no further with this experiment in employment.'

The look on Harry's face was a picture. Bitten off more of a mouthful than he'd realised in employing Lydia, hadn't he?

I'll be honest, there was a part of me that hoped she would just pack her bags and go. Things'd been simpler before she arrived. But, with my sensible head on, I knew that my life'd be a damn sight easier, in the long run, if I wasn't the only one trying to make Harry see sense.

'It was simply expedient,' she said, when Harry didn't respond. 'Having spoken to Miss Gwatkyn on Saturday evening, it seemed to me that there was a significant chance that Morgan Walters might do something like this. I didn't want to arrange a second inquest on your behalf, only to have to send letters cancelling it again the following day.'

Harry still said nothing and she shot a look at me. I nodded. *Carry on.*

'If my suspicions had been proved wrong,' she said, 'you'd still have had ample time to hold the inquest on Friday, as planned. But, if Billy Walters has been persuaded to say that he made it all up…'

She didn't need to say any more. Without Billy's testimony, the only new evidence was the erotic books and Harry wouldn't want to bring them to the attention of Llanddewi Brefi. On their own, they didn't give Nan and Ruth a reason to kill Rowland but even a sniff of their existence would ruin the girls' reputation.

Harry stalked over to the cabinet in the corner of the library, yanked it open with its usual squeak and pulled a decanter out, knocking glasses over in the process. He picked one up, poured himself a measure of something – brandy, I think – and drank it down in one gulp. Then he poured some more before good manners got the better of him and he held the decanter up. 'Either of you?'

We both declined.

I watched him carefully. He wasn't generally much of a drinker and I hadn't seen him like this before. He drank half the brandy in one go, put the decanter back and shut the cabinet. He had to nudge it with his knee to make sure it caught and I saw him lose his balance for a second.

'Am I going to have to justify every single request to your personal satisfaction in future?' He sounded like a defiant boy who knows he's lost the argument but can't let it go.

Lydia stood up and went over to him. 'Harry, did you really think that Morgan Walters was just going to stand idly by and let his daughter be ruined? He's a determined and resourceful man and I dare say Jonathan Eynon'll come out of prison to a tidy little sum when he's served his sentence.'

Harry swallowed the rest of his brandy and put the glass down with a thud that made me flinch. I knew it was difficult for him to judge how far away things were but he usually took more care than that.

He turned his back on Lydia and walked over to the library window. He wouldn't like the fact that she'd predicted what Morgan Walters would do when he hadn't. Harry prided himself on knowing what criminals were like. He might not've been a barrister for long but he'd been paid to defend any number of people and he was convinced that he could tell a born criminal from somebody who'd just been forced into crime by miserable circumstances. But they'd been London people, hadn't they, and London crimes? He was going to have to get used to the way Cardiganshire people thought and acted.

'Bellis will try and see Jonathan Eynon hanged,' he said, still looking out at whatever he could see in the late afternoon light.

'Not if you give him reason not to.'

The look he turned on Lydia Howell then made me wish I'd taken the brandy he'd offered. I wasn't used to an atmosphere like this. Couldn't breathe properly for the tightness in the air and I finally understood what was going on here. Harry's anger wasn't about Lydia's going against his wishes. Or not mostly about that, anyway. It was about her seeing things he hadn't. Being quicker on the uptake.

'And how will I do that?' he said, as if he'd much rather not know.

'Billy Walters's testimony,' Lydia said. 'I've transcribed it as far as I remember it and you and John can add to it if there's anything I've omitted. I've also written a short explanation of the kind of books Rowland and the girls were writing together. Send all that to the inspector. Make sure he understands that you're prepared to bring it forward as evidence if he thinks he can put Eynon on trial for murder. I don't think Morgan Walters would actually send his son into the witness box and ask him to perjure himself. Do you?'

Dear God, she wasn't one jump ahead of him, she was three.

–

I didn't see much of Harry for the next few days because Mr Ormiston kept me hard at it. Lydia was busy, too, and not always with Harry. She seemed to be keen to build bridges with Mrs Griffiths and I came in, one afternoon, to find the two of them with their heads together over what looked like a set of accounts.

She and Harry were civil to each other but, even by the end of the week, they still hadn't got back to where they'd been before the argument and I wondered whether Harry was considering ending their 'experiment in employment' before the three months' trial period that he and Lydia had agreed was over. If he did, the servants wouldn't like it. They'd all taken a shine to Lydia.

Then, on Saturday afternoon, Phoebe Gwatkyn arrived and changed everything.

'I'm sorry to appear on your doorstep without so much as a note beforehand for a second time,' she said, as Harry fussed over her and Lydia Howell asked the maid, Elsie, to bring some tea – for all the world as if she was the mistress of the house. 'But, in the circumstances, I felt that promptness was more important than politeness.'

Harry shepherded her to the comfortable chaise-longue. There were two in the drawing room and the stuffing in the other one was as lumpy as potatoes in a sack. 'You're more than welcome at any time, Miss Gwatkyn. I hope the circumstances to which you refer aren't too...?' He didn't seem to know how to finish that sentence so he just left it hanging.

Miss Gwatkyn picked up the carpet bag she'd brought with her and took out a blue paisley shawl. The drawing room was large and its fireplace was small so it was never very warm. '*Unfortunate* might be an apposite word,' she said, as she wrapped the shawl around her shoulders.

Lydia Howell sat down next to her and put a hand on her arm.

'Oh no, please don't concern yourself, my dear.' She patted Lydia's hand. 'It's just that I'm somewhat embarrassed.' She looked at Harry, then me. 'I'm not entirely sure what your intentions were for Nan Walters and Ruth Eynon, now that there's to be no second inquest.' Again, she looked at each of us in turn but we were still no help. 'However, I'm afraid they've rendered the question rather moot.'

'In what way?' Harry asked.

'They absconded on Thursday night,' she said. 'And I'm afraid they took the money you left in my keeping with them.'

Harry

It seemed that the first indication the Alltybela household had had of the young women's disappearance was a missing horse. When the grooms had risen at first light, one of their mistress's favourite hacks had been absent from the stable and a trail of hoof-muffling straw traced its path through the yard and into the fields behind.

I imagined Nan and Ruth making their way over the same dark fields that John and I had crossed with the boy, Lleu, on the night of the *ceffyl pren* procession. As they reached the road, had they looked back towards Llanddewi Brefi and their homes, saying a silent goodbye? For, surely, such a clandestine departure suggested that they had no intention of returning.

I wondered where they would go. With three hundred pounds they might travel anywhere they wished, set themselves up in business and never look back.

They would not stay in Wales, I was sure, for they would too easily be found here. Would they make for London? With Mr Gordon eager for more erotic tales from 'Nicky Revell', they might keep themselves in funds indefinitely.

But perhaps, given the circumstances, America was their most likely destination.

On their stolen horse, they could have been in Aberaeron by dawn on Friday, travelled to Aberystwyth by coach and thence by sea to Liverpool to embark across the Atlantic. Well provided for financially, they would not have to endure the notoriously unpleasant conditions in steerage but could take a decent cabin for themselves, though they might be obliged to wait a few weeks for a sailing that had berths available.

How would they fare in a city they did not know, prey to confidence tricksters, unscrupulous boarding-house owners and all manner of criminals? Somehow, I suspected that, between the two of them, they would manage tolerably well.

All these thoughts occupied no more than a few seconds as Phoebe Gwatkyn gave an account of how the stolen horse had come trotting home later in the day.

'They'd taken her bridle off,' she told us. 'And the note we found under the saddle said they hoped that, by not having a bridle to take hold of, she would avoid being laid hold of and stolen.'

'Did the note say anything else?' Lydia asked.

'A good deal. They were at pains to point out that the money, having been earned by the sale of books they had written, was rightfully theirs and that they hoped nobody would begrudge it. They also lamented the fact that they'd had to leave without saying goodbye, and thanking me for all I'd done for them.'

She fell silent but, before I could respond, she took up the thread once more. 'Now that I've had time to think about the whole affair,' she said, her words measured, careful. 'I wonder, actually, whether I didn't do the two of them a disservice in helping to educate them to the extent that I did.'

'Why?' I asked, taken aback.

'Because, as yet, there is so little employment for an educated woman in Cardiganshire. The education Nicholas and I provided raised their expectations and, when those expectations seemed unlikely to be realised, I fear they saw no alternative but to take matters into their own hands.'

Was she referring to the pair's flight from Alltybela, their complicity in producing pornography, or the circumstances surrounding Nicholas Rowland's death? It was suddenly clear to me that, at almost every turn, Nan Walters and Ruth Eynon had been faced with a stark alternative: give up their ambitions and submit to the fate ordained by their sex and station, or deploy their native intelligence and education in pursuit of something better.

'Surely our society and its treatment of women must shoulder some of the blame,' Lydia protested. 'If we were allowed to direct our own lives, give ourselves in marriage to whom we choose – *if* we choose to do so – those young women's lives would have been very different.'

As Lydia and Miss Gwatkyn continued in a similar vein, I turned in John's direction. And, seeing me shift my attention to him, he inclined his head toward me in acknowledgement. It was the closest I would ever come to being able to catch his eye and share a smile.

I wondered if John, like me, was seeing Nan Walters and Ruth Eynon in his mind's eye as they began their new life away from the confines of Llanddewi Brefi. Did he see them standing on deck together – *betgwns* discarded in favour of less obviously Welsh attire – watching Liverpool disappear over the eastern horizon before turning and looking westwards to their new world?

In my imagination, I could see the two of them quite clearly. Nan, sharp and determined; Ruth, an unstable compound of anger, intelligence and fear.

I could only hope that America – if that was, indeed, where they were bound – would afford them greater scope for their talents than their native land.

And that it would present them with fewer reasons to use those talents in their own defence.

Epilogue

From the Carmarthen Journal's *report on Cardigan assize courts.*

… Jonathan Eynon, a merchant seaman from the parish of Llanddewi Brefi, Cardiganshire, pleaded guilty of the manslaughter of schoolmaster Nicholas Rowland on the 27th April, in the course of an argument. The Cardiganshire Constabulary having brought aggravating circumstances to the judge's attention, Eynon was sentenced to be transported for a period of seven years…

Some historical notes

Places

As with the other books in the Teifi Valley Coroner series, where at all possible I've tried to use real places in *Those Who Know*.

The Talbot Inn in Tregaron is still there on the main square, though it's been extensively rebuilt and extended since 1851. Harry and John would think it much grander than the inn they stayed at.

The Black Lion, which also appeared in *In Two Minds*, is still going strong on the High Street in Cardigan.

It's a shame that the only pub I could find reference to in Lampeter in 1851 was also called the Black Lion. (Apologies to everybody who knows better – there is only so much time an author has for research!) I've taken a certain amount of liberty with the description of its coachyard and have described the inner aspects of the inn with reference to similar mid-century coaching inns rather than taking my description from any contemporary sources.

The Three Horseshoes in Llanddewi Brefi is a figment of my imagination, as is Miss Gwatkyn's Alltybela, though countless gentry mansions like it, many with additions from more than one period, peppered the countryside of the Teifi Valley.

Llanddewi Brefi is, as I hope people realise, a real place and the parish in which it lies is the largest in Wales. The village was immortalised by Matt Lucas and David Walliams in *Little Britain* but, contrary to the impression they gave, it is not in a mining area.

Early plans for St David's College (now the University of Wales, Lampeter) situated it, as Phoebe Gwatkyn suggests, in Llanddewi Brefi. However, despite Llanddewi's ancient history of scholarship, the college was eventually founded in Lampeter where land was provided for the purpose. The difference in size, status and prosperity of the two towns is, as John says, testimony to what having a university does for a place.

Wych Street and Holywell Street were, as depicted, the centre of London's pornographic publishing industry. As Gus tells John, publishers and booksellers in the area also published seditious literature but, following a government crackdown on sedition in the 1810s, publishers more interested in making money than in changing society had turned their attentions to pornography.

Loventium (or Luentium): In *Those Who Know*, Phoebe Gwatkyn identifies Roman Loventium as lying a little over a mile to the north and west of Llanddewi Brefi, where it is clearly marked on contemporary maps. *The National Gazetteer of Great Britain and Ireland, 1868* also sites it there. However, if you Google 'Loventium', you'll be told that it's near the Dolau Cothi gold mines, more than twenty miles away, in Carmarthenshire. Even more confusingly, the Wikipedia entry, whilst locating Loventium near the modern-day village of Pumsaint, near Dolau Cothi, gives its Welsh translation as 'Llanio' which is the name of the hamlet near Llanddewi Brefi where Miss Gwatkyn believed Loventium to be! If any classicists or archaeologists would like to tell me how this confusion has arisen, please get in touch via my website as I'd love to know.

Sarn Helen is, as Phoebe Gwatkyn tells Harry and John, the name given to various ancient tracks through the Welsh heartlands from south to north and the name may, indeed, come from the story of Macsen Wledig in the *Mabinogi*. I've seen the suggestion made that these tracks should be joined up into one national path or cycleway from north to south, something I would love to see, as anybody who has tried to travel from one end of Wales to the other, by any means, knows what a monumental task it is.

People

Henry Richard, mentioned in the book as secretary of the influential Peace Society, was a real person and is a son of whom Tregaron is justly very proud.

Simi Jones is not a real person but I should just say a word or two about his role as *plwyfwas*, or parish constable. In theory, after the establishment of the Cardiganshire Constabulary in the mid-1840s, the role of parish constable became defunct. However, change was slow to happen. People resented the 'new police' (a force which was, at any rate, thinly distributed across the county) and preferred to be policed by their own, as they had been for centuries. So, parish constables survived here and there, in the more remote locations, for some time after the constabulary's establishment, as long as – like Simi Jones – they were seen to earn their keep.

The Mabinogi

The *Mabinogi* (also known as the *Mabinogion*) with which Nicholas Rowland and his assistants take such liberties is, as Phoebe Gwatkyn rightly maintains, an undeservedly poorly-known collection of medieval and pre-medieval Welsh tales. In fact, I'm told (and who am I to argue) they represent the earliest known prose fiction in Britain.

The first popular translation of the *Mabinogi* into English from Middle Welsh was produced by the eminent linguist, industrialist, pioneering liberal educator, philanthropist and elite society hostess, Lady Charlotte Guest, in the early 1840s.

I must offer my sincere apologies to Lady Charlotte and all who love the *Mabinogi* for John's somewhat reductionist reading of the text and, more especially, for Nicky Revell's shocking treatment of the tales.

Pornography

As Harry says, writing pornography was not illegal and neither, strictly speaking, was selling it. The Victorians hadn't got around to being excessively prudish by 1851 (though they were getting there) and the Obscene Publications Act was not passed into law until 1857. Prior to that, the authorities had to rely on an 1838 amendment to the Vagrancy Act of 1824 which made it illegal to cause 'moral outrage' to the public by 'wilfully exposing to view, in any Street... or public Place, any obscene Print, Picture, or other indecent Exhibition'. The police did – fairly regularly – bring prosecutions against people like William Gordon but it was often difficult to do so successfully until the 1857 Act.

In general, in *Those Who Know*, I've referred to the literature concerned as 'erotic fiction' rather than 'pornography' as the latter term suggests, to the modern reader, something far more obscene – and possibly disturbing – than the volumes and photographs John saw on sale in Wych Street and Holywell Street.

The Report of the Commissioners of Inquiry into the State of Education in Wales

This 1847 report – in later years dubbed *Brad Y Llyfrau Gleision* or the Treachery of the Blue Books – is a county-by-county, parish-by-parish, school-by-school survey of every teaching establishment that the commissioners could find. It's incredibly detailed and, although it's now seen to be more than a little biased, the data collected still represents an enormous repository for the social historian. If you'd like to read it, it's available online, free. John's account of the Report, though somewhat prejudiced, is broadly accurate and Wales and the Welsh language are still recovering from its pernicious effects.

Acknowledgements

As ever, first and greatest thanks go to my beloved other half and first reader, Edwina, for all her endless support and constant positivity. The writing and editing of *Those Who Know* took place during a hectically busy year and a half which I would not have survived if Edwina had not basically taken up all the slack in our domestic arrangements and coped with my being, at best, distracted and, at worst, obsessed with getting stuff done. Thank you, my love, I literally couldn't have done it without you.

Huge thanks to Rebecca Lloyd and Emily Glenister at The Dome Press who are an absolute joy to work with and who have offered me enormous support and encouragement during the last year or so. Emily, thanks so much for your steadfast support during my mad tour of all the independent bookshops in Wales last year. Rebecca, your insightful comments have helped me make *Those Who Know* a far better book and I'm so pleased that you've got John and Harry's backs! I'm really looking forward to working with you on future books in the series.

Jem Butcher's covers for the series are wonderful and the one for *Those Who Know* is no exception. I'm so grateful both to Jem and to David Headley and the editorial team at The Dome Press for allowing me to have so much input into cover design – it's a real privilege for a writer to be listened to as everybody at The Dome Press has listened to my ideas.

In my writing life I am very fortunate to have made some wonderful friends along the way. Particularly important to me are the authors of the Macmillan New Writing crew:

Eliza Graham, Len Tyler, Aliya Whiteley, Frances Garrood, Tim Stretton, Deborah Swift and Roger Morris – our regular London meetings and intermittent online group chats are a huge support when things are tough and a great joy when we all have something to celebrate. I must also thank various Crime Cymru authors for their friendship and support over the last year. Particular thanks in this context must go to Katherine Stansfield, Bev Jones, Thorne Moore, Matt Johnson and Chris Lloyd.

Thanks also to the booksellers and festival organisers who have taken Harry and John to their hearts and introduced them to their readers. Particular thanks to Emma Corfield-Walters of Bookish in Crickhowell and the Crickhowell Literary Festival, Matt Taylor of Chepstow Bookshop, Beth at Victoria Bookshop in Haverfordwest, Inge Fullerlove, manager of the Aberystwyth branch of Waterstones and Jacky Collins (aka Dr Noir) founder of Newcastle Noir crime festival.

Almost last, but by no means least, to my family – Sam and Nancy, Rob and Flo, Mum, Dad and Jim. Thank you, my loves, for always being there and for not being surprised that it all worked out in the end. Your faith has always meant everything to me.

And finally, dear reader, if you have slogged your way to the end of the acknowledgements, thank you! Without you and all the other readers who have responded so enthusiastically to Harry and John, there would be no series and I would be a very sad author.

If you would like to contact me, please use the contact tab on my website: www.AlisHawkins.co.uk